Flight of the Angels

Allan and Aaron Reini

Cover Design by Michael Vincent

PUBLISHED BY HENDIADYS PRESS

ISBN-10: 0615716105
ISBN-13: 978-0615716107

To Becky and Jill:
Our best friends, faithful critics, and most enthusiastic fans.

Squadron Personnel

Pilots
Captain Dex "Deadeye" D'Felco
Commander Hagen "Sarge" Lebrian
Lt. Commander Lee "Ninja" Onigen
Lieutenant Jani "Rabbit" McLeod
Lieutenant Scot "Flash" Calgaro
Flight Lieutenant Geffory "Prince" Bennet
Flight Lieutenant Seltrice "Viper" Valani
Flying Officer Adahn "Ghazi" Manasser
Flying Officer Ravi "Sunfire" Voor
Flying Officer Purnima "Moonlight" Voor

Support
Lt. Commander Job Hansen, executive assistant
Flight Sergeant Drager St. James, chief mechanic
Ronnie Wilco, ops tech

Prologue

He stumbled, his breath coming in ragged gasps. Somewhere in the dimly illuminated halls behind him, the killer moved silently forward, relentless in its pursuit. Grasping the charred wound in his side, the man barely managed to keep his footing, lurching to his right into an even darker narrow hall. The stun bolt had done its job well. Even at full strength, he knew he couldn't have outrun the thing behind him. Now, as the painful, paralyzing effects of the shot radiated throughout his body, every agonizing step he took became slower.

Only one thought spurred him on. If he could just keep moving, if he could somehow lure it further away, he might buy the others enough time to hide, or even escape. He had to keep trying to run, to continue moving forward for her sake, for the children, for all of them.

The passage before him came to an abrupt halt, a solid security door barring his way. Trembling, he punched a code into the console. No response. He tried again. His tormentor had been thorough. There was nowhere to run.

Turning around, his back to the door, he saw it approaching, purposefully and silently. It moved without urgency—it had effectively stalked and cornered its prey. Knowing that the side arm he carried would be useless, he still drew the weapon and fired. The bolt bounced off harmlessly as the monster continued unimpeded. It stopped before him and stood fully erect—its rigid posture almost human. Lungs screaming, nearly blinded by pain, he fought to control his panic. There was no escape. He raised his pistol for one more desperate shot.

The predator produced a thin pointed rod of shining metal from its upper left appendage, thrusting it forward with lightning speed. Piercing his right shoulder beneath the collar bone, the rod continued outward, shattering his shoulder blade. Once through, four small hooks shot out of

1

the rod and dug into the back of his shoulder, making it impossible to wriggle off the implement. Screaming in agony, he dropped the pistol as the hellish fiend lifted him by the shoulder, his feet dangling inches from the ground. Writhing and struggling for breath, fighting the red-hot haze exploding in his brain, he heard the thing speak.

You are a Christian. It was not a question.

Somewhere, beneath his terror, beyond the pain, he found a resolve that he knew was not his own. "Y…yes," he answered.

You cling to an imaginary god and a dead religion. The voice had an ethereal, horrifying timbre, as if a thousand evil beings were speaking at once.

"I…I believe in God the Father Almighty, maker of heaven and earth," he gasped, in his fading consciousness calling upon the ancient creed to find the words. "I believe in Jesus Christ, His only begotten—"

Will you renounce your faith in exchange for your life?

It was a question he had been expecting his entire life, a question he had always hoped and prayed that he would have the strength to answer.

The strength came. "No," he groaned. "Go to hell."

Wordlessly, the creature raised another arm. Struggling against the impaling rod, wild eyed, he saw that the monster held a pulsating blade, moving close, so close to his neck. He closed his eyes.

Lowering its arm, the assassin retracted the hooks, letting the decapitated body of its victim slide to the ground. It turned and moved silently away.

Chapter 1

A pair of Angels soared through the heavens. Flying with unwavering precision and leaving shimmering purple trails in their wake, they would, for a time, appear to a distant observer as twin comets, leisurely traveling along their preordained path. This illusion would soon be shattered, however, by a sudden flurry of movement—the trails abruptly bending and slashing, tracing a series of brilliant yet fleeting symbols on the starscape. While uncharacteristic of celestial bodies, such erratic flight patterns had become commonplace for these Angels. Fallen from grace, they were accustomed to fleeing for their lives.

The pair rose in unison for a third time—carried not by supernatural wings of fire or light, but by man-made crebonite-encased thrusters. On a wordless cue, the climb fluidly transitioned into a dive, the two pilots—each an Angel, each an outlaw—massaging their sensitive flight controls as they hurtled their fighters through the void.

It was during this third dive that Captain Dex D'Felco experienced something that he had never before felt in the cockpit of his fighter—a jolt of panic. The cause was seemingly innocuous—a voice in his ear.

"Break left."

It wasn't the tone of his wingman's voice that shook him—on the contrary, she sounded as calm and composed as ever. Rather, Dex was startled to discover that he had been awakened from a mental haze, the last few moments of his existence lost from memory. The feeling of disorientation was brief but intense. It wasn't immediately clear how long he'd been drifting—maybe he had checked out for only a second or two, maybe longer. And, for all he knew, he might have remained on mental autopilot indefinitely had it not been for his wingman's intervention.

The instruction was repeated—this time with more urgency—and Dex obeyed without hesitation. What choice did he have? Given his current vulnerable state, he was completely dependent on his partner's judgment. At least Dex could take some comfort in knowing that he was in capable hands. There were few people, if any, he trusted more than Jani McLeod.

Tilting his side-stick toward his hip and then straight back, he pulled his fighter hard left. It was an exceptionally quick reaction, considering that he had just snapped out of a mental fog, but it wasn't quite quick enough. The whole of his fighter trembled as cannon bolts skipped off his rear shields. Still, despite his delayed reaction, Dex managed to keep his fighter just ahead of the tracers, pushing past the enemy as quickly as possible while avoiding any devastating direct hits. Sparing a glance out the right side of the canopy, he saw that Jani had fared even better, cleanly evading the arcing trails of red cannon fire.

Dex breathed a prayer of thanks for her safety before inwardly scolding himself. It was unbearable to think that he could have lost Jani because of his own lack of concentration—his own stupidity, really. He simply couldn't fathom how he had lost focus, especially when the situation was so dire. Ambushed from behind by four hostile fighters, he and Jani had been scrambling for their lives from the start of the engagement. To make matters worse, Dex was flying with a handicap. A cargo crate, bonded to the bottom of his fighter, had greatly reduced the efficiency of his ventral thrusters. It was tempting to jettison the crate, but his contact had said it was important. Dex could only hope the cargo was worth the headache it was causing.

As he jerked his fighter into another tight turn, Dex whipped his head around to peer out the back of the canopy. With his naked eye, he would have had difficulty spotting his pursuers amid the stars, but he was aided by his visor's Heads Up Display, which clearly highlighted the locations of the enemy fighters.

Each of the four rust-colored GF-44 Marauders was nearly twice as large as his fighter. Stacks of missile launchers bracketed each ship's cockpit, squeezing both sides of its rectangular canopy as though the Marauder's flight controls were an afterthought to its armaments. The back half of the fighter expanded into a massive engine compartment. From atop the blocky engines, two stubby wings extended down with cannons mounted above and below each wing tip. The Marauder was hideously armed and heavily shielded, but it sacrificed agility for strength.

By comparison, Dex's fighter—the S/A-81 Hornet—was small and sleek, its design harkening back to the atmospheric jet fighters of old. Twin

AI-530 engines, positioned side-by-side at the rear, powered the craft, their circular nozzles emitting brilliant purple light. Rising up from the front of the engines was the Hornet's most distinctive feature—a pair of vertical stabilizers that angled out in the shape of a wide-bottomed "V." With its speed, maneuverability, and top-of-the-line avionics, it was the most advanced fighter employed by the United Coalition Navy. The two Hornets may have been outgunned by the Marauders, but they were far from outmatched.

Spotting the Marauders, it took Dex only a split-second to assess their angle of attack and react accordingly. He turned hard right, sending his fighter directly across the flight paths of his pursuers. The maneuver brought him into the line of fire, but the danger was minimal. Running perpendicular to the Marauders, he raced by in a flash, too quick for the enemy to get off an effective shot. The pair on his tail, unable to match the nimble turn, were forced into a wider arc. In the lower right side of his cockpit, the three-dimensional battle map showed that Jani had once again given the slip to her pair of trailers as well. Now that they had a little breathing room, Dex knew that it was time to stop running. For all its intricacies, a dogfight could be boiled down to one basic principle—hunt or be hunted.

"Rabbit, sweep the Slugs," he said, ordering Jani to scan the Marauders for signs of life. Once spoken, however, the words sounded rather familiar. Dex wondered if he had already given the order, possibly while he had been less-than-focused on the situation at hand. He didn't have to wonder for long.

"Confirmed all four Slugs *still* cool."

Embarrassed, Dex replied quickly.

"Roger. Cleared hot."

This was troubling. How could he not remember giving such a critical order? How long had he mentally checked out? And how had he managed to survive a blackout in the midst of a heated dogfight? The final question was the only one he could answer definitively at the moment—he had survived, as he ever survived, by the grace of God.

For the first time in the engagement, Dex armed his cannons. The Angels' rules of engagement would not permit them to go weapons free until they had confirmed that there was no human life aboard enemy ships, and Jani had done just that, verifying that the Marauders were drones, flown by remote operators rather than pilots physically seated in the cockpit.

He quickly double-checked his battle map for other contacts, looking specifically for the control ship. It was a problem that had been nagging at Dex since the Angels' first encounter with the Marauders. As far as he knew, it was impossible to fly drones without a control ship somewhere in the vicinity, but he found nothing in the sector aside from Jani's Hornet and the four Marauders. Dex, though, didn't have the luxury of dwelling on the question. He had already let his concentration slip once—it would not happen again.

Circling with the Marauders, Dex could see that he was close to gaining the advantage, as was Jani. But in her dogged pursuit of one Marauder, she had allowed her target's wingman to slip away. Dex saw that the wingman was now turning sharply, attempting to get position behind Jani.

"Rabbit, bandit on your seven, high," Dex called, warning her of the trailing Marauder.

"Tally. Please advise."

Jani needed only a few more seconds to take out her target. She was wondering, then, whether she should break away or continue her attack under Dex's cover. Ordering her to break was the safer move, but it would cost her the opportunity for an easy kill. Anticipating the flight path of her pursuer, Dex determined that he could get the Marauder before the Marauder got Jani.

"Continue pressing. You're covered."

Dex turned directly toward Jani's fighter, letting his two bandits escape in order to engage the Marauder on his wingman's tail. As he turned, Jani's pursuer roared in front of him from left to right. Dex held his fire. Had he snapped off a shot, he might've scored a few glancing hits, but it would've done little to slow the hulking Marauder. It was better to save his cannon power for a sure kill. Holding his fire, though, was a calculated risk. The longer he waited, the closer the Marauder crept toward Jani.

He continued hard right, working his Hornet into the control zone— the imaginary cone-shaped area behind an enemy fighter, the area in which his weapons would be most effective. Stay in the zone and a kill was all but assured.

6

Skirting into the edge of the control zone, Dex shifted his attention to the pipper on his HUD. The light-green circle danced around as he manipulated the thumb control on top of his flight stick. The cannons on a Hornet were not locked forward but could be independently aimed, an advantage that greatly increased the potential size of the control zone—provided the pilot had a light touch. Some of the Angels ignored the function, preferring to keep their cannons locked in place after finding it all but impossible to aim accurately in one direction while flying in another.

Dex, however, had never struggled with that ability. He hadn't earned the call sign "Deadeye" for nothing.

Guiding the pipper with his thumb, he smoothly lined up the center dot just in front of the Marauder. Next came a gentle squeeze of his index finger, triggering an extended burst from his forward cannons. Two tight rows of yellow bolts lanced out from the nose of his fighter, crossing directly in front of the Marauder. He'd led the target perfectly.

Unable to turn away in time, the Marauder ran straight through the streams of yellow tracers. The bolts splashed across the fighter's invisible outer shell, pounding its shields to the verge of collapse. The Marauder engaged its afterburners in a desperate attempt to escape, but as it surged forward, a flurry of bolts slammed into its rear quarter, burning deep into its armor. Streams of vapor burst through the engine cowlings, shooting small sections of the fuselage out into space. Moments later, a series of internal explosions tore through the Marauder, splitting it into hunks of flaming wreckage.

As he pulled above the debris, Dex glanced at a small bar next to his pipper. Retreating from right to left, the gauge informed him of how much power was left in his cannons. Only a small fraction of the bar remained. He wasn't surprised—it took a healthy amount of sustained firepower to bring down a Marauder. While his cannons recharged, he checked his battle map just in time to see Jani take out her target.

"Splash one," she confirmed.

Dex looked forward through the canopy, searching for the telltale fireball, but a rhythmic tone in his cockpit snapped his attention back to his sensors. Dex realized that while he had been covering Jani, the first pair of Marauders had taken the opportunity to regain position on his tail. The tone meant that they were close to achieving a missile lock on his fighter. The Marauders, like the Hornets, were armed with several

Advanced Intercept Missiles. The AIMs—more commonly known as "Slammers" because of the violence of their impact—were a serious threat. Even at full strength, a fighter's shields could not deflect a Slammer.

Dex reacted immediately, pulling back on his stick. As he rose, he jinked right, then rolled back down, yanking back on the throttle as he dove. Over the course of several engagements, Dex had come to learn that, for all their skill, the drone's remote operators had difficulty recognizing and reacting to double moves.

Looking behind him, he was pleased to see that it remained a weakness.

The lead Marauder had overacted to his feint, committing hard right. It wouldn't take long for the Marauder to correct, but at least it bought him a few extra seconds. The second Marauder had stuck with Dex through the roll. However, anticipating a sharper, speedier turn, the fighter had blown past him, overshooting his position.

Dex pounced on the mistake. He toggled his weapons from cannons to missiles, his HUD illustrating the change by replacing the circle pipper with a diamond. With his Hornet on the near edge of missile range, and with the target turning so tightly, there was a possibility that his missiles wouldn't be able to maintain a lock. But with the second Marauder once again jockeying to get position on his tail, he didn't have time to get cute with guns. He lined the diamond-shaped pipper over the Marauder's bright orange engines and clicked his thumb-stick, identifying the target for his missiles. A half-second later, a solid tone indicated a lock, and he released two missiles in rapid succession.

"Fox one," he called, barely getting the words out before the glowing blue missiles closed the gap. The lead missile shot straight behind the Marauder's engines, failing to track the target. The trailing Slammer, though, arced sharply toward the Marauder, slicing through its shields and detonating against its engines.

Dex slammed his stick forward, wincing as he dove below the blinding white explosion. A fierce shockwave rattled his fighter, the impact violently knocking Dex's head to the left, as though someone had swung a wrench against his flight helmet. Adding to his headache were a fresh set of cockpit alarms announcing various systems failures. Before Dex could assess the damage, his fighter was once again rocked—not from the explosion above, but cannon fire from behind. Red tracers streaked past both sides of his canopy as the final Marauder unloaded on him. Out of the cacophony of alarms, Dex picked out one in particular—the friendly female voice reserved for the most serious of problems. She was cooing, over and over, "Shields, shields."

Dex tried jinking, rolling, anything to shake the Marauder, but his controls were lethargic. He lowered his hand, reaching for the yellow ejection handle. Dex knew that his odds of surviving a deep-space ejection were extraordinarily slim, but even worse were his odds of surviving a cannon barrage without any shields.

He closed his eyes as his fingers squeezed tightly around the handle. His Hornet shook again, and for a heartbeat, Dex wondered if he had waited too long to eject. But the impact hadn't felt like the others. It wasn't an immediate and vicious *thud*, but rather a wave that gently vibrated through his fighter. Dex turned and saw the Marauder exploding behind him. His fingers loosened from the handle.

"All clear, Deadeye," Jani reported.

His heart racing, Dex took a few deep breaths before addressing his wingman. A fighter pilot was not supposed to show signs of weakness— and that was doubly true for a squadron's captain. Steadying his nerves, he keyed the comm.

"What kept you?" he asked.

He knew Jani wasn't buying his show of nonchalance, but she played along for his benefit.

"I was curious—I wanted to see how many hits you'd take before punching out."

"The thought never crossed my mind."

He surveyed his cockpit. The HUD had disappeared from his visor, and his sensor screens had flicked off. It felt eerie sitting in the dark cockpit without his instruments emitting their familiar blue-green glow. The only display still functioning was the emergency systems screen, which operated with its own back-up power source. Dex flipped through the screens. His comm was functioning normally, and he'd be able to limp along with his engines, but that was about it. The remainder of the screens were filled with red type, identifying failures of varying degrees of severity. Before he could begin prioritizing the repairs, he needed an overview of the situation—something he couldn't ascertain for himself without sensors.

"My lights are out," he informed Jani. "What state?"

"Zero contacts, point four juice, all systems sweet." Dex imagined that she took special pleasure in reporting the last item—while his Hornet had been shredded, she had made it through the battle completely unscathed.

Despite the little jab, he was able to breathe a little easier following the report. Jani hadn't spotted any additional contacts, and she still had plenty of fuel remaining, as did he.

"How's your E?" she asked, concern creeping into her tone.

His ether-drive was one of the many systems marked with red type.

"Not good," he confessed. "Attempting a restart now."

The next few moments would be critical. The matter/antimatter-based ether-drive enabled the Hornets to jump between star systems. If the restart failed, he would be stranded out in space. Hitching a ride with Jani wasn't an option. A pilot took up every last inch of a Hornet's cramped cockpit—it would be physically impossible to squeeze in another body. Without the ether-drive, he would have to wait for the Angels to come back and pick him up in the squadron's light transport. If it came to that, he would have to pray that his oxygen reserves held out long enough—or worse, that the enemy didn't pick him up first.

"It's looking promising," Dex said, watching the restart progress on the emergency display. As he waited, he occupied himself with a series of systems checks. Even if his ether-drive became operational, he had to make sure that his Hornet could structurally withstand a series of jumps.

"So, you going to tell me what happened back there?"

It was the question Dex had been waiting for. He had been hoping that Jani hadn't noticed his mental lapse, but it had been a foolish hope. They had been flying together far too long for anything that significant to escape her attention. He wasn't sure how to respond. What was he supposed to say—that he had gotten bored and started daydreaming in the middle of a dogfight? How could he possibly fly with her again after admitting to such an egregious mental error? With no clear alternatives, he chose the only reasonable option—evasive action.

"You'll have to be more specific," he replied.

"You usually aren't one to repeat yourself."

"I was just making sure you were paying attention."

A long minute passed in silence.

"Well, the next time you plan on getting your bird shot up, make sure to let me know," Jani deadpanned. "I'll bring a book or something."

Dex was relieved that Jani seemed to be letting the issue drop—at least for the moment. And he couldn't entirely fault her prickly attitude. Not only was he evading her question—an entirely reasonable question at that—but the two of them remained stranded in hostile space. At any moment, another flight of Marauder's could drop into the system, and with his Hornet all but useless, she would have to fend them off by herself.

The restart cycled to completion. Dex exhaled, relieved to see the status of the ether-drive in green. He hurried through the remainder of his checks, becoming reasonably certain that his fighter wasn't going to split apart at the seams.

"Drive's sweet," he informed Jani. "Cleared to jump."

Dex activated the autopilot. When jumping into the ether, a Hornet would not allow the pilot to have manual control of the fighter. Even the slightest quiver of a finger on the flight stick could send the fighter radically off course. In order to ensure a safe jump, the autopilot had to maintain a true course for anywhere from five seconds to half-a-minute, depending on the length of the jump.

"I'm in the groove," Jani reported, affirming that her autopilot had achieved a true course. "Whatever's in that box better be worth the trouble."

"Roger that. Let's go home."

Chapter 2

The apartment, still dark at that hour, was tastefully decorated and had the faint pleasant ozone flavor in the air that spoke of the owner's affection for plants. Greenery of every kind filled open areas, effectively complementing the modern artwork adorning the walls. The soft strains of Mozart playing through hidden speakers in the ceiling were intended to bring sleeping occupants gently out of their slumber, refreshed and ready to face the day. That intent was lost, however, on the lone inhabitant of this apartment. He hadn't slept all night.

Darik Mason rolled over in his bed, slapped the lighting control with an open palm, and instantly regretted his lack of precision as the full brightness of the lighting panels assaulted his dilated pupils. Squinting against the glare, he let out a growl of frustration while furiously dialing the control down to fifty-percent intensity.

"Any time now," he muttered to no one in particular as the stupid thing took longer than he would have liked to respond. He was certain that he had adjusted the presets as late as last week, but the Household Controlling Unit seemed determined to return to its default settings. Finally able to open his eyes, Darik wearily swung his feet around to the floor and sat on the edge of the bed, trying to clear his head. He would have to take another look at the settings but knew it wouldn't be this week. Mechanics flew the worst looking shuttles, plumbers had the lousiest lavs, and this JenKore junior executive couldn't seem to find the time to figure out his own HCU.

Some executive, Darik thought. *What kind of executive ends up being chewed out by his boss twice in the same week?* The problems at work hadn't been his fault—as if that had ever stopped an employee from getting yelled at.

Rising to his feet, he reached for his handpod and switched off the Dream Weaver, an expensive little program that had proven to be a complete waste of money. The application was supposed to "program" his dreams based on pre-selected desires, locations, and scenarios, but Darik's preoccupied mind seemed reluctant to fully succumb to the Weaver's suggestions, resulting in some bizarre hybrid concoctions—two nights ago, he'd tossed and turned through an interminable employee conduct meeting on a secluded beach. He'd left a scathing product review but continued to give the Weaver a try, desperate for anything that might offer a reprieve from his restless nights.

He made his way to the lav where he finally caught sight of himself in the mirror. His dark brown eyes widened slightly—what he saw wasn't exactly the handsome, rugged look he was going for. Darik's longer sandy hair stuck out in several directions—evidence of his rough night. In addition, the skin beneath his eyes had taken on a decidedly darkened hue. Stress or no-stress, he needed to get his act together.

As he suffered through a shower that intermittently spanned the temperature range from icy to boiling, Darik tried once again to figure out what might have happened. There was simply *no way* the latest field malfunctions could have been his fault. Pulling his solid frame into a fresh business suit, he began to feel a little better. By the time he had finished his breakfast, he had to conclude that sometimes, despite his best efforts, things could still go wrong. And this had been one of those times. He would go in today, start fresh, and make it right.

Walking through the apartment's living room, he reminded himself that he didn't have a lot to complain about. Still in his early thirties, he had already climbed the JenKore ranks to a level that many of his university rivals would have envied. He took in his surroundings. The now properly adjusted lighting panels emitted a soft glow, illuminating the room's stylish furniture—a soft leather sofa and matching occasional chairs surrounded a dark faux-oak coffee table to the left-center. Several periodicals, covering subject matter from traditional rock-climbing gear to high-tech security innovations, rotated slowly above the table's holoprojector, flickering in a way that Darik always found relaxing. Even though he rarely had time to actually read them, he considered the decorative effect to be well worth the subscription price. The soft but provocative artwork occupying each wall were each tastefully framed in light zebrawood, perfectly complementing the darker wall panels. Almost everything was imported from off-world—the leather, of course, by necessity, the rest simply because Darik preferred it that way.

While it was all quite a bit more lavish than his current salary should have allowed, Darik considered these creature comforts essential. If he was ever going to reach the highest tier of JenKore, he first needed to look as though he belonged. He hadn't been born into the same privileges as most of JenKore's elite, and he worried that they viewed him as an imposter. And so, Darik was ever mindful of how he presented himself. The upscale apartment, the tailored suits, the luxury shuttle—he considered them all job requirements. He was, of course, uncomfortable with the amount of debt he had accumulated in order to maintain this lifestyle, but all of that would be taken care of with just a single promotion.

Darik would have preferred to linger in the comfort of his living room a while longer, but one of the periodicals caught his attention. A smiling, benevolent face beamed at him from the cover of *UC Industrialist*. Beneath the flattering portrait was the cover story's headline: *Social Responsibility vs. Profits—JenKore CEO and Philanthropist Kirrone Jenkins Explains How You Can Have Both.*

Darik shook his head ruefully. The JenKore CEO exemplified everything Darik wanted—everything he wanted to be. But there was no time for daydreaming. Undoubtedly, Darik's own immediate boss, Marcus Stirling, would be waiting for an update, and it wouldn't do for him to be late.

Stirling. Now there was a man Darik could live without. As much as Darik admired Kirrone Jenkins, he despised Marcus Stirling. The privileged, petty Vice President of Mining Operations was the person standing in Darik's way to the top. More than anything, Darik wanted to prove his own value to JenKore, get promoted—and then throw Stirling out on his ass.

Darik shook himself back to reality. Guys from a working-class background, he thought, aren't promoted automatically like Stirling had been. The only way Darik would reach his goals—the only way he would even have a *chance* at becoming an actual CEO like Jenkins—would be through a combination of incredible luck and extreme personal sacrifice. He was more than willing to make the sacrifice—he just needed to catch a break.

The periodicals flickered again, and the renewed sight of Jenkins's face rotating above his coffee table pulled Darik from his musings, reminding him that it was time to get to work. He drew a cleansing breath, refocused his resolve, and moved toward the door.

Another mirror adorned the wall near the front entrance, strategically positioned to give Darik one more opportunity to evaluate and adjust before heading out. The reflection now showed a tall confident Director of Mining Security. He filled out the suit nicely, retaining the conditioned tone of his more athletic university days. Even the faded rugby scar above his right cheek seemed to have taken on a more distinguished look. The professional in the mirror had every hair in place, shoulders squared, and was ready to take on the challenges of the day—whatever they might be.

As he prepared to leave, Darik, out of habit, checked his handpod again. He saw that he had a new message from that idiot Stirling. Feelings of inadequacy and trepidation came flooding back as he waved his finger over the icon, activating the retrieval system. Keyed and confident just a moment earlier, Darik waited for the message with his heart pounding, hoping that no further disasters awaited him this morning.

The message was brief but devastating. *Mr. Jenkins to see you in his office at 7:00. Four more units missing in last eight hours.*

Darik Mason leaned against a planter, digesting the information. Four more units? How could that be? And now he was being called in to explain the situation to Jenkins himself. It wasn't like this would be the first time, either. While Darik's encounters with Jenkins had been few, it seemed like every one of them, lately, had been to explain another shortcoming in his job performance. The previous meetings had not gone well.

Darik placed both hands on the planter, closing his eyes and trying to form a strategy—any answer that he could give to the explosively unpredictable CEO. At that moment his malfunctioning HCU chose to begin irrigation and pest control procedures. He backed away from the planter with an air of resignation and headed back to the bedroom to change, the front of his suit dripping with a mixture of insecticide and water. This was going to be a long day.

*   *   *

Dex D'Felco rolled his shoulders and turned his head left, then right, trying to maintain circulation in the Hornet's cramped cockpit. After their encounter with the Marauders, he and Jani had to endure an extended series of complex course changes, dropping out of the ether each time to realign before jumping again. What made it all the more exhausting was the fact that most of these changes did not take them any closer to home, but were simply a necessary routine to keep any potential pursuit from discovering the location of that home.

Another day in the life of interstellar fugitives.

Fighting the fatigue, Dex tried to keep his thoughts positive as he guided his ship through atmospheric reentry. The blue-green planet below had no official name. In fact, it did not yet appear in the *Downs-Boyum Register of Celestial Bodies* or any other comprehensive database. That's what made it perfect. Even if his instruments hadn't been fried in the ambush, Dex's bioscanner would have detected no life on the surface. A unique upper-atmospheric mix of heavy isotopes and strong magnetic patterns served to create a natural dampening field that effectively hid the planet and the two thousand-plus lives below from discovery. While obviously visible up close to the naked eye, the planet simply did not appear on long-range scans.

As Dex continued his descent through the field, he maintained comm silence, switching all of his now defunct instruments to passive mode out of sheer habit. Above and to his right, Jani did the same in her fighter out of necessity. Any emanations from either craft in the midst of the field could disturb its delicate balance just enough to reveal the secrets it hid below.

Nothing was ever easy. It should have been a simple cargo run, not a white-knuckle battle for their lives. The near-disaster of a mission had served as yet another reminder that even the smallest of errors or lapses in security could result in their discovery—and an entire fleet of Marauders swooping down on them. This train of thought brought Dex back to the question that had been nagging him during the entire return flight. Where *had* those Marauders come from? The route they had chosen to Vorina and back was obscure. The chances of running across a random patrol were almost nil. Yet the Marauders had been there on the return trip, waiting at their first course change.

As Dex's Hornet broke through the clouds, brilliant light from the system's yellow dwarf star streamed into the cockpit, obscuring his vision until the transparent canopy self-adjusted a split-second later, revealing the planet's single major land mass far below. Gray ice-covered mountains dominated the horizon to the east, and a large turquoise ocean occupied the west. In between lay his and Jani's destination, a small settlement nestled in the plains area, a few kilometers from the coast.

Even from this altitude, Dex could make out the distinct outlines of phirmium buildings. Blessed with exceptionally sharp eyesight, he was able to distinguish between the individual structures from a much greater distance than Jani could. Of course, her approach and landing instruments were still intact. Once she activated them below the dampening field, she could bring in her Hornet with her eyes closed if she chose. Dex, however, had no choice but to operate on manual control for the remainder of the flight. Setting aside his annoyance at the sluggish response of his banged-up Hornet as it descended through the atmosphere, Dex tried, instead, to enjoy the ride and the view.

Living quarters and supply warehouses surrounded the colony's commons—home to the marketplace and the church, which doubled as a small but necessary rec-center. Vast cultivated fields in alternating hues of green and amber checkered the plain to the east between the settlement and the ocean. Adjacent to and just north of the main colony, Dex could now see the squadron barracks, landing pads, and hanger. As he continued his descent, refueling stations, comm towers, and ground personnel came quickly into focus.

Other than this tiny pocket of manufactured civilization, fly-over scans had shown the planet to be uninhabited. Most of the remaining continent maintained climatic extremes inconsistent with sustaining human life, with temperatures ranging from -50 Celsius in the mountain region to +70 in the desert beyond. Only the small fertile strip below held any promise of habitability, and even that existence could be harsh, with hurricane-force seasonal storms frequently sweeping in from the ocean. But, despite the difficult environment, it was home, at least for now. Even though the planet was uncharted, the residents had been adamant that they wanted some way to refer to it. After the customary amount of discussion and in-fighting, they had finally settled on the designation *Pella*. The decision to name the planet, and their settlement, after the ancient Earth city to which many Christians fled in the first century had been suggested by the young Pastor Nathan Graham and had seemed to satisfy a majority of the colonists.

Confident that he was now below the dampening field, Dex reactivated what was left of his instruments, smiled a bit ruefully at how little help they were going to be, and prepared for final approach. His thoughts turned again to the ambush he and Jani had survived. Had they been spotted on Vorina and tracked? Although this seemed unlikely, Dex did not want to consider the alternative. He refused to accept the idea that the enemy's information could have come from within Dex's own forces, either intentionally or through an oversight of some sort. And right now, Dex was simply too exhausted to keep thinking about it. Yet he knew he would have to face the possibility and, if necessary, act upon it. With the security of the entire colony resting on them, the "Angels"—Dex's squadron—could not afford any lapses.

The Angels and the colony.

In the three years since their lives had become intertwined, Dex was certain that his pilots had seen more loss, battle fatigue, and frustration than most people endure in a lifetime. Friends lost, families separated, the constant threat of discovery and annihilation—it was enough to destroy people of lesser faith. But Dex knew his squadron—he knew their discipline, he knew their abilities, and he knew where their strength came from.

Throttling back his twin 530s, he eased over to ventral thrusters. His Hornet, though, dropped more quickly than expected, and he remembered that the thrusters were partially blocked by the cargo crate below. As he added more power to the thrusters, Dex again wondered what was in the crate. Food, medicine, fuel, living supplies—the colony's needs were many, and the cargo container was far too small for its contents to make a significant impact in any area. But it could only help. Deftly working his thruster controls, Dex brought his fighter in for a remarkably smooth landing, considering the condition it was in. Moments later, Jani's ship touched down lightly beside his. To dwell on the mountain of problems was pointless, Dex realized. They had a job to do—best just to focus on that.

Pulling off his helmet and shutting down life support systems, Dex fantasized about a hot cup of coffee and an even hotter shower. Glancing out of the cockpit, however, he knew it was not to be. Job Hansen, his executive assistant, was already approaching, organizer opened on his handpod and questions on his mind. Even as Dex hit the release on the canopy, Job's words rushed in faster than the outside air.

"Captain, welcome back. Here are a couple of things you need to know. The ROs at the water station have been acting up again, so we're on tight rations. We've had a few intermittent power spikes, and I have a request from a Mr. Granderson from the colony for you to...What the heck happened to your Hornet?" The tall, skinny Scandinavian rarely took a breath while he was speaking.

"We ran into a flight of Marauders before our second skip," Dex said, climbing out of the cockpit. "I took a hit before Jani blew one off my tail."

"Drager's not going to like it. He's having trouble keeping these birds in the air as it is."

"I'm fine, Job, thanks for asking..."

"Oh, yeah. Sorry, boss. But still, you know how Drager..."

As if on cue, Dex a heard an all-too-familiar anguished growl on the other side of his Hornet. Stepping off the ladder, he turned around reluctantly to face his flight sergeant. Drager St. James shuffled around the nose of the craft, carefully caressing the fuselage, emitting groans and clucking his tongue as he scrutinized every square inch of the hobbled ship. The stocky, balding sergeant didn't seem to notice Dex until his inspection placed him nearly at his feet. Seeing his captain, he snapped to attention.

"Sir!" Drager saluted, his clipped tones revealing a refinement that his soiled coveralls and three-day growth of beard did not. "May I ask you a question, sir?"

Dex sighed. "Go ahead, Sergeant."

"Captain, taking into account your considerable flying skills, your acumen in the cockpit, and your instincts in battle, sir, are you *intentionally* going out of your way to mess up my ships?"

Although he was in command, Dex knew better than to argue with the man who so skillfully kept the squadron flying with minimal facilities and nearly non-existent supplies. He looked Drager squarely in the eyes.

"Yes."

That seemed to satisfy the little flight sergeant. Nodding, he motioned to a couple of ground personnel, preparing to tow the Hornet into the hanger. Dex allowed himself a thin smile before turning back to his exec.

"Anything else, Job?"

"Yes, sir. There is a coded transmission waiting in your quarters. I have no idea how it got through. I wanted to ask..."

Dex interrupted him. "Thanks, Job. I'll take a look at it."

"You got it, boss." Job paused for an uncharacteristic moment. "Any idea what's in the crate?"

"Not sure. I didn't take any ventral hits, so it should be okay. Drager?"

"Already on it," a voice called from underneath the Hornet.

19

"Great," Job smiled. "Lord knows we could use the supplies—anything really. And boss?"

"Yeah, Job?"

"Welcome home."

As Job stooped down to watch Drager's progress, Jani passed behind him and whispered in his ear, "By the way, *I'm* fine, too."

"Oops, sorry. Welcome home, Lieutenant."

Drager, with some assistance from a crewman, lowered the crate and wheeled it over.

"Go ahead," Dex said, giving Drager permission to open the crate. If they had been following strict protocol, Drager would have first subjected the crate to a series of thorough scans to ensure protection against booby traps or harmful foreign agents. But this particular contact had never sent the colony anything harmful in the past, and indeed, sometimes the contents were time-sensitive.

Drager released the hatch, and the group peered inside. Three small white packages lay just beneath the cover, each labeled *phytochems*.

"Meds," Job exhaled. He made eye-contact with Dex, who nodded. "I'll take a package to the Gates family right away."

Job grabbed one of the packages and then stopped.

"There's something else in here." Job handed the other two packages to the crewman to put away in storage while Drager reached in and retrieved the extra item—a nondescript black box. Uncertain, he looked toward Dex.

"Let's see it."

Drager opened the lid, and Dex caught a glimpse of what was inside. The object, though, was less notable to Dex than the effect it was having on him. The instant the box was opened, his head and chest were assaulted with waves of pressure and heat. He suddenly felt queasy. His palms started to sweat, and the throbbing in his forehead was making it difficult to think clearly.

"Shut it," he all but yelled to Drager, who quickly complied.

Dex immediately felt as though he'd over-reacted, but seeing the discomfort on the others' faces, he wondered if they'd had similar reactions.

His forehead still cold with sweat, Dex did the best he could to steady himself.

"Job, see to the medicine." His executive assistant hurried off with the package. Dex then took hold of the black box from Drager. His flight sergeant seemed more than willing to part with it.

"And I'll take care of this."

Chapter 3

Nikky Weis was feeling edgy—not that this was anything unusual. As he monitored control screens in his cramped office deep in the bowels of JenKore's #3 Research and Development Facility, the idea of relaxing or even drawing a complete breath never occurred to him. His coworkers had never, in fifteen years, seen him loosen his collar, much less put his feet up on his desk. For that matter, they had not seen much of him, period. Nikky primarily kept to himself and did his job. And right now, his job consisted of watching the holodisplays before him for any anomalies they might reveal in the facility's complex control network.

With an almost rodent-like twitching, his eyes bounced spasmodically from screen to screen. A JenKore mug, half full of room-temperature coffee, sat on the desk beside him. He rarely finished a cup—it made him nervous. Every few seconds, his eyes would inevitably return to a small old-fashioned "flat" screen on his lower left. For the time being, it was blank except for the flashing cursor in the corner, but Nikky knew that at any moment it could spring to life with a new bit of interesting information. This data would never be saved in the system nor even on Nikky's own workstation. Such a back-up procedure would be far too risky. Any information captured on this monitor would be for Nikky's eyes only and then would be automatically deleted forever. Remembering it would not be a problem, of course. He had never forgotten anything in his life.

Nikky continued scanning the various displays, making mental notes to himself whenever he came across an opportunity to improve the efficiency of the system. He would then begin to work out the necessary codes for these changes while continuing to monitor the screens for any new information. At times, he would have several calculations formulating in his mind simultaneously, arranging thousands of characters in the precise order necessary for later input. He was also allocating a great deal of thought to a domestic concern—his pet turtle, Louise, was not eating as much lately, twenty percent below her normal intake.

An ancient keyboard occupied the desk space to Nikky's immediate left. While most user interfaces for JenKore employees consisted of either voice commands or the increasingly popular direct cerebral implants, there were still some functions where a simple keystroke was the most efficient way to input commands. This was usually accomplished through proximity detection units for the user's hands and fingers that were built into the workspace. Nikky's preference for the antique keyboard was considered among his coworkers to be just another odd quirk in his enigmatic personality. The truth was that excessive perspiration from his hands often threw off the proximity detectors and the cerebral implants gave him headaches—which meant that for Nikky, the anachronistic input method was a necessity.

The keyboard also served Nikky's purposes in another, less-than-official capacity. JenKore's system tracked every voice command, implant transmission, and proximity stroke in order to monitor each employee's efficiency and accuracy, the subsequent ratings often becoming the center of discussion and controversy during annual performance evaluations. Nikky's keyboard, however, was different. Any detailed inspection would show it was simply connected to and traceable by the control system, just as it should be. But with a quick sequence of keystrokes, the keyboard became independent, standalone, and anonymous. This was ideal for Nikky. He couldn't care less about his evaluation, but the setup made it easier for him to pursue his hobby.

It was because of that hobby that Nikky kept his left hand continually on the keyboard as he scanned the displays and performed the functions of his job. With one smooth motion he could take his keyboard offline, wipe his special screen clear, and return to online operation with absolutely no trace of an interruption. The personal subroutine he had been running on the small monitor would appear to show only familiar status data from a minor control function, unworthy of notice to any casual observers.

The monitor suddenly demanded his attention. Data was beginning to appear in a code that only Nikky could read. Scanning the information, he felt a rush of nervousness uncharacteristic even for him. This was going to be very interesting.

At that precise moment, Nikky heard the sound of his office door sliding open behind him. Reflexively, he keyed the sequence into the keyboard. The cryptic code instantly disappeared, leaving easily recognizable, standard characters in their place.

"Hey, Nikky." Seun Zhang, a junior analyst, poked his head through the door. "We're having trouble with the sync protocols on line fifteen. What's the access code to that diagnostic you ran last week that cleared it up?"

"Uh, that would be…" Nikky hesitated. It wasn't that he was nervous about the close call. It wasn't even that close. Even though he knew the answer to Zhang's question, Nikky preferred to make it appear as if he had to think about it. He swallowed hard and recited mechanically, "NW5719B3423-A."

"Thanks, Nikky. You're the best." The door closed as Seun retreated back into the hall. Immediately, Nikky whirled around to face the keyboard. His program was designed to intercept interesting information once, display it on his screen, and release it with a modifying time stamp to prevent the system from detecting the tampering. Ordinarily it was a one-time shot—if Nikky didn't read and memorize the data stream while it was on the screen, there was little chance of retrieving it again without risking detection. There were other analysts monitoring anomalies who were almost as good as he was.

He had only had the chance to read about a third of the screen before Seun's interruption, but what he had seen had piqued his curiosity. While continuing to monitor other displays and create codes for his normal job requirements, Nikky began to calculate ways to recapture the tantalizing data from the system's echo. If he could quickly pull it from the record of the network's fail-safe echo monitoring—a protocol designed to prevent someone from performing the exact undetected cyber eavesdropping he was in fact doing—he may be able to extract it unnoticed one more time.

Nikky realized that attempting such an extraction would be extremely risky. But if the data he had read so far was any indication of the rest of the captured stream, it would be worth it. Still devoting a sliver of his thoughts to Louise and her eating habits, Nikky began to mentally assemble the code for his next level of entry into the JenKore control system.

Nikky's hands trembled slightly as he took a sip of lukewarm coffee. It was all so very stimulating.

*　　*　　*

The box rested on his desk, closed.

Alone in his quarters, Dex sat and stared at it, unsure of how to proceed. He needed to take a closer look at the object—it obviously had been sent for a reason—but Dex wasn't anxious to repeat the same creepy experience he'd had in the hangar. As a man of faith, he believed in a spirit realm, but he had never before felt a spiritual force in such a tangible way. And, based on the brief but intense encounter, if he was dealing with a spiritual force, he was certain that it was not heaven-sent.

The longer he sat there, however, the sillier he began to feel. Wasn't he just working himself up over nothing? He was the commander of an elite fighter squadron. He'd flown dozens of combat missions. He had stared down death more times than he could count. How, then, could he be afraid to open a harmless little box?

Ashamed, he grabbed the box and opened the lid before he could stop himself. As before, the air around him immediately shifted—a tingling sensation crawled up his spine and pressure built against his ears. Dex wondered, though, if this physical response was of his own creation. It made sense, considering how much time he had spent psyching himself out, and as he reasoned through it, his body seemed to return to a more natural state, enabling him to look at the object in the box with a rational mind.

He had caught just a glimpse of the object in the hangar, and now he could confirm that it was indeed an ornate knife. It was long, perfectly symmetrical, and looked to be rather old, ancient even. The blade was composed of several layers—a dull, gray metal as the foundation, then silver, then gold, and then, most predominantly, another metal that Dex couldn't identify, colored a deep dark blue. Several inscriptions, indecipherable to Dex, ran up and down the blade, and embedded in its hilt was a single red gemstone. As a whole, the knife was well-crafted and held a certain entrancing beauty.

Dex figured that it was some sort of artifact, which made its presence in the cargo crate something of a curiosity. He couldn't fathom why the knife had been sent to him. It certainly wasn't a practical weapon for the squadron, and the colony had little use for ancient artifacts. It seemed like nothing more than wasted space—a shame since his contact's crates were typically packed to the brim with precious resources.

Dex closed the lid and slumped back into his chair, sore, exhausted, and stinking of sweat. He would have loved to take a shower using actual water, but the colony's strict rationing policies on Pella made such an option out of the question. It would always be possible for him, as the squadron commander, to pull rank and allow himself a few luxuries not available to the others, but he simply did not operate that way. Even though senior officers were not required to have roommates—an arrangement that fit well with Dex's unnaturally light sleeping habits—his quarters were no bigger, his furnishings as basic, and his water ration the same as everyone else's. He would have to settle for a simple ion shower, very effective for cleaning, but lacking any of the refreshing, invigorating benefits that a steaming spray of hot water would have provided for his tired body.

He rocked his head from side to side, stretching the muscles in his neck. The ambush and the long flight had taken their toll. Running a hand through a shock of medium length black hair, he rubbed a particularly sore spot on the right side of his head. The awareness of one ache seemed to lead to another. He slowly flexed his square jaw from left to right and back again, gingerly touching a tender area just below the cleft in his chin. Beneath the one-day stubble of his beard, a definite bruise was developing. The hits he had taken must have jarred him more than he'd thought.

He wondered, briefly, how Jani was doing in the aftermath of the battle. He figured that the lieutenant was probably in the gym, already working out the kinks from the extended hours in the cockpit. He considered walking down to check in on her. After all, a quick workout would do him some good as well. Jani would be already loosened up and undoubtedly looking for a partner for a couple falls of *Nuba-Jistsu*. Dex imagined her tying her red hair back, loosening up, stretching out...

He quickly decided against it. His relationship with his young wingman was complicated enough without entertaining those sorts of thoughts. It was obvious that Jani held a deep respect for him, but Dex sometimes wondered if her feelings went further than that. Even more worrisome, he sometimes wondered if, deep down, he felt the same way about her. But he simply could not encourage those feelings. Romantic relationships within a unit were a bad idea, inevitably leading to bad decisions—decisions, in the heat of battle, that could get pilots killed. He chased his own thoughts away as inappropriate and impractical. He was ten years older than she was, as well as her commanding officer, and that had to be that.

Besides, as beneficial as the workout itself sounded, Dex just wasn't up to it. Even the ion shower would have to wait. The coded message Job had mentioned demanded his immediate attention. Walking toward his workstation, Dex passed his small food prep area and noticed a pot of freshly brewed coffee. He smiled to himself. Job must have stopped in and keyed the brew sequence as soon as he heard Jani's and his approach in their Hornets. For all of Job's single-minded attention to duty rosters and inventories, he could be downright thoughtful in anticipating the little needs and wishes of his commander. At least the hot coffee would not have to wait. Dex poured himself a cup and sat at the terminal.

The message was indeed coded. Job had probably seen the decryption protocol query flashing on the screen when he started the coffee—such a detail would never have escaped him. Out of several possible options, Dex entered a personal code known only to him and the person he suspected of sending the message. His hunch was rewarded as the screen resolved to show a single unscrambled message:

NEW DEVELOPMENTS MUST DISCUSS 1900 HRS DP21A997

The message was simple enough. Dex's contact was someone he had never met, known to him only by the code name *Baker*. Other than that, he knew little else about the man, his entire knowledge of Baker having been pieced together out of clues from previous transmissions. Dex only knew that he was a man who had helped the colony and the squadron on several occasions; that he was obviously very wealthy, very well-connected, or both; and that he guarded his anonymity zealously.

Baker must have had something very important to discuss. Most of his messages were simply one-way transmissions about the availabilities of medicines, munitions, or other supplies for the colony. These messages could be pulsed in, compressed, and encrypted in a way that made them virtually undetectable to any outsiders. Many of the squadron's supply runs were initiated by these messages from Baker. His pattern was to send a coded message to Dex describing the place and time the critical items could be located, a name or description of a contact, and terms if there were any—most of the time the items were waiting for them with no payment necessary.

Baker's instructions had always been reliable, but the surprise encounter with the Marauders on the last trip made Dex a bit more cautious than usual. He had only spoken with Baker over a direct link on a couple of previous occasions. Such transmissions were risky both to Dex, who could not risk the colony's security by communicating on a more traceable two-way signal, and to Baker, who understandably did not want to be found in the position of helping the fugitives. Because of this necessity for high security, Dex rarely initiated these contacts himself. His role was to wait for a message, act on it if prudent, and then wait for the next one. Somehow, Baker was able to determine how the previous runs had gone without any replies on Dex's part.

Yet, it appeared that Baker required a two-way communication with Dex tonight. Sipping his coffee, Dex weighed the possible risks. He sincerely doubted that Baker had set them up on their latest run, yet someone had to have tipped off the Marauders to their route.

Dex sighed, tapping the rim of his cup with an index finger—the ripples on the coffee's surface distorting the message's reflection on the dark liquid. Baker, though unknown in person, had been their greatest ally since this whole mess had begun. Even if there was a breach in security, Dex would never uncover it by shutting off all communication. Besides that, the colony still desperately needed the contacts and supplies Baker had to offer. And, if Dex was being completely honest with himself, he was more than a little curious to hear Baker's explanation for sending the knife.

Dex glanced at his chrono—1830. He would have just enough time for that ion shower before the call came.

Chapter 4

The security measures at JenKore were extreme at any level, but the amount of scrutiny increased exponentially the higher one ventured up the Unity Tower, the home of JenKore's corporate offices. And, naturally, the office of President and Chief Executive Officer Kirrone Jenkins was located in the Tower's uppermost tier. Darik Mason had already passed through several checkpoints with verification procedures ranging from retinal scans to DNA analysis, obediently stopping at each to provide whatever password, print, or body part was required. He had suffered each of these delays and indignities so many times before that he hardly noticed the inconvenience anymore. Security procedures were just that—procedures. If you wanted to work at JenKore, you had to get used to the roadblocks.

This final roadblock, however, would require more of Darik's patience than all the others put together. Directly between Darik and his appointment with Mr. Jenkins stood the desk of Clara Kinsey, Jenkins's personal secretary. Darik glanced at his chrono. His appointment was in one minute. He had scrambled to make the rather unreasonable 7:00 a.m. start time, but now his fate was in Clara's bony little hands.

"Mr. Mason." Clara's monotone voice and sour expression gave Darik the impression that she regarded him with a contempt she would normally reserve for Christians or software salesmen. "Do you have an appointment?"

"Yes, Clara. I received a message this morning saying that Mr. Jenkins wanted to see me at seven."

"Well, no one told me." Clara sighed slowly, her breath creating a long oscillating whistle as it escaped through a gap in her clenched teeth. "I'll have to look it up. Have a seat."

With that, she turned slowly to her workstation and began an agonizingly long search through the various levels of her calendar for his appointment. Darik realized she was looking in vain. The summons to appear before Jenkins had shown up first thing in the morning, following an overnight disaster. Jenkins would not have run this appointment through Clara's calendar. She could look all she wanted—it wouldn't be there.

Darik would have taken a seat as Clara had ordered, except for two problems. First, he was far too anxious to sit. Second, Jenkins's outer office, with a sparse, antiseptic design, lacked the basic comforts of most reception areas—including chairs. Darik figured that Clara was trying to be funny—*have a seat*—but he chose not to comment for fear of dividing her attention. She was already taking long enough without any distractions from him. Instead, he stood at the desk, sporadically rapping his thumb against the cold metallic surface.

After what seemed to be several minutes, he sighed, unwilling to wait any longer. "Look, Clara, the appointment probably isn't in your calendar. He only contacted me this morning, and I don't…"

Darik's voice trailed off. The sight of Clara glancing menacingly up at him from her screen made his blood run cold. He took his hands off her desk.

Second after unproductive second ticked by. Darik tried not to pace, but he was growing steadily more nervous about the impromptu meeting. Four more of the M-2 units under his supervision had somehow failed again. He had tried to get more information on his way in to work, but none of his coworkers or contacts within the organization seemed willing or able to contribute anything of value. He was operating in the dark, though considering his recent record he was sure of one thing—this meeting was not going to be pleasant. But waiting for it was even worse.

Finally, after several lifetimes, Clara turned from her terminal. Without as much as a sidelong glance at Darik, she opened a comm.

"Excuse me, Mr. Jenkins, I'm so sorry to bother you, but Mr. Mason is out here, and he's insisting that—"

"Tell him to get in here." The irritation in Jenkins's voice was evident. "He's seven minutes late."

Darik consulted his chrono again. He had been standing at Clara's desk for exactly eight minutes.

*　　*　　*

The workstation sounded an incoming message alert just as Dex was returning from the lav facility up the hall from his quarters. Fastening the collar on his uniform tunic, he was pleased to realize that, despite the absence of water, the ion shower had actually refreshed him. The coffee hadn't hurt either. Dex now felt better prepared to handle whatever information Baker had to share. He knew that his mysterious ally would never initiate a rare two-way conversation unless the subject matter was extremely important. Settling into his chair before the screen, Dex adopted an official expression. Even though the encryption software would effectively obscure both parties' identities and appearances, Dex would remain careful to play this conversation by the book.

At first it seemed that his counterpart did not feel the same need for propriety.

"Hey old boy! How y'all doing?" The man on screen fairly shouted in exuberance as the picture resolved to show his image. While Baker's face was appropriately scrambled, Dex was able to note other details on the screen from the turtleneck sweater Baker wore to the various plaques and objects of wall art to the light clutter on the expansive desk. Despite Baker's folksy tone, Dex knew that the man behind the greeting was all business. As he had in previous transmissions, Dex felt a distinct impression that the image on his screen contained only the elements Baker wanted him to see and not a single detail more. Even the over-the-top southern accent, unaffected by the ever-present voice encryption, could have been genuine or simply have been generated. A quick glance at a readout at the bottom of his screen told Dex that the person addressing him did indeed match previous voiceprints of Baker. Beneath all the encryption and scrambling there were certain telltale signs in a vocal message, as certain as one's own DNA, that a person was not supposed to be able to fake. As far as his terminal was concerned, the man on the other side of this connection was who he was supposed to be.

Security protocol demanded that Dex make sure.

"Not good. My aunt has been ill," he replied.

"Right sorry 'bout that," the image on the screen responded. "Have y'all tried hot water and brandy? That'll fix her right up like nobody's business."

"I'll try it," Dex said, "but I've always found chicken soup works well."

"Sounds good to me." The electronic voice seemed to grow a bit more serious. "So, Dex, how are you really doing, my boy?"

In that short exchange, both Dex and Baker had confirmed their identities and assured the other party that their own end of the connection was secure. Any deviation from the preset pattern of questions with the right number of positive and negative responses would have caused both parties to immediately terminate the comm. In addition to this, Dex would have given the order for the fugitives to prepare for the possible discovery and invasion of the planet.

Instead, he relaxed ever so slightly. "Jani and I were ambushed on the med run."

"No kidding. You both okay?"

"My Hornet got shot up a bit, but we're all right."

"The medicine?"

"It's okay, too."

Dex half-expected Baker to ask about the knife next, but at the moment his contact seemed more interested in the details of the attack. "What was it? Marauders?"

"Yeah. Unmanned again."

"How about a control ship?"

Dex shook his head. "That's the funny thing. We could only track the Slugs. If there was another ship, it was beyond sensor range. But if that's the case, the lag time would make it pretty useless for controlling the Slugs or monitoring the actual fight in real-time."

Dex detected a trace of a smile in Baker's voice. "So, I take it none of them survived to go running back to mama?"

"No, Jani took care of the last one—the one that was on my tail."

"Give that little gal a hug for me, would ya?" Baker hesitated again. "You realize you may have a problem on your hands out there, don't you, son?"

Dex almost laughed. "You mean besides being on the run, trying to hide a couple thousand criminals, dodging Marauders, and trying to stay alive?"

"You know what I mean."

Dex did know what he meant. If there actually was an internal security leak, all of their lives could be in immediate jeopardy.

"Any suggestions?" he asked.

"I don't likely know what we can do except maybe try to flush 'em out with some bad info. Problem is, if they can track your moves, they might find out about any setup we would rig, too. Let me work on that one a bit."

Dex was determined to work on it as well, but watching the time count down on the display, and knowing that each second could bring them closer to detection, he also wanted to get to the point of the present conversation. "Baker, I don't think you risked a two-way to discuss my security arrangements."

"No, you're right, son," Baker replied, "but they are a consideration in the next drop I want to run by you. Dex, how would you like an entire *Charon*-class freighter filled with supplies for your little outpost?"

Dex wasn't in the habit of answering the obvious. "What do you have in mind?"

"I've got an older H-freighter. It's not exactly falling apart, but I can't justify keeping the old bugger out on legit runs. I could just mothball the thing, but I got to figuring—why not let you guys do a little acquisitioning out there? I could fill it up with all sorts of goodies from my normal sources and send it out on an automated run with a good comm hook-up back here. You guys hit it, make a few nice fireworks for my folks back here to see, and wham, y'all got yourselves a nice repairable freighter with enough treats inside to keep all them refugees of yours fat, happy, and healthy for a few months. In the meanwhile, because of the way we set up your shots, I'm happy, 'cause I've got transmitted comm files and maybe a few local witnesses seeing the darn thing blowing up. A total loss!"

"A total loss to your insurance company?" So far, Dex was not impressed.

"Aw shucks, son. I think I know you better than that." Baker actually sounded a bit hurt. "I know you wouldn't want anything to do with any insurance scam. To tell you the truth, neither would I."

"Then why would we want to make it look like we destroyed the thing?"

"Taxes, my boy! Taxes!" If it were possible, Dex's benefactor was showing even more exuberance than before. "The darn ship's so old I don't even have loss insurance on it. If I just take her out of service, I get nothing. But if she's attacked and destroyed out there, I can declare the thing as a total loss. Heck, if we fix it so you boys hit it in an enterprise zone, I may even be able to finagle a credit!"

Dex still wasn't convinced. "I don't know, Baker. It still seems wrong."

The voice encryption made Baker's sigh sound like paper caught in a fan. "Listen, son. It's high time you came to grips with something. Just who and what do you think you're fighting out there? This government may have taken the *illegal* stickers off your old churches down here, but they've still got all you folks who left labeled as fugitives. That's not even taking into account how annoyed they are with you over those little pieces of hardware you absconded with. There still isn't any amnesty for all those people who stayed out there when they were supposed to report back, and there certainly isn't any pardon for you and your squadron. And get this straight, Dex, there are plenty of people—military brass, intelligence agencies, civilian activists, you name it—who don't want you home, and they don't want you in prison. They want you dead! It's about time you got it through that thick head of yours that you are in a war, son..."

Dex felt blood rush to his hands and up his neck. He cut off Baker. "You think I don't know we're in a war? Do you have any idea what we go through every day? Do you know what we've lost—what we've given up?"

If Baker detected Dex's sudden rise in anger, his tone didn't reflect it. "Yes, son, I do know. That's why I'm suggesting this change in tactics. You need to step it up boy, or you ain't gonna make it."

Dex considered Baker's argument. "I don't know. The whole thing sounds pretty convoluted. Remember what happened the last time we tried to get too clever?"

Baker paused a moment, likely reflecting, as Dex was, on the losses the Angels had suffered a few months ago. When he finally spoke, there was an edge in Baker's voice. "Look, do you want the supplies or not?"

"Of course we want the supplies," Dex shot back, "but I just don't see why it's necessary for us to do something as overtly illegal as out and out piracy, even if it's just a put on. Why should we call more attention to ourselves and give them another reason to hunt us?"

Baker's tone softened. "Dex, you have to understand the situation here. It's getting more and more difficult to keep you folks supplied. Now you know me, boy, and you know I don't mind sticking it to the authorities and playing a little cat and mouse with 'em, but the simple fact is, I have to start coming up with some more creative ways of getting stuff to you. The watchdogs are all over my place. They suspect I've been helping y'all and are just waiting for me to slip up. I figure maybe if I take a couple of hits myself, like a hijacking gone bad—an attack that seems to blow up one my freighters—well, that might help to cool the heat a little bit."

Dex considered Baker's words. For the first time in the history of their covert relationship, the brash cowboy actually sounded concerned for his own safety. Dex knew that Baker was taking huge risks in supplying the squadron and the colony, and thought again about what it would mean to lose this powerful ally.

"Baker, we appreciate all you have done for us. Maybe we should just cool the transfers for a while." Dex knew the consequences of what he was saying. Besides the colony's constant need for medicine, supplies, and certain nutrients that they simply could not produce on Pella, the squadron itself required regular resupplies of fuel, munitions, replacement parts— the list went on and on. To back off on deliveries from Baker would put them all in a very difficult situation.

"Ah, heck son, it's not that bad," Baker countered. "I just told you, we simply need to get more creative."

"I'd like to help with that, Baker, but it still just doesn't make sense. I mean, the only actions we've taken out here so far have been in self-defense. It seems risky to show ourselves as aggressive attackers, even in a mission that we know is fake."

Baker returned quickly to his jovial, confident form. "C'mon, son, don't you think there are other outlaws running around out there? Who says the Angels have to be identified as the aggressors? There've been enough pirates hanging around the FSA border to force the government boys into declaring a tax incentive-laced enterprise zone just to get us businessmen to risk operating out there. So, don't you think it'd be easy to pass yourselves off as another bunch of 'em? Say, you don't happen to have a bunch of ghillie generators out there, do you—or someone who can rig 'em up for you in those birds?"

Dex was aware that Baker knew the answers to both questions. One of Baker's earlier transfers had contained, among other items, ten of the ghillie devices, brand new in the box. Designed to transmit a false sensor signal, they could theoretically be tuned to make the Hornets appear on enemy screens as any type of craft the Angels wished. While Dex immediately recognized their value, they were a new technology, and adapting them to the Hornets' complex systems had proven to be no easy task. But Dex knew, as Baker had implied, that given a pressing mission where the ghillies would be vital to its success, Drager and Ops Technician Ronnie Wilco would find a way to get it done. Reflecting on the devices' unannounced inclusion in an earlier shipment, Dex realized that his supplier had been planning this latest change in delivery tactics for some time.

The display showed less than a minute remaining in the "safe" window of their conversation. Dex sighed. "I'm going to need to think this one over, Baker. In the meantime, we haven't discussed the *other* item you had stashed in this latest shipment."

Baker looked puzzled. "What other item? What are you talking about, Dex?"

Dex held up the box with the knife. Even without opening it, just making contact with the outside of the box brought a subtle wave of revulsion throughout his body.

Baker didn't seem to notice. "Hmm. Never seen that before, son. What's in it?"

Steeling himself, Dex opened the box toward the screen, revealing the knife within. He was mildly surprised and relieved to note that the disconcerting effect of the knife was not quite so intense this time.

Baker regarded the box and its strange contents. "And you say that was stashed in the crate with the meds we sent you?"

Dex nodded.

"Dex, I can honestly tell you that I have absolutely no idea how that got in there. I take it you've already had your boys sweep it for tracking elements?"

Dex's stomach turned inside out, but not because of the knife's influence. If the knife, or even the box, concealed any kind of tracking device, the entire colony could be in imminent danger. Pella's natural dampening field prevented outside sensors from looking *in* but would do nothing to prevent a tracking signal from getting *out*. How could he have just glossed over an important detail like that?

"Uh, yeah. I'm getting it over to Ronnie and Drager as soon as we're done here. In the meantime, I'll give your latest mission offer some serious thought."

"Suit yourself, kid. I'll beam the particulars over to you at 2100, your time, in a compressed one-way shot. You can simply reply on the echo with the usual choices."

Dex would reply to the message with an omni-directional single burst of static exactly one millionth of a second long if he found Baker's arrangements acceptable or with two short bursts if they were not. Baker would monitor the exact frequency on which he had sent his original message for the reply. How Baker managed to discern and capture the static bursts among all the other cosmic noise was a mystery Dex wouldn't even attempt to unravel.

His ability to remain discreet, his resources, and his unblemished track record of assisting the squadron tempted Dex to trust Baker yet again on this new course. He would wait, however, for the details to be transmitted. Glancing once again at the now-closed black box, Dex felt none of the effects he had experienced earlier. If Baker didn't know anything about it, how *had* that knife found its way into the shipment? Dex wondered if perhaps this newest mystery was reason enough to pass on the freighter mission. No, he decided, he would proceed on facts and not on emotion. The knife was just that—a knife. Ronnie and Drager would check it over. If it concealed any trackers, they would respond quickly and deal with that fact. And if it didn't—if it was simply a weird artifact that had thrown him for a loop the first time he saw it—well, he certainly wasn't going to let some queasy feeling affect decisions that could keep the colony supplied.

"All right," Dex replied, "beam the specs, and I'll get back to you."

"Good enough, hot-shot. But mind what I say, Dex. Don't get too caught up in this what's right, what's wrong stuff. You don't fight a war that way, son, and if you don't watch it, one of these days that faith of yours is going to get you killed."

Dex actually smiled at Baker's rare reference to his Christianity. "How's *your* faith, Baker?"

"See ya, kid."

The transmission ended.

Chapter 5

Compared to the stark, almost sanitary outer office, Jenkins's inner sanctum was a study in expensive taste. From the walls paneled with a dark rare wood from Riksen, to the desk inlaid with the tusk-ivory of Argenian elephants, everything in the office spoke of its inhabitant's desire to find and possess. It was an office of power and position. It was the kind of office that Darik wanted desperately to have.

Despite his nervousness, Darik couldn't help taking in, once again, the ornate décor, accented by eclectic *objets d'art* from a hundred worlds, each individual piece worth many times more than his own annual salary. His eyes involuntarily paused to rest on a large sculpture a few feet to the right of Jenkins's desk. It was a bizarre study, sculpted from a metal Darik couldn't identify. The material had a bluish tint, yet it possessed an even darker quality that seemed to absorb all the other colors near it. Though motionless, it still gave the impression that one was seeing it from several angles at once. Darik was transfixed. The sculpture had an unmistakably violent feel to it. Yet there was something more, something almost sensual in its brutality.

"It's Travarian." Jenkins's voice shook Darik from his reverie. "Do you like it?"

"Yes, sir," Darik responded automatically, although he wasn't actually sure that he did like it that much.

"It came, in that form, from ruins on Travarus."

"Ah" was all Darik could find to say while nodding, perhaps, too agreeably. He was vaguely familiar with the legend of Travarus, but he recognized the idea of the ancient mythological planet to be exactly what it was—the stuff of fantasies and pre-adolescent fairy tales, like Atlantis, or Heaven. He felt a twinge of disappointment that someone he admired so much—someone he aspired to emulate—could be so taken in by such an obvious hoax, right down to purchasing a supposed "artifact" from some junk-peddling con man.

Of course, there was no way Darik would allow himself to show that disappointment or to indicate in any way that he disagreed with the imposing man standing before him. Kirrone Jenkins was an impressive figure. Tall and athletic, he was classically handsome and quietly intimidating at the same time. While the general public knew him well for his winning smile, engaging personality, and unmatched philanthropy, his own employees knew him better for his personal ambition, unparalleled drive, and exacting standards—and openly feared his harsh reprisals when those standards were not met.

Jenkins's expensive suit covered a middle-aged physique in prime condition—his daily 4:00 a.m. workouts maintaining almost non-existent levels of body fat. With his own athletic build, Darik was used to being the most physically fit person in any room, but standing in front of Jenkins, he couldn't help being conscious of his own deficiencies—a certain softness under his cheeks, a little extra pressure against his belt. He was certain that Jenkins was taking mental notes, so obsessed was he with the power of appearances. And from his tightly trimmed silver hair to the tips of his beluga-skin shoes, the man certainly radiated power.

The JenKore CEO gazed fondly at the sculpture as he continued. "That piece was found in an ancient temple. Most of the other artifacts were deteriorated, but this one remained in almost perfect condition. The arch-techs were able to piece together enough glyphs from the surrounding walls to speculate that it was a kind of centerpiece to the temple. They've concluded that it may have been a local god."

For the first time since he'd entered the office, Darik met the eyes of his employer. They were gleaming. Jenkins raised his thin eyebrows momentarily. "The glyphs indicated it was an object intended to receive sacrifice."

Darik endured this line of conversation like he endured everything else involving his superior. Not knowing what to say, he waited for Jenkins to conclude his idiosyncratic thoughts and move on to the subject at hand.

It did not take him long. "You have been involved in production of our mining M-2s for how long, Mr. Mason?"

"Two years, sir."

"And your area of expertise is?"

Darik was aware that Jenkins knew the answer to each question he was asking. He found himself wishing they would go back to talking about the bizarre artifact, which was still managing to captivate an uncomfortable amount of his attention.

"I am in charge of fail-safe and security protocols, sir."

Jenkins also continued to gaze at the artifact, keeping his eyes fixed on it as he continued.

"Explain to me what fail-safes and security protocols are supposed to accomplish, Mr. Mason."

Darik nearly rolled his eyes. He hoped Jenkins was enjoying himself. "Fail-safes are intended to prevent the M-2s from operating in any way contrary to their intended programming," Darik replied mechanically, "and security protocols are established to prevent the loss or catastrophic failure of any units in the harsh environments in which they operate."

Here it comes, thought Darik, *the question that ends my short, unremarkable career.*

"And how many M-2s have suffered this *loss or catastrophic failure* under your watch, Mr. Mason?"

Darik wanted to scream. He wanted to grab Jenkins by his expensive suit coat, pull him to within inches, and shout into that lean placid face that he already knew how many units they had lost. He wanted to explain through gritted teeth that if Jenkins really wanted progress on the security measures, they would need to provide him with better information than the garbage reports he was getting from the field. He desperately wanted to point out that no one—absolutely no one—could accomplish anything in the atmosphere of secrecy that surrounded the mining units. More than anything, and quite disturbingly, Darik wanted passionately to grab Jenkins and impale him on one of the many sharp points protruding from the "Travarian" idol.

Instead, he simply answered, "Twenty-three, sir."

"Twenty-three units," Jenkins repeated slowly. "Twenty-three supposedly indestructible machines, destroyed. The industrial equipment they were operating, all gone. The time to replace them, wasted. The potential for profit, never to be recovered…"

Previous experience had taught Darik that his best response to Jenkins's lecture was stoic silence. Eventually, his superior would come to the end of his thoughts, pause in the satisfaction that he had put a wayward subordinate in his place, and release Darik to return to the impossible task he had been assigned. He didn't intentionally tune Jenkins out, but as the CEO continued to speak, Darik found it increasingly difficult to stay focused. As words began to run together, Darik became less aware of what his employer was saying and more aware of an almost audible vibration coming from the bizarre sculpture near his desk.

The effect was hypnotic. Darik's heart began pounding in his chest, and his field of vision narrowed until he could see only the idol in front of him. It appeared to vibrate with an intensity and life of its own. The humming in his ears increased. He could not discern if he was actually experiencing the phenomenon with his senses or if he was simply having a hallucination brought on by fatigue, stress, and the stifling environment of Jenkins's office. No matter what the reason, Darik could not tear his gaze away from the idol. It dominated his thoughts, his vision, his attention. The object's protrusions, radiating out at different angles, seemed to move, blending with one another and stretching out toward him before receding again. All the while, the sounds increased in Darik's head, tunneling, unbidden, into his mind, into his soul. He felt his own will begin to weaken before the force of the strange object.

As the motion and sound grew even more intense, he began to discern additional sounds. Low and guttural, these new sounds stayed just beneath the surface of the idol's weird emanations. The sounds, at first, defied description, but then it occurred suddenly to Darik that they sounded almost like...voices. He could not make out their words—only that they called to him, producing both a feeling of dread, and desire. The dizziness increased, causing Darik to feel as though he would need to reach out to grasp the edge of Jenkins's desk to keep from falling.

As gradually as the effect had manifested itself, the illusion of motion coming from the idol began to subside. The low vibration faded, and the multiple discordant voices congealed steadily into one. It was Jenkins, continuing on as though nothing odd had occurred.

"...so it would seem you have a choice to make, Mr. Mason. Do you feel you have a future here at JenKore?"

Still feeling unsteady, Darik heard himself reply, "Yes, sir."

"Then it is well past the time you should be proving it." Jenkins's pale eyes narrowed even further. "I don't care what it takes, Mr. Mason. You are being paid to keep our M-2s in the field operational and out of danger. Utilize whatever resources are necessary. Recruit whoever you need to.

Do whatever it takes, but hear me—the next unit you lose will be your last."

Jenkins did not wait for a reply. Allowing his gaze to settle once more on the Travarian idol he added quietly, "You're dismissed."

Chapter 6

Dex never felt comfortable in the commons, and this morning's excursion set him more on edge than usual. Disciplined and regimented by nature, he preferred the secluded confines of the squadron barracks to the more populated, bustling atmosphere in the civilian section of the colony. By outward appearance, there was not a lot of difference between them—the lightweight but durable phirmium construction of every building gave the entire community a distinct military feel. But to Dex, the similarities ended there. The squadron base was a military operation with established rules of conduct and a chain of command. The rest of the colony, he acknowledged, was not.

Dex rounded a corner between a cafeteria building and a three-story living facility. With any luck, he might make his destination with minimal distractions. He didn't want to be unsociable—he just didn't have it in him to stop and talk with anyone. Last night had been lousy. He had struggled to sleep—that was nothing new—but once he had drifted off, the dreams had begun. Nightmares that he thought he had put behind him had returned with a vengeance—and a new twist.

That knife. What is it about that knife?

Following his conversation with Baker, Dex had immediately brought the thing down to Drager and Ronnie. Late into the night, the flight sergeant and ops technician had examined both the box and the knife within, finally declaring them to be one hundred percent benign. As far as the knife itself, while they acknowledged its strangeness and wondered aloud at its origins, neither one had mentioned being affected by it personally in any way. Dex, still feeling a little silly at his own reaction to it, hadn't pressed the issue.

Yet, even with the issue of potential danger from the knife apparently put to rest, the stupid thing had still managed to infiltrate his sleep. He tried to shake the sickening, foreboding feeling that still lingered from last night's restless visions and to concentrate instead on navigating the sudden crush of colonists that grew out of nowhere, flooding the path before him. Somehow, all two thousand of them must have decided to use this particular street this morning.

Two thousand colonists, Dex thought, and every one of them relying on the Angels for protection—and for leadership.

That was another reason Dex was uncomfortable in the midst of the colony. He had to remind himself to smile politely to passers-by, acknowledging their greetings without pausing to become trapped in conversations. Dex tried not to notice the hushed whispers.

Look! Isn't that the captain?

Ask him about the water.

What do you think he's doing down here?

Leave him alone, Harry. I'm sure he's busy.

Keeping his eyes mostly forward, Dex quickened his pace. He didn't notice a larger rotund man emerging from a side door until he nearly collided with him. The man, moving deceptively fast for his size, effectively blocked Dex's path, bringing him to a sudden halt.

"Captain! Captain D'Felco!" The man's breath carried a distinct fishy odor—evidence of a meal not quite finished. "I'm so glad I ran into you!"

Dex drew a breath and held it as best he could. Putting on his most congenial expression, he racked his brain trying to remember the guy's name.

"Ah…so good to see you, Mr.…uh…"

"Granderson." If the man was hurt by Dex's lack of recognition, he didn't show it. "Milo Granderson. I run the Senior Men's Fellowship. You remember! We get together every Tuesday in the main cafeteria."

Dex remembered now—and he knew where this was going. Granderson continued with enthusiasm. Smiling, he held up an admonishing finger and, if it were possible, drew even closer to Dex's face.

"We're still hoping to get you in as a guest speaker, Captain. You still have my contact info, don't you?"

Dex did have it, somewhere, under a pile of other data back in his office.

"Yes, Mr. Granderson." Dex tried to maneuver around him, but the guy was a planet. "I'll have to look at my schedule again. It's been a bit full, lately. As a matter of fact, I really have to be moving along..."

"Oh I understand, I understand," Granderson nodded, not understanding a bit. "Keeping us protected, bringing us supplies, leading the colony—it must be a lot to juggle."

"Yes, it keeps us busy." Dex fought the impulse to check his chrono.

"Well, the men would love to hear all about it. So what do you think about next Tuesday?"

"I'll check my schedule, Mr. Granderson." He patted a soft, fleshy shoulder in a feeble attempt to indicate the conversation was ending. "It's really good to see you again."

As Granderson opened his mouth to say something else, Dex noticed several more people beginning to gather. It was time to evac, or he would never make his meeting. Putting a bit more pressure on Granderson's shoulder, Dex feinted to his left. Granderson, predictably having at least one more thing left to say, moved to block him. Dex used the man's substantial momentum against him, slipping by on the right. Out of the corner of his eye, he saw Granderson recover his balance and then shoot him an enthusiastic thumbs-up, no doubt convinced that the speaking engagement was confirmed.

Dex gritted his teeth and continued his semi-brisk pace. He was a pilot—in command of other pilots. He had never considered himself to be any kind of *de facto* leader of the colony. In fact, he was on his way to see the man who, in Dex's opinion, really was their leader. Nathan Graham, however, did not consider himself a civil authority any more than Dex did. Graham preferred the simpler title of *pastor*.

Nearing his destination, Dex reflected that the colony hadn't always been without civil leadership. Back on Aphea, before they had ever encountered Dex and the Angels, the colonists had had a solid structure of government with a duly elected board of directors. These civil servants had been appointed to administrate all the nagging details of colony life, from housing and food production to conflict resolution. From what Dex understood, the directors had properly governed the colony, allowing Pastor Graham the freedom to concentrate on his own calling of spiritual leadership.

All of that had changed on the day the colony was attacked and forced to flee Aphea. While the Angels had arrived in time to rescue most of the colonists from certain destruction, the entire board had been killed in the initial attack. Since then, many of the decisions and day-to-day operations of the colony had fallen either upon Dex—with his access to supplies through the mysterious Baker—or Graham, simply because he was "the pastor." Neither man liked the current status quo, and while Graham had worked tirelessly to find men qualified to take up those leadership positions, the search had been slow.

Dex turned onto a side street which was decidedly less crowded than the main commons. Even so, it still seemed as though people were everywhere, with more than a few noticing him and stopping in their tracks when recognition dawned. Each furtive glance in his direction made him more anxious to arrive at his destination. Dex didn't care for the celebrity treatment—the last thing he or any of his pilots needed was a hyper-inflated ego. One didn't become an Angel without already possessing an over-abundance of confidence, and keeping his and his pilots' pride in check was difficult enough without the colonists fawning all over them.

He breathed a sigh of relief when he arrived at the young pastor's door. Ignoring the chime sensor, Dex simply knocked.

The door slid open immediately. Nathan Graham had been waiting for him. A little taller than Dex, but more slightly built, the dark-haired man of God flashed an easy smile, a counter-balance to the quiet intensity of his eyes.

"Dex!" he said with genuine warmth. The man's hospitality was legendary. "Come on in. Have a seat. I just made us some coffee."

Stepping through the doorway and out of the commotion of the street, Dex relaxed considerably. In the corner of the office, a small sofa—comfortable by colony standards—sat across a coffee table from an age-worn easy chair. Dex knew that Graham preferred this informal setting to meetings over a desk or conference table. Sliding onto the sofa and picking up a cup the pastor had placed on the table, he had to admit that while it wasn't *his* style—he doubted that it would be effective in a military environment—it worked well for his friend. He stretched out before sipping the coffee.

Graham regarded the squadron commander for a moment.

"So how are you, Dex? Are you doing all right?"

Dex started to give the usual, "*I'm fine*" response and then realized how foolish that would be. Nathan Graham knew him better than that, and wasn't he here to talk these things through?

Dex swallowed. "I've been better."

"You've looked better. How are you sleeping, Dex?"

Dex appreciated his friend's ability to get right to the point. "Not much. But you know that's normal for me."

Nathan cocked his head a particular way, giving Dex a somewhat sideways look. His tone was skeptical. "Yeah, sleeplessness is pretty normal for you. But I didn't ask *if* you were sleeping, Dex. I asked *how* you're sleeping."

Dex smiled ruefully. *How did he know these things?* "Okay. Okay. I'm not sleeping *well*. I mean, I was, for a while, until last night."

"And what happened last night?"

Dex took another sip of coffee, more to collect his thoughts than to enjoy the flavor.

"I had another dream, Nate."

"Like the other ones?"

Dex nodded.

"You want to tell me about it?"

"Not really." Dex met Nathan's eyes, knowing full well that answer wasn't going to fly. "All right, yeah, it was a *lot* like all the others. There I was, captured, bound. As usual, I couldn't escape—I couldn't even move. I was being interrogated and tortured. And it wasn't just me. I could hear the screams of the other pilots and other colonists. Whoever was doing this, I couldn't see them. Like always, they were just out of sight, in the darkness. I could only feel what they were doing to me and hear the agony of my friends. They asked me if I was a Christian—accused me of it is more like it. I wanted to say yes, and tell them that I was, but I couldn't. I just felt like if I simply denied it, I could make them stop—make it all go away. I could save my life, and the others as well, but I knew that it would be all wrong. My heart was pounding. It was all so vivid. I wanted to scream the truth at them. I wanted to shout out my faith, and to hell with the consequences. But then…"

Dex hesitated. He had intended to tell Nathan all about the knife, and how in his dream he had felt it pressed up against his neck, its sinister vibrations shaking his body and his faith to their core. He wanted to tell him how he felt the slicing pain and the blood beginning to ooze down his neck, but something made him stop. He skipped the description of the knife and instead shared the result it had brought.

"Then I caved, Nate. Like all the other nightmares, I took the coward's way out. I denied my faith. I denied being a Christian. I denied everything."

There was no judgment in Nathan's expression. "So did they let you go?"

Dex shrugged. "I woke up."

"So these dreams—they end with you denying your faith under duress. Is that what you think would happen?"

Dex shook his head. "I'm just not sure. I can't sit here, Nate, and honestly tell you how I would respond. Am I really that faithless? That ashamed?"

Seeing that Nathan was waiting for him to answer his own question, Dex decided to change the subject. "Anyway, my restlessness is probably more due to other concerns. One of the last things I did before turning in was wrestle over the details of our latest procurement opportunity."

Nathan, to Dex's relief, seemed okay with letting the other matter drop, at least for the moment.

"So, I take it you've heard from your contact again?"

Dex nodded, eager to discuss something less personal, more strategic. "This one's big, Nate. We could come away with an entire H-freighter, fully loaded."

He paused, letting the implication sink in. Pastor Graham didn't need to be reminded how desperately the colony could use those supplies, not to mention a large functional transport.

Graham nodded slowly. "An entire freighter full of supplies. Even for someone with your friend's connections, that's no easy pick-up. What's the catch?"

"The catch is that he wants us to steal it."

"Steal it?"

"Well, not actually steal it. For it to work out for him, it has to look like a typical pirate hijacking."

Graham shrugged. "And you're not capable of pulling that off?"

"Oh, we can do it." Dex smiled grimly, recalling how Baker had made sure previous deliveries had included everything they needed to pull off the subterfuge. "That's not the problem."

"Then what is?"

Dex set his cup of coffee on the table. "Nate, I'm just not sure where this is going. We're not outlaws."

Graham raised an eyebrow.

"Well, I guess officially we are," Dex admitted. "But that's not who we're supposed to be. And the further away we get from who we're supposed to be, the easier it is for us to believe their labels—to become what they say we are."

Graham remained silent, an old but effective method of allowing Dex to work through his thoughts. This time, Dex was willing to go along.

"I mean, one day we're sensor-masking the Hornets as pirate Adders and lighting up a freighter, next week we're firing back at any yahoo who takes a potshot at us, and finally…"

He paused again, gazing down at the liquid cooling in his cup.

"And finally?" Graham encouraged.

"And finally, we're out actively taking revenge for Aces and Smiley, for all the people you lost, and any other excuse we can find."

"Is that what you're afraid will happen?"

Dex looked at his friend for a long time.

"Nate, sometimes that's exactly what I *want* to happen."

The two friends shared a longer pause, dwelling on Dex's confession. Finally, Graham spoke softly.

"Dex, I think you know me better than to expect that I'm going to tell you what to do."

Dex smiled and shook his head. "No, you know why I'm here Nate. I need to pray through these things, and you're the only guy I can turn to."

It was Graham's turn to put down his coffee. "And you know I don't take that trust lightly, Dex."

They both bowed their heads.

Even though this moment of prayer was exactly what Dex had come for, and had, in fact, requested, he was still caught off guard by the sudden intensity he felt when his friend began to pray. It was a sense of presence, a sense of power, and a sense of assurance that Nathan's words were indeed being heard on high and that circumstances and events were being impacted in that very moment. It was a sensation that Dex rarely, if ever, felt in his own prayer life, and he wasn't sure if he found it compelling or frightening. Either way there was no denying that for a moment, concerns for the colony and the squadron and all of his personal doubts and fears faded in the light of what could only be the presence of God.

Dex hadn't necessarily been expecting clear answers—he couldn't pretend to understand the mysteries of prayer—but by the time Nathan and he said *Amen*, he knew what he was going to do, at least about Baker's mission. Dex reluctantly stood to leave. He was grateful for his friend's support and wished that he could remain longer, but another full day's worth of responsibilities awaited him.

Graham stood as well. "Dex, there's one more thing. Remember that passage from Exodus 18 we talked about last time?"

Dex remembered. The story of Jethro straightening out Moses' delegation skills had hit just a little too close to home.

"Dex, I'm going to say it again. What you are doing is not good. You're taking on too much. You've got good people around you—people you can trust."

Dex remained silent. How could he tell Graham about his other concerns—that he might have a security leak or, worse, a traitor in his squadron? He let him continue.

"You're tired, Dex. More tired than I've ever seen you. And no, it's not just the insomnia—that's only a symptom. You're exhausted. And when someone is exhausted, they make lousy decisions. You can't afford to do that. You have to give up some of this pressure."

Dex realized his friend was only trying to help, and even more, he knew that he was right. But he couldn't resist a sardonic nod toward the *other* corner of Graham's office, where the pastor's desk overflowed with water-ration requests, medical reports, crop projections, and neglected sermon notes.

"Finding some help, huh?" Dex good naturedly put a hand on Graham's shoulder. "And how's that working out for you, buddy?"

Nathan Graham smiled back at the pilot, the commander, his friend.

"Goodbye, Dex. See you at the briefing."

Chapter 7

Most weekdays, Darik spent his lunch hour working in his office where he would occasionally nibble on a cafeteria sandwich, if he ate at all. The exception was Monday, on which he had a standing lunch appointment with friend and JenKore colleague Eliot Liddle. The lunches had been Eliot's idea. He ate out every day and thought Darik might benefit from doing the same. "The office is a coffin—you gotta bust out and claw your way to freedom!" Eliot often argued, more or less in those exact words. And that was, in a way, precisely what Darik wanted. But going out for lunch was a far cry from doing field research. The lunches themselves weren't so bad—food was food, and Eliot was entertaining enough—but Darik found it difficult to enjoy himself, constantly harboring the uneasy feeling that he was wasting time or, worse, that someone would catch him wasting time. After enduring the first week of daily lunches, Darik had talked Eliot down to Mondays—an appointment Eliot jealously guarded.

That didn't stop Darik from trying to cancel after his disastrous morning meeting with Jenkins. He was in a rotten mood, and more importantly, he needed the time. With his job in jeopardy, Darik knew he needed to work harder, and longer, than ever. He grabbed his handpod and sent a message over to Eliot, informing him that he needed to cancel. Seconds later, his handpod lit up with a face-to-face comm request from Eliot. Darik reluctantly accepted. He hated wasting time with face-to-face comms—something he had made quite clear to Eliot which, naturally, had only increased the frequency of such requests.

Darik's handpod projected his friend's image. With his tanned face and short spiky hair, Eliot fit right in with the other trendy young execs in the JenKore marketing department.

"Hey, buddy. So what's this about canceling?"

"I just don't have the time today, Eliot. I'm in trouble over here, and I could really use the extra hour."

Darik saw Eliot inhale and then suddenly disappear, replaced by an upside-down view of an unkempt black desk. Unfazed, Darik spoke to the desk. "C'mon. It's not a big deal. We'll just—"

"No no, fine," Eliot said, reappearing. "Go ahead, cancel. It's your choice. But when I stop by your office later to complain, or comm you throughout the week to triple-confirm our next lunch, or drop by your apartment at night—and I remember where you live, by the way—so when I drop by to gripe about how my friend is too busy to see me, I want you to be thinking about whether that one little extra hour was really worth it. Again, it's your choice."

An hour later Darik found himself seated at a familiar table. The Black Swan, an upscale restaurant just a couple blocks down from the Tower, had a minimally designed interior, with tables and walls colored in whites and grays and a series of large windows that overlooked Compton. What set it apart from other restaurants in the financial district was that it employed an all human staff, even in the kitchen, rather than incorporating the cheaper and more efficient M-2 service models—and it charged a premium for that extra human touch. When it was his turn to choose, Darik typically opted for one of the Tower's automated cafeterias, which provided a cheap and speedy dining experience. But his friend preferred the amenities of finer eating establishments. As Darik rifled through the menu, Eliot was doing his best to charm one of those amenities.

"Shari, you've done something to your hair. I don't like it—too wavy. You'll change it back for me, right?"

"Sure, Eliot, I'll get right on that." The young waitress turned her attention to Darik. "Can I start you off with something to drink?"

Darik was still tearing through the menu. "Water will be fine."

"No." Eliot jumped in. "Don't enter that. We're having a bottle of Vorinian. White. You pick the year—and bring two glasses."

"All right, I'll be back with that in a second." Eliot's eyes lingered on Shari as she moved on to an old couple at the next table.

Darik lowered his menu. "It's barely past eleven."

"Relax. We're celebrating."

He could see that Eliot was still distracted by the young waitress. "What's the occasion? New shirt?"

Eliot mumbled his response. "No, I got this a couple weeks ago..." He watched Shari disappear into the kitchen and then shifted his attention back to Darik. "What were we talking about?"

"Vorinian before noon."

Eliot broke into a big grin. "Oh right. Today's a big day. They're launching the new campaign for JenOps this week. *Think Smarter, Dream Bigger*. They went crazy for it—huge bonus crazy."

Darik resumed looking at his menu. "I guess it's kind of catchy."

"It's going to be everywhere. They just threw it up on the city screens an hour ago."

"Yeah, I saw it on the way over. I was wondering how JenOps can make you *think smarter*."

"Who cares? Man, I love my job! You know what my next assignment is? I have to develop a new ad campaign for the handpods. They're giving me three months to do it. I came up with one last night while I was on the can. *Big Things, Small Packages*. There. Done. Three months of work finished in ten seconds." Eliot leaned in a little closer. "You can't tell anyone though, all right? I'm serious now."

"What, you're afraid someone's going to steal your slogan?"

"Are you kidding? It'd take a whole two minutes to come up with a new one. No, don't tell anyone I'm already done. I've got a sweet thing going here—all that's left is to fabricate a little market research, and then it's basically three months paid vacation."

"You're something, Eliot."

"Speaking of sweet things..." Eliot spotted Shari coming out of the kitchen, carrying a tray with a bottle, two empty wine glasses, and a large glass of water. Arriving at their table, she set the glass of water in front of Darik. "So you can keep your options open," she told him while opening the bottle and filling the two empty glasses with the pale liquid.

Eliot waved his hand dismissively at the glass of water. "You can drink that after the bottle's gone. We're celebrating, remember. Who celebrates with water?" He turned to Shari. "And you. You double-crossed me."

"Uh huh." Shari finished pouring and set the bottle on the table. "So are you two ready to order?"

Darik answered immediately. As usual, he was beginning to feel antsy about sitting down so long on his lunch break. "Yes. I'll have the turkey sandwich."

Eliot sputtered. "Turkey sandwich? You can get that at the Tower. Who comes to the Swan and orders a turkey sandwich? Seriously, Darik. We'll both have the rib eye, medium rare."

Shari gave a look to Darik, who shrugged and handed her his menu. At The Black Swan, famous for its exotic entrées and innovative flavor infusions, steak was as uninspired an order as a cold cut. But he knew there was no point in trying to talk Eliot into something more adventurous—he always ordered steak. As for Darik, he simply didn't have the time today to relax and fully enjoy the Swan's finer offerings.

Shari picked up Eliot's menu, unopened, from the edge of the table and walked briskly toward the kitchen.

"And don't you dare bring out any turkey sandwiches," Eliot called out after her. He chuckled and turned back to Darik. "Not bad, huh? Love those legs."

Darik was typically amused by Eliot's behavior, but today, he found himself growing more and more annoyed at his friend.

"Sure, she's all right," he said with an edge. "And now that I think about it, she kind of resembles Cristi a little bit, doesn't she? Same dark hair, blue eyes. Pretty close, don't you think? How's Cristi doing, anyway?"

"See, I know what you're doing here, but it's not like that at all. There's nothing wrong with being friendly to people."

"I didn't say there was."

"You could take a lesson from me, you know. You can get pretty far in life just by being a people-person. Take today for instance. I've been nothing but sweet and gentlemanly to Shari, and she's been lovely in return. But you, with your rude, surly demeanor—I don't think she even noticed you."

"She brought me the water."

"Oh right!" Eliot smacked the table in mock celebration, spilling some of Darik's water onto the white cloth. "Yeah, good for you. This is definitely the start of something special—I can feel it."

"Me too. As long as I don't get stuck paying her tuition."

Eliot looked genuinely surprised. "No. You think she's still in school?"

"I don't know. Too young at any rate—for either of us."

"Hmm." Eliot took a long drink from his wine glass and frowned. "Bleagh—terrible. Bad job by Shari." He grabbed the bottle and filled his glass back up to the top.

Darik sipped on his water. He enjoyed a good bottle of Vorinian as much as anyone—and looking at the year on the label, he was sure, despite Eliot's reaction, that it was a good bottle—but he knew he had a long day of work ahead of him, and getting tipsy with Eliot wouldn't make it any easier. He glanced at Eliot as he set his glass of water down, half-expecting a reprimand for not "celebrating properly," but his friend was distracted, glancing furtively over Darik's shoulder. Darik turned his head to look, but Eliot stopped him.

"No, don't turn around."

"What? What is it?"

Eliot lowered his voice. "I think that old couple behind you might be Believers. No wait—"

Before Eliot could stop him again, Darik turned and took a peek at the two old people quietly eating their meal.

Darik smirked and faced Eliot again. "You could tell just by looking at them, huh? That's pretty good. You know, you could've made a lot of money a few years ago."

Eliot kept his voice lowered. "No, shut up. I think I saw them praying. They both had their eyes closed."

"Maybe they fell asleep. They are pretty old."

"Please, don't use up all your wit on me. Save some for Shari."

Darik smiled and took another drink of water while Eliot kept glancing at the old couple.

"You don't see that every day, do you. I didn't think there were any left in the city."

Darik grunted, and Eliot continued. "It's actually kind of cute, don't you think? It must be nice to be so oblivious to the real world. I actually feel kind of sorry for them."

"Don't."

Darik's icy tone caught Eliot off-guard, and the two of them sat for a moment in silence. Eliot filled his glass again while Darik finished his water. He set the empty glass on the table and began nudging it around with his fingers. After taking it for a few trips back and forth across the table, he muttered, "It sure is taking your girlfriend long enough with the food."

"Oh, right, I forgot," Eliot said. "You're in some sort of hurry. What happened this morning, anyway?"

"I got called in to see Jenkins."

"Oh no. One-on-one?"

"Yeah. You've never been called in to his office, have you?"

Eliot shook his head. "No, I've met him a few times, but those were always in meetings. He never stayed long. I don't think he has much time for our department—which is fine with me."

"Well, you're lucky. I think he actually plans out how to make you feel as uncomfortable as possible, starting with the way he decorates his office. It's filled with all these weird artifacts and statues and stuff like that."

"Creepy bastard. So, what's the deal? What'd he call you in for?"

Now it was Darik's turn to lean in. "They lost four more units."

"No kidding? It's amazing you still have a job."

"Yeah, thanks."

"So what happened?"

Darik lowered his voice. "The reports say it's the same as the others—mining explosions. They're blaming my department's program."

"Huh." Eliot took another drink, and Darik reached for his glass of Vorinian for the first time. One drink wouldn't kill him, and he suddenly felt like he needed one. Eliot emptied his glass and set it down firmly. "Okay, you know I'm not an expert on these types of things, but doesn't it seem like there's been a freakish number of mining explosions lately? I mean, why are we mining in places that are constantly exploding?"

Darik coughed mid-drink. "That's a great question. They send their precious M-2s to mine the most dangerous places in the Coalition, then they act surprised when the machines break. And then they come yell at me. Fun job, huh?"

Eliot leaned back in his chair and clasped his hands behind his head. Darik recognized it as Eliot's "thinking" position. He wasn't expecting much. After a few quiet moments, Eliot shared his musings. "So, why are the M-2s breaking? What's wrong with your program?"

Darik closed his eyes momentarily before speaking, by his estimation, in a remarkably measured tone. "If I knew that, I wouldn't be in trouble, would I. It's so frustrating. Before this morning, I would've sworn on my life that the last upgrade was flawless."

"Yeah, I figured as much." Eliot blew his nose into a table napkin and then stuffed it in his pocket. "So it's obvious what you have to do, right? Get out there. Go see those units in action and figure out what's going on."

"Yes." Darik said it louder than he intended. Embarrassed by the attention he'd drawn to himself, he lowered his voice again. "Exactly. And that's what I've been saying. But Stirling shoots me down every time I bring it up. He says that the reports have all the information I need."

"Stirling? You still have to report to that moron? Screw him, and screw the reports." Darik had never heard Eliot speak with this sort of urgency, at least not about anything JenKore related. He marveled as his friend continued. "Maybe I don't know what I'm talking about, but it seems to me the first step in fixing these units should be finding out where they are and what they're doing. So take a few days and do a little fieldwork. And if you're worried about a low-life like Stirling or someone getting upset with you, well, Jenkins himself ordered you to fix this, didn't he? And that comes straight from the top. So, you either find a way to stop those machines from blowing up all the time or you're going to get fired anyway."

Darik had to concede that Eliot was making sense. He also didn't want to admit that fact to his friend, reasoning that his already enormous ego didn't need any more stroking. Instead, Darik muttered a non-committal, "Yeah, well, we'll see," and downed the rest of his glass. Eliot followed suit and poured himself another. Darik allowed his glass to be filled as well, then raised it and held it in place just short of his mouth.

"Why do we do it, Eliot? Why do we put up with all this crap? All the headaches and stress and long hours."

"That's easy. I do it because for me there are no headaches or stress or long hours. I have no idea why you do it. It must be the obscene amount of money."

Darik shook his head and smiled. "Must be."

They each took another long drink, and when they finished, Shari arrived with their meals—two identical steak meals and a smaller plate with half a turkey sandwich. She set the plates on the table, placing the turkey sandwich just below Darik's empty water glass.

"Enjoy your meals," she said, then turned and addressed Darik directly. "Would you like me to refill your water?"

Eliot jumped in before Darik had a chance to answer. "All right, Shari, that took some guts. I like that. But if you think I'm paying for that sandwich, you're crazy. Now, I don't know if that comes out of your pocket or not, and I don't want to hear it. The bottom line is, we ordered—"

Darik cut him off. "Hey, you know what? Don't worry, Eliot, I've got this one." He turned to Shari. "And yes, a refill would be great."

*   *   *

It was dark in Nikky Weis's office—he preferred it that way. Hunched over his workstation, he hesitated for a moment, drawing in a deep breath. In the days since he first discovered the elusive transmission—a data stream that he was forced to shut down before he could interpret the full impact of what he had seen—he had devoted more than a small amount of his considerable capacity toward finding a safe method of bringing it back for a more detailed analysis.

The puzzle had proven to be even more difficult than he had first imagined. He knew where the data was in the archives. He had the time stamp and location committed to memory. The problem would be pulling it back up on the echo without detection.

He released the breath into his cramped office space and drew another, his right pinky finger poised over the ancient *Enter* key. What he was prepared to do was dangerous and impractical—in fact, it was impossible according to any known theories of system management. JenKore's Echo Monitoring System—the system he was about to infiltrate—was originally developed for the United Coalition Navy during the conflict with the Frontier Systems Alliance. In the midst of that ten-year civil war, the UCN had uncovered the ease with which FSA agents were hacking their most secure military transmissions. JenKore's innovative echo monitoring had provided not only the UCN, but all branches of the Coalition military with the ability to know when their communication was being compromised, as well the precise location of the parties executing the subterfuge. Undetectable to the hackers, the system had rooted them out and helped to swing the balance of the conflict decisively in the favor of the UC. Not surprisingly, it also solidified JenKore's already strong position as the Coalition's top-grade military contractor.

In the forty-odd years since the Frontier War, and the relative peace that had followed, JenKore had parlayed its considerable war-time profits into a veritable empire of its own, diversifying into almost every area of Coalition life. No longer just a military contractor, JenKore now provided services and products ranging from city-wide security management to the manufacturing of so many of the conveniences Coalition citizens took for granted, from mass transit systems to the ever popular and versatile M-2 service units.

Nikky's main concern at the moment was that JenKore, while providing the basic Echo Monitoring System to the military, had kept its subsequent versions in-house, developing and refining the EMS over the past four decades into the absolutely impenetrable entity that it was today. No one in his right mind would try to infiltrate the system. The estimated time between such an attempt and discovery could be measured in nanoseconds. In essence, picking up an echo transmission, undetected, on this system was impossible.

Bringing his finger down on the *Enter* key, Nikky accomplished the impossible—or at least he hoped he had.

His eyes widened as the same data stream he had seen days earlier reappeared on the flat monitor before him.

He whistled softly in spite of himself. Still just a jumble of characters to most eyes, the stream coalesced in Nikky's mind into a series of images that both fascinated and terrified him.

What in the world was this doing on a JenKore data burst?

As quickly as the stream appeared, it reached its conclusion. Meanwhile, Nikky's brain had been counting down his window of opportunity. Knowing that nothing more could be accomplished by lingering, he terminated the probe with what he fervently hoped was time to spare. A quick diagnostic of the system status routines verified that, to the best of his knowledge, he had been successful. There were no alarms, no secondary protocols kicking in, and more importantly, no instant lock-down of his station with the inevitable pounding of security boots in the hall outside.

Always nervous by nature, Nikky had to fight an impulse to run. His mind was racing so much that he had to actually remind himself that he was in the middle of a shift. To leave now would draw exactly the kind of suspicion and scrutiny he had so far managed to avoid.

Hands shaking, he reached for his coffee. Partway to his lips, he changed his mind and set it back down. He missed the edge of the desk, and the half-full cup clattered to the floor. There was no need to clean it up—the floor automatically sensed the moisture, and microscopic channels opened to absorb the liquid.

Nikky retrieved the empty cup and set it more carefully in place. His heart was pounding. He had to settle down—this was ridiculous, even by his standards. No hobby was worth this.

Or was it. Beginning to breathe a bit easier, Nikky allowed himself a slow smile. In his years of surreptitiously monitoring JenKore's data bursts, he had never intercepted anything like this. Without a doubt, it was something he was not supposed to see, but he had apparently pulled it off.

An unrelated alert appeared on another monitor. Nikky sighed and diverted at least part of his attention back to doing some actual work. In the meantime, he allowed an even larger part of his mind to begin formulating his next steps. His initial shock at the contents of the data stream subsiding, he considered what he had seen. While he didn't know yet where it came from or why it was on the JenKore grid, one thing was certain—he was going to find out.

Chapter 8

Darik struggled to peel off the form-fitting omni-suit that fit just a little too snuggly to his form. Yanking on a particularly stubborn left boot, he again questioned whether this trip was worth the trouble. Finding a private transport to ferry him to Cacarus had not been difficult—but it had been expensive. And now, having seen the planet firsthand, Darik had to question why humanity had ever settled on such a desolate hunk of rock. Only under the broadest of definitions could Cacarus be classified as *habitable*. His edition of the *Downs-Boyum Register of Celestial Bodies* listed several charming features—*toxic atmosphere*, *arid surface*, and *unstable core* to name a few. The *Register* went on to note that in an isolated, self-sustaining environment it was, technically speaking, possible for humans to inhabit Cacarus. A lone outpost attested to that possibility. Established decades ago by JenKore, the outpost existed for one purpose— to mine the planet's rich phirmium deposits. And, so long as the depths of the planet yielded the valuable resource, humans would continue to live— if not exactly thrive—on Cacarus.

Darik, then, had not been expecting paradise—though he wouldn't have minded terribly if the four M-2s had malfunctioned in, say, one of Virgilia's luscious resorts—but it was the short walk from the landing pad to the outpost that fully convinced him that Cacarus was a special kind of hell. Exiting the transport, he had been greeted by a smothering wall of sand and dust. And though the transport had landed at midday, Darik stepped out into darkness, the swirling storm rising high into the sky, blotting out all but the faintest light from Cacarus's sun. After just a few unsure steps, he had completely lost his bearings. Bits of sand and rock pelted every inch of his body, stinging his arms and legs and crackling against his helmet's visor. Though he had been assured that the omni-suit was virtually indestructible, Darik couldn't help worrying about a fatal puncture. Fortunately for him, his suit remained intact, but it didn't take long for the unrelenting force of wind and debris to bring him to his knees. It was only there, on the ground, that he saw a faint glowing. If it had not been for a low-lying series of lights leading from the landing pad to the outer lock, Darik wasn't sure he would've been able to find the outpost— or make it back to the transport.

No one had met Darik in the outer lock, which was just as well with him—wriggling out of the omni-suit was embarrassing enough without an audience. With one final tug, the boot came free, and he stuffed the suit into a storage compartment whose door would not quite shut completely. As a matter of habit, he checked his handpod for messages. Seeing nothing of interest, he turned the device off and tucked it away. Prior to leaving Compton, Darik had told his secretary, Liana, that he would be working from his home office for a couple of days and that she should forward all incoming comms to his handpod. He didn't particularly like having to lie to Liana, but his trip to Cacarus had not been authorized, and the fewer people who knew about his excursion, the better.

Relying only on field reports, Marcus Stirling continued to blame Darik for the recent epidemic of M-2 failures. Darik and his staff had been ordered to work overtime until the program was fixed. And as far as Stirling knew, he was at his home office doing just that. But Darik was confident that his program was flawless—or at least it was flawless based on the data he'd been given. He was certain that the true error lay in the field reports. The reports had to be missing some critical piece of information, some variable that would explain how his program could continue to fail so miserably. And so, without Stirling's knowledge, he had come to the Cacarus mine—the site of the latest M-2 disaster—to find that missing piece of information.

A narrow corridor led Darik from the outer lock to a large room whose layout mirrored so many other generic JenKore offices. There was the reception desk guarding the room's entrance; the bland artwork on the walls, consisting mostly of Virgilian landscapes; the rows of desks and storage compartments; and the most telling characteristic of all, the spacious private office in the back that kept watch over the entire room. There were, however, two qualities that set this office apart from any other JenKore office Darik had seen. One, it was a complete mess. The desks seemed to serve no other purpose than to support piles of junk. Waste containers overflowed with trash, and directly in front of him, there was a sprawling stain on the floor of unknown origin. Two, the room was devoid of people. Though it was the middle of a workday, there was no one at reception to greet him, no workers at their desks, no manager milling about.

The office in general looked as though it hadn't been used for quite a while. A fine layer of dust covered most surfaces, including some of the junk piles. Darik began to wonder if the staff was on an extended holiday. Or worse, perhaps the outpost had suffered some sort of terrible accident. Because of the near-continuous planet-wide storms, communication between Cacarus and other planets was spotty at best. It wasn't inconceivable that a disaster at the outpost could go unreported to other worlds—though Darik, of course, had enjoyed no such luck with the lost mining units. And with only fifty or so workers stationed at the outpost, it wouldn't take much to wipe out the entire human population of Cacarus. Maybe hungry indigenous creatures had attacked. Maybe the air filters had malfunctioned and everyone had been poisoned—in which case, Darik himself would soon be dead. Maybe an earthquake had struck, and the living quarters had been swallowed into the bowels of the planet. With Cacarus, Darik didn't consider anything out of the realm of possibility.

His dark musings suddenly seemed very foolish as a man walked out of a door that Darik recognized as leading to the lav. The man was working at refastening his pants, which was no simple matter, given his substantial midsection. His entire head was colored a bright shade of red, almost as though his rumpled shirt collar were squeezing his neck too tightly. It took the man a few steps before he noticed Darik across the room. He stopped and stared at the visitor with a mixture of confusion and hostility. There was no greeting.

Feeling more than a little awkward, Darik broke the silence. "Hello," he said a little too loudly. Darik waved his hand slightly. "I'd like to speak with the site manager, if I could."

The man began walking again, keeping his eyes fixed on Darik. He exited out a back door without having uttered a single word. As he watched the fat man leave, Darik realized that it took a unique sort of person to work at the Cacarus mine. Though JenKore paid the Cacarus workforce exceptionally well, each worker had to sign on to a seven-year agreement—seven years of no natural sunlight, no fresh air, minimal communication with other worlds, and day-to-day working conditions considered among the most hazardous in the Coalition. Even Darik had to admit that in this case, money wasn't everything.

Three long minutes passed, and Darik began pacing around the front of the office. On his fourth trip past the reception desk, he slid into the chair and switched on the workstation. He would have preferred to have spoken with the site manager directly, but there were other methods of obtaining the information he needed. The display flickered to life and prompted him for a password. Undeterred, Darik pulled out his handpod and opened a file that contained thousands of JenKore passwords and their common permutations. Every JenKore executive had access to the list, and this would not be the first time Darik had used it to hack into a JenKore system. Back in Compton, he often pulled data from other departments— it was much easier and more efficient than getting bogged down with request submissions.

Gaining access to the reception desk terminal would be a simple matter of syncing his handpod and running a program that would rapidly insert each password one-by-one. The whole process would take only a few seconds. It was a basic hack that Darik had performed dozens of times, but never before had he felt such a surge of adrenaline. Then again, he'd never before hacked into a stranger's workstation in an abandoned office on an unstable planet whose inhabitants were, at the very least, not entirely friendly. As Darik finished syncing his handpod, he heard a noise on the far side of the office. He scrambled to switch off the terminal and looked up in time to see another man enter through the back door. Even at a distance, Darik could tell that he was taller than the first man and not nearly as obese, though his gut still hung noticeably over his beltline. He spotted Darik immediately.

"Can I help you?" he asked. His tone didn't sound very helpful.

Darik walked out from behind the desk to introduce himself, tucking his handpod away as he moved. "Darik Mason—I'm from corporate headquarters."

Although Darik had kept his trip a secret at the Compton offices, he saw no point in lying here. The man would undoubtedly check to verify his identity, and Darik hoped that his credentials would be enough to grant him access to the information he needed.

The man forced a smile and stepped forward, crushing Darik's fingers with his handshake. Topping the man's head were a few wispy strands of hair loosely slicked back, and centered on his round pale face was a bulging nose.

"Patrik Hedges, director of operations. What can I do for you, Mr. Mason?"

"I'm here to write a follow-up report on the M-2 incident."

The thin smile disappeared. "A follow-up report? What more is there to say? You guys sent us bad equipment, and it cost us a lot of money. The whole thing almost got me fired. I tell you, I'd like to meet the guy that programmed those worthless bastards."

Hedges's right hand was shaking ever so slightly by the time he finished speaking, and Darik was beginning to regret using his real name. Nevertheless, he forged ahead.

"Yes, Mr. Hedges, we understand that it was a significant loss for the mine. And that's why I'm here—to make sure this sort of thing doesn't happen again."

"Terrific. But that doesn't really help me now, does it? So why don't you just head on back to corporate and tell them that if they want their precious phirmium, they'd best stop screwing us over."

Darik took a moment to consider whether he should simply turn around and forget the whole thing—relaxing in his favorite chair and sipping a glass of Vorinian certainly sounded more appealing than dealing with Hedges and the rest of the unsavory outpost. But Darik knew that if he didn't get his answers now, then he might as well say goodbye to his title, his salary, his career, and everything else he'd worked for over the last ten years. Determined not to be beaten by this self-important bureaucrat, Darik rearmed himself. He leaned in and spoke to Hedges in a conspiratorial tone.

"I apologize for what happened, but I can assure you that your cooperation here will not go unnoticed. Compton might be able to arrange something—perhaps a new shipment of units…"

Darik had absolutely no authority to make such a promise, but, somehow, he had to get access to Hedges's records. He'd just have to sort out the rest later. Hedges, though, wasn't biting. "If it's more M-2s, you can keep 'em."

Darik didn't miss a beat. "Credits, then—compensation for all the inconveniences you've suffered on our account." As he spoke, Darik slid a credit chip into his hand. Instead of pocketing the unmarked chip, Hedges held it up at eye-level. At first, Darik feared that he had misread

Hedges—that some personal code of ethics was causing Hedges to reject the bribe. But then, Darik realized that Hedges just wasn't being very subtle.

"How much?" asked a frowning Hedges.

"See for yourself."

Hedges pulled out his handpod and inserted the chip. His eyes flickered with surprise before resuming their previous hostility. He tucked the chip away and mumbled, "Those M-2s cost me a lot more than that."

"And rest assured, more compensation is coming—provided I get the information I need."

Hedges looked hard at Darik, and then a slight smile crept at the corner of his mouth.

"Well, Mr. Mason, if you want to waste your time digging through old reports, who am I to spoil your fun?" Hedges led Darik to his private office and slid his handpod over a scanner to unlock the door. "Here, we'll use my office terminal—unless of course you'd prefer to use the one at the reception desk."

Darik's heart skipped as he tried to gauge the director's expression, but Hedges was already through the door before Darik could get a good read. Hedges took a seat behind his desk. He grabbed a nearby chair for Darik, knocking some clutter off the seat as he dragged it over. Darik, still feeling a little uneasy, tried to bury the last comment with a new topic of conversation. He nodded out the door.

"This office doesn't get a lot of use, does it?"

Hedges only grunted as he switched on his workstation. Darik took a seat while Hedges quickly closed whatever programs he'd previously left open. "So, what is it you're looking for exactly?"

"Let's start with the initial accident report."

Hedges flipped through a few displays until he reached the correct file. The report was old news to Darik. Four M-2s arrived the morning in question. After a summary inspection, they were immediately sent into the deepest shaft to begin operations. While cutting into a thick wall, one of the units opened a pressurized gas chamber. The ensuing explosion completely destroyed all four units. Darik, though, was certain that the report didn't tell the full story.

"I'm not seeing a name attached to the inspection. Do you know who was on duty that day?"

"Uh, yeah, that'd be Kuble. He handles all inspections. You two've already met. He's the gentleman you saw coming out of the can. So, what, you wanna talk to Kubsy?"

Darik pictured himself with the plump, taciturn man and foresaw that conversation going nowhere. "No, that's fine. I just needed the name for my records."

Hedges leaned back in his seat. "Anything else?"

"Yes, actually. The report indicates that all four units were within a twenty-meter radius at the time of the accident. Is it common procedure here to have your machines working in such close proximity?"

Hedges closed the report and shifted his weight toward Darik. "Are you telling me how to run my mine?"

"No, of course not."

"Oh, 'cause it sure seemed like you were just then. Tell me, what is it that you do again, Mason?"

Darik continued staring at Hedges's blank display. "It's my job to keep the M-2s safe and operational."

"Hmmm. And I don't suppose you've ever worked in a mine." Hedges was again flashing his toothy smile.

"No, I haven't."

"Well, I have—over thirty years. So, I think I know a little something about keeping my equipment in good working order. I also know bad programming when I see it, and those M-2s were about the dumbest piles of scrap I've ever seen. Hell, I could've detected that gas chamber with a handpod. So, don't go blaming my *procedures* when your machines take the very first opportunity to go blow themselves up." Hedges switched off his station. "If we're all through here, I've got a lot of work to do."

Darik stood up, blocking Hedges's path to the door. "Right. I certainly don't want to keep you. Just one more thing, and I'll be out of your way."

Hedges let out an audible sigh, and Darik took that as a cue to continue. "The report said that the accident occurred in Shaft Three."

"Yeah, what about it?"

"Well, I was wondering if I could have a look around down there—I can go by myself, obviously, if you and your staff are busy."

Darik expected an immediate rejection, and so he was surprised to hear Hedges mulling over his request. "Hmmm, I don't know—you're not certified, and there's insurance issues…"

Darik pulled out another credit chip.

"…but I won't tell if you won't." He motioned toward the main office. "Head out the back door and take a left. The signs should lead you the rest of the way."

Darik nodded and tossed Hedges the chip. As Darik exited the room, he heard Hedges call out after him.

"Just be careful, Mason. It can get a little dangerous down there."

*   *   *

The air in the shaft was foul—nothing at all like the odorless, sterile air that Darik normally associated with filtration systems. An info display leading into Shaft Three had informed Darik that an omni-suit was not required, but after spending just a few seconds in the shaft, Darik was already second-guessing that claim. The air was so heavy, so thick, that the filters had to be missing something. He just hoped that the *something* wasn't a life-threatening toxin.

A single row of running lights along the ceiling cast a bluish hue on the rocky walls. The relatively low light made it difficult for Darik to see anything in fine detail, not that he was looking for anything in particular. JenKore technicians had already scoured the accident site, and it was highly unlikely that Darik's untrained eyes would spot something that their instruments had missed. Still, Darik was more determined than ever to see the actual site, if for no other reason than to finally accept that his program was to blame.

Prior to entering the shaft, Darik had input the coordinates of the site into his handpod, and he was grateful for the map, as he would be hopelessly lost without it. Every fifty meters or so, the walls opened to reveal a possible new direction, each one seeming as endlessly long as the shaft Darik currently traversed. He was approaching just such a junction—the current shaft splitting off at an angle to the right while his handpod was instructing him to keep to the left. As he passed by the alternate route, he thought he heard a noise. He slowed his pace and listened intently.

And there it was—a low, throaty growl. He stood motionless, hoping to escape the notice of—whatever it was. The growling noise grew more intense as the thing approached the intersection. Darik knew he should do something—anything—besides just standing there, but his body had gone numb. He didn't seem to remember how to take a step, much less run.

He could hear it clearly now. Its loud growling vibrated through the shaft. Darik figured it couldn't be more than a few meters behind him. Fighting his body's natural instincts, he willed himself to turn around.

The first thing he saw were the eyes—six golden circles looking down at him through the darkness. The eyes were unnaturally bright, causing Darik to involuntarily wince away. He crossed his arms in front of his chest, bracing himself for the creature's attack. A few seconds passed. Darik, still momentarily blinded, listened for movement, thinking the creature might try to circle around him. But all he could hear was the continuous growling. The rhythmic growling. The mechanical growling. Darik's eyes slowly adjusted, and he saw that it was not, in fact, a living creature that stood before him, but an old Harvester mining unit.

The machine was massive, rising a full meter above Darik's head. Its lower appendages were twice as wide as Darik's torso, and its ultra-grade laser cutter made the M-2's industrial cutter look like a child's toy. While Darik was certainly relieved that he hadn't stumbled across a ravenous beast, he felt far from relaxed in the presence of the monstrous machine. Accidents were known to happen, and all it would take would be a faulty scanner or a bad bit of programming or even just one clumsy step for Darik to become another casualty of the mine. Darik carefully watched the slightest movements from the machine, looking for any sign of danger.

Whatever the Harvester had been scanning for, it seemed to be satisfied. It swiveled its bulbous head away from Darik and lumbered down the shaft, its large frame hunched over as though it were carrying a heavy burden. Watching the ancient Harvester plod away, Darik felt a newfound appreciation for the revolutionary M-2 design. The M-2 was exponentially more efficient than the Harvester, despite its slender human-sized frame. But it was its aesthetic quality that attracted Darik. Unlike other biped machines, whose movements appeared rigid and overly mechanical, the M-2 moved with a certain other-worldly elegance. Darik almost considered it wasteful that so many M-2s were employed for something as mundane as mining. Then again, he would be out of a job if they weren't.

The Harvester disappeared down the shaft, its rumbling diminishing to a distant hum, and Darik set off again. After a hundred meters or so, the shaft abruptly widened into an open area. A set of portable work lights stood in the room's center, illuminating a large hunk of twisted metal. Darik stopped and took in the rest of the room. A row of shelves along the right-hand wall held a variety of tools, and in a far corner, he spotted a makeshift cot. He stepped toward the bed, incredulous that anyone would sleep so deep in the shaft. After only a few minutes in the mine, Darik had already begun feeling a little sick; he couldn't imagine how someone could spend an entire night breathing in such rank, oppressive air.

"A fella gets used to it pretty quick."

Darik turned and was startled to see a man standing just a couple meters behind him. He was tall and wiry with bright blue eyes and hair buzzed so short that it took Darik a moment to notice that it was gray. Darik also couldn't help noticing that he was clutching a large blunt tool.

The man continued. "It's been a long time since I've seen a new face down here."

Without fully realizing it, Darik took a half-step back as he spoke. "I can imagine."

"Can you?" He searched Darik's eyes. Darik looked away, fearing that he'd offended the man.

"Well, I suppose not. I'm sure it gets pretty lonely here."

"It does." The man nodded and suddenly lurched forward. Darik flinched, and to his surprise, the man flinched in return. The man looked confused until he noticed Darik eyeing the tool in his hand. A smile spread across the man's face as he once again stepped forward, extending his free hand.

"The name's Franklin. What—you thought I was gonna bop you?"

"No. No, I, uh…" Darik trailed off. The truth was, that was precisely what he'd thought. He reached out and shook Franklin's hand. "Darik Mason—from corporate. I'm here to investigate the M-2 incident."

Franklin let out a single brusque laugh. "What M-2 *incident*?"

"You haven't heard?"

"I wouldn't say that, now. I hear plenty." Franklin made his way over to the work lights. On closer inspection, Darik recognized the large hunk of metal as the frame to a Harvester, albeit it a severely warped one. Franklin squatted down and ran his hand along the inside of the frame.

"So, what do you know about the M-2s?" Darik asked.

"There's not a whole lot to know on account of the fact that there never was any M-2s."

Darik wasn't sure he'd heard Franklin right. "What do you mean?"

"Just what I said—we never got any M-2s. A few days ago, all the workers here got a message saying that the mine was getting four new machines. Then the next day we get another message saying that all four machines were destroyed—right here in this shaft." Franklin looked Darik straight in the eye. "Now, how's there gonna be an explosion in this shaft without me knowing about it?"

Darik didn't have an answer. Franklin stood up and continued, waving his tool emphatically as he spoke. "Think about it—four machines and not a single scrap survives? These Harvesters are getting blown up all the time, and there's always pieces everywhere—believe me, I'm the one that's got to put 'em back together. Fact is, there was no accident, and there was no M-2s. If you don't believe me, go ask around. Not a soul in this outpost saw a single one."

Darik was scrambling to process this new information. It had to be nonsense—a lonely old man making up stories in order to seem important. Darik searched for a hole in Franklin's account. "What about what's-his-name? Uh, Kuble—he did a visual inspection of the units."

"He told you that, did he?" Franklin asked through a tight grin.

Darik felt his cheeks flush. "Well, no, not exactly."

Franklin turned back toward his machine. "Kuble didn't see nothing 'cause there was nothing for him to see."

Darik rubbed his temples. As much as he was reluctant to admit it, there was sincerity in Franklin's voice—a sincerity that had been noticeably lacking with Hedges. This frightened him. If Franklin was telling the truth, Darik didn't know what he was supposed to do with this information. A bad line of code he could've handled, but this was something else entirely.

"It just doesn't make any sense. Why would anyone want to fake a mining accident? And why here?"

"Beats me. All I know is I'm glad we never got those new units. I hear they're tough little buggers—virtually indestructible. They'd put me right out of a job. Now these Harvesters—a fella can rely on these." He kicked the twisted frame for emphasis, dislodging a small piece that bounced and rattled to the ground.

Darik couldn't help smiling in spite of the sharp headache that was rapidly forming in his forehead. Franklin's information had disturbing implications, but if what he said was true, then Darik was in his debt. He pulled out another credit chip—worth twice as much as the total he'd given to Hedges—and flipped it to Franklin. "Thanks for your help."

Franklin caught the chip and tossed it right back to Darik.

"Keep it. If there's one thing I don't need, it's money."

Darik didn't argue, tucking the chip away. Franklin adjusted one of his work lights, momentarily casting a shadow over his face. "If you don't mind, I will ask a favor though."

Darik hesitated before replying. "What's that?"

"You do what you can to keep those M-2s away from this mine."

Darik relaxed and smiled. "Right. Job security."

Franklin didn't smile in return. "Sure."

Darik tried unconvincingly to match Franklin's serious expression. "Yeah, I'll do what I can."

Franklin nodded. "Much obliged." He knelt down next to the Harvester frame and raised his blunt tool. Darik turned and left Franklin to his work. As he made his way back up the shaft, he walked to Franklin's steady beat—*clang, clang, clang*—slowly fading behind him.

*　　*　　*

Hedges closed the door to his office. He knew he had taken a risk letting Mason into the shaft, but he wasn't about to turn down free money. Besides, what harm was there really in letting Mason stumble around in the dark for a while? He would find nothing, of course, and what could he possibly do with nothing? Still, this was something *he* would definitely want to know about. Hedges took out his handpod and sent a request.

The small screen flickered to life. As usual, he offered no greeting. "What is it?"

Hedges glanced up at the door one more time and cleared his throat. "I thought you'd like to know we had a visitor today."

Chapter 9

The Angels awaited their captain in the squadron's ready room. They stood or sat in varying stages of alertness—some keeping an attentive eye on the entrance, others lounging and chatting more lethargically. The pilots approached their attention and adherence to the chain of command and military protocol with the same level of diversity that could be seen in the individual observations of their faith. While their shared convictions and choices had led them to the circumstances under which they were serving, they each expressed those beliefs in ways ranging from formal and conservative to casual liberality. In like manner, commitment and loyalty to the squadron and its commander, while evident, was practiced in ways as divergent as the members of the group themselves. Some showed strict, unquestioning allegiance to Captain D'Felco, following his every command or even suggestion to the letter. Others, while no less dedicated, were quicker to present alternatives, leaning towards the *as iron sharpens iron, so one man sharpens another* perception of command structure. The most vocal of this persuasion, Scot Calgaro, sat in a swivel chair in the back of the room, his feet positioned on another seat reversed in front of him. From this vantage point, he surveyed the room.

Eight pilots, each of them highly skilled in his or her own right—a couple that Scot would even consider near his own level. There was, of course, Lieutenant Jani McLeod, seated near the front in her ever-present position as D'Felco's wingman. Scot noted that even here on the ground, with Dex not yet in the room, there she was, poised and ready to run alongside her captain. An admirable trait, Scot had decided, however nauseating. Loyalty was one thing, but Jani's devotion to Dex bordered on the obsessive. For lack of a better term, Scot thought of it as a schoolgirl crush—a weakness in her personality that he just couldn't figure. He knew that she would never act on her obvious infatuation—not only would involvement with a senior officer be outside of protocol, but she seemed to have her own set of self-imposed rules about involvement with *any* other pilots. Plus, Scot had decided, she just wasn't that much of a risk-taker.

He smiled sardonically, remembering McLeod's early days in the UCN. He had first encountered her at flight school, where she had torn up the obstacle challenge, setting the course record in the process. She had obviously come from an athletic background, and noting the way she effortlessly bounded over the course barriers, Scot had referred to her as "The Rabbit." The name stuck, and much to Jani's annoyance, she would thereafter be known in the cockpit as Jani "Rabbit" McLeod. Preferring a more menacing call sign, but having little practical say in the matter, Jani had never really forgiven Scot for saddling her with the timid-sounding moniker.

Scot didn't care—he felt it suited her. He believed that as good a pilot as Jani was, she would never truly reach her potential until she learned to break some rules and let loose the creativity and competitiveness that he knew was boiling inside her. In fact, Scot had to admit to himself, as he admired once again her long red hair, confident blue eyes, and the particular way she stretched out her legs, that he wouldn't mind seeing her loosening up on a couple other restrictions as well. Forget the captain—he was too old for her anyway—but maybe she *would* consider getting involved with someone a little closer to her own age and rank.

At the moment, however, Scot simply watched dispassionately as Jani chatted with the pilot seated next to her. Commander Hagen "Sarge" Lebrian was a man Scot could respect. A full two meters tall and weighing at least seventeen stones, the man carried a command presence equal to his stature. He could fly with the best of them, and Scot could recall more than one occasion in which Hagen had put himself into harm's way to cover his squadron mates' tails. Scot figured Hagen to be in his mid to late 40s—he'd never dared to ask his exact age—making him the oldest member of the squadron. Scot couldn't understand why Hagen had never aspired to higher rank, even before the Angels' official fall from grace, but considering the quiet pride and excellence with which the commander carried his position as second-in-command, Scot wasn't going to spend too much time faulting Hagen his career choices. He was just grateful to have Commander Lebrian right where he was.

Not nearly as physically imposing, but occupying a greater portion of Scot's attention was Hagen's wingman, Flight Lieutenant Seltrice Valani. Slightly shorter and decidedly darker in complexion than Jani, Lieutenant Valani was the one peer whom Scot found a little intimidating—that was why she fascinated him. Noticing that she wasn't yet seated next to Hagen, Scot rose and casually crossed the room to where the fiery Sicilian stood. Her back to the wall, she was surveying the room with a slight scowl, as if looking for a fight. Scot swallowed once and sidled up next to her.

"Hey, Viper, how's it going?"

Valani stared straight ahead, replying in a cool tone, "Don't *Viper* me. I don't know how you managed to hack my personal log, but the message you left was *not* funny."

Scot assumed his most practiced, innocent expression. "Me? I don't know what you're talking about. Besides, that sounds more like something Geff would do."

"What's the difference? You're both a couple of no-brain, testosterone-fueled, arrested adolescents."

"Is that all you've got, Viper?" Scot asked, grinning as he leaned in. "You must be warming up to me."

"How many times do I have to tell you?" Seltrice continued to stare straight ahead. "You can call me *Viper* in the cockpit, but here on the ground, it's *Lieutenant Valani*."

"Hey, I don't get upset when people call me *Flash*."

Finally turning to face him, Valani eyed Scot incredulously. "You named yourself *Flash*."

Scot shrugged and turned back toward his seat, nearly bumping into Lieutenant Commander Lee Onigen. The squadron's third ranking officer surveyed Scot, his mixture of Caucasian and Asian features revealing little emotion beyond a certain intensity in his dark eyes. Behind him, Onigen's wingman, Flight Lieutenant Geffory "Prince" Bennet, stood smirking, obviously enjoying the moment.

"Trouble with your range finder, Lieutenant?" Scot could never tell whether Onigen's infrequent and tight-lipped smiles portrayed amusement, annoyance, or simple arrogance.

"No trouble, Commander. Just going over some flight details with Vip…uh, Lieutenant Valani here."

"It would appear, Mr. Calgaro, that you are flying solo."

Scot followed Onigen's gaze back behind himself. Seltrice had joined Hagen and Jani in the first row of seats.

Geff laughed. "That's Scot, Commander. He's naturally repellent—he must give off some sort of pheromone."

If Onigen was amused, he didn't show it. "Gentlemen." He nodded and left them to take a seat.

Scot gave his friend a scathing look. "Thanks, Prince. Next time Ninja Onigen comes breathing down your neck, I'll be sure to warn you, too."

"Aw, don't mind the commander." Geff was clearly still amused. "He was just messing with you. You have to get to know his sense of humor."

"What sense of humor? I've seen rocks with more personality."

"Flash, my man, I think you're just jealous of Ninja's and my kill record. Don't worry—you'll catch up eventually, once you whip Ghazi into shape."

Scot's eyes flashed, revealing just enough pain and anger to let his friend know he had crossed a line.

"Not funny," Scot said. He glared at Geff a moment longer and then returned to the back of the room, where he resumed reclining in his chair. Over to his right sat the Voor twins, Ravi and Purnima, while his own wingman, Adahn "Ghazi" Manasser, sat to his left. Not really in the mood to converse with Adahn, Scot regarded the twins instead.

Ravi and Purnima were as much a mystery to Scot as they were to rest of the squadron. Even as fraternal twins, the brother and sister still held a remarkable similarity in appearance to each other. Olive skinned with almost identically styled close-cropped, jet-black hair, both were slightly built—the similarities causing Scot, on more than one occasion, to mistake one sibling for the other from a distance, especially when their backs were turned. The Voors each held the rank of flying officer, the lowest in the squadron. Ordinarily, their ranks would preclude their assignment to the same element, with protocol demanding that each be paired with a more experienced senior officer as lead. Scot didn't fully understand Dex's decision to allow the two least experienced members of the squadron to fly alongside each other. The normally regulation-bound captain had taken the completely unorthodox approach that neither Voor would lead, but both would act as wingman to the other. Not being a slave to the rulebook himself, Scot didn't really care one way or the other. As long as they kept the Slugs off his six, Scot was fine with whatever the Voors did.

Technically, Scot realized, his own assignment was outside regulations as well. As a lieutenant, Scot was not supposed to be the lead pilot in his element. Glancing over at his wingman, Flying Officer Manasser, Scot wished for the hundredth time that things had worked out differently. It wasn't that Scot minded having the rare opportunity to fly lead as a lieutenant. That elevation confirmed his own assessment of his abilities, and he felt justified for having finally received the proper recognition. It was the circumstances behind his unofficial promotion that filled Scot with regret. He inwardly cringed once again at the memory.

Their names were Fran "Smiley" Simmons and Kevan "Aces" Adlerson—two excellent pilots, both lieutenant commanders, both gone in an instant. Scot and Adahn had been their wingmen on a long, complex mission in the Erebus system. The squadron's light transport, an LT-11 Raven, had been jumping in and out of the system, ferrying supplies to a hidden location while the Hornets patrolled around a deep space supply dump. Midway through the operation, four Marauders had appeared out of nowhere. Scot's Hornet had been disabled seconds after the Slugs dropped from the ether, and he had watched helplessly as the two leads were pounced upon, their Hornets vaporized before either pilot could eject.

Where the hell had Adahn been? The question had plagued Scot ever since. Had he hesitated? Dex, Jani, Hagen, and Seltrice had turned and engaged, destroying three Marauders and driving off the other, but it had been too late for Simmons and Adlerson. In the investigation and debrief, both Scot and Adahn had been cleared of any negligence. Scot had, in fact, been hit and disabled so quickly that he was lucky to have survived. Adahn's Hornet, however, had not so much as been grazed. Flight data had shown him to be just out of range and position to respond. It was ruled that he reacted quickly and appropriately, considering his position, but wasn't able to assist the lead pilots in time. Scot wasn't so sure.

In a time of conflict, urgent needs require that decisions be made quickly. With two senior officers gone, the word had come swiftly from Captain D'Felco. Lieutenant Scot Calgaro would assume the responsibilities of lead. His wingman would be Flying Officer Adahn Manasser.

Shaking himself from his unpleasant reverie, Scot glared again at his wingman. Whether it was his loyalties, his abilities, or even his faith, there was something about Adahn that he just didn't trust. That line of thought was interrupted by the sound of chairs scraping as each pilot rose and snapped to attention. Followed closely by Ops Technician Ronnie Wilco and the ever-present Job Hansen, Captain Dex "Deadeye" D'Felco entered the ready room.

"At ease. You may be seated." As Dex addressed the pilots, Job Hansen took a seat in the front row, and Ronnie Wilco assumed his traditional place at the ready room's IT console. Deftly moving his fingers over the console's proximity detectors, Wilco brought the room's holodisplay to life. The squadron's emblem materialized in the space just off to Dex's left.

"Angels, we have been given an opportunity to obtain much needed supplies for the colony, along with an even more valuable prize—an H-freighter, designation *Milk Wagon*. It is fully operational and will considerably enhance future supply procurement."

The nine seated pilots focused their attention on the display as an image of a *Charon*-class H-freighter replaced the squadron emblem. The reproduction of the bulky, roughly H-shaped ship rotated slowly, giving a full 360-degree view, with readouts noting shield strength and speed capabilities.

Scot ignored the details for the moment, knowing that all the relevant information would be transferred to his handpod for further study. His thoughts strayed, instead, to the importance of the freighter as a whole. Hornets made for poor delivery vehicles. Cramming meager supplies into their tiny stowage areas was laughably inefficient. Because of this, such runs were only made in emergency situations. For the majority of supply missions, the squadron relied on its light transport. The Raven could hold much more cargo than a Hornet, but its maximum capacity couldn't come close to that of a full-sized freighter. It would take the Raven dozens of trips to bring back as many supplies as the *Milk Wagon* could carry in a single run.

Scot knew that a freighter could also serve another, even more vital purpose. The Angels and the colonists shared a constant concern that Pella would be discovered and attacked. While each member of the squadron was willing to give his or her life to defend the colony, it would all be for nothing if the colonists couldn't evacuate the planet. An H-freighter wouldn't be able to accommodate all two thousand colonists, but it would be a start, possibly meaning the difference between a few hundred survivors and complete annihilation.

Dex continued. "This will be a full-scale sortie involving all ten Hornets. Each flight will have specific mission objectives leading to the successful capture of the target."

Murmurs of approval circulated the room. The Angels had grown weary of single-element medicine runs and other small-time supply missions. While important, these forays put pilots in danger without making any noticeable improvements in the colony's precarious situation. Dex and Jani's recent run had been a sobering example. The critical medicine had been obtained, but the captain's Hornet had been knocked out of commission for days. The pilots were itching for a full-squadron, meaningful operation, and it sounded like they were going to get one.

"Make no mistake," Dex said, anticipating his pilots' enthusiasm, "this mission represents a departure from our recent operations, but the same rules of engagement will apply. You will fire on unmanned targets only. Manned enemy craft, if present, are to be avoided with defensive maneuvers. Under no circumstance are you to fire on manned craft without express orders from Commander Lebrian or myself, and in that extreme situation, ordnance will be employed to disable, not to destroy."

While entirely expected, Dex's reminder dampened Scot's enthusiasm. It was no secret that he had a philosophic disagreement with the squadron's rules of engagement.

"With that understood," Dex paused, hinting at a smile as he surveyed the pilots, "we're going to get out there, drill some targets, grab a big prize, and fly again like Angels are supposed to fly."

Amid the general nodding and confirming glances among the pilots, Onigen raised his hand.

"Pardon me, Captain, but am I to understand that we will be stealing this freighter?"

"Well, we certainly want it to appear that way." Scot noticed that Dex was having difficulty reigning in his enthusiasm. He must have missed having the full squadron in action as much as the rest of them did.

"Flight Sergeant St. James and Ops Tech Wilco have been outfitting your ships with ghillie generators as well as modifying your IFF transponders to disguise your Hornets. Local sensor readings will show you to be flying old SF-33 Adders."

Several pilots chuckled. Geff pointed at Ronnie, giving him a thumbs-up. From behind the console, the affable ops tech returned a quick mock salute.

Dex continued. "With those changes in place, as long as we are in and out before any craft can get a visual, we should come off as ordinary low-life pirates."

Scot realized that Dex still hadn't fully answered Onigen's question. "Uh, Captain? Looking like pirates or not, aren't we still stealing the freighter?"

"The freighter is ours for the taking," Dex replied, annoyance creeping into his tone, having interpreted Scot's question as some sort of challenge. "The donor and circumstances are classified, but it is imperative that we make it *look* like it was commandeered. That's where the mission specifics come in. Besides being fully loaded with supplies, the freighter will have pyro-charges built into its exterior in the following locations."

Several points on the freighter's outer hull glowed green while indicators on the display showed the strength of each charge.

"As you can see, the charges are not strong enough to do lasting damage to the freighter, but targeting them with a low-powered burst should produce enough fireworks to sell the illusion."

The holodisplay showed a rather impressive representation of several Hornets firing a series of Vulcan cannon bursts at the freighter with spectacular explosions following the strafing runs. Scot had to hand it to Wilco—the kid had talent. The squadron was fortunate to have found someone with his unique skill-set in the colony. Most of the colonists, in Scot's experience, were pretty useless.

Ronnie, after taking an extra second to admire his work, switched the screen to tactical mode. The fully rendered ships were replaced by a system map with an as yet unnamed planet in the center. Traveling along an outgoing commerce lane, the freighter was represented by a simple yellow rectangle while the ten Hornets were rendered as smaller green triangles with accompanying call signs. With the full tactical map in view, Dex proceeded with the briefing.

"We will drop from the ether at these coordinates." As the information was displayed, Ronnie simultaneously fed each pilot's handpod data customized to his or her own Hornet with corresponding information pertinent to each wing or lead. "Rabbit and I will proceed as a two-craft flight, designated Angels One. We will make the first strafing run, targeting these pyro-charges."

Two triangles broke toward the rectangular freighter. This time there were no clever effects. The tactical rendering was all business.

"The four remaining elements will set up a perimeter. Sarge and Viper will team with Sunfire and Moonlight as Angels Two." The Voor twins nodded in silent acknowledgement to Hagen and Seltrice. "Ninja and Prince will fly with Flash and Ghazi as Angels Three. Each flight will execute recon pattern Alpha, scanning for incoming contacts."

The eight remaining triangles began to circle the freighter, four fighters in each group, performing the patrol. The recon pattern would look like a reasonably organized pirate maneuver to anyone watching on sensors. More importantly, it would also place the Hornets in an effective defensive position against any unexpected visitors—a distinct possibility, Scot mused, considering the Angels' recent track record.

"As Rabbit and I complete the first run, Angels Two will break for the freighter. Rabbit and I will take their place in the defensive patrol. At this point, since the freighter will not be sustaining anything but superficial damage, it will be necessary to bring it to a standstill for boarding. Sarge's and Viper's Hornets will be loaded with full complements of Leeches. They will use these to target the freighter's engines on their strafing run while Sunfire and Moonlight cover their work by lighting up the next four pyro-charges. The Leeches will drain the freighter's engines, slowing it to a stop and giving the impression that it has been disabled by the strafing runs.

"Angels Three will engage next, igniting the most powerful charges, giving the impression that the freighter is becoming more damaged with each run. Ninja and Prince will rejoin Angels One and Two on the perimeter, deploying partial chaff and micro-jammer screens. Our objective is to create some cover while leaving enough room for sensors to still see a bit of the action. Meanwhile, Flash and Ghazi will execute the next phase of the operation. Commander Lebrian."

Acknowledging Dex's introduction, the burly ebony-skinned commander stood. "In the wake of the explosions, Lieutenant Calgaro and Flying Officer Manasser will double back and dock with the freighter here." The tactical display zeroed in on the freighter's aft quarter, indicating a pair of docking ports on the ventral surface, one on the left side and one on the right.

"Securing their Hornets, they will board the freighter and proceed down the parallel corridors, meeting at the bridge one hundred meters ahead."

Ronnie had once again made a neat job of it. The holo zoomed to an interior view with a pair of amber lines running along the two long corridors of the "H" before converging at the front of the ship. Scot, however, was not thrilled with the prospect of being separated from Adahn. He could just imagine his wingman all alone in the dark corridor, getting jumpier with each step, waving his side arm at every shifting shadow. Scot made a mental note that before he turned the corner to the bridge, he would be sure to announce his presence loud and clear.

Hagen continued. "During this time, the pyro-charges will continue burning with increasing intensity while releasing secondary explosions at timed intervals. This will accomplish two objectives. First, to outside observers and sensor scans, the freighter will appear to be on the verge of final, catastrophic destruction. Second, the pyrotechnics will cover Deadeye's and Rabbit's final approach, where they will pick the Leeches off the freighter's engines with precise low-powered cannon fire.

"Once on the bridge, with engine power returning, Lieutenant Calgaro will take control of the freighter, using command codes that are being transferred to his handpod now. Officer Manasser will take ops. His first objective will be to engage the freighter's shields, encompassing the two docked Hornets and securing them for the jump. Once field integrity is established, they will immediately engage the freighter's E-drive, jumping to the first set of prescribed coordinates. All remaining fighters will detonate Slammers in the wake of the *Milk Wagon*'s ether jump, finalizing the illusion of the freighter's destruction. Needless to say, timing will be critical."

For the first time since the briefing began, Adahn made eye-contact with Scot.

"Piece of cake," Adahn whispered.

"Walk in the park." Scot leaned back, once again placing his feet on the seat in front of him. Despite the added silliness of the pyrotechnics and ghillie generators, the whole thing seemed pretty easy—not even Adahn could screw this one up.

Hagen concluded his portion of the briefing. "As with any EVA operation, the boarding party will carry side arms with stun clips. Once inside the freighter, you will be operating in very tight quarters with limited visibility. While we do not anticipate resistance on this mission, gentlemen, it is our expectation that you will prepare for the unexpected.

Therefore," he said, leveling his gaze at Scot and Adahn in the back of the room, "remember your hand-to-hand combat training."

Scot winced. Hagen's brutal sessions had certainly left their mark— or rather marks.

Dex turned to address the squadron again. "Standard etherspace security protocols are in place. Coordinates for each jump will be sent to your Hornets via encrypted data bursts. As always, if any Hornet is lost, captured, or rendered out of communication, you will not be able to find your way back here to Pella. If that is the case, we wish you Godspeed."

Scot understood. The security of the colony required that no pilot could carry the entire flight plan at any given time. Dex and Hagen alone knew the final coordinates of the colony's adopted planet. The capture and torture of any other personnel, while horrifying, would ultimately prove to be unproductive.

"With that in mind," Dex said, pausing to nod at the entrance where Pastor Nathan Graham waited, "Pastor?"

The young spiritual leader of the fugitive colony entered the room. His demeanor was anything but military. While he, like the rest of them, bore the weight of responsibility to the colony, his smile and easygoing manner conveyed a peace that many of the squadron members envied.

"Angels, I'm going to ask you to stand, if that's all right." The pilots, trained as they were in military commands, were also quite accustomed to Graham's softer requests. The man of God held a completely different, but no less powerful authority than that of their captain. The pre-mission prayers were something each pilot genuinely appreciated.

Asking them to bow their heads, Graham led the squadron in prayer for safety, wisdom, restraint when possible, and force when necessary. He prayed that each would know the power, presence, and guidance of the Holy Spirit, and would return safely with the successful completion of their task.

As was their tradition, the squadron snapped back to attention at the word *Amen*. Dex addressed them one final time.

"All other flight and mission data is on your handpods. I suggest you start studying. Operation Milk Run launch is at 1600 hours today. Dismissed."

As the pilots began to disperse, Scot saw Ronnie, Job, and Hagen exchanging a few words in hushed tones, mild concern written across their faces. All three of them had been part of the initial planning stages with

Dex, which meant that the captain must have sprung something new on them. When Ronnie stepped away, Scot caught his arm.

"What was that about?"

Ronnie seemed preoccupied. "Oh, it's nothing. Captain D'Felco just moved the mission up by twelve hours." Scot could see the long list of tasks already forming in Ronnie's head as he spoke. "I'd better get to work."

Chapter 10

Compton had the most iconic skyline in the Coalition. This was thanks in large part to the authorized cityscape, which had been carefully crafted to highlight the skyline's striking symmetry. In the ubiquitous marketing image, both ends of the horizon sprouted up into tall buildings, which gradually morphed into skyscrapers, each side growing taller at approximately the same rate until the two rows met in the center—at the feet of the Unity Tower. To those who had never seen the Tower in person, it was difficult for the silhouette to capture the scale of the immense structure, but the careful observer would notice that it dwarfed nearby buildings that, in their own right, were among the tallest in the Coalition. Millions of people who had never set foot on Earth were familiar with the silhouette—and to them, the Unity Tower *was* Compton.

It had always been a source of great pride for Darik that he worked in the Coalition's most famous building. Whenever he could spare the time, he made a point of taking an external lift up to the Tower's second tier. He took a certain pleasure in watching the city shrink beneath his feet—the sense of power was exhilarating.

Today, however, Darik felt neither pride nor exhilaration during his morning commute. Rather, he was weighed down by an almost tangible heaviness as he made his way through the heart of the city. He had lived in Compton for almost all of his adult life, and never before had he experienced anything close to claustrophobia. Now, without any sort of warning, he had become paralyzed with it. His personal shuttle, flying on autopilot close to ground level through the financial district, seemed to have inexplicably slowed to a stop. The buildings on either side of the street, each so familiar to Darik, suddenly appeared alien to him. It was almost as though they had somehow shifted position, closing in around him, offering no avenue of escape. And in the background, the Tower, rather than rising majestically through the clouds, hovered over him—leaning so far that it was on the verge of toppling over and crushing him along with all of downtown Compton. His heart pounding, Darik shut his eyes for a moment and took a couple of deep breaths. When he returned his attention back down to ground level, he saw that traffic had resumed its normal flow, each building flying past in a blur, just as it did every other morning. He was embarrassed by the intensity of his relief.

Darik blamed Cacarus for his dismal mood. The site visit was supposed to have cleared everything up, but he had left the planet with far more questions than answers. And with Jenkins himself taking a sudden personal interest in JenKore's mining division, Darik didn't have the luxury of time to sort things out. Worse, he now had absolutely zero margin for error. One bad decision and Jenkins wouldn't hesitate to purge Darik and his entire department.

He was running a few minutes late when his shuttle arrived at the Tower, forcing him to take one of the speedier internal lifts. The lift was already over-crowded when he stepped on, which—combined with being randomly selected for a full-body scan at the Tier-Four security checkpoint—left Darik stewing in a mixture of hostility and self-pity by the time he arrived at his floor. Striding aggressively through the main office, he was fully prepared to snap at the first person who looked at him the wrong way. His acidic temper, however, dissolved ever so slightly when he spotted Liana across the room. She flashed him a bright smile, and Darik altered his path toward her, deciding that it would be rude not to check in with his secretary after his extended absence from the office. As he stepped up to Liana's desk, any lingering unpleasant memories from his morning commute were instantly rendered vague and unimportant by her warm, sincere greeting.

"Welcome back, Darik. We missed you around here."

"No one ever misses their boss. But thanks anyway, Liana. It's good to be back." He shuffled around her desk. "Any news around here?"

Liana's slender fingers raised a display filled with abbreviated notes.

"Well, let's see. You missed one terribly important meeting…" Liana glanced up at him, and he shot her a knowing grin. It was not a coincidence that his absence had coincided with the department's interminable monthly budget meeting. Liana continued, "And Mr. Stirling stopped by. He wanted a progress report on the new program."

The heaviness began to creep back into Darik's chest. Marcus Stirling, the esteemed Vice President of Mining Operations, rarely took the time to come down to Darik's office unless he was in trouble.

"What did you tell him?" Darik asked, trying to mask his concern.

Liana looked him directly in the eye. "I told him the truth—that you were at your home office working tirelessly on the update."

Darik felt a fresh wave of guilt for lying to Liana about his trip. "And what did he have to say?"

"Nothing that bears repeating…" She offered a thin smile, attempting to show Darik that it wasn't a big deal, which, naturally, made him feel even worse.

"I'm really sorry about that, Liana. I promise to make it up to you."

"You most certainly will."

It took Darik a moment to realize he was blushing. "Well," he said, stepping away, "I'm sure I have a ton of work waiting for me."

Darik fumbled around for his handpod as he walked the half-dozen paces from Liana's desk to his office. Unlocking the door, he was greeted with the familiar sanitized odors wafting out of the room. But as he moved through the doorway, he couldn't shake the sense that something was wrong. It wasn't anything overt—the room just seemed a bit off. He took a couple of soft steps, allowing the door to slide shut behind him. After a few still seconds of observation, he began to notice the tangible little changes that his subconscious had instantly detected—a chair up against the wrong wall, his workstation turned off rather than on standby. He leaned over his desk and triggered a comm.

"Liana, was anyone in my office while I was away?"

"Not that I know of. Is something wrong?"

"No—just wondering. Thanks."

It was possible that he had decided to break his routine and shut his station down before the trip. And it was possible that he had met with someone in his office prior to leaving—someone who pushed his chair up against the wrong wall. Possible, yes, but he didn't remember either happening that way.

Then again, what reason could someone have for snooping around his office? Anyone with enough clearance to key into his door would already have access to his files through the network. Besides, Darik didn't have anything to hide—except, of course, his trip to Cacarus. But there was nothing in his office that would even hint at that.

Cacarus—that hellhole of a planet and the center of all of his recent troubles. He turned on his workstation, waiting patiently for the start-up displays to cycle through—one of the reasons he preferred to keep it on standby. As soon as he was able, he pulled up the logs for all recent M-2 shipments. It didn't take him long to track down the four mining units in question.

Their journey had been simpler than most—or at least that's what the logs led him to believe. The four were assembled in the enormous orbital manufacturing station over Bacchus, the "birthplace" of over two-thirds of JenKore's M-2s. The log then showed that they had been shipped directly from Bacchus to Cacarus, hitting all the necessary checkpoints along the way.

This was an essential piece of information. All M-2s were programmed with a series of fail-safe protocols. The relevant fail-safe here was that if an M-2 was not in an exact location during a certain window of time, the machine was supposed to immediately shut down and emit a distress signal. Overriding this protocol was occasionally necessary—most often to accommodate shipments that were running behind schedule—but that decision was supposed to begin and end with Darik.

He was now almost certain that the M-2s had never arrived on Cacarus, but if that was the case, he should have received four distress signals when the machines missed their checkpoints. The alternative was that, somewhere along the line, the M-2s had been reprogrammed. However, only a handful of executives had the authority to override the program, and why anyone would go through all the trouble of secretly rerouting a handful of mining units was beyond him.

A flashing comm request from Liana interrupted his train of thought. Darik accepted the comm.

"Yes?"

"I'm sorry to bother you already, but Mr. Liddle is here to—"

Darik clearly heard Eliot's voice butt-in. "It's *lie-DELL*, sweetie, not *little*."

Liana resumed, pronouncing his name the same as before. "As I was saying, Mr. Liddle is here to see you. Should I tell him you're terribly busy and he needs to make an appointment like everyone else?"

Darik smiled, thinking of the look Eliot must've given her.

"No, it's all right, Liana. Send him—"

Eliot strode through the door before Darik had a chance to finish. He was shaking his head back and forth with an exaggerated air of disapproval.

"Well, well, well. Look who finally decides to show up to work."

"Says the man who's never worked a full day in his life."

"Not true," Eliot replied while grabbing the chair from the side wall. "I know for a fact I've worked at least three—maybe more."

Darik leaned back and folded his hands over his waist. "So what brings you by so early? Lunch isn't for, what, another three hours?"

Eliot plopped down into the chair. "Can't a guy just stop in to see his friend? Is that some sort of crime?"

Darik knew that Eliot was only joking, as always. But his mock indignation held just enough of an edge that Darik felt the sudden need to apologize, more or less.

"No, you're absolutely right, Eliot. I'm delighted by your presence. My life is empty without you—a black hole of despair."

"Well, now," he grinned, "that's more like it."

"So, what've you been up to?" Darik asked while casually flicking through the messages that had piled up in his absence. "Anything happen while I was gone?"

Eliot peeked over his shoulder and saw that the door was still open since he had not yet cleared the proximity detector. He half-stood out of his chair and pressed the manual control to slide the door shut. Turning back to Darik, he brought his voice down a level.

"The office has been buzzing about you. Rumor was you got fired. I knew the truth, of course. How'd that go, by the way? You were off on your field research, right? Where'd you go? What'd you find out?"

Eliot's face grew more and more expressive as he spoke, and normally, Darik would've been amused by his friend's ability to rile himself up. But there was something in Eliot's sudden eagerness that didn't sit quite right with Darik. *What is with this day?* he wondered. First the claustrophobia during his commute, then his rearranged office, and now Eliot acting unusual. Or was he just becoming paranoid, reading too much into every little thing? Eliot was his friend, after all—a friend who, only a short time ago, had seemed sincere in his desire for Darik to uncover the truth. Now, he was simply asking a few follow-up questions. What was wrong with that? Yet, as he watched Eliot lean in expectantly, awaiting an answer, Darik knew that he had to trust his gut.

"Actually, I just took some time to work from home. And, the more I think about it, I'm not sure I'm going to go into the field after all. Truth be told, the program *could* probably be improved in some areas. And besides, there's no point in me irritating Stirling any further, right?"

Eliot took a moment to consider what he'd just heard and then gave a couple of slight nods before speaking. "Yeah, that's probably for the best—although I'm always in favor of irritating Stirling." He clasped his hands together and raised his voice to its usual volume. "Now, for the real reason I'm here—you'd better keep a closer watch on Liana."

Darik raised an eyebrow. "Is that so?"

"You better believe it. There was a pack of middle-management pukes hovering around her desk while you were gone. I tell you, it's those bangs—so long, so dark and…mysterious. She has those guys whipped up in a frenzy, and from the looks of it, their intentions are less than honorable."

"And how exactly do you know all that?"

Eliot seemed surprised by the question. "I kept my eye on her, naturally. I felt it was my solemn duty to you in your absence."

"I'm in your debt, Eliot."

"I live to serve." He stood up. "Now, if you'll excuse me, I have a lot of work to ignore."

Darik smiled and waved him out of the office. As he watched Eliot exit through the doorway, he thought about sending a quick message to Liana, warning her that Eliot was probably on his way to harass her. Then he realized that Eliot was probably the one he should've been warning.

The door slid shut, once again blocking out the ambient noise from the outer office. Knowing that a backlog of work awaited him, Darik instinctively reached for his workstation but then hesitated, making a conscious decision to sit instead for a moment and soak in the stillness. He reflected on the odd turns his life had taken in the past several days—his meeting with Jenkins, the trip to Cacarus, and now this strange morning. The more he replayed the events through his mind, the more he realized that, despite his best efforts so far, he *still* didn't have any idea what was going on. If the frustrating trip to Cacarus had proven anything, it was that Eliot's advice at the Black Swan was still essentially correct. Darik was being kept in the dark, and his entire career depended on finding out what was *really* happening to those M-2s.

But maybe, while Eliot had been right about the need to dig further, he had been wrong in thinking that Darik should investigate the M-2s at their intended destination. Cacarus had turned out to be a dead end, but if nothing else, he now understood that the problem needed to be approached from a different angle. He stared at the now idle workstation. Maybe, with the right access, the answers could be found a little closer to home.

Darik broke his impromptu meditation and reactivated the workstation, flipping immediately to the JenKore company directory.

Utilize whatever resources are necessary, Jenkins had said. Darik realized that his next move, while necessary, was going to be risky, possibly illegal, and definitely beyond his own skill level. He was going to need some help.

Chapter 11

Nikky had no intention of sleeping. There was far too much to think about. His hack of JenKore's echo monitoring had been tricky, even for someone with his extensive skills. Ever since his first encounter with the data stream and Seun's poorly timed interruption, he had worked frenetically at his station, compiling a code that would make the echo data he intercepted from the stream appear to remain dormant and archived, even as he had attempted to pull it up for a single real-time read. There was, by his thinking, a 98.2 percent chance that he had pulled off his latest subterfuge undetected, but Nikky was not comfortable with those odds. Any detection of his excursion behind the firewalls of JenKore security, even a hint of an anomaly originating from his area, would bring unwelcome questions and scrutiny.

An intensive security investigation would inevitably bring the discovery of Nikky's cyber-eavesdropping hobby. This would lead, at best, to termination from employment or far worse, if he actually believed some of the rumors circulating about JenKore's unique disciplinary actions. He had always written them off as so much paranoid gossip, but now, walking the darkened back streets of East Compton to clear his head, Nikky was beginning to believe that the rumors could be true. He imagined an ominous figure crouching in every alcove, a JenKore security enforcer waiting just beyond the illumination of each street light. Jumpy, even by his standards, he reached into his jacket pocket yet again, fingering the tiny stunner he was carrying. The silly low-powered weapon had been a gift, of all things, from his mother. She'd argued that if Nikky was going to stubbornly insist on living in the seedier part of the city, he at least needed to be able to defend himself. He had never carried it before tonight.

It wasn't merely the fear of discovery that had Nikky planning to skip his customary three hours of nightly rest. Along with the danger, there was also a compulsion, a feeling of curious excitement that he couldn't contain. The echo monitoring hack had worked. He had been able to recover and read the entire data stream that he missed earlier and, of course, he had now committed it to memory. To anyone else, the data would have been unreadable. It was just a series of indecipherable characters firing across the screen. Nikky, however, was able to pull together and interpret that information to form a mental picture as clear as an ordinary human being would view a holoproduction. Nikky was sure of what he had seen. What he didn't know was what it had meant.

The data had originated off-planet—of that, Nikky was certain. But the picture it formed was so unusual, so bizarre, that Nikky almost began to doubt his own interpretive abilities. That, Nikky realized, would be foolish. He had never been wrong before.

But what was that visual doing in a JenKore data burst? Could it have been a contraband horrofix piece that some tech had been viewing and stupidly allowed to go out on the system? It couldn't have been, he decided. Any unauthorized garbage like that would have been filtered, trapped, and traced before the offender had time to clean out his desk. Besides, the data just didn't have the amateurish markings of the usual muerterotic industry trash. What Nikky had seen had been real, and it had been official. Something unusual, something horribly wrong was going on within JenKore, and Nikky was dying to find out more. The nocturnal walk had been effective—his mind was made up. It was only 10:00 p.m. He would make a quick stop back at home to feed Louise, and then he would be back at his workstation, digging deeper.

He turned the corner to the street where his modest flat was located. Stepping around the piles of trash, he mounted the short flight of stairs leading to the front door. As he reached out to key in his access code to the building, he sensed movement out of the corner of his eye. It wasn't his imagination this time. Two men, large in build and wearing nondescript dark suits, stepped out of the shadows of the entryway.

"Nikky Weis?" Both men moved toward him. Nikky noticed with unease that in the darkness he could not see either of their hands—or any weapons the street thugs may have been carrying. He slowly pulled away from the door's key pad and placed both hands in his pockets, his right hand tentatively grasping the stunner.

"Wh…who wants to know?"

"JenKore Security. We'd like you to come with us."

This was far worse than mere street thugs. He wanted to know how they'd found him out, not that it would have any bearing on his fate. He would be taken in, interrogated, and disciplined. And based on what Nikky had seen in the data burst, he did not want to explore what form that discipline might take. He only had an instant to decide. Nikky's hand shot out of his pocket with alarming sluggishness. His pitiful weapon was halfway up when the agent closest to Nikky pressed a sleeker, more powerful, and much more professionally handled stunner against his neck. Nikky went down in an instant.

"Idiot," the agent remarked to his partner. "C'mon, give me a hand."

*   *   *

Scot Calgaro shuffled between stacks of metallic-blue crates as he weaved his way toward the squadron's armory. *Armory*—an optimistic label if ever he'd heard one. It was, in reality, little more than a single weapons locker tucked in the back of a dim closet next to cleaning supplies and crebonite paint canisters. The contents of the locker were as pitiful as its location—a rack of Hagg-Sauer BP-105 pistols and battery clips, a half-dozen stun grenades, three demo charges, and two assault weapons. The first assault weapon—an old beat-up Klobb SMG—was as inaccurate as it was ugly. The second—a top-of-the-line Hagg-Sauer BR-614 with attachable holosight—was an unexpected recent addition, appearing unceremoniously in a crate of med supplies. The battery rifle gave the locker at least some small measure of respectability, but it still didn't hide the fact that the colony was woefully ill-prepared to defend itself against a ground attack. One good rifle, a dozen pistols, and zero heavy weapons to defend two thousand people. If ever it came to that, it wouldn't be a battle so much as a slaughter.

That's why keeping the colony's location a secret was the squadron's highest priority—and why the possibility of a traitor was so disturbing. The Angels had never been formally briefed on the potential security leak, for obvious reasons, but rumors were abundant. Three ambushes on the last five runs—that was more than just bad luck. It was during one of those recent ambushes when the squadron lost Fran and Kevan, and God help him, Scot thought, if he ever learned who betrayed them. Scot had the utmost respect for Dex as a fighter pilot, but he completely disagreed with the way he was handling—or, rather, not handling—the security situation.

Scot knew that if he were in charge, he wouldn't rest until the guilty bastard was found and brought to justice.

Entering the supply closet, Scot was surprised to find Adahn Manasser, his wingman, already rummaging through the locker. As the two pilots assigned to boarding and hijacking the freighter, both Scot and Adahn required special equipment. Scot, however, had already obtained the locker's keycard from Dex. He had been planning to pick through the equipment first and then give the card to Adahn, but it looked as though Adahn had somehow beaten him to it.

"How'd you get in there?" Scot asked brusquely. He was pleased to see that he'd startled Adahn, who turned awkwardly to face the door. Scot noticed that he was holding the new battery rifle.

"Oh. Hi, Scot. Commander Lebrian gave me his card."

It figured. As the only member of the squadron with infantry experience, Hagen was in charge of the weapons locker, and it was no secret that he was frustrated by the squadron's current lack of preparedness on the ground. It was out of this frustration that Hagen had found an unlikely companion in Adahn. Despite their difference in age—Hagen was almost twice as old as Adahn—they'd discovered common ground in their shared obsession with physical fitness and combat training. They ran together, lifted, trained with firearms, and sparred hand-to-hand, developing the kind of bond and trust that comes with pushing one another to the limit. So, it was no surprise to Scot that Adahn had managed to weasel the keycard from Hagen.

Scot nodded at the rifle. "Pretty slick, huh?"

Adahn frowned. "Not really—it has an excellent grip."

Before Scot could determine whether or not he was joking, Adahn raised the weapon to his shoulder. Scot flinched with the sudden motion, reaching for a side arm that he did not yet possess. It was immediately clear, though, that he was not in danger. Adahn had kept the rifle consistently pointed at the far wall. Scot felt both a twinge of embarrassment for his overreaction and resentment toward Adahn for making him feel embarrassed.

Adahn, for his part, was peering enthusiastically down the sight, his right cheek nestled gently against the stock.

"The holosight is fantastic. Good magnification. And it's multi-spectrum, so it can peer through walls. You want to see?"

"I've seen one before," Scot lied.

Adahn lowered the rifle, cradling it in his hands. He slowly pivoted back around to face Scot, avoiding direct eye-contact. "So, I guess you get first pick from the locker, seeing as you're the ranking officer."

Scot fought back a smile as he casually stepped toward Adahn. "Yeah, as a matter-of-fact, I do." He nodded at the rifle. "Let's see it."

Adahn looked pained as he reluctantly handed over the weapon. Scot held it up, angling it back and forth against the dim light above, admiring its trim design. He then placed the rifle in the locker and glowered at his wingman.

"We're boarding an unmanned freighter—not storming an Alliance compound. A big rifle like that's just going to get in the way. Use your head, Ghazi."

Scot all but spat out the call sign—a reference to Adahn's Middle-Eastern heritage—as though it were an insult. His wingman, however, seemed too distracted to notice.

"So," Adahn began slowly, "you're not taking the rifle?"

Scot rolled his eyes. "Go ahead. Knock yourself out. I'm sure it'll be a lot easier getting those engines started with a rifle slung over your shoulder, bumping into everything."

Adahn didn't waste any time retrieving the rifle. Scot, meanwhile, searched the rack of seemingly identical pistols for his personal favorite, set apart by a scuff mark toward the bottom of the grip. After he found and inspected his pistol, he grabbed a stun battery clip—the only kind of battery Dex permitted on missions requiring firearms. Scot kept half an eye on Adahn to make sure he grabbed a stun clip as well.

When they were both satisfied with their equipment, Scot closed the locker door, double-checking to make sure it was secure.

"We don't want anyone stealing our stun batteries," he smirked.

"Or the demo charges," Adahn added seriously. "Those could be very dangerous in the wrong hands."

Scot ignored him, focusing his attention instead on a stack of cases in the corner. He flipped open and closed several of them, moving and restacking the cases until he found what he was looking for.

"There you are," he said, reaching in with both hands and pulling out a couple of flares.

"What do you want those for?" Adahn asked, hovering over Scot's shoulder.

"Give me some room, will you?" Scot demanded as he snapped the case shut. Adahn shuffled back a few paces, and Scot continued. "Auto freighters operate on emergency lights to conserve power. I figured it'd be helpful to, you know, see what I'm doing."

"Yeah, I know," Adahn said, "so bring a flashlight, like me. You'll blind yourself with those flares. They're made for deep space—not to light up a room."

Scot flipped one of the flares in his hand. "I'm not going to blind myself. Look, you can dial down the power right here. And I'd rather drop one or two of these on the floor than lug around a flashlight the whole time. Between that and the rifle, how much stuff are you planning on carrying anyway?"

Adahn considered for a moment before answering. "As much as I need."

"Wow. Profound," Scot said, heading for the corridor. He paused at the door. "Just make sure that junk doesn't slow you down. I'm serious, now. This thing's got to go off without a hitch. You know how badly we could use that freighter."

Adahn stood up straight and squared his shoulders, and Scot was reminded of how physically intimidating his wingman could be. "I'll do my job," Adahn said. "I'm just trying to be prepared."

"Well," Scot said, turning away. "I guess there's no harm in that." He stepped out, pacing briskly to his quarters to do his own preparing for the mission. Adahn remained in the supply closet for a few extra moments, tracking Scot down the corridor through the holosight on his rifle.

Chapter 12

The dimly lit storeroom had not been Darik's first choice for a meeting place. While it was necessary to keep this initial contact under the radar, he would have preferred to show his guest a bit more hospitality than a single chair in a cinderblock-walled room on the third sub-level of an unused JenKore warehouse. Meeting openly in his office was, of course, out of the question, so Darik had initially planned for this rendezvous to occur in a quiet back room of a local dive where they could at least sit comfortably and enjoy a decent meal.

Those plans changed when he received the call that the recruit had resisted and was being delivered without the benefit of free choice—or consciousness. No matter how out of the way the little bistro had been, and how discreet the ownership, Darik was not going to take the risk of a passerby seeing a limp form being dragged through the back door. He had the security codes to a nearby warehouse, and because of its mothballed status, Darik knew that the reassignment of its security feed and sensor bandwidth to other, more active projects wouldn't arouse undue suspicion. He had sent the necessary commands to the security system from his handpod and then shot back a terse message to his one-time agents, ordering that his guest be rerouted to the new location.

That guest was now slumped awkwardly in the room's single chair, a rickety wooden throwback that looked like it might collapse at any time. Why the devil had he resisted? The agents had reported that they had no alternative but to incapacitate him. Looking at the gaunt, mousy form, Darik was fairly certain the men had been overzealous, but all the same, he hadn't objected to their binding the unconscious figure's hands and feet securely to the chair before they left the two of them alone.

Darik regarded the rodent of a man. He had carefully selected him from hundreds of candidates, but now, seeing him in person—his diminutive frame slumped over, his pasty skin reflecting under the light of the ceiling's single illumapanel—Darik had his doubts. The little cretin didn't seem capable of tying his own shoes, let alone pulling off the kind of work that he had in mind. But there was no time to second guess his decision now. Nikky Weis was beginning to wake up.

His head, which had been lolling on his right shoulder, came slowly upright, sending a glob of drool dribbling down his chin. His eyes opened and gradually refocused, panic spreading across his face as he took in his surroundings. Nikky lurched in the chair, straining against the bindings.

"Take it easy," Darik said, stepping into the light. "I'm not going to hurt you."

"Th…then why am I tied up?" Nikky asked. Any defiance Darik heard in Nikky's voice was undermined by the way he fumbled over his words.

"That's your fault, not mine. What kind of moron pulls a stunner on a security agent?"

Nikky's mouth again began moving long before the words came stumbling out. "A moron who doesn't want to get arrested."

Darik frowned—that was the last thing he'd expected to hear. Perhaps he didn't know as much about Nikky Weis as he'd thought. "Arrested? For what?"

Nikky swallowed before answering. "How am I supposed to know?" he muttered. "Security men don't always need a reason."

Nice try, Darik thought. He was well aware of JenKore Security's shady reputation, having worked in the department for a number of years. But he didn't for one second believe that Nikky's ill-advised tussle with the agents was born out of simple paranoia. He had seen the look in Nikky's eyes—the little man was definitely hiding something. And if Nikky was indeed dabbling in illegal activity, it made him a potential liability. Darik's plan was tenuous enough without Nikky bringing along extra, unwanted attention.

On the other hand, Darik was fast approaching the point of no return. Nikky had seen his face, and if he didn't know his identity already, it wouldn't take someone with his resources long to find out. There was, of course, one alternative—a way to keep his identity a secret, a way to start over with a new recruit. But Darik wasn't quite ready to consider that option. It would be less complicated, and decidedly less messy, to proceed ahead as planned.

Darik exhaled loudly, making his contempt clear. "You weren't getting arrested, you idiot. I just wanted to talk to you. Those agents work for me."

"And who are you?"

No turning back now. "My name is Darik Mason. I work in JenKore's Mining Division—security and fail-safe protocols."

"And what do you want with me?"

"I have a job offer for you. It's a chance to use your talents more effectively—and make more money at the same time." Now that he had begun, Darik pressed forward with some enthusiasm. "Nikky, it's an opportunity for someone of your abilities to finally be appreciated."

"*Appreciated.*" Nikky looked down at the bindings on his wrists and ankles. "You have a funny way of showing it."

"Okay, all right." Darik held his hands up. "If I take those off, do you promise to behave yourself?"

"Do I have a choice?"

Less than you think. The security agents had handed Nikky's sad little stunner over to Darik as though it were some kind of justification for the force they had used. It was a pathetic little piece, but Darik had kept it in his right pocket for this meeting, just in case. Stepping over to a crate on his left, he picked up a small remote, waving his thumb over a command. The bindings released with a snap, falling to the floor.

Nikky began rubbing his ankles and wrists. Keeping his eyes lowered, he mumbled, "So, what is this job you're talking about?"

As the tension dissipated and as Darik's body came down from the initial surge of adrenaline, he realized that his stomach was rumbling. "I'll tell you all about it," Darik said, "but first, are you hungry?"

"I could eat," he replied indifferently. With his waif-like physique, it appeared that Nikky didn't make mealtimes much of a priority.

Reaching into his jacket, Darik keyed a handpod message to the two agents waiting down the hall, informing them that they were through for the night.

"C'mon," he said, turning toward the door. "I know a place."

*   *   *

The owners of Bistro Riservata were not the curious type. Alphonse and Josephine Brobergo, the older couple who ran the quiet little Italian place several blocks from Compton's more lavish downtown restaurants, didn't really care what your business was as long as you shared their love for finely crafted, traditional pasta dishes. In a time when so many establishments had succumbed to the trend for synthesized, low-calorie mockeries of time-honored cuisine, Al and Josie had stuck to their convictions, shipping in authentic ingredients to create mouthwatering dishes from recipes handed down over generations.

It was, however, an expensive proposition, and their profit margin was practically nil, a fact reinforced by the outward appearance of their restaurant. Alphonse had never been a big fan of maintenance in the first place, preferring to concentrate on the finer arts of the kitchen, and with finances being tight, the exterior had fallen into a state of dismal disrepair. With its peeling paint, half-darkened signage, and neglected planters under grimy, bar-protected windows, the restaurant blended in seamlessly with the other buildings on the street. To potential customers, there was nothing in the Riservata's appearance that would suggest the warm hospitality and exceptional food waiting within. This restriction of sales volume didn't bother Al and Josie in the least. They preferred the slower pace over financial success and the fierce loyalty of their regular customers over the snotty pretentiousness of the truqué cuisine crowd.

As one of those regular customers, Darik found Bistro Riservata to be the perfect place to relax over a fine meal. While the menu always appealed to his discriminating palate, it was the lack of crowds and the discreet atmosphere of the place that best fit his needs—especially tonight. Not that the Brobergos were standoffish—they were two of the most outgoing and welcoming personalities Darik had ever met. But somehow they managed to combine their outstanding hospitality with a diplomatic appreciation for their patrons' privacy. Accustomed as he was to a professional life in which it seemed everyone was looking over his shoulder, Darik found their lack of curiosity into his personal affairs refreshing.

Walking through the front door with Nikky in tow, Darik momentarily set aside his concerns for confidentiality and allowed himself to once again soak in the unique ambiance of the bistro. Tantalizing aromas from the kitchen instantly filled his nostrils, reawakening the grumbling in his stomach. The soft traditional Italian music playing in the background had a distinctive metallic timbre, emanating from magnetic coil speakers mounted in the acoustic tile ceiling. Incandescent fixtures illuminated the small dining room, creating a much warmer glow than lighting panels ever could. In one corner, a large man with dark curly hair was hunched over a dais, chewing on an actual pencil and staring intently at a ledger book, as if he were willing the numbers to suddenly line up and make sense. Hearing the door chime, he looked up, his face breaking into a huge smile of recognition.

"Ahhh, Mister Darik!" Alphonse quickly stepped out from behind the podium, wiping his hands on a stained apron before spreading them out in greeting. "We were so afraid that you would not be making it tonight!"

"Yes," Darik replied, grasping and shaking one of Al's hands in order to avoid the otherwise inevitable bear hug and cheek kissing. "We were a bit delayed."

"*No materia*! We still have the room you wanted reserved in the back for you, eh? *Josie*!" His voice rose several decibels, calling to his heavily set, dark-haired wife and business partner who had been chatting with a couple other patrons in the sparsely populated dining room. "Look who finally dragged himself in!"

"*Benvenuto*, Darik!" This time Darik was unable to preempt the enthusiastic physical greeting, submitting instead to Josephine's tugging at his cheeks. "It has been too long. And who is this guest you are bringing to us?"

"This is Ni…" Darik stopped short, sensing Nikky stiffen next to him. "This is a…friend of mine. I've told him all about your *Penne Rustica*. I hope it's not too late."

"Nonsense!" Alphonse inserted himself back into the conversation. "What's one or two more sticks on the fire for Mister Darik and his good friend?" The ancient wood-burning oven was another element that kept Bistro Riservata on the verge of bankruptcy. Acquiring real pine and smuggling it into the city was a huge expense, even before the necessary bribes to local eco-enforcement inspectors. Alphonse, however, remained steadfast in his conviction that it was the only way to bake proper pasta dishes. There would never be an IR oven in his kitchen while he was alive.

"Come, come," Josephine said, taking Nikky by the arm. "Alphonse! Get yourself back to your kitchen. This one here could use some fattening up." She gave Nikky's arm a little squeeze and led them down a short hallway.

The room was small, nothing more than a couple of tables and chairs tucked away from the main dining area. The décor was understated but classic, from the Sicilian landscape wall art to the red and white checkered tablecloths. The effect was completed by half-melted candles in empty teardrop-shaped wine bottles in the center of both tables. Most importantly, for Darik's purposes, the room was private.

"So what will it be then?" Josephine pulled a worn pad from her apron. "*Penne Rustica* for both of you, eh?"

Darik was famished. "For me, yes please, Josie." They both looked at Nikky.

"Uh, could I just get some plain spaghetti?"

Josephine smiled broadly. "Oh, *miele*, you are going to love our spaghetti. We have marinara sauce, alfredo, tomato and basil, garlic butter sauce, and *L'oh mio*," Josephine paused, crossing her arms over her chest while looking heavenward, "we have Alphonse's special recipe, a red sauce with sausage made with our own Sangiovese. So good, every one of them. Which one would you be liking?"

"No sauce, just plain spaghetti, please."

Josephine stopped smiling. "Plain spaghetti?" She narrowed her eyes.

"Yes, please."

"No sauce?"

"No. No sauce."

Darik could see Josephine's fingers tightening around her pencil. "And how about a bottle of that Sangiovese you mentioned?" he said hurriedly. "Alphonse is an expert vintner," he added to Nikky, hoping to smooth the moment over.

Josephine noted the order on her pad. "Yes, we have a very good twenty-six," she said distractedly before turning again to Nikky. "And I suppose it's water for you then?"

"Yes, please."

Josephine left the room. Moments later, Darik could hear a muffled but animated conversation coming from the kitchen. Not understanding Italian, he couldn't quite make out the words, but he had the impression that the language was colorful. Looking back at Nikky, he forced a smile. "I suppose you're wondering why I asked you here," he began.

"Kidnapped me, you mean."

Though Darik didn't wish to alienate Nikky, he couldn't help being a little exasperated. "Would you get off that already?" He gestured to the room around them. "This, *this* is where those agents were going to bring you. I just wanted to sit down, have a nice meal, and talk to you about a little project I have in mind."

Nikky leaned forward. "Why me?"

"Your file." Darik pulled out his handpod and turned it toward Nikky. "Expert systems analyst, IQ beyond measurable stats, never once late with a single task, most completed in half the time of your peers." Darik had spent so much time with the file, he could have recited the information from memory. "But yet, with all that, only average reviews and wage increases, and not one recommendation for promotion. I found that…interesting." Darik's eyes formed the last statement into a question.

"Maybe I just fell between the cracks." Nikky returned Darik's level gaze.

"I think you *like* falling between the cracks, Nikky. I think you have made a career of flying under the radar. You've got abilities that could write you a ticket anywhere, but for some reason, you don't want to be noticed."

"My own business," Nikky said dismissively. He sat back in his chair before adding quietly, "Why should you care?"

"I care, Nikky, because you may be exactly the guy I'm looking for. I have some research that needs to be done, important research. But before I can—"

The two men were interrupted by Josephine bursting back onto the room, bearing a cart laden with bread, salads, olive oil, and a wine bottle. Displaying no trace of her former annoyance, she began to work a corkscrew into the top of the bottle.

"And how are my two *ragazzi* doing?" She pulled the cork and filled Darik's glass with the richly colored red wine. Nikky didn't bother objecting when she filled his glass as well. Pouring some of the olive oil on a small plate, she mixed in a few grinds of black pepper and then turned and produced two generous plates of salad.

"Alphonse says your dinner will be ready in a few minutes. In the meantime, enjoy." She smiled and turned back toward the kitchen.

Dipping a piece of bread in the olive oil and pepper, Darik continued. "Okay, here's what I'm saying. This research goes deep, deep into my own division. Something is going on, and I want to find out what it is. But I can't do the research myself. I'm too close to the situation, and frankly, I don't think I have the skill to pull it off undetected. That's where you come in."

Nikky chewed passively on a lettuce leaf. "Again, why me?"

"Because I don't know where this investigation will lead. If it gets ugly, I need to know that the guy I've got digging won't turn into some kind of whistleblower. I need someone who will find the information I need and then let *me* deal with it. That's the only way this will work. You strike me as the kind of man who doesn't have a lot of loyalties either way. And again," Darik added, hoping to stroke Nikky's ego, "everything in your file says that you are the best."

"Assuming I was interested," Nikky paused from chewing the wet lettuce, leaving a small bit of dark green on his chin, "what exactly would I be looking for?"

"Before I can tell you that, I need to know if you *are* interested."

"I can't tell you if I'm interested until I know what I'm looking for."

Darik sighed. "At some point, we're going to have to start trusting each other."

"You first." Nikky leaned forward across the table. "You seem to know a thing or two about me. But I know this about you. You seem to need me a lot more right now than I need you, this meal, or this conversation." Nikky pushed his chair away from the table.

Darik considered his options. He could threaten the little troll. He could tell Nikky that he was under suspicion for illegal activity and by tomorrow dozens of JenKore internal affairs agents would be crawling all over, around, and inside of Nikky's workstation. He could promise him that whatever little secret Nikky was concealing, whatever was keeping him in his tiny subterranean alcove at JenKore, would soon be discovered and revealed, causing his safe, private world to come crashing down around him. Darik could do that, but he got the impression that if he really wanted to recruit this guy, coercion was the worst strategy he could use.

"All right, relax." Darik saw Josie approaching with a huge plate of penne pasta, shrimp, grilled chicken, and smoked prosciutto with creamy cheese sauce in one arm and a bowl of plain sauce-less spaghetti in the other. "Just sit down and eat. I'll fill you in on the details—then you decide."

*   *   *

Nikky still hadn't slept. Unless the hour or so he had spent unconscious from the effects of the stunner counted, he had been up for

105

over twenty-seven hours. Now, following his unsolicited and unexpected late-night dinner with Mr. Darik Mason, he was finally back on his original quest. Leaving Bistro Riservata on foot, he smiled with the realization that the conditions of his search had not changed dramatically with the inclusion of this new task. If Mason was right, there was something very unusual going on at JenKore, and now, Nikky had authorization to dig deeper into whatever it was.

How much that authorization would be worth if he were caught was another matter. Mason had made it clear that their conversation had never officially happened. There would be no payroll position, no department transfer, and absolutely no record of their business transactions.

This wasn't a problem for Nikky. He had dismissively acknowledged Darik's promise to covertly reallocate UC credits from a small security sub-account to Nikky's personal Transnet site. The personal payment details bored him. He reasoned that Mason had a lot more to lose than he did, so the tracks would be covered well enough. Besides, he had enough personal ID-cryption built into his own accounts to thwart any curious investigative efforts. Nikky was far more interested in the access this new project would allow.

Darik had reached into his pocket during dinner, producing a very small nondescript oval disc. Even though he had never before seen one in person, Nikky knew that he was looking at a JenKore executive-level Access Code Generator. Looking at the display on the three-centimeter-long device, he committed to memory a series of complex codes it emitted. Those codes would permit the user of the ACG much deeper access into JenKore's security grid—deeper than even Nikky, with all his special abilities, could access on his own.

The catch was that the codes changed every thirty seconds, would not be repeated and could not be transferred to a data chip or any other storage device. JenKore protocols mandated that at the executive security level, the correct code had to be input by the user during the interval in which it was active. Half a minute later, all executive user codes would be useless and new codes would be generated by each user's ACG. Any attempt to copy the internal files of an ACG would trigger the automatic erasure of that unit and its invalidation on the system. This fail-safe, designed to ensure that only the registered user of an ACG would be able to utilize it, was further complicated by the disc's internal proximity detector. All JenKore execs were required to keep their code generators within ten meters of their person at all times. Any violation of this rule would result in deactivation of the ACG, along with instant detection and discipline of the offending party.

"Aren't you going to write them down?" Darik had asked incredulously. Nikky understood his concern—he had probably taken a great risk even showing him the disc.

"No, I got it," Nikky had said, watching a series of ten different codes flash on the display before Darik finally secreted the ACG back into his pocket. Whatever else was going on, Mason had done his homework well. No one else in Compton would have been able to memorize the passing codes, much less use them to predict the future behavior of the ACG. No one else on Earth would have had enough insight into the rhythms and nuances of the JenKore mainframe to be able to extrapolate from those ten codes a seemingly undetectable pattern in their random generation. And no one else in the entire Coalition should have had the ability to then predict an entirely new series of codes at a given moment in time that would not only be valid, but untraceable back to any particular junior executive, like Darik Mason. Halfway back to his flat, Nikky had already worked out the algorithm in his head.

Mounting the steps outside his building, Nikky suppressed a shudder at the memory of his earlier encounter with the JenKore security goons. He worked his head back and forth, massaging the charred and still tender area of his neck. Nikky considered just how hazardous this latest development had become. Mason had laid out his responsibilities for the M-2 mining units—units that were supposedly experiencing destructive failures in the field, but were, in fact, not arriving at their designated sites. Mason was clearly frustrated over the absence of any solid information related to where the units were actually going and what was happening to them. Nikky's task, then, would be to use his projected, untraceable ACG sequences to hack deeper into JenKore's system, gather solid intel into the diversion and disappearance of the M-2 units, and then get out undetected. Nikky had accepted Mason's offer and assignment with a casualness that belied his real concerns. If this little piece of corporate espionage were detected, a stun-shock would be the least of Nikky's problems.

He keyed the access code into his building. Mason had clearly understood the risks as well. As he began a series of more complex lock sequences at the door to his own flat, Nikky smiled again at the recollection of Darik's self-centered concern for his own personal wellbeing.

"Why worry about projecting fake codes?" Nikky had asked. "If you were right there with me, I could get in with your ACG and still cover the tracks. It's really not that difficult, you know."

"No!" Darik had loudly insisted. Nikky distinctly recalled seeing a bit of penne pasta stuck in his teeth. "I don't know you, I haven't met with you, and you do not work for me. You just do whatever you need to with your make-believe passwords to get yourself in. Then, you find what I need and get out clean. Do not contact me. I will find you again, you got that?"

Nikky entered his apartment. Yeah, he had "gotten" that. Louise was paddling around the pool in her aquarium, seemingly agitated at Nikky's long absence. The old turtle ambled from the water to an empty food dish, sending Nikky what he was sure were accusatory glances in the process.

Nikky was fine with Mason's insistence on separation and secrecy. He was even more pleased to now have locked in his mind a series of access codes that he could use to go practically anywhere he chose in JenKore's system. Grabbing a tattered box of food sticks, he absently dropped one next to Louise and triggered the *Replenish* command on her hydration unit.

He would get Mason the information he wanted, all right. But in providing Nikky the access he needed to spy for him, the young exec had also given him exactly what he wanted most. Nikky hadn't breathed a word to Mason about his recent data interception. And now, he had the tools he needed to dig even deeper into that elusive echo. With the projected ACG codes, he would finally be able to extract the entire feed undetected and satisfy his insatiable curiosity as to its origins.

A holopic on his wall captured Nikky's attention for a moment. It contained the smiling images of four people. In the holo, Nikky stood with his mother and his now-deceased stepfather and half brother. His half brother, Louise's original owner, had his arm around Nikky's shoulder. His stepfather and mother beamed proudly at their two sons.

They had been happy—Nikky remembered that—but it had been so long ago. Nikky was grateful that Louise was still with him. After his mother had broken the news that the two had been killed in a transport accident off-planet, the old turtle became his trustworthy companion and a reminder of happier days.

His eyes moved over the holopic to the soft features of his mother. She was more carefree then—not so angry and suspicious. Nikky patted a pocket holding her recent gift—the stunner that Darik had returned to him at the conclusion of their dinner.

Nikky took a final look around his flat. Satisfied that Louise had enough food and water for a day or two, he reactivated the security system, locking down the apartment before setting out in search of answers—for Mason, and for himself.

Chapter 13

Dex replayed the mission plan on his multi-function display for the tenth time, not to calm his nerves—which were remarkably steady despite the rapidly dwindling ETA to Ceres—but rather to give his eyes something else to focus on other than the white nothingness of etherspace. Dex hated traveling through the ether, especially alone, disturbed by the illusion of complete and total isolation. He knew that Jani's Hornet was only a handful of meters off his starboard wing, but when he looked out the canopy in her direction, he saw nothing but unblemished white. There were no shadows, no ripples, not a single point of reference to prove he was even moving at all. Dex had long ago conquered his fear of etherspace, but he could never completely shake its disquieting effect.

There were rumors of freighter pilots who had gone mad from spending too long a time in the ether. Dex didn't doubt the rumors. On the other hand, neither did he overly worry about the adverse effects of etherspace on his pilots, for two reasons. One, he limited single jumps to six hours—well within the recommended safety guidelines. And two, the Angels were all experienced travelers, and they knew well enough to keep busy. Some brought books. Others watched pirated holofilms. A few took advantage of the long hours of silence for prayer and meditation. Years ago, Dex had tried praying during etherspace jumps, but he eventually gave up on it. He could never get past a certain mental block. The ether was too empty. It seemed to be a place where God couldn't hear him— maybe even a place where God didn't exist at all.

A series of soft beeps coupled with a vibration in his seat informed Dex that he was one minute away from dropping into the Ceres system. He switched off the alarms and toggled his main display from the mission plan to sensor readouts. The screen turned blank—in etherspace, there was nothing for his sensors to detect. But once his Hornet dropped from the ether, the sensors would be invaluable for monitoring the status of the *Milk Wagon* and tracking the possible approach of the four Scorpion police fighters from the outer moon of Ceres—the only known rapid response force in the system.

For the first time during the long jump, Dex raised his eyes and stared straight into the vacant ether, only because he knew that in a few seconds there would be much more to see. His Hornet's E-drive automatically powered down, which coincided with a small dark circle appearing in front of his fighter at a great distance—or at least what looked to be a great distance. The black circle didn't stay small for long. Dex could never decide if he was rushing toward the hole or if the hole was rushing toward him—either way, the white ether was quickly overtaken by the familiar darkness of sub-ether space. Ceres was directly ahead, turning in an instant from a small speck of dull-light amid the bright stars to a hulking planet that filled Dex's canopy, approaching so rapidly that it seemed, for a moment, that Dex might slam straight into it. But the hazy green world halted just as quickly as it had appeared. Traveling safely at standard speed, Dex unlocked his flight stick, taking manual control of the Hornet.

His sensor screen lit up with flashes of images and data. Dex noted the safe arrival of the Angels—Jani to his right, the rest in formation close behind—and spotted the target, Baker's H-freighter, directly ahead. And then his stomach dropped. His sensors detected seven ships in the vicinity. Two Scorpion fighters were circling the *Milk Wagon*, undoubtedly part of the local rapid response force. In addition, he counted five gunships—four of them right on top of the Scorpions.

Dex scarcely had time to process this new development when he heard a crackle through the comm. It was Jani.

"Deadeye, Rabbit. Tracking five Rhinos. Weapons are hot."

"Roger," Dex replied as evenly as he could, hoping that his agitation wasn't evident over the comm. "Angels, hold course."

Dex cycled through the gunships on his sensor screen. The JenKore-built GN-55s were large—four times the size of the Hornets. In addition to standard cannons and launchers, the gunships were outfitted with four manually operated burst turrets—two above the long broad wings and two below. The burst turrets fired powerful spreads of cannon bolts, ineffective at great distances but devastating at close range. Dex shifted his attention from the main sensor display to his battle map. Oddly, one of the gunships stayed a good distance apart from the others, avoiding the battle. The other four were swooping over, under, and around the freighter, their turrets pounding the two Scorpions.

Jani confirmed Dex's readings. "The Stingers' shields are failing."

"I'm detecting wreckage from two other Stingers and three Rhinos," Onigen added.

Scot jumped in. "My parrot's squawking nonsense," he reported, indicating that his IFF transponder had received an unregistered response from the gunships. "Looks like pirates—and I'm guessing they're not the pretend kind."

Hagen brought the outburst of chatter to a halt. "Orders, sir?"

Dex considered the situation. He had once again led his squadron into some sort of trap. Baker's freighter was all but lost, and if he ventured any closer to those gunships, his squadron would likely be lost as well. The choice was clear—turn around, jump out, and be grateful to have escaped alive. And yet, as he continued to observe the battle map, watching the desperate flight of the two Scorpions, he found himself speaking a different order into the comm.

"Angels, new objective. We will escort the Stingers to Ceres. The Rhinos are warm—most likely manned with crews of six, so continue dry. Instead, maintain a lock on the Rhinos—the threat of incoming Slammers might be enough to spook them into running."

Scot chimed in again. "What about the *Wagon*?"

"We'll worry about the freighter once the Stingers are clear. Understood?"

Dex's question did not immediately elicit a response, and he wondered how his pilots were taking the orders. He was sure that none of them would object to a rescue mission, but increasingly as of late he'd been hearing grumblings about the squadron's rules of engagement—namely, the standing order not to fire on ships with human life aboard. He knew that some of his pilots thought that the order needlessly complicated missions, putting the squadron in greater danger than necessary. And Dex conceded that it was a valid argument. In this case, it would certainly be a lot safer for the Angels to tear through the gunships with a barrage of Slammers, not to mention it would increase the Scorpions' chances of survival. But, safer or not, the order was in place for a reason, and Dex would not compromise for this mission or any other.

Scot broke the silence. "Yes, sir. Who knows—maybe these pirates aren't the fightin' type."

The responses were considerably less sarcastic from the rest of the pilots, who acknowledged with a single click into their comm units. Dex wasted no time in targeting the nearest gunship. His visor's HUD highlighted the gunship's location with a translucent red box that included numbers on distance and shield strength. Though Dex could just now make out the freighter with his naked eye, the gunship was still beyond visual range—too far for his cannons but well within missile range. The red box slowly drifted across his HUD from left to right. He checked his battle map and saw that the gunship was flying in a loose circle around the freighter. Toggling his weapons from cannons to missiles, he guided the diamond pipper over his target, clicked it in place, and waited for a lock.

Something about the gunships troubled Dex. It was more than just their presence—rare was the mission, as of late, that did not include some form of ambush—rather, it was their tactics. The gunships had maintained the same flight pattern since the Angels had arrived, circling the freighter while they tangled with the Scorpions. If this were a trap, Dex reasoned, the gunships should have broken off by now to engage his squadron. Could this have been merely an unfortunate coincidence, catching a random band of pirates in the middle of a raid? Whatever the case—trap or coincidence—the gunships, at the moment, appeared strangely indifferent to the arrival of the Hornets.

The red target box continued its slow journey across the right side of the HUD. Dex made a slight course adjustment to keep the gunship in front of him. A rhythmic beeping indicated that his missiles were close to achieving a lock—which meant that warning alarms should have been blaring in the gunship's cockpit. And still, the red box maintained its lazy arc. Dex rechecked the battle map and noticed, to his amazement, that none of the five gunships were taking evasive maneuvers.

Scot sounded surprised as well. "Do these guys have some sort of death wish? Wait, what the—I lost him!"

Dex's target vanished as well even as Scot was finishing his outburst. The red box disappeared, along with information on the freighter, the other gunships, the Scorpions, and his squadron. All that remained on Dex's HUD was the diamond pipper, essentially useless without targeting information. He checked his sensor screen and battle map. Both were blank. He was flying blind.

Dex soon discovered his comm system still worked as several pilots voiced their surprise. "Whoa!—Target faded!—My map's blank!—The freighter's gone!"

Dex attempted to regain hold of the situation. "Can anyone tell me what just happened?"

"My lights are out," Geff reported.

"Yeah, we know," snapped Seltrice. "Everyone's lights are out. Deadeye wants to know *why*."

"And I'm sure *you* know why," Geff shot back.

"That's enough," Dex scolded. The Scorpion pilots weren't going to hold out much longer—if they weren't dead already. Without sensors, it was impossible to know for sure. "I need answers."

Purnima spoke up for the first time. "Deadeye, Moonlight. Just before our lights went out, Sunfire and I detected a small object near the freighter. We weren't sure what it was."

Dex knew better than to ask Purnima how she had known that Ravi had detected the object as well. There were more pressing concerns at the moment than the curious behavior of the Voor twins. Chief among those concerns was the small unidentified object that seemed to be creating such havoc. It didn't take Dex more than a few seconds to figure out what had happened. He addressed the squadron.

"The Rhinos have deployed a jammer pod." Only once before had Dex encountered a jammer pod—a powerful device but one used sparingly in combat because its effects were indiscriminate, blocking all sensors within a certain radius. "They know we can't lock on with our Slammers when our lights are out, so they're baiting us into a knife fight. And that's exactly what we're going to give them. Cannons are cleared hot—but use restraint. Shoot to disable, not to kill."

Adahn, Scot's wingman, entered the comm. "How are we supposed to find the Rhinos without lights?"

"My guess is they won't stray far from the jammer, which Moonlight tells us is near the freighter. If you get disoriented, use Ceres and the *Wagon* as your bullseyes." Dex knew that it was vital for the Angels, unaccustomed to flying in space without the aid of sensors, to maintain a couple points of reference. "Keep visuals on each other and call out the Rhinos. And if you tally the jammer, do us all a favor and splash it."

As Dex finished giving the orders, he swiveled his head around the canopy to get a feel for the location of the other Hornets. The tight formation made him realize just how much he took for granted the little things his sensors provided—collision detection for instance. He noticed the Hornets were slowly drifting apart as the pilots, perhaps subconsciously, added a little breathing room to the formation.

Dex charged his cannons—his HUD responding to the change by switching the pipper back to a circle—and turned his attention forward to the freighter. Silhouetted against the enormous green backdrop of Ceres, the freighter was becoming increasingly easy to make out, its bow angling toward the approaching Hornets. Dex strained to find the other ships, shifting his eyes up and down, back and forth. He created gunships out of the shifting atmosphere of Ceres or Scorpions out of tiny imperfections in his canopy. The longer the gunships remained unseen, the more paranoid Dex became, imagining that the pirates had somehow circled behind the squadron undetected. He began glancing straight above and behind.

A series of bright flashes near the *Milk Wagon* eased Dex's fears. He followed a burst of cannon fire—a deep red distinctive to JenKore models—back to its source, a gunship just now visible hovering above the freighter. Two more appeared to the left of the *Wagon*, and another below and to the right.

Jani confirmed the gunships' locations.

Hagen reminded the squadron to keep an eye out for the Scorpions.

Dex softly voiced a quick prayer.

And the Angels screamed into battle.

The two gunships on the left side of the freighter took a wide angle of approach, attempting to flank the squadron. Hagen, Seltrice, and the Voor twins broke formation to intercept them. Onigen and Geff also broke off to chase the right-most gunship, which was making a run toward the freighter, its lower turrets rhythmically discharging.

"Tally one Rhino engaged offensive with a Stinger, heading zero-three-one," Onigen reported, seeing that the gunship was pursuing one of the Scorpions.

"Roger, Ninja. Press the Rhino. Flash, shadow the Stinger." Dex was hoping that Scot and Adahn could cover the Scorpion long enough for Onigen and Geff to disable the gunship.

"Roger," Scot replied as he and Adahn turned right in unison. That left Dex alone with Jani to engage the final gunship—at least, the final visible gunship. He knew an unseen fifth gunship was still lurking somewhere on the fringes of battle. Dex and Jani's more immediate adversary turned directly toward them, all four of its burst turrets blasting away. They easily dodged the first few volleys, though evading the tight spreads of red bolts proved to be increasingly difficult as the two Hornets roared closer to the gunship. And there was little room for error. In close-quarters, a single burst could punch through a fighter's shields. A second burst would rip the fighter to shreds.

Rising and dipping to avoid the steady onslaught, Dex guided the light-green pipper over the gunship, and, despite the sporadic pitching of his fighter, held it firmly in place over the target. He squeezed off a short burst. His cannons hummed as two narrow rows of yellow bolts streaked forward. But instead of dispersing over the gunship's shields, as Dex expected, the bolts tore into the hull. A second burst from Jani's Hornet nearly vaporized one of the topside gunners.

"Rabbit, shields are down. Check your fire."

"Just giving him a little scare."

"Be careful," Dex tersely replied. He normally didn't mind the occasional glib comment from Jani, but he didn't want to encourage carelessness when human life was at stake.

Dex switched to rear-targeting, and a small window appeared in the bottom corner of his HUD, a feed from his Hornet's rear-mounted camera. A Hornet's rear cannons were most often used as a deterrent against trailing bandits rather than as an offensive weapon, but Dex, perhaps more than any other Angel, had confidence in his ability to make any shot from any angle with any of his cannons—forward or rear.

The gunship was now menacingly close. He could see the individual turrets swiveling, trying to get a bead on his fighter. Dex punched his throttle forward, and not a moment too soon, as a fresh volley of red bolts passed just behind the tail of his Hornet. He sped underneath the port wing of the gunship. The two ventral-side gunners turned to track him, but he was by in a flash. Dex's rear-targeting window showed the gunship pulling up in an attempt to flip around. But the gunship, while able to attain an impressive top speed with its high-powered engines, was anything but agile, and its turn was laborious. The bright orange-tinted engines loomed large in Dex's rear-window, presenting him with an easy target. He lined up his shot just forward of the engines and fired.

His rear cannons ripped through the gunship's aft quarter. A series of small flashes gave way to a much larger explosion. The flames rapidly spread forward, briefly engulfing the entire ship and causing Dex to worry that he had grievously violated his own primary order, taking not one, but six lives. But the fire quickly burned out, leaving the gunship mostly intact aside from the charred, twisted remnants of what used to be its engines.

"One's disabled," Dex informed the squadron. "It's about half a klick forward of the *Wagon*. Keep your distance—the turrets are still hot. Ninja, what's the status on those Stingers?"

"Still have a visual," Onigen said. "Flash and Ghazi are attempting to saddle on their wing to provide additional cover."

"Yeah, if the morons would ever sit still long enough to let us," Scot added.

"You can't blame them," Jani said. "For all they know, we're just more bandits."

"Well, if they'd just pull their heads out of...wait, holy—!" A loud rattling obscured the rest of Scot's transmission. Dex was all too familiar with the sound, caused by a ship buckling from a nearby explosion.

"Flash, status. Are you two all right?"

"Yeah yeah, we're fine, Ghazi's fine." The words were pouring out. "One of the Stingers is down, just obliterated right in front of us. Looked like a Slammer—it came out of nowhere!"

"It couldn't have been a Slammer," Geff said. "It's impossible. The jammer pod is keeping the Rhinos' lights out, too."

Seltrice couldn't help herself. "So you're calling Flash a liar?"

"No, I'm just stating a fact. A jammer blocks all—"

"Shut up, you idiot, it doesn't matter," Scot blurted out. "The Slammer didn't come from one of the Rhinos. I told you, it came out of nowhere—away from the engagement."

"Flash, Ghazi—no, all Angels break toward the freighter, now!" Dex nearly shouted the order while inwardly cursing his stupidity. How could he have ignored such an obvious threat? Responding to his own command, he adjusted his course, maneuvering his fighter closer to the freighter. He confirmed that Jani did the same and then continued in a steadier tone.

"There's a fifth Rhino lurking just outside the range of the jammer. He's feeding information to the other bandits. Plus, it looks like he's taking potshots at anyone who strays within range. So stay close to the *Wagon*—we couldn't lock on to the Rhinos at that range. Let's hope he can't get a lock either."

Dex knew that the Angels couldn't hide around the freighter forever—they were going to have to take out that fifth gunship. He would have liked to have let loose the entire squadron after the cowardly gunship, but he couldn't, in good conscience, abandon the final Scorpion to fend off the other gunships alone. Dex figured he could spare two pilots from the furball. He was about to ask for volunteers when Purnima beat him to it.

"Deadeye, Sunfire and I request permission to locate and engage the outer Rhino."

"Granted. But remember that until you clear the jammer's range, you won't be able to detect incoming Slammers—that means no warning alarms. So keep your head on a swivel."

"Roger."

Dex glanced out the left side of the canopy and saw Purnima's and Ravi's Hornets simultaneously speed off in opposite directions.

"Moonlight, Sunfire, check your wings—you're drifting."

Ravi answered, followed immediately by Purnima.

"Roger, sir. We know."

"It's all right. Trust us."

Splitting up was a risky strategy. Though it would cut the search time in half, it also meant that one of them would be racing toward the hidden gunship without a wingman. That meant one less pair of eyes to spot incoming missiles. Dex hoped the Voor twins knew what they were doing.

The departure of the Voors left Hagen and Seltrice at a severe disadvantage. Under normal circumstances, two Hornets could hold their own head-to-head against two gunships. But in the current close-quarters slugging match, the odds heavily favored the gunships. Dex checked in with his second-in-command.

"Sarge, status. Do you need assistance?"

"Stand by."

Hagen's voice was steady, but by no means did Dex take that to mean that he and Seltrice were safe. Hagen was always calm under fire. In the background, Dex heard Hagen's fighter shudder from multiple missile launches. He wasn't sure what Hagen was hoping to accomplish by launching his Slammers. One hit would obliterate a gunship, which would be a blatant violation of his orders. Nevertheless, Dex held his tongue for the moment. He had always trusted Hagen's judgment in the past, and he would do so now.

Hagen resumed speaking. "Hold on—hold on—got him! Rhino two is down."

118

"Sarge..." Dex began, but stopped himself, determined to give Hagen the benefit of the doubt. Hagen, sensing Dex's hesitation, put his captain's mind at ease.

"I got him with my Leeches. Stopped him dead in his tracks."

In the chaos of battle, Dex had completely forgotten Hagen and Seltrice's original mission—to drain power from the freighter's engines. Their Hornets had been equipped with Power Draining Missiles, or "Leeches," which could just as effectively drain power from the gunships, as Hagen had just proved.

"Sarge, what state?" Dex was wondering how many PDMs Hagen had remaining.

"I'm winchester Leeches. Sorry, sir."

"Roger. Good work."

Dex couldn't blame Hagen for using all twelve Leeches. Shooting ballistic missiles, unguided by sensors, it was a testament to Hagen's skill that he was able to score a hit at all. Still, it would have been helpful to have a few extra Leeches at his squadron's disposal. Seltrice's Hornet was now the only one armed with the suddenly invaluable PDMs.

Confident that Viper's Leeches would give Hagen and Seltrice the upper hand over the other gunship, Dex turned his attention toward the remaining Scorpion. But first, he had to figure out where exactly it was. There had been a lull in cannon fire, which, while fortunate for the Scorpion, made it difficult for Dex to get a visual on the small fighter. He hoped Scot and Adahn were still trailing it.

"Flash, status."

"The Stinger shook us off his tail, but I've still got a visual. He's making a pass behind the *Wagon*."

"Roger. We're on our way."

In unison, Dex and Jani turned to intercept the Scorpion on the far side of the freighter. Scot spoke up again.

"Deadeye, Flash. I just got a good look at the freighter's engines and saw about a half dozen Leeches. It's at a standstill. Looks like those pirates did most of the work for us. You know, we could still—"

Dex knew where Scot was headed and cut him off immediately.

"You and Ghazi stay with that Stinger. Is that understood?"

A sharp burst of static drowned out Scot's response. The comm continued to crackle with interference before giving way to a panicked voice.

"I'm hit!" It was Geff. A brief silence followed the transmission. Dex instinctively glanced at his battle map before remembering that his sensors were still jammed. He was about to call for a report from Onigen when, to his relief, Geff reported in himself.

"I'm all right. Shields are down, but I'm good."

Onigen addressed his wingman. "Prince, bandit diving for the freighter. Break right—I'll cover you."

"Tally. Wait, I've got this." Geff's response surprised Dex. He was deliberately disobeying Onigen, chasing after the gunship in a damaged fighter.

Onigen spoke more forcefully. "Negative, Prince. Disengage and—whoa! Hold your fire!"

"My stick's sluggish!" Panic was creeping back into Geff's voice. "I'm losing control!"

"Prince, pull up!"

A vicious rattling echoed through Dex's cockpit, signaling the second large explosion of the battle. After a few moments of silence, Onigen gave the report. His tone was somber.

"The Rhino's destroyed. My apologies, sir. We were…imprecise. I take full responsibility."

"And Prince?"

"I'm still here, sir."

Dex breathed a quick prayer of thanks. Nevertheless, his squadron had crossed a serious line. He did not hesitate giving the next order.

"Angels, guns are cold. No one, I repeat, no one fires on the Rhinos—except for Viper."

Seltrice was clearly surprised.

"Me?"

"You still have a full payload of Leeches, correct?"

"Yes, sir."

"Then grind that fourth Rhino to a halt. Sarge, cover her. Rabbit and I will intercept and cover the Stinger. Everyone else, hunt down that jammer."

Dex's Hornet skimmed along the port side of the freighter, its dull gray plating looming large over the right side of his canopy. As he approached the freighter's stern, he expected to make visual contact with the Scorpion. Instead, appearing suddenly from behind the freighter, the Scorpion made contact with him, firing a few quick shots from its cannons before screaming by just a few meters overhead. His shields held against the light volley, and Dex turned hard left, trying to get on the Scorpion's tail.

The appearance of the Scorpion and Dex's sudden maneuver seemed to catch Jani by surprise, and she couldn't quite match Dex's tight turn. Her Hornet, forced into taking a wider arc, would now have trouble catching up with the speedy Scorpion. Dex realized he was going to have to cover the Scorpion without his wingman.

"Deadeye, bandit, your ten, high," Hagen said, informing him of a nearby gunship.

Dex had stuck with the Scorpion through another tight turn, and now the Scorpion's pilot was holding a steady course toward Ceres, hoping to outrun his pursuers. Generally, that would have been a good strategy for the speedy Scorpion, but this particular course was bringing it directly underneath the diving gunship. Dex turned to his best weapon.

"Viper, I need your help with this Rhino."

"I'm blind. Where are you?"

"*Wagon*'s stern, port side. Follow my tracers."

Dex fired his forward cannons in the general direction of the gunship—which was well out of range—so that Seltrice could follow the yellow bolts from him to the target. Dex then drained his cannons and rerouted the power to his engines, needing every bit of extra juice to catch up to the Scorpion. Time was running out, and the gunship, with its powerful engines, was having significantly less trouble closing the gap.

"Viper, status."

"Still out of range," Seltrice replied.

"Fire one anyway. Maybe it'll scare him off—or at least distract him."

"Roger," she said. Seconds later, she called out, "Fox two."

Dex looked back over his left shoulder to track the flight of Seltrice's Leech. The stubby green-glowing missile overtook Dex's position in seconds. Seltrice had done an excellent job anticipating the flight path of the gunship, and for a moment, it appeared as though she might've scored a one-in-a-million hit. But the missile proved to be too fast, flying through the point of intersection well in front of the gunship.

The gunship's pilot had certainly seen the near miss, but there was no visible reaction from his ship, which continued diving on an intercept course. The Scorpion's pilot likewise held his course, seemingly oblivious to the fast-approaching gunship.

Dex switched to a universal comm channel, which would broadcast to all ships in the area. For security purposes, the Angels rarely used open channels, but Dex was getting desperate.

"Scorpion, you have a gunship closing in—your ten, high. The Horn—the Adders are friendlies." Dex caught himself, remembering that the Hornets were employing ghillie generators to make them appear as Adders. So far removed were they from the original mission plan that the detail had nearly slipped his mind. "We can cover you, but you must turn back toward the freighter immediately."

Dex waited, but there was no response. The Scorpion continued on what was essentially a suicide run. Jani spoke up on the secure channel.

"Deadeye, Rabbit. I've got a shot at the Rhino's engines. Permission to engage."

"Negative. Return to the freighter. That's an order." Dex emphasized the last bit, knowing that, given the chance, Jani would do everything possible to harass the gunship. And without the ability to fire and defend herself, she would most definitely be killed in the process. In the distance, he saw her fighter break off pursuit.

Dex, using every last bit of rerouted power, had nearly reached the Scorpion, but he appeared to be too late—the gunship had closed within firing range.

"Viper, now's the time for those Leeches."

"Fox two—I've got a pair on the way."

Seltrice had scarcely finished her transmission when the gunship's turrets opened up on the Scorpion. Dex engaged his Hornet's afterburner reserves, jolting his fighter forward, helping him make up the extra distance between him and the Scorpion. He positioned his Hornet directly above the Scorpion, placing himself in the path of the gunship. The turrets poured down on Dex. In an instant, he was surrounded not by the darkness of space, but by blazing fire. A rapid succession of flashes blinded him, and his ears rang from the thunderous impacts. One burst slammed into the canopy, jerking Dex forward in his seat. Only his safety harness kept his head from cracking into the instrument panel. Delirious from the blow, Dex was not fully aware that he'd lost his dorsal shields, and yet, by instinct, he rolled the exposed side of his Hornet away from the gunship. Another burst rocked the belly of his fighter, collapsing the remainder of his shields and leaving his Hornet completely defenseless.

Dex's head involuntarily tilted back on his right shoulder. Though the concept had little meaning in space, he felt as if he were upside down. Looking up in a daze, he saw the Scorpion drifting away, pursued by the lumbering gunship. He saw two shimmering green lights streaking through the stars. One and then the other closed within a few meters of the gunship before passing by. He saw the gunship hover over the Scorpion. A final burst ripped the tail clean off the fighter. The two sections of the Scorpion floated apart before each exploded into a thousand fiery bits. He saw two Hornets rising up toward the belly of the gunship. The lower turrets continued to pump out red death until two more Leeches ground them to a halt. He saw Seltrice's Hornet launch its entire payload of Leeches at the gunship, the last missile at near pointblank range, until there was no doubt that she had drained every last bit of power from her attacker.

He heard a voice. It was Hagen.

"You all right, sir? You took some nasty hits."

Aside from a persistent ringing in his ears, Dex was starting to come around.

"I'm fine, Sarge. How's she look?"

"Not too pretty."

For the second time in two missions, Dex was forced to consult his emergency systems display. The screen was full of red type, confirming Hagen's concise evaluation of the state of his fighter. Shields, missile launchers, and rear cannons were all beyond immediate repair. His left engine was out, and his right was dangerously close to failing as well. If Dex had one bit of good fortune, it was that his E-drive had once again escaped critical damage.

"They got the last Stinger," Hagen said.

"Yeah, I saw."

After a brief pause, Seltrice asked the question that was undoubtedly on everyone's mind.

"Orders, sir?"

The mission had been a bust from the start. Having failed to either secure the freighter or rescue the Scorpions, there was absolutely no reason to stick around and risk further disaster.

"We bugout," Dex replied. "Immediately."

It was clear from Jani's tone that she didn't care for the order.

"Sir, Flash said the freighter's stopped. We could still grab it, now that things have cooled down some."

"Not a chance—not with our lights still out. For all we know, there could be more hostiles headed our way as we speak. No, the mission's over. Angels, form up and prepare—"

"Moonlight, archer archer! Five, high!"

Dex, having been so caught up in trying to save the Scorpion, had forgotten about the Voor twins and the fifth and final gunship. With his sensor screens still blank, he had no idea where the Voor twins were or how he could help Purnima with the incoming missile. At the moment, all he could do was listen.

"No joy!" Purnima called back, informing Ravi that she couldn't see the missile.

"Don't panic. I've got you covered." Ravi seemed on the verge of panicking himself—though he managed to keep his instructions clear. "Continue run, then break hard right on my mark."

Dex figured that Ravi must have been tracking Purnima's Hornet and the missile with his sensors, which meant that he was out of range of the jammer. Dex had a lot of questions for Ravi, but he kept his mouth shut. Interrupting Ravi now would be a death sentence for Purnima.

"Still closing on your five..." Ravi said, urging his sister to spot the missile.

"No joy...no joy..." Purnima's voice echoed ominously through Dex's cockpit—if she couldn't see the missile, she would have no hope of avoiding it. Yet, despite the grim situation, he heard Ravi begin speaking in softer tones to his sister, momentarily forgetting—or purposefully neglecting—to use her call sign.

"Nima, listen. Close your eyes a moment...there. You know where it is. Now open. Can you see it?"

"I...yes! I see it! Tally."

"Now, wait for my mark...a little closer...wait...wait..." Ravi's voice trailed off. Purnima called out in her brother's silence. "Ravi—?"

"—Go go go!"

Dex faintly heard the telltale rattling over the comm system, and he feared the worst. But Purnima's voice soon put those fears to rest.

"Trashed—it missed."

"Good," Ravi said, "but don't relax yet. There's another pair on the way."

It would take Ravi a few seconds before he could determine the flight path of the missiles and instruct Purnima accordingly. Dex took advantage of the brief window of opportunity.

"Sunfire, Deadeye. I need the exact location of that jammer."

"Sir, I need to—"

"Quickly, Sunfire."

Dex understood Ravi's reluctance to even momentarily break concentration from his sister—she would be dead right now if it were not for Ravi's clear-headed instructions. But she wouldn't be able to dodge every Slammer, and the gunship would just keep firing away until forced to do otherwise. Dex was not about to allow the squadron to go weapons free—not after the incident with Geff. Therefore, the only other course of action was his original plan—lock on to the gunship and hope it fled. But getting a lock was the hard part. Though Ravi was out of the jammer's range, he wouldn't be able to do it. First, it would take him too long to circle around the jammer's area of influence to get within range of the gunship, and second, he had to devote all his attention to guiding Purnima. And, of course, Dex and the others couldn't lock on until the jammer was disabled.

"I can't get an exact fix on the jammer—it's moving around too fast."

"Give me your best guess."

"It's definitely sticking beneath the freighter, toward the bow. It's close, too—just a couple meters from the hull."

"Roger, Sunfire. You heard him, Angels. Take it out."

Dex watched Jani and the others race past his limping Hornet on their way to the freighter. Ravi wasted no time in resuming his role as Purnima's guardian angel.

"Moonlight, two Slammers, your eleven, low. They're spaced five seconds apart—you won't be able to dodge them both. You're going to have to shoot one down."

"Deadeye, Ghazi." Dex was surprised and irritated to hear a voice belonging to someone other the Voor twins coming over the comm channel.

Adahn continued. "Sorry to interrupt, but I've lost Flash. He's disappeared."

"Roger. Now stay off comm," Dex barked.

"Yes, sir. Sorry, sir."

Dex knew that reprimanding Adahn for again cluttering the channel with his apology would be counter-intuitive. He instead focused his thoughts on his missing pilot. It was possible that, without sensors to keep track of one another, Scot and Adahn had simply become separated. But Dex quickly dismissed that idea—Scot was too skilled a pilot to let that happen. It would have been easy for Ravi to locate Scot's Hornet with his sensors, but Dex had no intention of again distracting him.

Besides, Dex suspected the answer all along. He wanted to give Scot the benefit of the doubt—someone as smart as Scot couldn't possibly do something so outright stupid—but he couldn't shake a certain sinking feeling the closer he got to the freighter. And then he saw it. Toward the stern, docked beneath the portside airlock, was Scot Calgaro's Hornet.

*   *   *

The first thing Scot did upon boarding the *Milk Wagon* was turn off his earpiece. Adahn was an idiot, but even he would eventually figure out that he no longer had a wingman. And when that happened, the last thing Scot needed was Dex and the others breaking his concentration by hollering in his ear the whole time. It was going to be hard enough to single-handedly hijack the freighter.

He climbed up out of the hatch and found himself looking down a long corridor. Like most automated ships, the interior was dark. Every ten meters or so, an orange emergency light illuminated a small patch of the ceiling, but the lights were so dim, Scot could scarcely see the floor in front of him, much less what lay ahead down the corridor. Fortunately, he'd anticipated just such a problem. Reaching for his belt, he unhooked one of the compact flares he'd taken from the squadron's supply closet back on Pella. The flares, as he'd pointed out to Adahn in the armory, had a wide range of power settings, capable of piercing the darkness of deep space or softly illuminating a small room. Before the mission, he had spent a fair amount of time in his quarters calibrating the settings until they were just right. Unfortunately, he wasn't aware that after an extended period of inactivity, the flares reset to their default setting—full power. Scot ignited the flare and was instantly blinded.

He dropped the flare at his feet and stumbled into a bulkhead. Opening his eyes, he could see nothing but white light. He pulled out his side arm and waved it in front of him, listening intently for any would-be assailants.

Scot was most likely the only person on the ship, but if any of the pirates had boarded the freighter, he didn't want to be caught with his pistol in the holster. He closed his eyes and tried to listen for footsteps, but all he could hear was a constant high-pitched whine. Scot dropped to his hands and knees and felt around for the flare on the ribbed metal floor. The flare, while powerful, did not emit a tremendous amount of heat, allowing Scot to graze it with his fingers, pick it up, and dial down the brightness without burning his hands.

He reopened his eyes and still saw mostly white. But soon he was able to distinguish shapes—the contours of bulkheads, the outlines of doorways on his left. The once unbearably bright flare now emitted a soft white glow. He still couldn't see all the way down the corridor, but at least he could now make out his immediate surroundings. As he moved, the pale white light cast eerie shifting shadows along the corridor. Scot slowly made his way forward, his left hand carrying the flare as a kind of torch and his right hand aiming his pistol at the awaiting darkness.

*   *   *

Dex's Hornet crawled along the underside of the freighter while Ravi still tirelessly called out instructions to Purnima.

"Just a little more—good. The first Slammer should be dead ahead."

"Tally."

"Trash it."

Dex anxiously waited for some sort of response. Hearing the constant threats against Purnima had physically worn him down, reducing his arms and legs to jelly. He rarely tensed up so much in battle, but this was different—he wasn't accustomed to being a mere spectator.

"One's trashed!" Purnima exclaimed.

"Good—now dive on my mark. Use your burners." Ravi's voice reached an entirely new pitch. "Now! Go go go!"

Dex could hear the afterburners roaring in the background of Purnima's transmission.

"Missed again."

Purnima had been kept alive through some remarkable teamwork with her brother, but the gunship would not relent, continuing to launch missile after missile. And it would take just a single Slammer. She had been fortunate so far, but Dex knew that it was only a matter of time before one caught her.

He flew past the bow of the freighter and immediately began the agonizingly long process of turning his fighter around. The only way he could help Purnima was by taking out the jammer. But as hard as the jammer had been to locate, it had proven to be even more difficult to destroy. At only a meter wide, the black, elliptical jammer was a miniscule target. And it never stopped moving, with multiple thrusters propelling it erratically back and forth, almost as though it were bouncing off the sides of the freighter.

To further complicate matters, all available Hornets had converged in the immediate vicinity of the *Wagon*. It made things a little crowded, particularly underneath where the deep outer edges of the H-freighter served to funnel the Hornets into a tight alley, made even tighter by the presence of Scot's parked Hornet. The other pilots had certainly figured out what had happened to Scot, but there had been no comments on the matter. The Angels understood that any excessive chatter would hinder Ravi's instructions to Purnima.

Adahn's fighter raced in front of Dex from left to right, cutting perpendicular to the freighter, while the others were making parallel runs. For a moment, it looked as though Adahn's new approach would pay off, as he seemed to have a good bead on the jammer. But the moment he fired, the jammer bobbed down, easily evading the volley. His flurry of bolts continued past and peppered the freighter, tearing a number of holes into the portside hull and setting off a chain reaction of explosions. As fire rapidly expanded over the hull, Dex couldn't believe his eyes—an entire freighter was in the midst of being destroyed by a lone, isolated cannon burst. He could only hope that Scot would somehow be able to make it out before the engines exploded and disintegrated the entire ship.

But the explosions faded as quickly as they'd begun, and the freighter remained intact, aside from the minor hull damage caused by Adahn's cannon burst. Dex realized that the fireworks show had been another holdover from the original mission. Pryo charges had been planted in advance all along the freighter's hull as part of the ruse to make it appear that Baker's freighter had been destroyed in a failed hijacking. At least they now had proof that the show would've been convincing.

A second barrage from Adahn likewise missed the jammer and nearly clipped the tail of Seltrice's Hornet. Dex admired Seltrice's restraint in keeping off the channel, though Dex was certain Adahn would be hearing about that one later.

The transmissions between the Voor twins grew even more intense as yet another Slammer homed in on Purnima. It was clear from the strain in their voices that they were both nearing the breaking point. To make matters worse, Dex wasn't certain there would be a reprieve. The Angels had made no progress against the elusive jammer, making pass after pass in vain. Dex was doubly frustrated because he had yet to fire a single shot at the jammer—his damaged fighter still crawling on the edge of firing range. There was, however, one advantage to his glacial speed—it gave him ample time to observe the jammer, and Dex thought he may have detected a pattern in the pod's seemingly random flight.

Finally skirting into firing range, Dex waited for the jammer to reestablish its pattern. After jinking left and dipping down, Dex was confident the jammer would bob up. He lined the pipper above the jammer and fired. The jammer, however, didn't cooperate, dodging left again, while Dex's shot missed by a wide margin.

Dex could've sworn. Instead, he fired again, an extended burst aimed directly at the pod's center. The two rows of yellow bolts bracketed the jammer, streaking so close, on either side, that Dex momentarily lost sight of the pod amid the bright tracers. But the flashes soon subsided and still the jammer remained unscathed.

Dex again pulled the trigger and held it in place. He danced the pipper in circles around the jammer with little consideration for pattern. The multiple bolts seemed to form two continuous lines, waving wildly around in the general vicinity of the jammer. Dex saw several Hornets break off from strafing runs, keeping their distance from the unpredictable stream of fire from Dex's fighter. They didn't have to worry for long, as the uncommonly heavy barrage was rapidly draining the battery power of his cannons. Dex knew without glancing at the little bar gauge that, at the current rate, he only had a few seconds of fire left. Even so, he kept the trigger depressed. The jammer pod dodged right just as Dex aimed left, sending his bolts in the wrong direction.

And then the stream of fire abruptly stopped—the forward batteries having dried up. Dex looked on helplessly as his final few shots traveled well wide of the mark. But then the jammer, in a flash, veered left, miraculously bringing it directly into the path of the final few bolts. Dex didn't have to see the small explosion to know that he destroyed the jammer—the proof was in the displays that suddenly flashed to life, bathing his cockpit in the familiar blue-green glow.

There were dozens of things Dex wanted to check all at once, but he made sure to give one order first.

"Angels, paint the Rhino!"

Dex scanned the battle map for Purnima. He found her just in time to see her fighter narrowly roll beneath yet another missile—the last one, Dex hoped. By now, the gunship's cockpit would be shrieking with warning alarms as every available Hornet locked on. If the gunship's pilot had any sense, he would stop focusing on Purnima and start taking evasive maneuvers. After all, he had no way of knowing that the Hornets never intended to fire their missiles.

As Dex waited to see if the gunship would call his bluff, movement at the edge of the battle map caught his eye. Dex zoomed in to identify the new arrivals, but Hagen beat him to it.

"Deadeye, Sarge. A squadron of Stingers is inbound from Ceres."

As if to confirm, a voice broke in over the universal channel.

"Area traffic, power down your weapons and stand by for escort."

Dex replied through the open channel. "Ceres police force, be advised that the Adders are friendlies." This time, he remembered right away to refer to the Hornets' disguises. "We disabled four outlaw gunships in an attempted rescue of your personnel."

Not that it made a difference in the end to the dead Scorpion pilots, Dex thought solemnly. The gruff voice on the other end of the channel seemed to agree that the Angels' efforts in this case were irrelevant.

"Reduce speed and head to oh-eight-four. Failure to comply will be viewed as a hostile act, and you will be fired upon."

The channel closed. Dex's battle map indicated that the Scorpion squadron was about four minutes out—plenty of time for the Hornets to turn around and jump out of the system. There was just one problem—the Angels were missing a pilot.

"Flash, report in." Dex was hoping for an answer, but he did not expect one. If Scot had been brazen enough to violate orders and board the freighter, then he certainly wasn't going to feel any obligation to check in with his commanding officer. The channel remained silent. Each wasted second brought the Scorpions closer—Scorpions whose pilots were undoubtedly seeking vengeance for the loss of their four friends.

Hagen had had enough of Scot's nonsense. "Sir, permission to board the freighter and retrieve Flash."

"Denied. Flash, respond. There's a hostile squadron inbound."

There was still no response, and Dex concluded that Scot must have turned off his earpiece. Maverick or not, Scot would never purposefully put the squadron in danger. But by remaining on the freighter, he was doing just that.

"Deadeye, Rabbit." Jani was never one to be easily rattled, but she sounded worried now. "I just conducted a tight sweep of the freighter. Sir, Flash isn't the only one on board."

*   *   *

Scot had picked up the pace after a few explosions rocked the freighter. He wasn't sure if the hits had been part of an attack or just stray fire, but either way, he didn't want to be caught standing still if the freighter went up in flames.

Briefly, after the explosions, he had turned on his earpiece to get a read on the situation outside. All he'd heard was Ravi calling out instructions to his sister. Scot had been forced to turn it off—it had been too debilitating. He was worried for Purnima, but he knew the best way he could help her was to get the freighter moving and complete the mission. He wasn't leaving without the *Wagon*—even if the squadron left without him.

Scot was nearing the end of the corridor. Ahead, there were a few more doorways to his left, and at the end, a right turn led to the bridge. Scot angled his flare to cast more light on the corner, revealing nothing but nondescript bulkheads. Slowing his pace again, he listened carefully. He was certain that there were no pirates aboard, but if there were, they would likely be in the nearby bridge, working to override the freighter's automated controls. Normally, the engines would have provided a constant droning, but they had been disabled by the gunships. An air circulation system worked softly in the background, and the dim orange lights emitted a faint hum, but there was little more. The loudest noise, by far, was Scot's own breathing.

And then he heard it—a footstep. Scot froze. The sound had not come from around the corner, as Scot had expected, but rather from behind him, back down the corridor. He knew that taking the time to turn around and face the intruder could cost him his life. Scot paused ever so briefly to consider his next move, and then he acted.

Without looking, Scot threw his flare behind him with a fluid backhand motion. The flare skidded across the floor, illuminating the figure as it slid past, and came to a stop a few meters behind him. Casting off the flare shrouded Scot in a thick and sudden darkness. Using the momentum from his throw, he whirled around and dropped prone to the floor.

As he dropped, several shots rang out, each high-pitched blast sending a deafening echo down the tight corridor. At the relatively close distance, the bright red bolts had been too fast for Scot to see, but he certainly felt them. There was a searing sensation on his right temple, and his right ear burned like it was on fire.

Scot grunted as he was hit but restrained himself from crying out. He fell hard to the floor, knocking the wind out of him, as several more shots whizzed over his head and struck the bulkhead behind, each setting off a flurry of sparks. Ignoring the pain, Scot stretched his arms forward, aiming his pistol up at the attacker. The man, backlit by the flare, made an easy target. Scot squeezed off three rounds.

All three blue stun bolts struck the man—two in the stomach, one in the chest. On impact, the stun bolts caused area muscles to violently spasm and then shut down. The man doubled over and crumpled to the floor, moaning in agony. Scot pushed himself up. As he stood, his head began throbbing, and he remembered that he'd been wounded. He reached for his right ear with the palm of his hand, but at the slightest contact, fresh waves of pain coursed from his head down through his chest, causing Scot to jerk his hand back.

He turned his attention back down the corridor, where the flare cast its flickering white light on the fallen man. Scot slowly made his way forward, carefully eyeing every door along the way in case anyone else decided to jump out.

When Scot reached the man, he was surprised by what he saw. The man was smaller than he had looked in the silhouette. His pale face was clean-shaven while his dark brown hair was parted to one side, giving the man an almost boyish appearance. This was not the gruff, battle-hardened pirate Scot had expected.

A pistol lay next to the man. Scot picked it up and looked it over. It was a standard military issue Hagg-Sauer BP-105, identical to Scot's own side arm, except this one hadn't been loaded with a stun clip—Scot had the burn on the side of his head to prove it. He stuffed the pistol into his flight suit. When he looked up, he noticed an open doorway a couple meters ahead and to the right, near the flare. Scot backed up against the wall and shuffled toward the open door, his pistol drawn and ready, pointed at the deck. Inching toward the unseen room, the thought crossed his mind that perhaps the rifle with the holosight wouldn't have been such a bad idea after all.

At the edge of the door, Scot craned his neck to peek one eye into the room. There was just enough indirect light from the flare for him to differentiate between shadows, and he spied a small section of the room before pulling his head back. He repeated the move, each time spying a little more of the room. When Scot was certain that it was clear, he pivoted into the doorway—swinging his pistol forward just in case—and entered.

The room was small, designed as crew quarters for manned missions, with bunk beds on the left wall and a tiny shelving compartment on the right. But, now that he had a closer look at the interior, Scot noticed something that clearly had not been in the original design—he could see out into space. Around a dozen head-sized holes were punched through the hull. Scot guessed that the freighter had gotten in the way of an errant cannon barrage. The mangled wall twisted in on itself at odd angles—only an emergency force field kept it from completely collapsing.

There was shrapnel everywhere—jagged hunks of metal strewn across the floor and thin shards deeply lodged into the sidewalls and bunks. As Scot surveyed the wreckage, a thought suddenly occurred to him. He moved toward the door, but his feet stumbled over something, causing him to lurch forward and tumble toward the hazard-laden floor. He caught himself on a corner post of the bunk beds and regained his footing, grateful that his hands had avoided any protruding bits of shrapnel. He looked down to see what he had tripped over.

Sticking out from underneath the lower bunk was a small silver case. Taking another quick glance at the doorway, Scot crouched down and opened it. Its thick padded lining held only a single object—a black disc just a little larger than Scot's hand. He wasn't sure what to make of it. He was reasonably certain it wasn't a bomb—what would the pirates stand to gain from blowing up the freighter? But neither did it look like a tool that would help restart the engines or override the freighter's flight controls.

Scot was at a loss. The object appeared to have no practical use for hijacking the freighter.

Then it clicked. What if the pirates had never intended to steal the freighter in the first place? The object was beginning to look familiar. Scot remembered seeing a similarly shaped object years ago in a reconnaissance course at the academy. There was now no doubt in his mind—he was looking at a tracking device.

He stood up and walked—more cautiously this time—to the door. He had some questions for the man lying in the corridor. It was then that Scot realized something had changed—the moaning had stopped. Scot rushed into the corridor, fearing that the man had crawled away and disappeared. But it was quite the opposite. The man had not moved an inch, and indeed, was completely still.

Scot hesitantly stepped forward for a closer look. Bathed in the white glow from the flare, it would've been impossible for the man to look any paler. His flight suit was soaked a dark red over his midsection, and Scot saw that there was blood on his hands. There was a small tear in the flight suit over the upper abdomen. Scot knelt down and delicately felt around the area, the wound still oozing blood, until he found what he had expected—a long jagged piece of metal, identical to those strewn about the crew quarters.

"Wrong place at the wrong time," Scot muttered. He moved to check the man's vitals, confirming what he already knew to be true—the man was dead.

*   *   *

The Scorpions had closed to less than a minute out when their squadron leader issued his last message over the open channel.

"This is your final warning. Stand down or we will engage."

Dex knew it wasn't an idle threat. Moments ago, the Scorpions had overtaken the final gunship, which had been making a mad dash for the freighter, presumably to pick up the man they'd left aboard. And perhaps a prisoner as well, Dex thought grimly. Regardless of the reason, the gunship had held a straight course for the freighter, closing the gap as quickly as possible. But it never stood a chance outracing the lightning-quick Scorpions. And when the Scorpions caught up, the gunship had not been destroyed so much as obliterated. Every one of the twelve Scorpions took a run at the gunship, even after it had started to break apart. Not a single scrap survived.

And now the Angels were the focus of their bloodlust. In a straight-up fight, the Scorpions would've been no match for the Hornets. While the Scorpions had superior raw speed, the Angels held advantages in maneuverability, firepower, and, most importantly, training. But if Dex had not authorized his squadron to use deadly force against a band of pirates, he certainly wasn't going to do so against a police force.

Dex had waited for Scot long enough—perhaps too long with the Scorpions closing so rapidly. He gave the order.

"Angels, form up and jump out. Ghazi, you're on Rabbit's wing."

Jani didn't miss the significance of taking on Scot's wingman, Adahn, as her own. Not only did it mean abandoning Scot, but it also left Dex as the odd man out.

"And we're both on your wing, sir." Jani wasn't asking.

"Negative," Dex replied. "I'm staying behind to evac Flash."

"Yeah, that's not happening," Jani stated matter-of-factly. "You stay, we all stay."

Several other pilots voiced their affirmation, and Dex realized he was going to have to deal with this recent bout of insubordination in his squadron—if they made it out alive.

"This is not open for debate—" Dex started, but another voice cut him off before he could finish.

"Flash here. The freighter's no good. They're tracking it. The lone hostile on board is dead, but I found at least one homing device—there could be more."

If Dex was relieved to hear Scot, it didn't come across in his voice, as he all but screamed his next order.

"Disembark now! We've got a dozen Stingers with their fangs out!"

"I'm on my way," Scot replied evenly with no hint of urgency—or apology.

Dex reigned in his tone as he addressed the rest of the squadron.

"Angels, we wait for Flash. The Stingers mean business, so take defensive action. Continue dry—do not fire on the Stingers."

Dex was well aware of the very real possibility that his orders could get some, if not all, of his pilots killed. The Angels had lost pilots before, but those had been against unmanned Marauders. Therefore, Dex's strict rules of engagement had never directly contributed to a pilot's death—yet.

He wasn't sure how he would respond if that happened—if he would break the rules for the safety of his squadron. While so far he hadn't had to make such a choice, he realized that their good fortune could not continue indefinitely.

The Scorpions first reached Hagen and Seltrice, and a pair broke formation to engage the two Hornets. On his battle map, Dex watched Hagen lead Seltrice through a sequence of scissors maneuvers designed to place them on their pursuers' tails. Though they weren't allowed to fire, the safest place to be was still on the Scorpions' six. The rest of the Angels would soon attempt similar maneuvers, except for Dex, whose damaged Hornet made him essentially a sitting duck. His only chance of survival rested on Scot making it off the freighter before the Scorpions made it to him.

His map showed the rest of the Scorpion squadron pairing off as they chose their targets. None appeared to be headed in his direction, and Dex figured that he probably wasn't a priority target. The Scorpions began firing, their bolts colored the same yellow as the Hornets', a trademark of all fighters designed by Aurora Company. There were no warning shots— the opening volley came fast and heavy with several bolts scoring glancing blows against the Hornets. The Scorpions' cannons were not as powerful as the gunships' burst turrets, but it would still only take a handful of hits to knock out the shields on a Hornet.

Dex zoomed in and out on his battle map, checking the status of his pilots. He allowed himself a smile when he saw that Hagen and Seltrice had managed to get behind their pursuers, no doubt frustrating the two Scorpions to no end. Onigen, Geff, and the Voor twins had more or less achieved a stalemate, suffering an occasional stray hit, but mostly just circling with the Scorpions for position. It was Jani and Adahn that Dex was worried about. They had attracted a flight of four Scorpions and were scrambling to survive, both of their shields on the verge of collapsing. And there looked to be no escape as two of the Scorpions were positioned squarely on their tails.

This was the moment Dex had been dreading—his pilots in mortal danger when a few words from him would likely save their lives. He knew there were very good reasons behind the squadron's rules of engagement—reasons, he was certain, that must have made a lot of sense in the comfort of his quarters back on Pella. But now, sitting in the cockpit, watching his friends come under fire with no realistic hope of saving themselves, those reasons seemed distant and elusive. He could not fathom, in that moment, how his self-imposed rules could possibly be more important than the lives of his pilots.

His eyes remained fixed on Jani's Hornet. Despite her desperate maneuvers, she continued to take a beating. There were simply too many pursuers for her to evade—if the tactical situation remained unchanged, she would be gone in a matter of seconds. And with that realization, the haze in his mind evaporated—he knew what had to be done.

Dex triggered the comm. "Angels, cleared hot." He didn't bother telling his pilots to shoot only to disable—the Scorpions were so small and lightly shielded that any direct hit, regardless of location, would be lethal. With that consideration in mind, he reopened the universal comm.

"Ceres police force," he said, his usual business-like tone underscored with a hint of menace. "Disengage now or you will be destroyed."

As if to punctuate the point, several Angels—Jani included—fired short cannon bursts. The bolts missed their targets—warning shots, Dex surmised. He knew that his pilots would not be eager to destroy police fighters. But he also knew that if the Scorpions continued pressing, his pilots, given their new freedom, would do whatever it took to defend themselves. Dex prayed that the Scorpions would ease off—otherwise, the situation was going to get ugly in a hurry.

The Scorpions began defensive maneuvers after the initial burst of fire from the Hornets, but they quickly re-gathered themselves and continued pressing the attack. Whether they were incredibly brave or stupid, the Scorpion pilots showed no intention of fleeing from the engagement. Checking his map, Dex noted that his pilots were showing remarkable restraint. They could've splashed half the squadron by this point if they'd wanted to, but they were using their cannon fire primarily to intimidate— not destroy.

His damaged Hornet still on the edge of the battle, Dex contributed the only way he could at the moment—he armed his missiles and aimed the diamond pipper over the lead Scorpion on Jani's tail. The Slammers quickly achieved a lock. Dex badly wanted to launch the missiles, to kill the Scorpions that had pushed Jani to the brink of death, but he was determined to give the pilots one final chance to save themselves. After a moment of indecision, the Scorpion and his wingman broke away, taking evasive action. Dex slowly lifted his finger from the trigger.

But there was little time for Dex to enjoy the small triumph. By locking onto the Scorpion, he had exposed himself as a potential threat. Two Scorpions had broken from the furball and were closing on him fast. He turned and punched his throttle forward, squeezing all the power he could out of his wheezing right engine, trying to buy himself even a few extra seconds. But it wouldn't be long before the Scorpions caught him. And when they did, Dex was sure they would give him the same harsh treatment they had given the gunship.

And then, finally, the transmission came.

"I'm out. Let's go."

Dex had never been so grateful to hear Scot's voice. He breathlessly gave his final order.

"Hold up. First we have to splash the freighter. Release ordnance and jump out at will."

Even though the mission had been a complete and utter failure, Dex had a responsibility to protect Baker. There was more than enough evidence on the freighter—with a cargo hold full of smuggled supplies—to link Baker to Dex and the fugitive colony. The freighter had to be destroyed. Even so, Dex felt a twinge of sadness as he gave the order. There were a lot of supplies on board that the colony desperately needed—food, clothing, medicine, even expensive replacement parts and ordnance for the Hornets. But the greater loss was the freedom the freighter would have provided the colony in obtaining and transporting future supplies. It was a terrible waste. Still, Dex thought sardonically, at least Baker would be getting the fireworks show he wanted—albeit a real one.

"Fox one," several Angels reported as they launched their Slammers. Their sector of space lit up with dozens of glowing blue missiles. The Scorpions frantically scattered, unaware of the intended target of such a potent barrage. The first few Slammers cut clean through the defenseless freighter. A dozen more set off a series of explosions—these ones, very real—that rapidly coalesced into a massive fireball. The last few Slammers vanished into the center as the outer flames began fading out, revealing only stars and empty space where the freighter had once been.

And the Angels disappeared into the ether.

Chapter 14

Early that morning, heavy clouds began taking position over Compton, and by midday, the city was blanketed in a thick haze of gray. The slow build-up continued throughout the day until sunset, when, as if on cue, the clouds opened, releasing a hard, steady rain that continued well into the night. The sharp points of light that typically dotted the cityscape on a clear night now shimmered through the windows of Darik Mason's shuttle, blurring and expanding into a broad canvas of red and gold and blue. A command flashed on the dashboard, prompting Darik to switch to autopilot due to poor visibility, but he maintained manual control, guiding his Perseus LX luxury shuttle through the high rises of midtown Compton. Given the opportunity, Darik preferred to fly manually, reasoning that he should make use of the "precision control system" he had paid so much for. Such opportunities, though, were rare, with the majority of his commute spent downtown in the financial district—a mandatory autopilot zone.

Glancing at his rearview displays, Darik accelerated and rose into the lane above, settling in snugly between a metro-bus and an open-cockpit airbike. After riding closely on his tail for a few seconds, the airbike pulled up along Darik's left side. He could see the driver's face—hard and weathered, though partially obscured by a tangled mess of hair matted on top by the downpour. Through the strands of hair, the driver stared intently at Darik, envying, no doubt, the dry, luxurious comfort of his Perseus. He then shook his head and punched the airbike's accelerator, cutting Darik off before ducking, illegally, under the metro-bus.

"Idiot," Darik muttered. Airbikes were dangerous enough without maniacs like him swerving to and fro in the middle of a thunderstorm. The weather conditions did not pose much of a hazard for Darik, however.

Even on manual control, his shuttle had so many fail-safes installed that he wasn't sure he could crash it if he wanted to.

Departing from the Unity Tower that evening, he had certainly felt like giving it a try. After successfully keeping a low profile for the past few days, he had finally been cornered in his office by Marcus Stirling. The first thing the vice president had done was jam his door open, ensuring that the entire office staff was an audience to their meeting. He then proceeded to rip into Darik with an almost comical ferocity. Amid the torrent of curses and expletives, Darik was able to decipher the message—he had until the end of the week to figure out the M-2 problem, or else Jenkins was going to fire them both. As he stood there, absorbing the insults and occasional spittle, Darik seriously considered doing absolutely nothing the rest of the week, just to see Stirling get canned. But, despite the enormous satisfaction that would bring him, Darik wasn't quite ready to sacrifice himself, regardless of how worthy the cause may be.

And in truth, Darik was closer than ever to figuring out what was going on with the M-2s. That fidgety little analyst, Nikky Weis, had been worth every credit. After their initial meeting at Bistro Riservata, it had taken Nikky less than a day to confirm, once and for all, that the four M-2s had been reprogrammed, never arriving at the Cacarus mine. A couple of days after that, Darik received a message on his handpod.

I have new program. Meet at B.R., 9 pm. Be ready to pay.

Darik's elation at the apparent breakthrough had been tempered by two concerns. One, he had expressly told Nikky not to contact him. And two, it appeared as though Nikky was going to use the new information as leverage for more money. As Darik dwelled on the first concern, he realized that perhaps Nikky contacting him wasn't such a big deal. After all, if Nikky was hacking into JenKore's most secure networks, he could probably be trusted to send an untraceable message to Darik's handpod. As for the second, his mood oscillated depending on how much he estimated Nikky would ask for.

The number, as it turned out, ended up being just a touch above zero— or, more precisely, the price of another meal at Bistro Riservata. The end of the message had simply been Nikky's way of saying that he didn't want to pick up the meal tab—something Darik was more than happy to do, considering the value of Nikky's information. The fact that Nikky was willing to give away the program as part of their original agreement either made him very honest or very stupid. Or, perhaps, he was genuinely interested in following the trail of information and didn't wish to alienate Darik. Whatever the reason, Darik had been delighted to have the new program in his hands.

Then he opened it.

"What is this?" Darik asked, looking at the strange code on his handpod. "This isn't an M-2 program."

Nikky nibbled on hard roll. "I never said it was an M-2 program."

Darik glanced into the main dining area, wondering how long it would take the nice young couple to notice him strangling his companion.

"Then what is it?"

"It's the program the M-2s were using."

Darik took a single calming breath before responding.

"Nikky—what are you talking about?"

As he prepared to speak, Nikky accidentally inhaled a handful of crumbs, starting a coughing fit that lasted well over a minute. The interlude gave Darik the opportunity to study the program more closely. While most of the program was unintelligible, he began to identify a few familiar bits and pieces that did, indeed, resemble an M-2 program. He began to grasp what Nikky was getting at.

"You're saying that this is the program the four M-2s were operating under when they were destroyed."

Nikky, his face flushed from the persistent coughing, nodded his head.

"And this new program was installed *after* they were shipped from the Bacchus station?"

Nikky nodded again.

"Well, why didn't you say so?"

Darik stood up and tossed a credit chip on the table, leaving enough for the meal and, as always, a generous tip for the Brobergos.

"I'll be in touch."

Darik had gone straight home and dissected the program. After several laborious hours of reading line after line, he was able to uncover most of the original M-2 program, including all the fail-safes his department had created. This didn't surprise him. Whoever was reprogramming the M-2 wouldn't want to start from scratch with basic functions such as mobility and detection. However, rather than remaining intact, these original commands were chopped up and scattered amid volumes of new code.

Darik was able to decipher portions of the new code—commands for threat identification and the like—but an alarming portion of the new program completely baffled him. He wasn't simply looking at a new program, but an entirely new programming *language*—a language he couldn't even read, much less interpret.

After some cursory research, he took a few stabs at translating the language, but it remained impenetrable. His eyelids were beginning to sag as the hours rolled well past midnight, and he got in the habit of flipping past any extended sequences of the foreign language. He was scanning one such sequence when a number caught his eye. The series of digits looked familiar, and Darik realized it was a set of coordinates—a location order. He felt a rush of blood move up his neck as he entered the coordinates into his handpod. Finally, he was going to find out where the four M-2s had actually been shipped and, presumably, destroyed. Perhaps this latest piece of information would be enough to solve the mystery of his missing machines.

The excitement quickly wore off, however, when he saw the result—Bellona, a backwater planet near the frontier whose only point of interest was a small orbital manufacturing station owned by JenKore. Some additional research revealed that the station produced industrial laser cutters for mining units in local systems.

Darik was dumbfounded. Mining M-2s were shipped from Bacchus with their laser cutters already installed. He could see no possible reason, then, for M-2s to be shipped to a station that manufactured laser cutters. It seemed like an enormous waste of time and money—resources that JenKore did not lightly squander.

He sat in the dark for a long time, his home office illuminated only by his workstation display and the city lights that diffused through his polarized windows. He wrestled with what to do next. He could certainly go to Bellona, just as he had gone to Cacarus, but he had a feeling that he would keep running into dead ends until he knew the answer to the most nagging question—*who?*

The question frightened him. Whoever it was had enough security access to completely reprogram JenKore's signature product. Whoever it was had enough resources to create an entirely new programming language. And whoever it was had gone through a lot of effort to keep all of this a secret. Darik had a suspicion that if he actually did find out *who*, it could cost him more than his job.

These thoughts still weighed heavily on Darik's mind days later as he finished his commute. Nearing his building, he initiated the landing sequence. The autopilot retook control, lowering the shuttle onto the upper-tier landing pad. He popped the hatch before the engines had fully powered down and stepped out into the rain. He was immediately met by an M-2, gliding up to him through the mist. Its approach was so silent and its appearance so sudden that Darik would have been terribly startled had he not been expecting it.

The machine opened a weather shield over Darik, protecting him from the elements.

"Good evening, Mr. Mason," the M-2 said through a layered, processed voice. The technology had long been available for machines to produce human-like vocal tones, but, like synthetic skin, eyeball sensors, and the like, the feature had never caught on. Apparently, man was not quite ready to accept machines that looked and sounded exactly like him.

Darik nodded, knowing that the machine was scanning for a response to its greeting. After a few brisk paces, he entered the building while the M-2 retracted the shield and bounded back through the rain to oversee the parking of Darik's shuttle and await the next arrival.

The building's upper lobby was empty as usual, but Darik felt watched nonetheless by the eyes of dozens of scanners, ensuring that he belonged in the building. At times, Darik felt the security measures were a little much, but he preferred excessive protection over the alternative. He knew there were plenty of people out there who hated men like him—men who drove luxury shuttles and lived in expensive high rises. Those people, like the long-haired man on the speeder, were consumed with envy, and they would violently lash out if given the chance.

Darik entered a lift and depressed the touch pad, which scanned his prints and routed the lift to his apartment. The door opened directly into his entry room, and Darik was annoyed to see that his apartment's Household Controlling Unit was still malfunctioning, failing to detect his presence and switch on the lights.

Shedding his overcoat, he reached over and pressed the manual panel. The HCU did not respond.

He pressed the panel more forcefully, but his apartment remained bathed in darkness. Darik threw down his coat and marched over to a small glowing terminal. He pulled up the illumination settings, selected the proper brightness, and pressed the *Execute* command a little more firmly than necessary. The lights flicked on, though they appeared somewhat dimmer than the percentage he'd selected.

Darik let out a weary sigh. He had put it off long enough—tonight he was going to have to buckle down and reprogram the HCU.

Turning around to retrieve his coat, he was startled to see a man standing by the door.

"Good evening, Mr. Mason."

He was a tall man and sharply dressed. His broad shoulders filled out a charcoal gray long-sleeved shirt that tightly hugged his form down to his trim waist. His head was completely bald, though he did not appear more than a few years older than Darik, and his jaw-line was sleek, without any hint of excess fat. But, even with so physically imposing a stature, the man's most striking feature was his eyes. They were as pale as ash, and they had locked onto Darik, never moving once from his face. The man seemed comfortable where he stood, almost as though Darik were the stranger in the apartment.

Darik broke from the stare, his heart racing. The man raised his right arm, and Darik saw that his overcoat was draped around the man's forearm.

"You dropped your coat."

Darik's head was spinning, the words barely registering.

"Who are you?" Darik spoke, his voice scratching through a suddenly dry throat.

"I'm Travarian," the man said, holding his gaze. "Does that mean anything to you?"

Only that you're a lunatic, Darik thought. Claiming to be an inhabitant of a mythical planet, he may as well have announced that he was half unicorn. Darik, though, kept his mouth shut and simply shook his head.

"In that case, call me Graves."

Darik gave a slight nod as his mind raced through his options. He did own a stun pistol—an illegal souvenir from his days in general security—but it was locked away on the top shelf of his bedroom closet. There were knives in the kitchen, but he doubted he would have an opportunity to make a break for them. He could have initiated a call to the police on his handpod, except that the device was in a pocket in his overcoat, which was still hanging over the intruder's arm. His last hope was that this "Graves" had somehow tripped an alarm along the way—but that was a long shot. The fact that he was standing in his apartment was proof that he was clever enough to bypass some of the city's most advanced security systems. Darik's only option was to give the intruder what he wanted and hope that it wouldn't cost him too dearly.

"What do you want?" Darik asked, managing to inject a measure of authority that he most certainly did not feel.

"Well, first, I want you to take your coat. I would not want to be accused of thievery."

Graves tightened his lips, looking as though he was holding back a smile. Darik's anxiety began to be replaced by anger. Was this some sort of sick joke? Keeping a watchful eye on Graves, he stepped forward and clutched his coat.

As he pulled it away, Darik noticed some sort of sheath strapped to Graves's right hip. A covering flap made it impossible for Darik to see what was inside, but he was terrified nonetheless, fear washing over him in fresh waves. Or was it fear? The powerful sensation felt familiar, something he had recently experienced. It wasn't raw fear—nothing like the terror he'd felt in the mines of Cacarus just before the Harvester had emerged from the shadows. This felt different, deeper. He was drawn toward Graves and the sheath in particular. He was being pulled in.

And he remembered. It was the same pull he had felt in Jenkins's office, a pull toward the idol. Now that he remembered, the pull didn't seem quite as strong now as it had then, but it was undoubtedly the same sensation. And he was having just as much difficulty focusing on anything other than the object of attraction.

Graves stared into Darik even as Darik remained fixated on the sheath.

"We work for the same man. You understand this now."

Darik nodded.

"And we work toward a common end."

Darik heard the words, but he didn't understand. He nodded anyway.

"You are here for a purpose, Darik Mason."

Darik nodded quickly, hoping Graves would finish and be quiet. If only he could get near the sheath. He craved to open it and touch whatever was inside. Graves placed his hand on the sheath, hiding it from Darik's vision. Rage welled up within him, and for a moment, he was ready to launch himself at Graves and take what was his. But the urge faded as his mind began to clear. He looked up again at Graves, whose eyes still had not wavered. He spoke a final time.

"Now, do your job." With that, Graves turned and departed, taking the lift down as if he were any ordinary guest.

Darik stood in a daze in the middle of his apartment, unsure of how to process what had just happened. The thought eventually crossed his mind that he should call the police and report the break-in, but he had a suspicion that his visitor operated above the law. Besides, Graves had implied that he worked directly for Jenkins, and Darik was in enough trouble with the CEO without trying to incarcerate one of his lieutenants.

He wandered over to a chair, running their brief conversation over and over in his mind. The more he concentrated, however, the hazier certain portions became, until all he could remember with any degree of certainty were Graves's last words. *Do your job.*

His entire body suddenly felt weak, coming down from the surge of adrenaline, and he collapsed into the chair. One thing was abundantly clear—Graves's visit was a direct result of him poking around the M-2 mystery. This was precisely the kind of incident he had feared—why he had been reluctant to find out who was behind the M-2 reprogramming. Apparently, he had uncovered too much already. If someone could break into his apartment undetected to deliver a message, they could also do much worse. Perhaps that unspoken threat *was* the message. But, in a way, this knowledge made his next decision all the easier.

Turning over the coat in his arms, he found the right pocket and pulled out his handpod. As he waited for the comm to be accepted, he noticed that the lights had risen to an uncomfortably bright level. The HCU would have to wait a while longer.

"Yes?"

"Nikky, I need to know who reprogrammed those M-2s, and I need to know tonight."

Chapter 15

Dex switched off the holoprojector and slumped back in his chair. He had been replaying and studying the Milk Run mission from every conceivable angle. Each Hornet was equipped with a three-dimensional flight recorder, making it possible to catch almost every detail of a battle or mission for later analysis. Typically, this data was compiled and fed to the ready room for Dex, Hagen, and Onigen to evaluate. The information was then condensed and recompiled into a recap session for the entire squadron. Each pilot was expected to participate in an honest discussion of strengths and weaknesses, and of tactics, both effective and ill-advised. Following a successful mission, these sessions were often light-hearted with good-natured challenges being traded among the group. After a failed or aborted mission, the debrief could be brutal. When Kevan and Fran had been lost, the process was almost unbearable. Yet, Dex knew that it was after such failures that the post-mission analysis was most important. A hard look at what went wrong could save lives the next time out.

As important as these post-mission training sessions were, Dex felt that this one, following the disastrous Milk Run, would have to wait. When it was time to review the feed, he hadn't wanted anyone else there. Things had gone wrong from the start. Pilots had disobeyed or ignored orders, and people had died as a result of his squadron's actions. Dex was determined to have the first look to sort out exactly what had happened. Even though he knew it was a ridiculous notion, he wanted to personally analyze the data in painstaking detail, as if that would somehow result in the freighter's successful capture, bring back the lives of the lost Scorpion pilots, or spare the men on the destroyed gunships. The past five hours, however, had revealed nothing new. The same images played over and over, each time with the same results.

Dex's holoprojector recessed silently into the desktop. Closing his eyes for just a moment, he considered that perhaps Nate had been right. Maybe he was taking too much on himself. But who else could he trust? A single lapse in judgment would spell disaster for not only his squadron but the entire colony. It was a crushing responsibility, and he was more and more frequently finding the invisible weight almost too much to bear. It hadn't always been this way. Not that long ago, he had been living his dream—and then God revealed a sudden change in plans.

*   *   *

It was three years earlier. Captain Dex "Deadeye" D'Felco had reached what many pilots in the United Coalition Navy would consider the pinnacle of achievement. He was in command of a squadron, and not just any squadron, but the elite 714th of the 501st Fighter Wing. The "oh-one" boasted most of the top pilots in the UCN, but only the best were assigned to 714th Fighter Squadron—which, as every Navy pilot knew, meant the privilege of flying the S/A-81 Hornet. At two-and-a-half billion credits apiece, the Navy's most advanced combined space and atmospheric fighter was strictly limited in production and assignment. There were only twelve Hornet squadrons in the entire Coalition, and Dex was honored that the Angels were numbered among them.

The squadron's name itself paid homage to another historic group of Navy pilots, who in the late twentieth and early twenty-first centuries had flown an atmospheric-bound fighter which also had borne the nickname "Hornet." These pilots performed what at the time were amazing precision aerobatics, pushing the F/A-18s and their own bodies to their utmost tolerances, delighting crowds who would flock to air shows and exhibitions to see them. Young men and women with aspirations of becoming Navy pilots could imagine themselves as members of the Blue Angels. Though the purpose, focus, and governing authority of the squadron had undergone much evolution since then, Dex was proud of the tradition and history that accompanied the name.

Recently, however, the "Angel" designation had begun to carry another connotation, or so it seemed to Dex. Never comfortable with blatant displays of evangelism, Dex had always been rather careful regarding his Christian faith and how he carried himself in his work. While he had never made a secret of his beliefs, he had not been overtly vocal about them either. In a steadily eroding socio-political environment for believers, Dex preferred to quietly live by the imperative that whatever he did, he should do with care and excellence as unto God—a conviction he applied particularly to his service. He was well aware that fighter pilots were often perceived as arrogant and self-absorbed, which made him all the more determined to fly not for his glory, but for the Lord's. So far, that dedication and integrity had served his career well. He made the rank of captain at an early age, his uncommonly good eyesight and superb gunfighting abilities earning him his "Deadeye" call sign along the way.

His fast rise through the ranks had not provided Dex with many opportunities to form close friendships with peers—not that he minded all that much. The higher his rank and responsibilities, the more Dex preferred to relax in the evenings with a good book rather than spend a night on the town with other officers. Command was often lonely, and Dex had come to appreciate the solitude.

He made exception, however, for Captain Jonathan "Bulldog" Buhl. Dex could remember sitting with his friend in one of Old Seattle's ubiquitous phylline cafes, gazing across the waters of Puget Sound, his half-drunk cup of coffee growing lukewarm on the table before him.

"Well, you're a load of fun tonight, D'Felco," Jonathan said through a grin. "C'mon man, spill it. What's on your mind?"

Dex regarded the lights across the bay—the nighttime glow of Rainier Airbase had filled the sky over Bainbridge Island as long as he could remember. In the past, it had always represented a source of security and purpose for him. Tonight, it provided little comfort.

"I don't know, Jon. I don't want to be paranoid, but it all seems just a little too coincidental. Do you know what I mean?"

If Jonathan did know, he wasn't letting on. "Nope. Haven't the slightest. Why don't you enlighten me?"

Dex sighed, sipped at his coffee, and recoiled from the tepid brew. "Okay, it's like this. You know that Hagen, Jani, Kevan, and I have all been with the squadron since I was promoted. Obviously, we're all Christians."

"Obviously." Jonathan refilled his own teacup with scalding water from a thermal unit. The orange-cinnamon aroma of Market Spice tea wafted from his cup.

"Well, over time, Hagen had been talking with Seltrice. *She* gets saved, and you know how she can be. Next thing you know, she's got Lee and Fran in a Bible study and *bam*—we've got seven Christians in the same squadron."

"Still not seeing a problem here, buddy. You should see what it's like in my squad. I'm all alone out there."

Dex accepted a refill from a passing server. His coffee replenished, he warmed up to his subject. "But here's where it gets strange. Over the next couple of months, the transfers begin. Davis is gone, Calgaro is in. Then, a couple weeks later, goodbye Seneca and Rueger, hello to Bennet and Manasser."

"Don't tell me, let me guess." Jonathan's serious expression was undercut by traces of a smirk. "The brass decided to balance out your squadron with a few more worldly characters?"

"No, that's just it." Dex looked directly at his friend. "They transferred all the unbelievers *out*. The pilots who transferred in are all Christians, Bulldog."

Jonathan sat back in his chair. "Whoa," he said, exhaling slowly. The normally easy-going pilot was all business now. "So, what do you think is going on?"

"I'm not sure. It could be as simple as Command believing that they would be a better fit with the Angels. Or…" Dex hesitated.

"Or they're putting people together where they can keep an eye on them," Jonathan said, finishing Dex's thought. "Dex, there's no doubt that we're not the most popular people on the planet right now. With the bombing in Dubai last month, and all that crap the Phelpsians have been pulling, the council's just looking for an excuse to slap the restraints on again."

Dex had to agree. Too many times in recent history, Christianity had been restricted or even declared illegal—usually in response to the actions of one or two radical fringe groups.

"It's funny, isn't it," Dex said, his gaze wandering again to the soft glow across Puget. "They closed the last re-ed camp seventy-five years ago, but they haven't torn a single one down. It's like they're waiting."

"I think you need to watch your back, Dex. If something's going to happen, it could happen quickly. Did you know that Prop 413 has been reintroduced in council?"

Dex nodded grimly, and Jonathan continued. "And this time, I think it might actually have some support. We're going to have to keep our eyes and ears open. Anything else unusual happening around your squad?"

"Well, that's the other thing. We have two more new transfers coming in tomorrow. It's very hush-hush, with sealed orders that I won't even see until morning. This one's coming from pretty high up. If we're being monitored, why trust us with a priority-one security assignment?"

Jonathan frowned. "Unless they're sending in moles, you're thinking?"

"Honestly, I'm not sure what I'm thinking, Jon."

Jonathan leaned forward, his voice dropping to a conspiratorial whisper. "Well, Deadeye, it could be worse, you know."

"How so?"

"They could be transferring *me* into the Angels." He held up his teacup in a mock toast.

Dex finally smiled and returned the gesture. "That, my friend, really would be the beginning of the end."

*   *   *

Dex had been up early the following day. Always a light sleeper, even prone to fits of somnambulism, he found that his late-night coffee excursions with Bulldog never affected his nighttime patterns one way or the other. At 0500, he was wide awake, and by 0600 he was disembarking from a transport before a massive hanger on the west side of Rainier Airbase. A blue and gold emblem fixed above the mammoth hanger doors announced the building's designation as the terrestrial home of the 714th Fighter Squadron, a.k.a. the "Angels."

Entering through a smaller man-door on the right, Dex paused to admire the twelve Hornet fighters parked inside. It was quiet in the hanger, with only a handful of ground personnel puttering about in the cavernous interior. Even at rest, the Hornets seemed to pulsate with an impatient energy, as if at any moment they would engage thrusters and explode right through the hanger's retractable roof. Each fighter had its pilot's call sign painted just below the canopy—call signs that some, like "Flash" Calgaro, really prized. Others, such as "Ghazi" and "Prince," merely tolerated their nicknames, while "Rabbit" and "Ninja" didn't care for theirs at all. Pilots, Dex mused, never had much say over which call signs they would be given.

Hornets eleven and twelve were missing the bright yellow lettering. Fresh silver crebonite paint where the names would normally be located reminded Dex why he had arrived at the base early. The sealed orders concerning his two newest pilots were waiting for him. Pulling himself away from the main hanger, he walked purposefully down a side passage to his office.

As expected, the workstation on his desk flashed a message indicating that the orders had arrived. Placing his right palm over the desktop proximity detector, Dex allowed his handprint to be scanned, breaking the electronic seal. The display lit up, showing a single enclosed file rather than the two he had expected.

Dex reached out and touched the holographic file with his fingertip, revealing the contents within. The images of two very young pilots, male and female, emerged from the file. So similar were their features and facial expressions that it was immediately evident they were brother and sister. The text below their holopics confirmed Dex's guess.

Ravi and Purnima Voor, Dex read. *Call Signs: "Sunfire" and "Moonlight," fraternal twins. Rank: Flying Officers. Date of Birth: not available. Family: not available. Home Province: not available.*

Dex frowned and leaned forward in his chair. With a quick motion, he scrolled down through the entire bio. Every other entry—military history, commendations, reprimands, training, previous assignments, even serial numbers—all read the same: *not available.*

Shaking his head in disbelief, Dex arrived at the bottom of the curtailed list. A final file was labeled with a single word: *Orders.* He opened it with an exasperated poke and did not like what he read.

His orders were to evaluate the Voors, putting the young siblings through intense simulations and the most demanding of live-flight exercises. He was to monitor and report on their performance, making note of any strengths and abilities they demonstrated, especially those that exceeded normal response times and accuracy ratings. Following the evaluation period, they were to be delivered back to UCN Command for reassignment. The Voors were to be immediately qualified together in Hornets, bypassing any individual training under a senior officer. Most distressing of all, the evaluations of the twins were to be based upon their abilities flying as an element—without direct supervision.

Forget that, Dex thought, shutting down the display. *No history. No information on qualifications. No explanations. Just put them in a couple of Hornets and let them play.*

Dex stood to leave. The orders had set the Voors' arrival for 0700 at Pad 37. He had made his decision before reaching his office door.

Emerging from the hallway at a fast clip, he nearly ran into Hagen Lebrian.

"You're with me, Commander." Dex wasn't usually so curt with his second-in-command, but his annoyance spilled over into his demeanor. Hagen joined Dex on his right, matching his brisk pace step for step.

Sliding behind the controls of a ground transport, Dex waited for Hagen to join him in the passenger seat. He fired the engines and raced from the hanger.

Hagen regarded his commanding officer. "Care to tell me what's going on, Captain?"

"Not sure, Hagen." Dex eased up on the accelerator. There was plenty of time to get to the pad, and he needed to get his temper back under control. "We're meeting our new recruits. I just read their file."

"You didn't like what you read?"

Dex snorted. "I'm not sure *what* I read. There wasn't anything there. You should have seen them, Hagen. They couldn't have been more than seventeen or eighteen years old. Why in the world does Command want them in the Angels?"

Hagen shrugged. "Do you suppose they're Christians? It would fit the pattern."

Dex thought for a moment. "This one's different. The brass isn't planning on having them stay. They want us to strap those kids into Hornets, run them through the paces, and assuming they don't auger in somewhere, ship them back like they're some kind of property."

"Are they qualified in Hornets?"

"I don't know, Sarge. The briefing didn't say." Dex accelerated again, the transport nearly clipping a corner traffic beacon. "But it doesn't matter. They start in T-68s like everyone else. After that, it depends on them."

Dex and Hagen were waiting when the Trident personnel carrier touched down on Landing Pad 37. Two figures with matching olive-drab duffels slung across their shoulders emerged from the carrier's ventral hatch. If anything, the twins looked even younger in person. Setting his jaw, Dex met his newest transfers at the foot of the Trident's ramp. The two pilots snapped to attention.

"Ravi and Purnima Voor reporting for duty, sir!"

153

Dex wondered if their speaking in unison was an attempt at being cute. He dismissed the thought. "At ease. As you have the same surname, I will be primarily addressing you by call sign. It is my understanding that you prefer to fly together. That is not going to happen. At least, not now."

He nodded toward Hagen. "This is Commander Lebrian." Dex leveled his eyes at the female twin. "Moonlight, you will be training under him." He shifted his attention to her male counterpart. "Sunfire, during your evaluation period, you will be assigned as my wing. All of your flight training, simulations, and squadron exercises will be under our direct supervision. The decision as to when and if you'll be upgraded to Hornets will be ours and ours alone. Understood?"

The puzzled expressions on Ravi's and Purnima's faces indicated that they did not fully understand this sudden change in their assignment.

"Sir?" Ravi spoke for both of them.

"You got a hearing problem, mister?"

"No, sir!" Both Voors snapped back to attention.

Hagen indicated the waiting ground transport. "Stow your gear, officers. We'll show you to your quarters."

As the flustered pilots hustled to obey, Hagen raised an eyebrow to his commanding officer. "I don't know, Dex, they seemed all right to me."

"We'll see, Sarge. We'll see."

*　　　*　　　*

Dex recalled that the following several weeks had revealed nothing noteworthy about the Voor twins. While their soft-spoken, respectful demeanor hadn't made them any enemies in the squadron, their flying skills hadn't won them any fans either. In their training runs, both had shown competence, but their response time, accuracy, and decision-making scores were decidedly below the Angels' exacting standards. Flight after flight, with Ravi on Dex's wing and Purnima on Hagen's, the two had been sluggish and uninspired, causing some of the other Angels to question their presence in the squadron.

Scot had been the most outspoken. "I don't get it, Captain. They're not horrible, but seriously, what are they doing flying with us?"

Dex was not in the mood to discuss the situation with the hot-headed lieutenant. "They're trying, Scot. Our job is to give them a chance."

"That's easy enough to say right now. But if the FSA fires up again, and we find ourselves in a shooting war, I need to be able to trust those kids to keep bandits off my butt."

"Do you have a point, Mr. Calgaro?"

"Yeah, I do. They're not *Angels*, Captain. And somebody has to tell that to the brass."

"Your concern is noted, Lieutenant. That will be all."

Dex left his conversation with Scot with the nagging impression that the brash pilot was probably right. Command had been pressing him for progress reports on the Voors, and Dex's evaluations had been noncommittal. He had seen nothing in their performance to convince him that the two should be placed in Hornet cockpits, let alone be allowed to fly as an element. He decided that his first instincts had been correct. Ravi and Purnima would be allowed one more test flight in T-68 Talon trainers. If they didn't show dramatic improvement, and he had no reason to believe they would, Dex would report that the Voors had washed out of training. He would not risk squadron equipment or personnel any further in a failed Command experiment.

Jani was waiting for Dex at the hanger. With Hagen's light infantry background, he was often called upon to conduct ground ops training exercises off-base. He had departed earlier that week with Adahn, so Dex had selected Jani to assist him with the final training exercise.

"Ready to go, Lieutenant?" Dex was looking forward to flying with his own wingman again, even if she was paired with Moonlight. "Where are the trainees?"

Jani shrugged in the direction of the Talons. "They're already strapped in. I'll give them this much, Captain, they're eager. How'd their pre-flight briefing go?"

"Well," Dex said uncertainly, "they know what they're in for."

Jani paused, her face showing some apprehension. "This is it for them, isn't it."

Dex knew that Jani had grown fond of the twins. She had worked tirelessly the past week to coach not just Purnima, but both of the young charges, offering tips and suggestions for the final training run, providing them with whatever gouge she had available.

"Yeah, Jani, it has to be. That's pretty much what I said in my last report. Scot and Job will be in ops, monitoring the flight. They'll have the data compiled by the time we land. If the scores don't add up, they'll wash out."

"Well, let's get it over with then." She climbed into the cockpit of her own Talon. Moments later, with Dex on lead, all four pilots left Rainier Airbase far below.

"Form up." Dex checked his instruments and found Ravi in the appropriate position on his wing with Jani and Purnima trailing on his right. The final training course began nine kilometers directly over the airbase. He would lead the Voors on a series of high-speed maneuvers, following a trail of beacons to the target, which would have to be destroyed in a single pass with V-cannons. It was a difficult course, a challenge for even the best sticks. Dex didn't give the Voors much of a chance.

"Remember, points will be deducted for straying too far from your lead. Watch your range finders—and try not to bump into us."

Jani's voice entered the channel. "Twenty seconds. Report in."

"Sunfire, ready."

"Moonlight, ready."

"Rabbit, ready. Vector confirmed. Here we go, Deadeye."

"Roger. First turn in four, three, two, mark."

The four Talons roared past the first of ten suspended navigation beacons. Pulling through the turn, Dex lined his craft up on the next beacon ten kilometers away. Travelling well beyond supersonic speed, the four craft reached the marker in seconds.

"You're straying, Sunfire. Tighten it up." As Dex pulled a nearly ninety-degree turn around the second nav-beacon, he spared a quick glance at his map. Ravi had already drifted twice. Purnima, on Jani's wing, was faring better, but she, too, was skirting the edge of the required parameters. With more challenging maneuvers waiting, it was doubtful either would finish the exercise with a passing score.

"C'mon, Moonlight, stay loose." Jani's coaching was far more encouraging than Dex's. As predetermined, she and Purnima moved forward to lead through the next maneuvers. "Points three and four approaching. J-flip on my mark—two, one, go."

Dex watched Jani's and Purnima's ships, meters ahead, flip 180 degrees and dive straight down toward the earth, nine kilometers below. He knew that they would immediately pull out of their dive and snap sharply to starboard, rotating another ninety degrees to reorient on the next marker, half a klick lower in altitude and at a neat right angle to their previous course.

There was no time to watch their progress, however. He and Ravi executed their own J-flip a split-second after their squadron mates. Pulling out of the turn below, Dex was gratified to note that both trainees had flown sharply on their lead officer's wing.

"Okay, one more J-flip, left. Shackle at the deck."

"Roger, Deadeye," Jani replied. If there was a trace of nervousness in her voice, Dex knew it was on behalf of the Voors. This was the most challenging maneuver in the exercise. With all four Talons in tight formation, they would flip at the sixth marker and dive toward the seventh. At that beacon, they would pull up to port while simultaneously crossing each other's path. They would then emerge from the aerobatic in formation, lined up for a serpentine run past the remaining three markers to the waiting target sphere.

Beacon number six loomed into view, its traditional red and green lights flashing in the darkened troposphere. Pulling into the J-flip, Dex saw the beacon rush past his canopy. With Ravi still on his right wing and Jani and Purnima dead ahead, he set his focus on beacon seven, one-half kilometer below.

The dive consumed no more than a second. Even with the Talon's dampening fields in place, Dex could feel the g-forces as all four craft pulled up. Leveling off, both pairs began their double cross pattern just as they passed below the glowing seventh beacon.

A bright flash suddenly filled Dex's cockpit. Temporarily blinded, he felt a sickening impact that he instinctively knew was his Talon striking Ravi's just below him. Dex felt his helmet strike the side of his canopy. His ship was in a flat spin.

Furiously blinking in an attempt to regain his sight, Dex fought for control of the damaged craft while his mind raced to access the situation. What had happened to the others? The flash hadn't come from any of the Talons. It had come from above them—from the beacon.

Dex's vision began to clear just as he managed to pull his T-68 out of its spin. A quick check showed that his instrumentation was out. He punched a reset, yielding no results. His engines were engaged, but the flight stick was sluggish. Dex quickly surmised that the impact with Ravi's ship had damaged the Talon's outdated hydra-optic flight control system. But why the devil were his instruments out? What was that flash?

Dex didn't have time for analysis. With no sensors, sluggish controls, and zero ship-to-ship communication, he still had to somehow find his pilots. Pushing forward on the flight stick, he coaxed the Talon into a dive and scanned the surrounding distance through the canopy. His unusually sharp eyesight helped him spot Ravi's and Purnima's Talons immediately. Both were stable and heading in opposite directions a klick below him. Apparently, the flash and collision had knocked them off course, but both seemed flight worthy.

He next tried to locate Jani. Straining to see into the distance, he finally made out the shape of her ship, two more kilometers below the Voors.

Dex's stomach lurched. He recognized the sight of a dead ship in free fall.

Frantically, he pushed the Talon steeper into its dive, but the slow response confirmed what he already suspected. He was helpless to assist his disabled lieutenant. The Voors could possibly reach her, but if they had suffered the same instrument failure, chances were they didn't even know where she was.

Desperately, Dex punched the reset again—no response. "C'mon, Lord!" he cried out. "This is stupid!"

Something vibrated in the thigh pocket of Dex's flight suit. Reaching down, he grasped his handpod—an extra piece of non-flight-approved equipment that he had uncharacteristically forgotten to leave behind at the hanger.

Job Hansen's image was on the pod's display. Knowing that its ambient setting would be useless through his flight helmet, Dex flipped up his visor and pushed the handpod as close to his ear as possible.

"Job! What's going on? Are you tracking Jani?"

The exec spoke quickly. "We saw the whole thing. It was beacon seven. As near as we can tell, it exploded as you passed, throwing out an E-M pulse. Engines are active on ships three and four, but Rabbit's are out. Lights and comm are out on all ships. The only reason I can talk to you is that handpods operate on theta band. I played a hunch you might have yours when it wasn't ground-checked with the other three."

"Can you contact the Voors? Can you give them Jani's location?"

"Negative, Captain, their pods are right here. Dex—there's nothing we can do."

"No…" Dex watched helplessly as Jani's ship continued to fall—the earth only a few thousand meters below.

"Can she eject, Job?" he asked, already knowing the answer.

Job answered quietly. "No, sir. T-68s had their eject function routed through the master bus. An EMP would take it out. I'm not reading it as active." There was a pause. "They fixed it on the T-70s."

Dex wanted to pound his head against the canopy. He cursed the outdated Talons. He cursed his own stubbornness for not having his trainees up there in Hornets, like they were supposed to be. He cursed the brass for sending him the Voor twins in the first place.

The Voor twins. Far below, Dex saw Ravi's and Purnima's Talons suddenly execute simultaneous flips, each ship peeling off its opposite course. The two young pilots screamed toward each other in matching dives, their flight paths threatening to collide. Meters apart, they neatly adjusted direction and gained more speed, rushing downward, wingtip to wingtip, in the direction of Jani's falling ship.

"Job!" Dex yelled into the handpod. "You said they had no comm!"

"They don't, boss. No ship-to-ship, no sensors. They've got nothing. Whatever they're doing, they're on their own."

Jani's Talon continued its freefall. She was seconds from impact—the rugged terrain of Olympic Coalition Park rising quickly from below. As Ravi and Purnima closed on their target, Dex continued to dive after them, hopelessly out of range, but transfixed by what he was witnessing.

Five hundred meters from the ground, both Voors reached Jani's ship. Drawing even closer together, the twins' wings overlapped one another, forming what Dex could only imagine was a makeshift cradle. Matching their speed to Jani's descent, Ravi and Purnima guided their Talons beneath hers. Dex could see both craft shudder as the falling ship smashed down upon them, but somehow they maintained control.

With three ships locked together as one, the mad plunge continued. Slowly, the arc of descent began to flatten—the twin Talons battling against the momentum of the fall. It was a battle that was impossible to win. They were too close to the ground. They were not going to make it.

Suddenly, Dex understood the twins' plan. With one perfectly timed firing of their ventral thrusters, Ravi and Purnima coaxed an infinitesimal bit of additional altitude out of the T-68s. Hurricane Ridge flashed by beneath the interlocked craft, the sparkling waters of the Juan De Luca Straight directly in front of them.

The three Talons, still locked, descending, and traveling perilously fast, streaked just over the treetops and out across the expanse of water.

Meters above the surface, the Voors cleanly separated, allowing Jani's Talon to glide down and splash roughly, but intact, near the middle of the straight. Performing opposite matching turns, they rose above and began circling her position.

Dex shook his head. It was a long moment before he could speak. "Job. They made it. It was unbelievable. Her ship's resting north of the park in De Luca. Send a medevac, but honestly, Job, I think she's going to be okay."

Dex was surprised to hear the reply come from Scot rather than Job. "Uh, roger that. We've got help on the way. But Captain, there's something you should know." Scot's voice sounded strained. "We've got company."

The handpod connection went dead.

*   *   *

Dex entered the ops center at a dead run. He had circled the downed Talon long enough to see Jani pop open her canopy and wave weakly to the sky above. Then, the moment the medical transport arrived and came to a rest in the choppy waters, Dex turned his own damaged ship back toward Rainier Airbase.

Bursting into the ops center, he pulled up short. The first person he saw was Scot, sitting in a chair near the comm unit. He was nursing a light bruise on his right cheek and wearing a darker scowl for the looming MP goon who had apparently given it to him. A broken handpod sat on the table before them. Job sat stiffly in another chair toward the back of the room—another MP standing over him. Two more enforcer-types took up additional space in the room, their posture indicating that they were still looking for another excuse to bust some heads.

In the center of it all stood a UCN air commodore. Above the requisite ribbons and badges decorating the senior officer's uniform, Dex immediately spotted an insignia indicating his attachment to the Department of Security and Strategic Development. The man coolly regarded Dex's sudden intrusion into the room. Protocol required Dex to come to attention in the presence of the VIP, but somehow he didn't feel like it. He wanted answers.

"Scot, Job, what's going on here?"

The commodore stepped forward. "I believe I can answer that, Captain. My name is Pickett. My team and I were on base to conduct a level-one priority intervention in your training exercise. While monitoring the test, we detected that your exec was using a handpod to break the comm silence we had so carefully engineered. We arrived here and...persuaded him to cease communication."

Dex glanced at Job. The slightly built Scandinavian's rueful expression told him the persuasion had not been polite.

Pickett continued, his expression deadpan. "Once the experiment had reached its successful conclusion, your Lieutenant Calgaro here decided to take it upon himself to break silence again. I'm afraid my own lieutenant took exception to his behavior."

"The freak nailed me as I was talking to you, Captain. The cowardly son of—"

"Easy, Lieutenant." Dex could see Scot bracing to spring from his chair. Barely able to contain his own anger, the last thing he needed was Scot's temper igniting the volatile situation. "You and Job are dismissed. Get back to your quarters, get cleaned up, and I will meet with you later." He turned to face the seemingly impassive air commodore. "Request permission to speak with you, sir. Alone."

Moments later in his office, Dex waved at a control, closing the door behind himself and his unannounced visitor. Pickett turned and addressed him. "All right, Captain, we're alone. What's on your mind?"

"Permission to speak freely, sir?"

"As always, Captain D'Felco, that will depend greatly on what you intend to say."

"Fine." Dex was well beyond caring whose feathers he ruffled or what it might mean for his career. His pilots had been put in danger, Jani had nearly lost her life, and it was becoming increasingly apparent that the entire accident had been engineered. "Am I to understand, sir, that the explosion of the beacon was intentional?"

"That is correct."

"An explosion in close proximity to my pilots in the midst of a tight maneuver? An explosion that caused a collision between our ships and intentionally knocked out all communications at the same time?"

"As I said, Captain, that is correct. What is your point?"

Dex wanted to punch that smug face in. "With all due respect, sir, are you insane? Those are *my people* up there. Where do you get off placing them in jeopardy like that? All four of us could have been killed."

The commodore held up a hand, cutting Dex off. "That's enough, Captain. How do I justify this test? I don't have to. The Voor pilots were sent to you for strict evaluation of a particular skill set. You were under orders to fly them, in Hornets, as an element, under adverse conditions. In spite of those orders—under some misguided safety concerns, according to your reports—you chose instead to waste time with minor training exercises in Talons—Talons that are quite expendable, by the way. You were content to muddle along at a snail's pace in this initiative. I was not. Your refusal to follow orders led to this intervention, Captain."

Dex was seething. "I could not, against my better judgment, put my pilots unnecessarily at risk. It is my responsibility to protect them. Those kids were not ready, sir."

"Captain, you have no idea what *ready* means when it concerns those two assets. We were confident that the Voor pilots were never in any real danger, even from this test. All of our research has indicated they would respond exactly as they did at the moment of the explosion. We simply needed to be sure. As for your Lieutenant McLeod, having her life in jeopardy, well," he smiled, and not benevolently, "determining whether they could actually save one of you was an added bonus to the test, wasn't it."

"And if they hadn't saved her?"

"Then we would also have discovered what we needed to know."

Dex couldn't believe what he was hearing. "What is it about those two? Why would you risk lives just to prove they can fly together?"

Pickett stepped close, meeting Dex eye to eye. "That, Captain, is none of your concern. You will obey your orders. You have seen enough today to allay your concerns about their abilities. You will get the Voor pilots into Hornets and complete your assignment. Is that understood?"

It wasn't, but Dex responded the only way a man with authority, and under authority, could. He snapped to attention.

"Yes, sir!"

The commodore held his gaze for a moment longer, then nodded and stepped toward the door. Stepping into the hall, he hesitated and turned to face Dex.

"Oh, and Captain, one more thing. Why do you think your squadron was chosen for this test? Don't flatter yourself with misguided ideas about skill or reputation. You were chosen because it doesn't matter what happens to you. Your entire squadron doesn't come close to the value of those two assets. You and your pilots are expendable, Captain, as expendable as those outdated Talons.

"Change is coming to Earth, D'Felco. It's coming to the entire Coalition. Do not make the mistake of thinking that we don't know who you are and what you stand for. If you and your cohorts continue to hold on to your narrow, intolerant beliefs, you will have no place in this society or this Navy. Soon you're going to have to make a choice. Remember that, Captain, the next time you begin feeling so self-righteous."

Pickett left, the door sliding silently shut behind him. Dex stood there at a loss. He knew the political climate was rapidly turning against people of faith. But what was that warning all about? Did Pickett know something, or could he simply not resist one final bigoted parting shot at Dex? Unaccustomed to inactivity, Dex decided to pursue what information he could right at the source. He changed quickly out of his flight suit. He would check in on Jani and then pay a visit to a pair of surprisingly adept young pilots.

*   *   *

As flying officers, Ravi and Purnima were allocated a small two-bedroom apartment in the base's housing complex. While many siblings would loathe the close proximity of shared quarters, Dex was not surprised that the twins seemed to prefer this arrangement. Nothing about the Voors was ordinary, from their sketchy military dossier to the remarkable flying prowess he had witnessed that morning. Dex was grateful for the skill they had shown—they had saved Jani's life—but he was also determined to uncover the truth about the enigmatic pair. He squared his shoulders and keyed the door chime.

Ravi answered the door. At the sight of his commanding officer, he quickly came to attention.

"At ease, Sunfire." Over Ravi's shoulder, Dex could see into the apartment's common room. Purnima had been sitting on a sofa but quickly rose when she saw him. "May I come in?"

"Of course, sir." Ravi stepped aside to let Dex enter. The twins were both wearing casual off-duty track suits—the unisex cut of the sweats further blurring the already minute differences in their appearance. Purnima was now standing at attention as well.

"Relax, Moonlight. Maybe we could all sit down?"

Both twins nodded gratefully and settled side by side on the sofa. Dex chose another chair across from them. Taking in the rest of the room at a glance, he noted the sparse décor. While it was common for transferring personnel to carry little in the area of personal belongings, he was struck by the total absence of mementoes. There were no holopics on the wall, no little trinkets on the shelves, nothing anywhere to remind the occupants of home. He noticed that Purnima had been watching an info-feed. She flicked a remote to shut off the broadcast, giving Dex her full attention.

"First of all, I just wanted to make sure that you two are okay."

Purnima answered. "We are fine, Captain. Is Lieutenant McLeod going to be all right?" The two leaned forward in unison, waiting for his reply.

"Jani's going to be fine. They wanted to keep her overnight for observation, but she was having none of that. When I got to the med center, she was already on her way out the door. She mentioned something about a hot bath—and she would see you two in the morning."

Ravi nodded. "Lieutenant McLeod has been very kind to us. We are glad that she was not seriously harmed."

"Thanks to you two," Dex said. "That's actually one of the reasons I'm here. I wanted to thank you for saving Jani's...uh, Lieutenant McLeod's life."

Ravi and Purnima exchanged glances. Purnima answered for them. "Thank you, Captain. We were only performing our duty. Besides," she said, hesitating for a moment, "I felt responsible. It was my Talon that collided with her."

"Belay that," Dex interrupted. "Rabbit and I were at the top of the formation when the beacon blew. As near as we can tell, our ships were forced down onto yours. It's a wonder you two were able to maintain control at all, much less regroup and coordinate a rescue..."

Dex paused, meeting the eyes of each of the young recruits. It was time to get to the truth.

"I checked with Flight Sergeant St. James. Both of your Talons suffered the same instrument blackout from the E-M pulse that mine did.

What you accomplished—diving together and rescuing her like that—was simply impossible without comm or sensors. I want to know how you did it, and I want answers now."

The Voors did not respond immediately, but they did not look away either. There was nothing in their expressions to indicate duplicity or guile. Dex had to hand it to them—these kids could play it cool.

Ravi answered slowly. "Captain, we would like to tell you more, but we cannot. Sir, our orders—"

"Yeah, you have orders. Well I have orders to put you in Hornets." The two of them immediately perked up as Dex continued. "And after what I saw today, I'm just about ready to do that. You'll have to pass the sim, but I get the feeling that if I let you take it together, you won't have any problems."

The twins actually smiled for the first time. "But understand this," Dex said, instinctively lowering his tone. "Before I let you move one step further, you are going to level with me. I want your history, your qualifications, and most of all—I want to know why I should fly you together as an element. What's so special about you two?"

The smiles faded as quickly as they had come. Dex took a breath.

"I asked you a question, Officers. It's really very simple. You tell me everything—right now—or I will have no choice but to send you back to Command and let you become someone else's problem."

It was mostly a bluff. Dex was in enough hot water with the brass over the Voors already. Sending them back without a complete evaluation was not an option. But he was playing off an intuition about these two, and watching their expressions change, he knew he had been right. Where there had been smiles a few moments ago, he now read outright fear on the two young faces.

"Captain," Purnima pleaded, "please don't send us back. We *can't* go back."

Ravi seemed equally alarmed at the prospect. He turned to his sister, reaching out to grasp her hand. "It's going to be all right, Nima."

"No," Purnima shook her head. "Not again. I can't do it."

Dex softened. Whatever was going on, he had suspected that the twins wanted desperately to stay with the Angels. He hated himself for having to threaten them, but if he were to put them up there with the entire squadron, untested and as a pair, he had to know what he was dealing with. The problem was, Dex realized, that these two "assets" were to be returned to Command at the conclusion of their evaluation, regardless of the outcome.

He would have to deal with that when the time came. They appeared to be genuinely terrified, and everything within Dex urged him to protect the young brother and sister.

Ravi turned his gaze from Purnima back to Dex. There was no longer fear in the young pilot's eyes, nor anger, as Dex might have expected, but hollowness. "Captain, we know how this works. We know you have your orders. But you can't possibly understand the fate you will be condemning us to if you send us back."

Dex leaned closer to the frightened pair.

"Then tell me," he said. "Tell me what's going on."

They told him.

*   *   *

"Let me get this straight, Dex." Hagen couldn't hide his surprise, glancing over at Lee Onigen—the two having been called in for an impromptu meeting. "Now we *are* going to be pairing the Voors up—in Hornets?"

"That's right, Hagen. Lee checked them out in the simulator." Dex knew his second-in-command would be as incredulous as he had been. He still wasn't completely confident in the new arrangements himself. "They passed together with identical one hundred and twelve percent efficiency ratings. As of tomorrow, they fly in ships eleven and twelve."

Hagen whistled softly. "Must have been one heck of a week."

Onigen slid a small data chip across the table. "This is the flight data from their last Talon run. The recording is incomplete—most of it coming from base scanners after the pulse—but I recommend you watch it when you have a chance. It's…impressive."

Dex smiled at the rare compliment from the lieutenant commander. A perfectionist by nature, Onigen was not easily impressed.

"How does someone score a hundred and twelve in the sim?" Hagen asked.

"I don't know." Onigen's thin dark eyebrows arched slightly as he answered. "When I ran them separately, Sunfire scored a seventy-eight, Moonlight higher at eighty-two—the same range as the ratings they'd been getting in the Talons. Then the captain asked me to run them through a sim together—that's when they scored one hundred and twelve. I checked the diagnostics and had them run through it again—same scores. So then I ran them through a completely different scenario and the score was—"

"Let me guess," Hagen interrupted, rubbing his temples. "Both of them got one hundred and twelve?"

"It was eerie."

Dex stepped back in. "Gentlemen, here's what's going to happen. The rest of the squadron is not going to understand having two rookies flying together. The twins are pretty popular right now after rescuing Jani, but based on their T-68 scores, there's still not a lot of confidence out there. I'm going to need you to back me on this play."

Hagen smiled wryly. "That would be easier, Captain, if we knew a bit more of the story."

Dex knew how his senior officers felt. "Not yet, Sarge. Hopefully, I'll be able to fill both of you in at some point, but for now, I'm going to have to ask you to trust me on this one."

Before Hagen or Onigen could answer, the desk comm unit buzzed. It was Seltrice.

"Sirs, this is Lieutenant Valani. I'm sorry to bother you, but we're all in the lounge, and there's something going on here that you need to see."

*   *   *

The squadron's recreation lounge was designed to provide ample opportunity for fatigued personnel to relax and recharge. Multi-dimension game chambers—in sizes capable of accommodating from one to a dozen players—lined one wall. For the more traditionally inclined, remarkably well-preserved pool, foosball, and ping-pong tables occupied a large portion of the floor. In the center of the expansive room, a well-equipped but comfortably furnished vending area offered a wide assortment of refreshments, ranging from coffee to more refined phylline stimulants and tranquility beverages.

Atypically, each of these diversions was completely deserted. Dex, Hagen, and Onigen arrived to find their pilots—as well as Drager, Job, and a handful of other ground personnel—in the back of the center, gathered around a holodisplay. Geff Bennet saw them approach. Rising to attention, he caught the attention of the rest of the group, who followed suit.

"At ease, everyone," Dex said, acknowledging the gathering. "What's going on?"

"Take a look, Captain." Geff nodded in the direction of the display. It was broadcasting a Coalition info-feed. A nightmarish image of burning buildings played out before them. Amid the wail of sirens and the flashing of beacons, they could see people scattering while uniformed enforcement officers advanced on them. Several bodies were lying motionless on the pavement.

Superimposed on the display, the ever-present *Live* graphic was accompanied by text indicating that the images originated in London. A heavily accented British correspondent provided the voiceover.

"Peter, again, what began as a small but vocal demonstration by a group calling themselves the Kensington Christian Alliance has erupted into a full-scale riot here in the Brompton area. Authorities have closed the Gloucester Road and South Kensington underground stations. All pneumatic lines have been halted, and reinforcements are being brought in from as far as Islington and Hoxton in an attempt to quell this brutal uprising."

"Uprising? Brutal?" Scot shook his head while the display showed a young woman being stunned by an enforcement officer. She fell to the ground, twitching from the shock effect. "It looks like the e-cops are doing just fine in that department."

"Quiet, Flash!" Seltrice snapped at him. "We're trying to listen to this."

Even as she spoke, the holo changed. While still live, the feed from London retreated to a small corner of the display. Three additional images from Atlanta, Tokyo, and Buenos Aires, each revealing similar scenes of destruction and violence, appeared in opposite corners. The foreground of the display resolved to reveal a serene, well decorated info-feed set. Four commentators—the pilots immediately recognized them as this particular network's panel of experts—sat around a stylish conference table. In addition to the anchor—Dex couldn't remember his name, "Peter" somebody—the panel consisted of a famous holoflick starlet; her husband, who was a former member of the United Coalition's Terran Council; and a very vocal spokesman for People United by Peace and Tolerance.

As the anchor addressed the camera, the holo effectively gave the impression that he was speaking directly to each viewer, regardless of the presentation angle.

"If you just joined us, that's the scene from London, just one of several locations where aggressive protests have broken out, almost simultaneously. Authorities have been hard-pressed to control these riots, and all indications are that the violence is spreading."

He turned to his co-hosts. "Could these outbreaks be related? Is there a unifying factor behind them?"

The starlet spoke first. "Of course there's a unifying factor. You have the Kensington Christian Alliance, the Southern Christian League, Christians for an Independent Japan, and all those other groups. What is the common denominator in all of them? Only one word stands out, Peter!"

The other panelists laughed, in sharp contrast to the horrifying scenes behind them. After a moment, the PUPT spokesman adopted a somber expression and raised a hand to silence them.

"Peter, for years our organization has been advocating a return to policies of peace and sanity. We envision a community where the sort of religious intolerance these groups represent would not be allowed to grow and infect others. We are calling upon the Terran Council to act swiftly in ratifying Proposition 413 so that these fringe elements, and all who align themselves with them through action or belief, can be removed from the mainstream and not be allowed to further upset the delicate socio-emotional balance of the planet."

The former council member interjected. "But you need to remember, Karl, Proposition 413 isn't just designed to remove these radicals from society. It's intended to help them. I personally have been in contact with my former colleagues on the council, and they assure me that the measure includes stipulations for re-education and rehabilitation of every religious extremist here on Earth and in the colonies."

The starlet's eyes grew misty. "Can you imagine it, Peter? A world— no, make that *worlds*—with no conflict, no intolerance, nothing to stand in the way of our true human potential, and all because we had the courage to deal with this problem now, in our generation. Why, our children will—"

The display went blank.

"Hey!" Several pilots turned toward Scot, who stood holding the remote.

"I don't know about you, but I've heard just about enough of that crap." Scot pointedly set the remote down on a table.

"Some of us were still watching that!"

"Who made you lord of the holo?"

"We need to know what's going on."

"Aw, it's all the same lies anyway."

"Give me that remote. At least I'm going to—"

"Take it easy, Viper."

"You take it easy! If we're—"

Hagen banged his fist on a table and held up his hand. As the room fell silent, he turned to Dex.

"Thank you, Commander." Dex took a breath. "We've seen enough for now. Speculation at this time is pointless, and we're not going to start relying on the info-channels for direction. If you want to discuss this, fine, but we will do it as a unit, and we will proceed with order. Now, who has something to say?"

Geff raised a hand. "Captain, if that proposition passes, they're not going to be rounding up just the fringe religious groups. They'll be reopening the camps and expecting every single Christian to report."

Scot drummed his fingers on the remote. "If you ask me, Geff, that's exactly what this is about. How do we know those protests were even real—or that those Christian groups were behind them? Anyone could have engineered them, just to give the Terran Council an excuse to act."

Dex stayed silent. He had taken a seat, allowing his team to work through this themselves for the moment.

Job spoke up. "This may not be much of a comfort, but my understanding is that as Navy personnel, we all fall under Command jurisdiction and would be exempt from any forced internment."

"And be ordered to round up the others?" Fran Simmons usually had one of the squadron's most positive dispositions, so the intensity of her statement took the others aback. She lowered her eyes. "I'm sorry, but I don't think I'd be able to do that."

Several pilots nodded their agreement.

"Wait a minute." Kevan Alderson was sitting next to Fran. "I tend to agree with Smiley, but don't you think we're getting a little ahead of ourselves here? I mean, we're talking about how we would respond to orders we haven't even been given. UCN Christians betraying other believers, friends turning in friends, family against family—do you really think that's where this is headed?"

Drager St. James had been sitting quietly near the back of the room. Not usually very talkative, he spoke quietly. "Yes. That *is* where this is going. My father was a Christian—my stepmother wasn't. You have to understand, they were in love. They had been together for years. But the last time this stuff started to flare up, when I was just a kid, he strongly believed that we needed to get off-planet. I remember my parents fighting about it. In the end, my father and I left, but my stepmother and brother stayed behind." Dex could see the pain in the flight sergeant's eyes. "Eventually, I made my way back to Earth. My father never did."

"Did you ever look up your family when you returned?" Jani asked.

"No. The way we left, the things I heard them say to each other—it just didn't seem right. That's what these conflicts do. They tear families apart."

"Captain, may we say something?"

Dex hadn't noticed Ravi and Purnima when he had arrived. Had they been there all along? He nodded to them. "Go ahead."

Ravi appeared to be choosing his words carefully. "Purnima and I do not fully understand the faith you all seem to share. There are so many aspects to your life and responsibilities here in the squadron that we still must learn. But we do understand oppression. We understand what it means when your lives, your choices, even your own bodies are not your own."

Purnima continued her brother's thought. "You must preserve your freedom, no matter what the cost."

Jani broke the silence that followed. "So what do we do now, Captain?"

Great question, Dex thought. He stood.

"We respond like officers and personnel of the United Coalition Navy. We do our duty. We protect our citizens. We fly like Angels. If and when the situation changes, we trust God to guide us in the decisions we each must make."

For Dex, it was an uncharacteristic outward expression of his faith. He did not, as a rule, use his position as captain to imply any kind of spiritual leadership over the squadron. But these were uncommon times, Dex decided.

"Until that time," he said quietly, "we pray."

As a united family, the Angels stood together to pray. Ravi and Purnima, near the outside of the group, bowed their heads respectfully.

*   *   *

171

Dex could remember very little detail of the days immediately following the riots. Activity, both in the squadron and on the geo-political level, had settled back into a more familiar pace. Ravi and Purnima had proven themselves quite adept in Hornets, much to the surprise of the rest of the Angels. Their training was going well, the pilots were warming to the new pair, and Dex had actually begun to relax a little.

Leaving the hanger on a chilly fall evening, he reflected on that day's training exercise. The Angels had participated in a much-anticipated combat simulation against the 904th Fighter Squadron. As one of the few other Navy squadrons assigned Hornets, the "Knighthawks" were a natural rival, and the inevitable trash talk and baiting between them and the Angels had been ongoing since the engagement first hit the calendar. With evenly matched numbers and neutral starting positions, the two teams had squared off beyond Saturn's orbit in an engagement that, above all else, would establish bragging rights for the foreseeable future.

Dex was more than pleased with the outcome. His entire squadron, including the Voors, had performed exceptionally well, outmaneuvering their opposition to the final tally of seven Knighthawks losses to the Angels' two. Dex had to admit that he was looking forward to the joint debrief he would have with Captain Walters. He would take a certain guilty pleasure in deflating some of the Knighthawk commander's arrogance—all in good fun, of course.

Dex felt so good, in fact, that he allowed himself to temporarily set aside some of his worries. Global tensions, suspicions of Command's motives, and even concern over the fate of his squadron diminished considerably in the post-flight euphoria. For the moment, the new additions were working out, his team was coming together, and Dex was simply enjoying the feeling that the Angels were on a roll.

Those feelings evaporated when he saw Jonathan Buhl's face. His friend had only recently returned from deployment with his own squadron, and he and Dex had planned to get together again in Old Seattle later in the week. Instead, Jonathan was waiting for him outside the hanger. Dex could tell that something wasn't right. He had never seen his friend look so haunted.

"What's wrong, Bulldog?"

"Walk with me, Dex. We need to talk."

Taking the cue, Dex walked silently beside his friend until they were completely out of earshot of the other personnel exiting the hanger.

Jonathan finally broke the silence. "It passed, Dex. We got the word during your exercise. Prop 413 goes into effect immediately."

"Immediately? I really thought things were cooling off."

Jonathan shook his head. "No. Apparently the issue was never dropped in the council. It took them a while to hammer out the details, but now that they've passed it, they're moving quickly."

He paused as two petty officers passed them, heading in the opposite direction.

"As UCN, we got the word first," he continued. "I'm sure you'll have a priority-one waiting for you in your office. The news hits the civilian channels tomorrow morning."

Dex didn't really want to ask, but he had no choice. "So what are the details?"

"Pretty much what we suspected. They released the list of faith-groups that are considered to be *Religious Extremists* and, surprise surprise, *Christianity* is number one—no subdivisions or qualifications. All resident Earth Christians will have forty-eight hours to report to re-ed camps. Off-world colonists have two weeks to return. Any registered Christians who do not report in, or unregistered *religious extremists* who are suspected of hiding their affiliation, will be considered criminals and subject to arrest and prosecution rather than internment."

"Prosecution? At what level?"

"Failure to comply with Proposition 413 will be a fourth-degree offense against the United Coalition, Terran Council." Jonathan tonelessly recited the edict. "Punishable by—"

"I know the punishment for level four." Dex let his frustration show. The early evening dampness of the Pacific Northwest wasn't solely responsible for the chill he was feeling. "I'm sorry."

Jonathan looked ahead into the fog rolling off Puget Sound. "Don't worry about it, Deadeye. We're all feeling the pressure."

Dex shoved his hands into his flight jacket. "My exec, Job, thought that UCN personnel would be exempt. Is that part true?"

"Yeah, as long as we follow orders. I'm sure they figure that a compliant Christian under Command authority is as good as a re-educated one."

"Most of the Angels have said that they won't be a part of any enforcement orders." Dex kept staring straight ahead. "I can't say I blame them. I'm not even sure what *I'm* going to do."

Jonathan grabbed Dex's arm, stopping him mid-stride.

"I'm leaving, Dex. And I wanted to let you know. I've had forged ID codes for myself and Janet and the boys for a while now. There's a transport leaving tonight from Kent, and we're going to be on it."

Dex processed this new information. "Where will you go?"

"We're heading for one of the colonies. I can't tell you where, but some of Janet's family are there, and they've already let us know that they wouldn't be returning if the proposition went through."

"So that's it then—the end of your career, your life here?" Dex considered his friend's plan. From the UCN's point of view, it was desertion, plain and simple. Under normal circumstances, it would be unthinkable, but now it sounded all too familiar. "I have to say, leaving is a possibility for everyone. I know some of my pilots have talked about it. I've even thought about it myself, Jon." He smiled humorlessly. "How much room is there on that transport?"

Jonathan met his friend's eyes. "Dex, it's none of my business what you decide. I don't know why I'm even saying this, but I think you may want to consider staying right where you are."

Lighting panels along the walkway blinked on as the last daylight gave way to night. The glow of the artificial light revealed Jonathan's earnest expression.

"Go on. I'm listening."

"It's like this, Dex. You've been driving yourself crazy wondering what the brass is up to concerning your squadron. You've been seeing a conspiracy everywhere, like they couldn't wait to get you all together just to take you out."

"As I recall, Bulldog, you agreed with me."

"And it could still be true, but think about it. As a Christian, I'm all alone in my squadron. You guys all have each other. Command may have stuck you together, and they probably have a shady ulterior motive for doing it. But if all the garbage with Prop 413 was coming, it was going to hit you one way or another, whether you were all in the same squadron or not."

"You're losing me here, Jon. What's your point?"

"My point is the brass might have their own reasons for grouping the Angels together, but none of this has been a surprise to God. I've got to bugout, Dex. It's not an easy decision. I know I'm giving up everything. But I also know it's what I have to do. Now, like I said, it's none of my business what you decide, but as your friend, I think you need to seriously and prayerfully consider something."

A malfunctioning lighting panel was flickering just over Dex's shoulder. The strobe effect increased the look of intensity in his friend's eyes.

"All right. What do I need to consider?"

"You need to allow for the possibility that the Angels were brought together, and that you were placed in their command, for precisely this situation. You're not just responsible for yourself—you're responsible for that entire squadron and who knows how many others. God has something in store for you, Dex. I'm sorry, but I just can't shake that feeling. I wish I could be around to see it, to stand alongside you, but I can't."

"Jon, if you're saying I need to be some kind of stand-out, some kind of *voice* for Christians, here in the military..." Dex pictured himself standing before a tribunal, shamefully fumbling for the words, doubting their power even before they formed on his lips. He shuddered. "If that's what you're thinking, Jon, you've *got* to know I'm the wrong guy."

"Dex, I don't *know* anything right now. I just hope and trust that *you'll* know when it does happen, and you'll still be in a position to do the right thing." Jonathan glanced at his chrono. "I've got to get going. Promise me you'll think about what I said before any of you make any snap decisions."

Dex had his doubts, too many to count, but he realized that was the last thing Jon needed to hear right now.

"I will, Bulldog." Dex held out his hand. "Take care of yourself, all right?"

Jonathan grasped the offered hand, pulling his friend into a warm embrace just as the faulty lighting panel finally winked out.

"Count on it, buddy. You take care of yourself, too. And watch over those Angels."

A moment later, Dex was alone in the darkness.

*   *   *

When Dex returned to his office that night, there were two high-priority messages waiting for him. The first had been just what Bulldog had predicted—an announcement regarding the adoption of Proposition 413, complete with enforcement details and timetables. Dex quickly scanned through the lengthy communiqué before saving it. He intended to study the details later that night before briefing the squadron in the morning. Touching a finger to the second message icon, he displayed its contents.

Dex slumped back in his chair. *So much for Jonathan's personal prophesies.* The communication had been concise in its brutality. He reread the orders twice before picking up his handpod.

"Hagen. I know it's late, but we need to get the squadron assembled. I've got news."

"They're all up, Captain. They've been hearing about 413 and are waiting to get the official word. They're all a little on edge, Dex—not that I can blame them."

Dex sighed. "Have everyone report to the ready room. It gets worse."

*　　*　　*

"What do they mean *decommissioned?*"

Dex hadn't expected Scot to take the news well. The lieutenant stood in the ready room, his fists clenched, looking every bit as though he might march down to Command and tell them what they could do with their orders. From the expressions on the other pilots' faces, Dex could see that Scot was not alone in that sentiment.

"Sit down, Scot. It means exactly what it sounds like. Effective immediately, the Angels are disbanded. Launch codes on the Hornets and all squadron flight equipment have been disabled."

"So we're grounded then?" Adahn Manasser shook his head. "Why would they *do* that?"

"Don't you get it?" Seltrice flared at the Jordanian. "Not *grounded*. We're *disbanded*. It's over."

Geff Bennet looked around the room. "If that's true, Captain, what are we supposed to do? What's going to happen to all of us?"

Pilots, ground personnel, and civilian support staff all turned their attention to their commanding officer.

"Tomorrow morning, 0800 hours, each of us—senior officers included—is to report to Command for reassignment."

"Reassignment." Lee Onigen had his chin in his hand. "Why don't I like the sound of that?"

Scot had returned to his seat. "Because it's exactly what we were afraid of. They're breaking us up. They want us separated so each of us plays real nice, follows orders, and helps them with their little round-up."

Kevan Alderson eyed him thoughtfully. "I'm not so sure. I mean, yeah, it sounds bad, but don't people get reassigned all the time? Before we go jumping to any conclusions here, let's remember our oaths, our careers."

"I said it before, and I still mean it." The fierce set of Fran Simmons's jaw gave her remarks a clipped tone. "I will not be used to arrest other Christians. I don't care if I have to resign. I'll just—"

Kevan turned on her. "Smiley, if you resign, then *you* go to the camps. *Any* of us who check out are open targets."

"Then I'll run. I'll get off-planet."

Several heads nodded in agreement.

"What are you going to do? Take a Hornet?" Seltrice rejoined the fray. "We've got no launch codes, remember?"

"I'm not stupid, Viper! There are other ways off-planet, you know."

"And every one of them will brand you as a traitor and a criminal. Is that what you want?"

Tempers continued to rise, prompting Dex to nod at Hagen. It was time to step in. Just as the burly commander stood to his feet, Dex felt his handpod vibrate with an incoming message. Glancing down, he read the simple text.

BE ALERT. BAKER.

Baker? Who in the world is Baker? And how did he get my pod address?

The mystery would have to wait. Hagen's imposing presence had quickly brought the squadron back to order, but it was clear that everyone was still on edge.

Dex spoke deliberately. "I won't tell any of you what personal decisions you should make. Frankly, this entire situation is unlike anything we've ever had to deal with. Each of you faces a tough choice. After tomorrow, chances are none of you will be under my command. And it sounds like some of you are considering not being here at all. I can understand that. But until that time—until you make that decision or are reassigned—I expect each and every one of you to respect the commitment you have to each other."

Dex looked over the assembled squadron. He nodded to Drager, seated near the back of the hall with some of his ground crew. Job was closer to the front, off to the right. The exec returned Dex's grim smile. Dex's sweeping gaze took in Ravi and Purnima, then Scot, Geff, Onigen, and Adahn. He made eye-contact with Fran and Seltrice before coming to rest on Kevan, Hagen, and finally Jani.

"Some of you have been with this squadron for a long time. You've covered each other's backs, and mine, more times than I can count. Others have been around a shorter time, and some we've barely gotten to know. But the way you've come together these past few weeks—the way you flew today—no matter where you end up, I want you to remember this. You have served in the finest squadron in the Navy. You have lived up to that tradition, and you will always be Angels. No matter what you decide, honor that legacy, and honor each other."

The squadron's blue and gold emblem was splashed across the wall behind Dex—below it were holos of various craft flown by the Angels, from the current S/A-81 Hornet all the way back to its namesake, the original F/A-18. Hagen looked up and whistled softly.

"All that history. And it all comes down to this."

Jani spoke for the first time. "Well, at least our last run was a good one."

"You got that right, Rabbit." Scot stood. "Captain, with your permission?" He indicated a door to the left of the ready room. The building's well stocked galley was just beyond it.

Dex smiled. Scot was right—perhaps a small ceremony was in order.

"Sure. Permission granted."

After containers had been distributed, seals cracked, and portions dispensed, everyone gathered near the front of the hall. Scot raised a glass.

"To the final flight of the Angels. Steady hands, weapons free, into the fray, as one, go we."

Every assembled Angel, from ground crew to pilot, raised a salute in return, and with that, the festivities commenced.

At first, Dex wasn't sure if he had been sleepwalking again or not. The squadron's impromptu final celebration had lagged deep into the night. At some point, he had politely excused himself and left the toasts and memories to the more nocturnal members of the group. Like most squadron captains, Dex maintained small quarters on the base in addition to his larger home in Keyport. That night, he had been grateful to make the short walk back to the officers' barracks, where he had struggled to finally fall into a fitful sleep. What little rest he managed was suddenly and harshly interrupted by a piercing tone from somewhere in the darkness. Dex shook his head—the urgent, pealing clarion sounded familiar.

It took him only a moment more to clear the disorientation—his years of training kicking in. The tone he was hearing was emanating from his handpod. It was the squadron's scramble signal.

Scramble? How can we be called to scramble? We're not even active.

The pod sat on a desk where Dex had tossed it earlier. In addition to the insistent, pulsating alert signal, the pod flashed red, on and off, filling the room first with an eerie crimson glow, then darkness.

Crossing over to the desk, Dex noted a wall chrono. It was just after four in the morning. He picked up the handpod, simultaneously silencing the offending noise and triggering the display.

As expected, it was a scramble code, with no further information. Standard procedure called for all pilots to immediately assemble in their fighters. Further orders would await them in the cockpit.

Without pausing, Dex began throwing on his flight suit, his mind racing while his body obeyed a routine it had performed hundreds of times before. Seconds later, the pod buzzed again. It was Hagen. Dex keyed the unit over to ambient sound and continued dressing while he spoke.

"What've you got, Sarge?"

With the pod set to ambient, Dex could clearly hear Hagen's voice, seemingly just inside his ear.

"I've got a scramble code. I take it you got it, too?"

"Yeah. I'm responding right now."

"So you think it's legit? We're supposed to be decommissioned. What's this all about?"

Dex didn't slow his preparation. "I don't know. It could be some kind of emergency. I doubt that it's a drill. I guess we'll find out at the hanger."

"Do you think that's wise? I mean, are we even supposed to respond? If they...hold on a minute."

The pod went silent for a moment. Already suited up, Dex grabbed a gear bag, scooped up the pod, and headed out the door. In the hallway, he heard Hagen come back on the line.

"Captain, I've got every pilot in the squad buzzing me, asking what we should do here. They all got the same signal. What should I tell them?"

"Tell them to follow protocol, Sarge. Get them to the fighters. For now, we obey orders. But Hagen...stay sharp."

It took Dex less than two minutes to sprint from the barracks to the hanger. Scot and Geff were already there. From their appearances, Dex correctly surmised that they hadn't yet made it to bed.

"What do we got, boss?" Scot asked.

"I'm not sure, guys—stand by." The remaining pilots were entering the hanger. Everyone was moving double time, and Dex could see the same curiosity in their eyes as he had seen in Scot's and Geff's.

He raised his voice. "All pilots, in your fighters. Follow procedure. Check your mission feed for orders. Use comm channel seven, encryption India niner-five Delta for discussion. Launch only on my order. Understood? Move!"

The Angels scrambled into their cockpits. Strapping in, Dex quickly began the Hornet's fire-up sequence. As the subtle vibration of the fighter's powerful engines filled the cockpit, he activated the multi-function display.

Dex frowned. The familiar UCN emblem had been replaced with a blank text screen. He read quickly as information began to appear.

Dex: All of your pilots are receiving this same information. The decision to proceed belongs to them as well as you.

Twelve hours ago, an assault force was launched. Intended target is a Christian colony on Aphea. This assault force is NOT an official United Coalition Navy operation. Black ops are suspected, but there is no authorization for this action. The forces behind this attack are ruthless and intent on the eradication of the entire colony.

Coordinates and the flight plan to Aphea are being transmitted to each fighter, and full weapons function has been restored. New launch codes are available at your command.

The colony has been alerted. They are evacuating on a single colony transport, but they will have no defenses. If you successfully intervene, encrypted coordinates to a safe haven will be transmitted. Your responsibility will be to rescue and escort the colony transport to the new coordinates.

Flight time to Aphea is 6.2 hours. Assault force ETA is 6 hours. Any delay will mean the extermination of the colony. Two thousand lives depend on your decision.

The new launch codes will be cancelled in 120 seconds. After that, it will be too late.

- Baker

Again "Baker." Who is this guy?

A countdown timer appeared where the mission briefing had been. It already read 118 seconds.

Dex slammed open his comm connection and keyed the proper encryption. He was reasonably confident that only the squadron could hear him.

"All right, Angels. We have less than two minutes. Options?"

Hagen's voice, scrambled by the protocol but still recognizable, came on the channel. "Captain, I can't trace the source of the briefing. I have no idea how it got there."

"Stand by, Commander." Dex played a hunch. Flipping to another channel while maintaining the encryption, he attempted to contact his faithful executive assistant. "Job, are you online?"

"I'm here, Captain. I've got Drager and four of his crew here with me. We're in Hanger Two, looking at the same feed you got."

"Can you trace it, Job?"

"Negative, Captain. We have no idea where it came from. The only thing I can tell you is that it *definitely* is not UCN. Wherever those launch codes came from, they are not officially authorized. I'll keep working on it, but I'm sure that somebody other than the brass is pulling the strings on this one."

"Stand by, Job." The countdown timer now read ninety-eight seconds. Dex flipped back to the squadron channel. "All pilots, we cannot confirm these orders. They are not UCN. We don't have the luxury of time here, people. If you have opinions, I need them now."

There was a brief pause while precious seconds ticked off the timer.

"Captain, Viper." Even in the pressure of the moment, Dex noted that Seltrice had switched over to her call sign. He sensed that the lieutenant was instinctively gearing up. "I think I speak for the others when I say this. We've trusted you this far. It's your call. Whatever you decide, we're with you."

Dex responded quickly. "Appreciated, Viper, but I'm not sure you *can* speak for everyone this time."

Kevan Alderson was the next pilot on the comm. "Aces here. I know I've been pretty outspoken about keeping our options open here at home, but there could be lives at stake now—brothers and sisters at risk. With all due respect, the decision may not actually be yours or ours. We've got responsibilities that outweigh our UCN oaths, Captain. I say we respond."

Dex heard Scot on the channel. "Hey, let's not forget—the brass basically cut us off at the knees a few hours ago, anyway. Let's go for it."

One by one the other pilots weighed in with their agreement. With just under a minute remaining on the timer, Dex realized that he hadn't heard from the squadron's newest and quietest members.

"Ravi, Purnima. This isn't necessarily your fight. You can walk away right now if you want—no questions asked."

As if he had been waiting to be addressed, Ravi responded. "Captain, I think you will understand when I say that Moonlight and I prefer to take our chances with you rather than remain behind."

Dex nodded. He did understand. The timer now showed forty-two seconds remaining. Dex needed to decide quickly, but there was one more consideration. He switched comm channels again.

"Job?" he asked quickly, already knowing the answer, "any luck on that trace?"

"No new info, Captain. If you're going to make the call, it's going to have to be on faith."

Dex couldn't help recalling his conversation with Bulldog—a conversation that had taken place only hours earlier, but seemed like an eternity past. What had he said? *You're not just responsible for yourself— you're responsible for that entire squadron and who knows how many others.*

"Job, if we launch, what will you do?"

"Not to worry, Captain. You're not going to believe this, but we're sitting in the LT-11 right now. It's been loaded up with a few supplies and seems to be good to go—ready for new codes and all."

Dex was beginning to believe it. Whoever this "Baker" was, he or she seemed to have taken care of everything, perhaps a bit too neatly.

"Flying the Raven? Can you and Drager handle that?"

Dex could hear the amusement in the exec's voice. "Hey, we haven't forgotten all of our basic flight training, boss. We can handle it. Trust me, Captain, everyone who is supposed to be here is already on board."

Twenty-three seconds remained. Dex knew what Job had meant. The four personnel inside besides him and Drager had to be the ground crew's other remaining believers. Only the Christians had received the scramble code. This was either a conspiracy to nail them all together, or perhaps Bulldog had been right after all.

Dex reached a decision. Aware that his next action would mean running off with well over thirty billion credits worth of Coalition property, he set his jaw and activated the new launch codes. His display confirmed that the codes were indeed being transmitted to each Hornet and to Job inside the light transport.

The countdown displayed fifteen seconds. Encryption no longer mattered. He switched to an open channel in order for the pilots and the Raven crew to hear him at the same time.

"All personnel. This mission is a go—repeat—a go. Prepare to launch."

Jani came on the channel. Free from the distortion, Dex could hear the emotion in her voice.

"Dex, you realize if we leave now…like this…Dex, we're never coming back."

"Understood, Lieutenant. Launch on my mark. Three, two, one— launch."

The hanger trembled as the powerful craft rose in pairs—each Hornet skyrocketing into the atmosphere, each Angel leaving Earth, home, and freedom far below.

Chapter 16

"Remind me again why you needed *me* on this little field trip."

Sitting against a damp wall in a poorly lit tunnel in the middle of the night, Darik was beyond annoyed. He had specifically instructed Nikky that he wanted nothing to do with the actual hands-on details of their corporate espionage—that was the whole point behind showing him his ACG. Darik couldn't quite understand, then, why it was necessary for him to be physically creeping around twenty-three levels below street level in JenKore's #3 Research and Development Facility.

"Shhh!" Nikky Weis held up a single finger that Darik could barely see. "One more pass," he said, his voice scarcely even a whisper.

Darik could hear the scrape of an automated maintenance unit crawling along the corridor one level up, only inches above their cramped space. Nikky had informed him that while maintenance units were not primarily programmed for security duty, they would report in and possibly trigger an alarm if they detected any unauthorized personnel prowling the halls. And Darik and Nikky were certainly unauthorized.

Darik once again patted the cargo pocket of his utility trousers, still not quite accustomed to the unfamiliar bulk of his stun pistol. It had been nearly a decade since he'd last fired the weapon. Like all JenKore Security personnel, he'd gone through mandatory firearms training. But since he'd entered the department on the administrative track, Darik's training had been minimal, and now, years removed from his security days, he was struggling to remember even the basics. He fervently hoped that his weapons proficiency, or lack thereof, wouldn't be put to the test.

The grinding noise of the unit subsided as it continued down the unseen corridor. Nikky raised his voice ever so slightly.

"Like I said in my message, I need your help. I got as far in as I could from my station upstairs. The only way to dig further is to directly tap into the system from down here, past the normal firewalls. If I had pushed any further from my office, the lock downs would have taken weeks to unravel. And when they did, my signature would have been just sitting there pointing back to me."

Nikky paused to wipe away a glob of sticky black liquid that had dropped from a pipe and congealed on his balding forehead. "And pointing back to me, boss, means pointing back to you."

Darik considered the little tech. He didn't care much for this recent attitude, or the not-so-veiled threat that any discovery would bring the two of them down together. His mind was forming a response, containing various physical threats and promises of abject ruin for the tech if such a breach should occur, when Nikky grabbed his arm.

"Okay. This will be the best opportunity we get." Nikky scurried to the left and squeezed his thin body beneath a series of conduits that crossed the tunnel. Free on the far side, he urged his employer to follow.

Darik knew he carried considerably more bulk than his companion, and the space looked extremely tight. Cursing Nikky under his breath, he dropped onto his back and pulled himself under the rigid pipes.

"Damn it, Nikky! I'm stuck." His belt had snagged a sharp conduit clamp, holding him in place and scratching him every time he tried to move. Lying there still—pressed beneath the rows of pipes, his back soaking up the wet floor—Darik felt a creeping panic.

"Relax." Nikky pulled a mini-beacon from his belt and illuminated the space around the pipes. "You're just a bit hung up. I think I can reach from here."

Nikky leaned in uncomfortably close and snaked his thin arm between the conduits. Darik could feel him rummaging around near his belt buckle. The offending clamp dug further into his abdomen with every move of Nikky's hand.

"Once we're out of here," Darik grimaced, "I'm definitely going to kill you."

"If we miss this window, you may not have to." Nikky continued to work, his shoulder now pressed tight against the wall of pipe. "Even after we get the name you are looking for—*if* we get the name you are looking for—I still have to cover our tracks and clear a sec-path out of here." He grunted with exertion, pushing down and back on Darik's belt. "And we only have a short time to do that. When the system cycles at 4:00 a.m., it's going to…There!"

Darik felt his belt slip past the clamp. Exhaling completely, he resumed his struggle, inching himself forward along the floor. There was a ripping sound, accompanied by another stab of pain as the clamp took one more gash out of his right thigh. Finally free of his confinement, he pulled himself to a sitting position next to Nikky.

"Tell me," he panted, recovering his breath and examining his wounds. Most were merely scratches, but he couldn't help wondering what kind of nasty infection he would get from the putrid moisture pervading the tunnel. "Tell me that we are *not* leaving the way we got in."

"Don't worry." Nikky reached for an access panel above them. "If your ACG does its job and I can get to the right systems, we can walk out of here right under their noses."

"And if not? What if your plan doesn't work?"

Nikky's hand paused on the panel's handle. "Just how important is getting this name to you?"

"Important enough to get me down here with you."

Nikky turned the handle, bringing a rush of air as the panel popped open into the corridor above. "Well, lucky for you, my plans always work. C'mon."

The corridor was only slightly more illuminated than the utility tunnel and nearly as dingy. While maintenance units regularly patrolled the deep recesses of JenKore facilities, there was rarely occasion for actual human traffic. All the same, security scanners abounded—any one of which would detect and instantly report their presence. In addition, each doorway had its own crimson alarm beacon with an accompanying siren—another symptom of JenKore's excessive security obsession, an obsession that Darik felt surpassed healthy precaution and bordered on paranoia.

Nikky had specifically chosen this unorthodox point of entry because it would place them exactly between the locations of two scanners, but just out of the range of both. Darik didn't know how Nikky had discovered this soft spot in the security grid, nor did he appreciate the disgusting, claustrophobic route they had taken to get there, but he had to admit that it had worked.

"Well, no alarms so far." Darik rubbed his legs, trying to restore circulation.

"Right." Nikky was rummaging through a small pack he was carrying. "Not that we'd hear them down here anyway."

"Terrific." Darik leaned against a wall. "So what happens now?"

"Now I have to take out that scanner over there. The junction we want is in its range. Oh—here we go."

Nikky produced the object of his search. The small rectangular device looked innocuous enough to Darik. Nikky set it on the floor and touched a button on its top. A single red light began to flash.

"What does that do?" Darik moved closer for a look.

"Shhhh!" Nikky hissed, moving him back with a sweep of his arm. "Don't speak, don't move. Just stay perfectly still."

Darik was sick of getting shushed at every turn. He was about ready to forcefully make that point, but the deliberate way Nikky reset the device's button indicated that his instructions may have been important. He held his peace for the moment.

After several seconds, the flashing red light turned a solid green. Nikky released his breath and faced Darik. "The emulator makes a scan of the empty hall in front of us. Once it's done, it projects a counterfeit signal to the scanner so we can walk into its range undetected. If we move or talk when it's scanning, even if we're behind it, it would pick us up and project *that* signal to the scanner." He reached down to retrieve his gadget bag. "Don't think we want that, do we."

Darik regarded the tiny device dubiously. "So how long have we got?"

"The signal has about a five-minute life, but that's not our biggest problem. I told you that the entire system cycles at four. That's when the memory dump pushes everything to the master back-up. When that happens, the file we're looking for will be gone."

"Gone?"

"Well, not gone, but out of our reach. But that's not all—the same cycle runs a quick diagnostic of the system. These scanners will reset, and we'll be visible. And that auto cycle happens in..." He consulted his chrono. "Three-and-a-half minutes."

Darik's eyes bulged. It would've been helpful to have known all of that before getting himself trapped in a maze of unauthorized sub-levels.

"Then why," he seethed, "are we wasting our time *talking about it*?"

Nikky shrugged. "You asked."

Before Darik could get another word in, Nikky moved—too deliberately for Darik's tastes—to a panel about ten meters down the corridor. Once there, he reached into the carrier bag and pulled out a small tool. Humming to himself, Nikky switched the tool's power on. Darik rolled his eyes as the tool began to hum at exactly the same frequency as

Nikky's tuneless melody. Working around the edges of the panel, Nikky paused every few centimeters to adjust the micro-tool's output while altering his own hum at the same time. Finally, he stopped as the panel gave way with a satisfying *click*. Darik could have sworn he heard Nikky click his tongue at exactly the same moment.

"So that's it? We're in?" Darik had begun obsessively consulting his own chrono while Nikky worked. They had just over three minutes remaining.

"Not quite." Once again, Nikky was rummaging about in the bag. "This panel isn't a normal junction. We're beyond the firewalls, so there aren't any access points down here. We'll have to create one."

"And how are we going to do that?"

"With this." Nikky held up a narrow gleaming cylinder about eight centimeters long. Now working quickly, he attached a lead from the cylinder to what Darik easily recognized as a small holoprojector. He then snapped the cylinder open—Darik hadn't noticed any hinges in the smooth surface—and closed it around a series of fibroc cables in the exposed chamber.

"This should allow us to get in undetected, read the data you're looking for, and get back out," Nikky explained.

"*Should* allow us?" Darik leaned in further. "You're not sure?"

"Nope." Nikky activated the projector. The familiar JenOps logo— with Eliot's new, banal slogan superimposed across the bottom—sprang to life in the space in front of them. Darik assumed that was a good sign.

"Where did you get that thing? I worked Security for years, and I never saw anything like that."

"You wouldn't have." Nikky fiddled with the device as more characters cascaded across the holo. "I just built it last night."

"So I take it this is the first test?"

"No. Do you have your ACG?"

It seemed an odd request to Darik. Nikky, after seeing the device in Bistro Riservata, was able to generate his own valid codes—he had proven that ability in obtaining the new M-2 program. Darik didn't understand, then, why Nikky needed the physical device. But with the clock ticking down, now wasn't the time to begin raising objections.

"Of course," he said, reaching into his pocket and producing his Access Code Generator.

"Thanks," Nikky said, then, anticipating Darik's concerns added, "the counterfeit codes could only take me so far. Down here, past the firewalls, I need the real deal."

And now, Darik finally understood his role on this little excursion. Since the ACG could never be more than ten meters from his person, Nikky had needed him to accompany the all-important device. *Nothing more than an errand boy.*

Nikky took the ACG from Darik and inserted it face down into a port in the cylinder. "*Now* this is the first test."

With little fanfare, the projector dropped the JenOps logo. In its place, thousands of characters began to race across the display. Darik couldn't make sense of them, but Nikky was nodding, taking it all in. Occasionally, he would murmur. Finally, he whistled appreciatively.

"Oh, for crying out loud!" Darik hadn't come all this way just to try to interpret Nikky's cryptic facial expressions. "What are you seeing?"

"Take a look at this, boss." Nikky tapped a rhythmic sequence on the cylinder—no buttons were visible on it—and the flurry of characters on the monitor slowed considerably. "You've been looking for info on those M-2 mining units. We know they've been reprogrammed, right?"

Darik nodded.

"Did you know they're being physically modified as well?"

This wasn't news to Darik. "Right. *All* M-2s are modified. They're used for everything. I've even heard of a child-care modification being considered."

"Yes, but these aren't your typical mods. Look."

As Darik watched the screen, his head began to spin. *What the devil?* Nikky displayed diagrams and schematics showing bizarre changes to the M-2s—advanced communication modules, threat identification subroutines, and most noticeably of all, wicked-looking external appendages. Darik knew the M-2 units down to the core. He knew their design, their capabilities, and their programmed duties, but there was nothing in these modifications that he recognized—and very little that had anything to do with any of their hundreds of intended functions.

"So, like we thought, someone *is* grabbing these units and reprogramming them. And now we know that they're also adding some unusual physical modifications. But who? And why?"

Darik had simply been thinking out loud, but Nikky interpreted the questions as his next command. "Well, let's take a look." He tapped the cylinder again. A section of the screen showing the M-2's modified logic system grew larger until it dominated the entire display. The amount of data was staggering. "I don't know, boss. It would take longer than we have to sort through all of this." Nikky moved to tap the cylinder. "Maybe if I—"

"Wait." Darik pointed to a corner of the display. "What's that?"

"It looks like some kind of list." Nikky tapped a different spot on the cylinder, and the display changed again. "Whoa…nice catch."

Thousands of names with attached holos flashed across the display. None of them meant a thing to Darik—nor did the list seem to have much impact on Nikky. Every few hundred images or so, one or two would appear bordered in red, but apart from that small detail, there was little else of note about the parade of unfamiliar bios.

Darik was growing concerned about the time again. The list did not appear to have anything to do with JenKore personnel. He didn't see the point of scanning it any further if it wasn't going to yield the name he wanted. He was about to say so when he heard Nikky take a sudden sharp breath. Something on the screen had caught his attention.

"What? What did you see?"

"Nothing. I just think we should be getting out of here."

In their short time together, Darik had found Nikky to be a rather poor liar. He wanted to press the issue further but a glance at his own chrono told him that Nikky was right. They had just under two minutes until the system cycled.

"Okay," Darik said, handing Nikky a blue data chip. "Grab what you can, and let's get out of here."

Nikky began coping files onto the chip before turning the cylinder back around. "Just one more thing, boss."

Manipulating the device again, he ran the image back several screens. A new group of names and holos appeared in the space before them. Darik grunted as he surveyed the information. He had a vague recollection of some scuttlebutt regarding a Navy captain who had absconded with an entire squadron of multi-billion credit fighters a couple years back. The name and image of Dex D'Felco definitely rang a bell. Judging by the names and ranks displayed, the other images on the list had to make up the rest of D'Felco's deserters. Nikky whipped through the list with characteristic speed, flipping past several dossiers, two of them bordered in red. While this sidebar was interesting, Darik couldn't imagine why it was worth prolonging their exposure.

"Okay, that's it." He nudged Nikky. "Time's up. Let's go."

"Yeah, boss, I think you're right." Nikky touched the cylinder again, and the projection winked out.

"Uh-oh."

"*Uh-oh*? What do you mean, *Uh-oh*?"

"That, uh, wasn't supposed to happen." He tapped the cylinder a couple more times. The projector rested quietly on the floor, uncooperative and dark. Nikky's tapping increased in urgency and force. Still nothing.

"So what does that mean?"

"It means I haven't cleared a path out yet. And the system is going to reset right about…now."

On cue, Darik heard a very distant alarm. Moments later, he could just make out the sound of personnel transport equipment on the move. The sound grew louder with each passing second.

"Nikky, we have to go…*Now!*"

"Just give me another second, boss. I can fix this."

Dex grabbed Nikky's shoulder, spinning him around. With his other hand, he reached into his pocket, pulling out the stun pistol.

"Uh-uh. You had your chance. Now we do this my way."

*   *   *

"*Now we do this my way.*" Brilliant, tough guy.

Darik had used the pistol to disable every scanner he could find in the corridor. He had been moving farther up the hall to continue his target practice when Nikky softly commented that each sensor he took out was actually making the distant alarms *louder*.

Now, the two were crouched in a small maintenance room, listening as a group of security personnel approached. From the sounds reverberating beyond the door, Darik could tell that it was a sizeable response force.

Nikky was hunched over the door's locking mechanism, punching codes and jamming it from the inside. "So, how's that *blast our way out of here* plan working out for you, boss?"

"Hey, it got us this far. Those scanners were marking us." Darik was pacing in the cramped space checking and rechecking the battery power on his stun clip. "If I had left it up to you, we'd still be sitting back there trying to figure out how you screwed up. We'd be staring at a dead projector, and they'd walk up and *Bam*—game over."

"Instead, we're sitting here in a janitor's closet waiting for them to walk up and *Bam*—game over?"

"And yet, I haven't heard any ideas from you."

Nikky turned and eyed the ductwork over Darik's head. "As a matter of fact…"

Darik followed Nikky's gaze. "No," he stated flatly.

The rectangular ventilation duct was barely large enough to accommodate Nikky's slender frame, which meant that for Darik, it would be yet another impossibly tight squeeze. All the same, as the volume of pursuit grew louder in the corridors beyond, Darik realized they had no choice.

He sighed. "So how do we get in?"

"There don't seem to be any access vents in here." Nikky craned his neck, searching the smooth polished metal for any points of entry. "You see anything?"

"Nothing here." Darik surveyed the far side of the duct, away from the door. "Hold on a second. Let me try something." Fumbling with the pistol's settings, he dialed the stun battery down to its lowest setting. He placed the muzzle flat against the duct surface and pulled the trigger. Fortunately, the low power setting doubled as a sort of silencer—the pistol only emitting a faint wheezing noise with the shot. More worrisome was the echo that traveled through the ductwork upon impact. But with few other options remaining, Darik determined that the extra noise was worth the risk. He repeated the procedure a couple dozen times, moving the pistol over a few centimeters with each shot and hoping that the sound would be lost amid the commotion in the halls outside.

"Okay, this last part's going to be louder." He flipped the pistol around in his hand, intending to use the grip as a makeshift hammer.

"I'm on it." Nikky had returned to fiddling with the lock while Darik was punching holes in the duct work. "These locks are all connected…just one more code…get ready."

Nikky keyed a final sequence, activating the crimson beacon above their locked maintenance door along with a very audible alarm. Ordinarily, that should have alerted every guard in the corridor to their location. However, at the same moment, every other door beacon and alarm in every hall in several levels above and below sprang to life as well. The cacophony was deafening.

Darik took his cue and swung the pistol several times, bashing in the duct metal between the punch holes until it began to tear away. He reached for a jagged, separated corner and pulled hard. After a few good tugs, the metal tore away, leaving a nasty-looking but passable ingress into the duct. He tossed the chunk aside and waved his pistol.

"Like I said, we do it *my* way." Darik smiled, then cupped his hands together to give the small tech a boost. "You first."

Nikky entered the duct without much trouble. Darik's entry required considerably more effort. Without Nikky to boost him, he had to jump, brace his hands against the sides of the duct, and slowly inch himself up into the tiny space. By the time he lay fully inside, gasping the dusty, oppressive air into his lungs, his clothing was in tatters, and he felt as though the skin along his chest, arms, and legs had suffered a similar fate.

"You all right?" Though he couldn't see Nikky's face, Darik could have sworn he was grinning.

"No, I'm not. Do you know where you're going?"

"Yeah, I've got the schematics memorized."

"Then go already."

Without further comment, Nikky took off, scurrying his way down the duct. Looking at the tech's rear end and feet disappearing into the darkness, Darik was amazed at the speed Nikky displayed.

Just like a rat.

Ignoring his discomfort, Darik followed as quickly as he could. He was greatly relieved when, about twenty few meters farther, the duct entered a slightly larger junction, perpendicular to the one they had entered. Both he and Nikky were now able to move along on hands and knees. Darik soon realized that they were traveling along one of the facility's main arteries. Every few meters, vents would allow in some light as well as a surreptitious view of the hall below. Guards were still moving about in the midst of the sirens and flashing red lights, opening every door that was not locked and forcing every one that was. Suddenly, the alarms and flashing beacons ceased their commotion. Freezing in place, Darik and Nikky could clearly hear a couple of guards on the other side of the duct, only inches away.

One guard's voice sounded like gravel in a blender. "Finally. That racket was driving me nuts."

Darik didn't recognize him. It had been worth a try—an old friend could have gone a long way toward getting them out of this mess. But he knew that the odds of seeing a familiar face were slim. JenKore Security was an enormous department, and it had been years since he'd left.

The man's partner sounded younger, obviously the subordinate in the relationship. "What do you think's going on?"

"Probably just a couple of cyber dinks thinking they're big stuff busting in down here. Wanna brag to their friends."

"Or it could be a false alarm. We've had enough of *those* lately."

"I hope not. I haven't had an excuse to crack open any heads for a while. Besides, didn't you see those scanners? Use your head, kid—false alarms don't disintegrate hardware."

Darik winced to himself as the guard cleared his throat and spat. "No, they're down here, and I'm in the mood to teach someone a lesson."

"We have to find them first. Chief says we've got alarms on fifteen levels now."

"We'll find 'em. Where can they go? We've got all the lifts and stairwells blanketed. It's just a matter of time now. C'mon."

The two guards moved further up the hall, banging open doors as they went. Raising a dusty finger to his lips, Darik motioned Nikky for silence and then pointed along the duct. It was time to keep moving.

The pace was maddeningly slow. With the alarms silenced, Darik had to fight the temptation to move quickly, a mistake he knew would generate enough noise to reveal their whereabouts. He knew it was just a matter of moments now before the door to the room they had vacated would be forced open. Darik was thankful that their makeshift access point to the ventilation system had been out of direct view from the room's doorway. With any luck, the guards would glance in, see the room was empty, and move on.

They kept crawling, listening intently as the search for them intensified. The crawl space widened even more as they entered an intersection between another pair of ducts. Nikky paused for a moment and leaned against the metal wall. Darik spoke in a soft whisper.

"This is useless. Even if they don't find us, we're twenty-three levels down. And you heard the guard—the lifts and stairs are being watched. We need a new exit strategy."

Nikky's voice, naturally soft, was barely audible. "I think I can get us back up to ground level. It will be a good climb, but we can get there from here. The key is that they don't figure out we're in the vents."

"As long as they don't find the hole we made, we should be all right. It's out of the line of sight from the door."

"You hid the scrap metal you tore out, right?"

Darik could have shot himself. "Damn. Okay, let's just keep moving. Which way?"

Nikky hesitated. "Uh…not really sure here, boss."

"What do you mean *not sure*?"

"I mean, this junction doesn't match the schematics. They must have made a change during construction. It happens."

"So you don't know. Then *guess*."

"Why didn't you say so? This way." Nikky scurried off to the right.

Nikky's guess eventually proved to be correct—though Darik didn't care much for the result. After endless turns and tight squeezes, they arrived at the tech's intended destination. Gazing through a grate, Darik could see the lift-shaft just beyond.

"Now let me get this straight." Darik paused as yet another lift whizzed by, shooting upward at a frightening speed. "You're suggesting we open this grate, pop out into the shaft, and just climb on up to ground level?"

The roar of a second lift descending on the path right next to the first drowned out Nikky's reply, but he nodded his head in assent.

"And you don't see a problem with that plan?" The first lift shot by again, accentuating Darik's point.

Nikky was unfazed. "We'll just have to dodge them."

"Dodge them."

"Yes—dodge them. Look, the lifts themselves are monitored, but the *shafts* are not. This is the only chance we have."

The second lift flew past on its way back up. All JenKore lifts were equipped with internal dampening systems that allowed them to travel at extremely fast speeds and to stop instantaneously at selected levels without damage or discomfort to the occupants inside. The speeds at which they moved made the idea of sharing a shaft with two of them totally preposterous. Darik could recall seeing a similar situation in a holoflick, in which the hero had simply jumped on the lift's roof and ridden it to the top. It all looked so easy on screen, but in real life, such a stunt would accomplish nothing but a quick death.

"I can't believe this. We should be out of here by now." Slumping against the wall of the duct, Darik turned to Nikky. "What was so important? You were supposed to be clearing a sec-path out, and instead you kept surfing that personnel list. What were you looking at?"

"Do you really want to know?"

Darik stared at him. "No, I'm making conversation because I'm bored."

Nikky ignored the sarcasm. "That series of names—it's not just some census roster. It's a list of *targets*—all of them off-world. Someone is targeting UC citizens."

"Targeting? Targeting for what?" Something stirred inside Darik, telling him that he already knew the answer.

"For elimination. The red ones were marked as completed."

Darik digested this information. "Okay, I get that. But you must have had that information as soon as you saw the list. Why did you have to keep poking around?"

Rather than answering, Nikky began to pry open the grate. "The lifts aren't running as often now. This is our chance."

The grate, never intended to prevent someone from entering the shaft, snapped free easily. Nikky scrambled through and began to climb. Following him, Darik got his first full glimpse of the interior. He caught his breath as he looked down. Even though they were already twenty-three levels below the ground, the rest of the shaft still seemed bottomless. Far below, he could see one of the lifts at rest. At any moment, it could begin its ascent, with the two of them right in its path. The two lifts traveled along several rails built into the shaft walls. Darik noticed that Nikky, already several meters above him, was using open slots in the rails as makeshift ladder rungs. Steeling himself, he grasped one of the slots and pulled himself the rest of the way into the shaft. For a terrifying moment, his legs flailed for a foothold. Finally, his right toe poked into a slot below, stabilizing his position. He looked up as he began to climb.

"Twenty-three levels, huh?"

"We'll make it," Nikky called down. "Besides, I'm not sure we—"

A roaring sound, accompanied by an upward rush of air, cut off any further conversation. Darik looked down, confirming his worst fear.

"Oh, crap."

The lift below them, so many levels down a moment ago, was ascending with dizzying speed.

"Nikky, *move!*"

Darik reached to his right, grabbing a handhold on the next rail over. Releasing his left hand, he awkwardly twisted around and groped for another rail even farther away. He missed once, then found his grip. His right wrist was now twisted painfully as he dangled between two rails. He let go, more from pain than intent, and his momentum carried him another half meter to the right, just as the lift rushed by. The airflow alone nearly sent him tumbling down the shaft.

Darik looked up. Nikky had just made it out of the lift's path as well.

"That was too close."

"Uh, look out—here comes the other one."

"Oh, come on!" After avoiding the first lift, the two of them were now hanging onto the second lift's rails. Looking up past Nikky, Darik could see it descending at the same speed the first lift had gone up. Nikky was already scrambling back to the left.

Wincing against the pain in his right wrist, Darik negotiated the same rails he had just taken back to his original position. The lift plummeted past, nearly grazing his right shoulder in the process.

"Hey, boss?" Even the wiry Nikky seemed out of breath.

"What?"

"I'm beginning to think this wasn't such a good idea."

"No kidding." Darik was already exhausted, and they had barely gained even one level. "Just climb before they start up again."

The words were not even out of his mouth when they heard the all-too-familiar roar of lift number one beginning its descent.

"Back to the right. Move!" Darik grunted and swung over again. This time, with more advance warning, both men made the shift with time to spare. Lift number one was still several levels up, and they were safely clinging to the rails of number two. Darik was about to congratulate himself on getting the hang of this when the second rushing sound from below joined in unison with the roaring from above.

"Oh no…"

Glancing down erased any doubt. Lift number two was on its way back up. Worse yet, judging by their speed and distance, the two lifts would pass each other right where Darik and Nikky were hanging. Horrified, Darik realized that there was nowhere to go. There were no safe rails and no space in between the lifts. Darik remained still, figuring that it was better to be slammed into by the car speeding upward than to be crushed or sent plummeting to the bottom by the one headed down. Either way, Darik decided, they were dead. As lift number one shot down on his left, he closed his eyes and braced for the impact from below.

Nothing.

Releasing his breath, Darik looked down. Both lifts had stopped just below them. It was only a short reach for Darik to gently step down onto the roof of lift number two. Nikky joined him a moment later. He heard the lift doors slide open and voices drift up from the hall below.

"You three—come with me. We found a hole in the ducts. They're in the ventilation system."

"Riggs and Lance, head up to HQ. Our comm is out."

Darik shot a quick glance at Nikky, who knowingly tapped his gadget bag. Somewhere along the way, he had managed to knock out communications. Darik smiled in spite of himself. The voice continued.

"Tell them to send as many men as they can to sub-level twenty-three and to monitor all vertical shafts. They may be trying to climb out."

Darik leaned in close to Nikky and hissed, "If they start monitoring these shafts, we're toast. Can you disable the scanner inside the lift from here?"

Nikky shook his head. "No. It would have to be taken out manually." He nodded at Darik's stunner, which was hanging askew from a torn pocket. "You know...*your way*."

Darik drew a breath. "Got it." He paused to quietly rip away a shredded section of his shirt and tie it around his face like a bandana. This close, he didn't want to be recognized by the scanner before he blasted it. He then remembered to dial the power back up on his stun battery. The last thing he needed was to squeeze off a couple of perfect shots only to realize that the low powered rounds only succeeded in giving his targets an irritating itch.

Hearing the doors slide shut, Darik reached for the access handle embedded in the lift's roof. In another moment, the lift would shoot upward—the g-forces outside making any further movement impossible. He took a single deep breath, and then in a seamless move—surprising even himself—he ripped open the hatch, targeted the two guards inside, and squeezed off two quick stun bolts, dropping both men to the floor. As the lift shot upward, he swung himself through the hatch. Nikky, not wanting to be outside the moving car, managed to drop in right behind him.

There was no time to waste. Darik popped up onto one knee, located the lift's scanning sensor, and fired. The device emitted a shower of sparks as the lift continued its ascent.

Darik's exhilaration at having successfully taken out the guards was tempered by a foreboding thought. "Damn," he muttered, "there's no way I was fast enough. That scanner picked up everything." He looked at Nikky and shook his head. "They're going to be waiting for us."

*   *   *

At ground level, several well-armed security personnel formed a semi-circle around the lift doors—weapons drawn. The security chief smiled. With the comm down, he didn't know exactly what was going on down there, but he did know two things. One, from the scanner's final seconds of feed, he knew that two idiots had just stunned a couple of his men and were on their way up in the lift. And two, from the bonus he was going to get for wasting them, he knew he would finally be able to get that new Adonis shuttle he had his eye on.

He was mentally picking out colors when the lift arrived.

He was considering adding some expensive options when the doors opened.

He began to reconsider ways to keep his old shuttle running when he saw what was inside. Except for the two unconscious guards, the lift was empty.

*   *   *

"Well, that was a colossal waste of time."

At a phylline cafe several blocks from the JenKore facility, Darik stared ruefully over his cup of coffee. It was just after six in the morning. He was shivering from exhaustion, from nerves, from the falling adrenaline, from the cool morning air—the precise cause was irrelevant. The important thing was to find a way to pull himself together. The first step would be to get cleaned up and into a fresh change of clothes. The filthy, shredded apparel he had been wearing was stuffed in a bag at his feet. He tugged at the collar of the shirt he had borrowed from Nikky's office. It was two sizes too small, and its color defied any conventional label, but it was better than walking around in tattered rags.

And at the moment, he really couldn't have cared less how ridiculous he looked. He just wanted to stop by his apartment, take a shower, put on a real suit, and report to work in an hour looking like someone who *hadn't* spent the night crawling around in JenKore's restricted areas. Fortunately, the #3 Research and Development Facility was not a responsibility of his department. If it had been, he would have been expected to be onsite last night, helping coordinate the search rather than being the subject of it. Sipping the steaming coffee in an effort to re-stimulate his brain, he was also thankful that he wasn't the one who had to spend the day filing the report. For the head of the R&D security division, the log work from last night's fiasco was going to be staggering.

"I wouldn't exactly call it a waste—we got the files on the data chip." Across the table, Nikky munched on a stale scone, his decaf untouched. "And we got out, didn't we?"

That much was true. When the lift had started its rapid ascent, Darik had slammed a final fresh stun battery into his pistol, intending to go out in a blaze of glory.

Nikky's hand on his arm had stopped him.

"Hang on, boss. There's another way. The scanner's out. They can't track this lift. We don't *have* to go to ground level."

A moment later, Darik understood what Nikky meant. The tech had popped open the lift control panel, deftly pulled a couple of fibroc cables, and prepared to place them into different inputs. Watching the rising level display intently, Nikky waited for just the right moment and jammed the cables home.

The lift car had screeched to a sudden halt—apparently the dampening system had disengaged with the fibroc cables—bouncing Darik about a half meter off the floor and leaving his stomach tickling his tonsils. The lift doors opened, and Darik had tumbled out. A moment later, Nikky followed before sending the lift back on its way without them.

Nikky smiled, his thin eyebrows arching.

"My floor," he explained.

Back on the same level as his office, it had seemed like child's play for Nikky to avoid scanners and work their way back to his cramped little work space. Once there, he had simply used his ancient keyboard to both cover their tracks and clear an unmonitored path out of the building. Nikky's fingers had flown over the keys, only hesitating once.

"What's wrong?" Darik found himself suddenly accustomed to reaching for his pistol, even in the relatively safe confines of Nikky's office.

"Well, our faces show up in quite a few of these scans, and they're already logged in the system."

"So, after all that, we're busted anyway?"

"I didn't say that." Nikky's index finger rested over the *Enter* key. "I'm going to have to purge the entire log for last night."

"Can the deletion be traced back to you here?"

"What?" Nikky had sounded offended. "No way. It's just that…"

"It's just what?"

Nikky swallowed. "Well, it's just so…it's just so…*amateur.*"

"Oh for the love of…just *do* it."

Fifteen minutes later, they were sipping coffee at the cafe. Darik was still depressed.

"Yes, we got out. And I have *total* confidence in you that no record exists of our ever being there, but…"

Nikky was making a habit of ignoring Darik's sarcasm. "Oh, it's better than us not being there. I left a half-dozen scans just deep enough under the purge for a good tech to pull them. Those scans will have a couple of fake ID images imprinted on them. They'll spend all of their time looking for a couple of cyber-dinks who only exist in one of my sim games."

Darik shook his head in surprise. "I thought you said it would be too amateur."

"I said the *purge* would be amateur. I didn't say *I* was."

Darik stood up to leave. "All the same, Nikky, the entire thing was a disaster. We went through all that, crawled around like rats, nearly got our heads busted in, and for all that, we didn't get the name we were looking for."

"Oh, don't worry about that. I think I can still get the name. I've got another idea."

"Yeah?"

"But you're late. You better get going—don't want to raise suspicion at the office, right? I'll work on it and get back to you."

Darik checked his chrono and realized that Nikky was right. The details would have to wait. He nodded to Nikky and left.

At the table, Nikky finally took a sip of his decaf. Yeah, he could get the name. He'd find out all about the name. He'd find out all about *both* names.

Chapter 17

The door chime shook Dex from his reverie. "Yes," he said reflexively. Looking up, he saw a rather sheepish Ronnie Wilco poke his head through the doorway.

"Uh, sorry to bother you, Captain, but I was heading in this direction and Commander Lebrian asked if I would check in on you. Your comm's been off for a few hours, and he knows you have a couple items on your agenda this afternoon."

Dex had completely lost track of time. Glancing at his chrono, he saw that he had only a handful of minutes before a pair of critical meetings with two of his pilots. Once again, Sarge had saved his tail.

"Thanks, Ronnie." The ops tech stepped to one side as Dex grabbed a portable holo-unit and rushed out the door. A couple strides down the corridor, Dex paused and looked back.

"Hey, Ronnie. You got a minute?"

"Sure, Captain, what do you need?"

"Just walk with me."

Ronnie fell in step as Dex resumed his quick pace.

"I was just thinking about Aphea. About the attack..."

Ronnie slowly nodded, picking up the thought. "We didn't have very much warning in the colony. It was complete chaos, everyone trying to board that old cruiser at once. By the time we got off-planet, it was too late—the Marauders were all over us. I thought we were dead for sure."

Dex shook his head, recalling how close it had been. The colony's cruiser had already been severely damaged by the time the Angels had emerged from the ether.

Ronnie continued. "But then you guys showed up and made short work of them. It would have been kind of fun to watch if we hadn't all been scared out of our wits."

"It seems to me, Ronnie, that you were too preoccupied at the time to be scared."

The cruiser's captain had been killed with the Marauders' first volley of Slammers, the missiles cutting effortlessly through the old ship's under-powered shields. Dex remembered his first impression had been that they were too late. The Angels arrived to find the cruiser drifting and completely dark except for several glowing points visible deep within the craft, remote fires that had not yet been extinguished by exposure to the oxygen-free vacuum. Other than that eerie, silent iridescence, the cruiser looked dead in space. As the Angels engaged the Marauders, Dex had tried to establish communication with the lifeless craft.

After several attempts, he finally heard a surprisingly calm voice crackling over the comm. The voice informed Dex that they were a bit busy on the cruiser's bridge, then went on to say that if the Hornets would kindly dispatch the fighters who were shooting at them, he would see to rebooting the cruiser and preparing it for an ether jump. Dex would later learn that the voice belonged to young Ronnie Wilco who, racing to the bridge, had discovered the lifeless crew and had assumed command of the cruiser. At the time of Dex's repeated queries, Ronnie had been engaged in some imagination-defying jury rigging of the cruiser's life support and flight control systems. Even as Dex acknowledged Ronnie's reply, he had observed interior and exterior lights on the cruiser beginning to flicker back to life.

Still walking stride-for-stride, Dex and Ronnie turned down a side corridor. The room where Dex would be meeting with his pilots was at the end of the hall. Geff Bennet was probably already waiting for him.

That's fine, Dex thought. *Let him sit on ice for a while.*

"To this day, I still don't know how you held that bucket together for the ether jump, Ronnie, let alone how you got it down here in one piece."

Ronnie never seemed to take himself or his abilities all that seriously. This quirky modesty was one of the qualities Dex liked about the young man.

"Well, Captain, I had been in charge of the colony's ground systems. We kind of held them together with bond-clamps and channel tape. How much different could the cruiser's hardware be?"

Dex smiled. *A lot different.*

Ronnie continued. "Besides, I really didn't get the ship down in one piece, did I."

"No," Dex agreed, "but you did manage to save a lot of lives." The damage to the cruiser had been extensive. After Dex had transmitted the encrypted coordinates for the jump, Ronnie had somehow been able to coax it into etherspace intact. But upon emerging above the colony's new uncharted home, it was evident that the battered craft could not survive reentry.

Dex had contacted the cruiser the moment they had dropped from the ether. The report had not been good. Ventral thrusters were offline, the landing sequencer was fried, and hull integrity was compromised in most places—nonexistent in others. On top of that, life support had failed near the end of the jump. There were only minutes of oxygen supply remaining. The cruiser had to land quickly, one way or another, but landing was seemingly impossible. Yet, in spite of this, the young tech in command of the cruiser—responsible for two thousand lives, including his own—sounded upbeat.

Ronnie had informed Dex that he had an idea. Back on Aphea, during one of the planet's frequent radium storms, the colonists had reinforced a failing shelter by hard-wiring the colony's lone polarity-lifter through the structure's duranium skeleton. The magnetic pulses of the lifter had reinforced the supports enough to outlast the storm. At the evacuation, that same polarity-lifter had been one of the first vital pieces of equipment loaded onto the cruiser, and Ronnie was frenetically working to tie it into the ship's hull structure.

Dex had been sure of two things. One, he didn't have a clue what Ronnie was talking about, and two, this was a tech to be reckoned with. *Get yourself and those people down alive, kid,* he had thought, *and you've got a job with this squadron.*

Dex stopped before the door of the meeting room. "The landing may have rattled a few bones—and I'm pretty sure the trail of destruction you left is visible from space—but everyone survived." He nodded in the direction of the colony. "These people wouldn't be here right now if it weren't for you."

Once again, Ronnie deflected the praise. "Captain, I don't think you had me walk with you in order to discuss my piloting skills."

"No, you're right. There's a detail from that day that's been nagging at me all this time—I don't know why. Anyway, I thought maybe you could help. Back in the Aphea system, during the battle, you still had sensors online, didn't you?"

"You bet. That was one of the only systems that didn't go red on the first hit. That's how we knew you guys had swooped in with your Hornets."

"Did you happen to detect another ship in the system? Besides the Marauders, I mean."

Ronnie considered for a moment. "There was another ship, yeah. A C-230 transport, but it was just hanging back, not really doing anything. We really didn't give it much attention."

"Did you get any kind of scan on it? Any clue as to what it was carrying?"

"No, Captain. I guess I always kind of assumed it was carrying ground troops for the invasion. Like I said, we didn't give it a lot of attention. We were a bit preoccupied at the time."

Dex sighed. It had been a long shot. The Angels' scans of the C-230 had been inconclusive. If Ronnie was right, and the transport had been carrying troops, Dex should have been able to detect the passengers. The mystery had been gnawing at him ever since—it went against his thorough nature to leave any detail unresolved. Dex realized, though, that he was foolish to think the old cruiser would have picked up anything that the Hornets' hyper-sensitive scanners could not. He placed a hand on Ronnie's shoulder.

"You definitely had your hands full. And this colony will never forget what you did for them. I may not get a chance to say it enough, Ronnie, but I appreciate you."

As Dex turned to enter the meeting room, Ronnie gave him a knowing look.

"Have an effective meeting, Captain. I'll be praying for you."

"Thanks, Ronnie. I will."

*   *   *

Geff Bennet was waiting for Dex in the meeting room. The flight lieutenant stood to attention as his commander entered. Dex briefly considered having Bennet remain standing, then decided otherwise. Some of his more hotheaded pilots needed to be reminded of their place, but there was no need for such games with Geff—he couldn't have appeared any more contrite.

"At ease, Lieutenant. Have a seat."

Geff gratefully accepted the offer to sit back down, but his expression showed that he was far from feeling *at ease*. He waited in silence.

Taking a chair across the table from Bennet, Dex placed the portable holo-unit on the surface between them.

"Before we begin this briefing, Lieutenant, do you have anything to say about your performance on the mission?"

Geff eyed the holo-unit and swallowed hard.

"Sir, I sincerely regret the destruction of the gunship and the loss of lives on board."

Dex stood to his feet, slamming his palms on the table top as he rose. "You're *damn* right you regret it! Your ship was damaged. Your controls were sluggish. You had no business going in with guns blazing, but you had been lit up and you were *mad*."

"I'm sorry, Captain. I let my emotions get the best of me."

Dex could sympathize. He had certainly made his own mistakes in the past, and he had to live with the consequences of those rash decisions—which is why he was so determined not to let Geff or any of the others make those same mistakes. He took a long breath and sat back down.

"I expected better of you, Geff. Our rules are in place for a reason. We are not in a declared state of war. We do not fall under the authority of any governing agency. We are in a defensive posture, and our job is to protect and provide for this colony—not to seek out conflict, even with hostiles."

Geff lowered his eyes. "That can be difficult in the heat of a mission, sir. When they're shooting at us, well, it's hard to do nothing."

Dex allowed himself a hard smile. "Tell me about it. I am fully aware of the risks each and every pilot in this squadron is taking, but understand this, Lieutenant—our lives are expendable. Our values are not. Yes, I authorized lethal force during the Milk Run, but that responsibility has to fall on me. You pre-empted that decision and took those lives on your own. Let me ask you, how does that feel?"

Geff slowly looked up. "Captain, I feel like I'm going to have to live with that for the rest of my life."

Dex considered telling him about the Artemis incident. The engagement had occurred years ago when he and Hagen were a couple of up-and-coming lieutenants in the "Gunslingers," a frontier squadron with a reputation for finding trouble. During a skirmish in the Artemis system, Dex had crossed the fine line between aggression and recklessness, allowing vanity to cloud his judgment—and it had cost him and the Gunslingers dearly.

But he decided against confiding in Bennet. Dex simply wasn't ready to reopen those old wounds. And maybe he never would be. Instead he met the young lieutenant's eyes.

"I know you will, Geff. Believe me, I know."

A small proximity indicator near the door told Dex that his next appointment had already arrived and was waiting in the hall.

Dex continued. "We all made a difficult decision that day we left Earth. I believed then, and still do, that it was the right decision. But if we begin to believe, for even a moment, that all of that somehow gives us the right, or the authority under God, to begin carelessly *taking* lives in some kind of vigilante war, then we're no better than…"

Dex paused. He glanced down at the holo-unit. He could begin the playback of Bennet's flight data, but somehow it seemed unnecessary. Dex had watched and re-watched it dozens of times. He still couldn't be absolutely certain whether Bennet had *intended* to destroy the gunship or if his damaged targeting controls had simply turned what he had thought would be a good disabling shot into something more lethal. Onigen had attempted to take responsibility as the element lead, but Dex wasn't buying it. He was convinced that, intentional or not, Geff's rashness had caused him to cross a very important line. Dex knew what he had to do, but if his pilot was to fly again, he needed him to understand *why* he was doing it.

"How much Earth history have you studied, Lieutenant?"

Geff appeared surprised by the question. "Some, I guess—as much as anyone else at the academy."

Dex stood once more. Geff followed his lead, coming to attention.

"Here are my findings. You pressed the attack on the gunship after your fighter was damaged beyond your ability to properly control it. While doing so, you disregarded a direct command by your lead to disengage. Your actions resulted in the loss of six lives aboard that gunship."

Geff once again lowered his eyes. "Yes, sir—I understand."

"Lieutenant Bennet. You are grounded until further notice. During the time of this disciplinary action, you are confined to quarters. Your assignment while under confinement will be to refresh your knowledge of Earth history, particularly Eastern-Western religious conflicts. Job is sending the reading list as we speak."

Dex kept his expression firm as he regarded the young pilot. "Take a good look at those events, Lieutenant. Remind yourself what can happen when men regard life as cheap and operate under the misguided belief that God is somehow honored by their bloodshed and destruction. As long as we are out here, on our own, we will not cross—no—we will not get anywhere *near* that line. If you want to fly with this squadron, you need to decide what kind of pilot—what kind of man—you intend to be. You are dismissed."

"Yes, sir." Bennet turned toward the door.

"And Geff…"

Bennet faced his captain again. Dex picked up the unneeded holo-unit, flicking off the power as he placed it in his pocket.

"Report back to me with that decision, and we'll discuss getting you back in the cockpit again."

"Yes, sir. Thank you, Captain."

Bennet saluted and left. Through the open doorway, Dex could see his next guest, Scot Calgaro, pensively waiting for his turn.

While Dex had allowed Geff Bennet to be seated during his meeting, he would allow no such comfort to Calgaro. Still wearing a dermo-patch over his right ear, the talented, but so often misguided lieutenant entered. He remained stiffly at attention as Dex dressed him down.

"You disobeyed direct orders." Dex's voice grew louder with each charge he leveled. "You abandoned your wingman in the middle of an engagement, and your cowboy tactics put the entire squadron at risk."

Scot continued to stare straight ahead as he spoke. "Captain, that freighter was still salvageable. All I wanted to do was—"

"Did I give you permission to respond, mister? Did I ask you a question?"

"No, sir."

"Then listen, and listen well, Lieutenant. I don't care what you thought about the freighter. I don't give a damn what you wanted to do, and I am not interested in your evaluation of the mission. You were out of line. You boarded that freighter, alone, against orders. And while you were screwing around, your squadron mates—your *friends*—were fighting for their lives. You entered into an unknown scenario with no backup and ended up in a lethal engagement with a hostile." Dex indicated Scot's bandaged head. "An engagement that could have gotten you killed, Scot. What in the world were you *thinking*?"

Scot waited a beat and cleared his throat. "As I said, sir, the freighter was still intact. I knew you guys could handle the Rhinos. I mean, c'mon, those four *police force* Stingers had taken out three of them before we even got there. To leave the prize at that point would have meant we came all that way for nothing." He paused again before adding under his breath, "Like so many other missions..."

Dex regarded Calgaro once again. How many times had they had conversations similar to this one? Only a few years older, Dex felt his authority under constant scrutiny by the brash pilot. Usually, Dex was able to set the subtle insubordination aside, taking it in stride as an almost necessary component of Scot's personality—the opposite side of the same coin that made him such a natural fighter pilot. But on this last mission, Calgaro had gone too far. He met Scot's gaze with an icy stare.

"You have something on your mind, Lieutenant? Let's hear it right now. You couldn't possibly be in any more trouble."

Scot did not waver. "Captain, we can't keep taking these losses. The rules of engagement are a joke. We go out, we get attacked, and we run like rabbits. Believe me—the others are talking. Everyone is sick to death of getting beat up and not shooting back. Listen to me, Dex. This squadron *needs* a clear victory. We all thought this freighter would be it. When I saw it slipping away for no good reason, I just had to do something."

"No good reason?" Dex struggled to keep his voice under control. "No good reason? Our intel was fouled, there were hostiles *and* friendlies swarming the area, and we were flying blind with no sensors to tell them apart!"

"And yet, in spite of all that, Captain, we could have *still* pulled it off. But you wouldn't let us!"

Dex had heard enough. If it was possible, he pressed even closer to Scot's face, their noses almost touching. "That, *Lieutenant*," his clipped tones emphasizing Calgaro's rank, "is *not* your call."

Dex drew himself back. "You are grounded. If I do let you fly again, and right now I'm having a hard time imagining that, your days as a lead are over. As of now, I'm taking Adahn as my wing. If you ever get back into the cockpit, you'll fly under Lieutenant McLeod."

Scot looked devastated. Dex knew that he had taken great pride in his lead status. After all the ribbing he had given Jani about her second-tier placement in the squadron, it was going to be humiliating for Scot to have to fly on her wing.

Dex continued. "And while I'm trying to think of a reason why I should ever allow you in a Hornet again, you can plant yourself in your quarters with your roommate, Mr. Bennet. I'm sure you two will have plenty to discuss. You are dismissed, Lieutenant."

Scot turned to depart. At the door, he hesitated and turned back to Dex.

"Captain, with your permission, there is one more thing I'd like to discuss."

"Go ahead."

"You know how I said that the local yokels had already taken eight *pirate* gunships down to five by the time we got there? How does that happen? No reasonably trained force, in gunships no less, should take those kinds of losses. I mean, they had a two-to-one advantage, and they lost it—to *police Scorpions*."

Dex had been bothered by the same detail. It just didn't add up. Even with the jammer pod, the gunships had not been able to fully press their advantage.

"Go on, Lieutenant."

"We've run into pirates before, out in the FSA, and I've got to say that these guys didn't fight like any pirates I've ever seen. They were either completely incompetent, or else they weren't who they appeared to be. And if they were pirates, what was the point of planting a tracking device on board? Their objective should have been the same as ours—to just grab the freighter and run."

Once again, Scot was vocalizing the exact concerns that had been nagging at Dex, but he kept his thoughts to himself.

"So noted. Anything else?"

"Yeah, there is one more thing, but you're not going to like it."

"Why should that be any different from the rest of this conversation?"

"All right, here it is. The hostile that died on the freighter—he was no pirate, Captain. He just didn't look the part. I know appearances can be deceiving, but he was just a kid. Clean cut, real soft—nothing like the usual roughnecks. This whole thing just isn't making any sense."

"Okay, Scot, you've made that point. What am I not supposed to like?"

"After the engagement, I grabbed his side arm. It's stowed in my locker back at the hanger."

Dex digested this latest information. "You procured a combatant's weapon, brought it back to base, and didn't bother to report it." Dex shook his head. Why didn't any of that surprise him? "Can you at least tell me why?"

If Scot hadn't looked uncomfortable before, he did now. "I honestly don't know. When we got back, I knew I was in trouble no matter what. So I had a lot of things on my mind at the time. After I stowed it, I pretty much forgot about it. But now I'm thinking it might help. Maybe we can trace the serial imprint and try to figure out just who the heck those guys were."

"You pretty much *forgot* about it? Or do you mean you just held on to it until you thought it could be useful to you?"

"Like I said, I was in trouble either way, wasn't I?"

Dex regarded his pilot for several seconds. He had already grounded him and confined him to quarters. What else could he do? Throw him in the brig? Beat the hell out of him? It all sounded pretty good.

"All right, bring the side arm to my quarters—discreetly. And then get your rear end back to your own."

Scot saluted and departed without another word. After the door slid shut, Dex slumped back into his chair. Scot had been right about one thing—the squadron *did* need a victory. He knew the pilots were fed up. Morale was slipping. All they did was sit back and protect, wait and hope. What kind of plan was that? But how could they plan to fight an enemy when they weren't even sure who that enemy was?

Dex was angry enough at Scot to throttle him. Yet, he had to admit, Scot's stupid act of boarding the freighter had ended up revealing the tracking device on board. It was clear by now that the gunships had not been manned by ordinary pirates. Someone had known enough about the mission to put together a pre-emptive attack on the freighter and to place the device on board, undoubtedly with the objective of tracking the ship back to the colony. He shuddered, imagining what would have happened if the Scorpions hadn't intervened or if he hadn't moved their own mission timetable up. The Angels would have grabbed the freighter, and by now, the colony would have been discovered—and quite possibly destroyed.

Where were they getting their information? Scot's grabbing that weapon might have been a Godsend in the otherwise screwed-up mission. Dex really didn't care at the moment why Calgaro had withheld that information until now. He just wanted to see if the side arm could be traced. Perhaps it might finally reveal some clue about who exactly was pursuing them.

Unfortunately, squadron resources for that kind of forensic work were woefully inadequate. Retrieving a weapon's unique, embedded serial signature was a simple enough matter, but tracing it back to its source required access to databases far removed from their colony home. To complicate matters, Dex was certain that this would be no ordinary trace. He believed the side arm could bring him some much needed answers, but he was also sure its origins would not be easily retrieved. Dex needed help from someone with extraordinary resources and unlimited access, and he knew what that meant.

*   *   *

It seemed to Dex that Baker had been expecting his call. The fact that Dex rarely initiated these contacts should have created a heightened level of caution and security, but Baker had hurried through the usual protocols, impatient to get on with the conversation. The instant their exchange was verified as secure, his next question fairly burst over the channel.

"So what in the world happened out there, boy?"

Even through the encryption, Dex could hear the concern in his benefactor's voice.

"We're not sure yet. It was a bust from the start. I'm sorry—we lost the freighter."

"Aw hell, son. I'm not worried about the freighter. I was writing it off anyway, remember? It is a shame you didn't get your hands all those supplies, though. No, I'm talking about all the company you folks had out there."

"Yeah, it was pretty crowded."

Baker leaned in toward the screen. "I don't suppose we're chalking up all that activity to coincidence, are we?"

Dex shook his head. "No, it wasn't a coincidence. We had already aborted the freighter objective when one of my guys ended up boarding it anyway—against orders. I'm ready to fry him for that, but the upshot is that he ended up finding a tracking device on board."

"Come again?"

"He discovered a tracking device. If we had simply taken the freighter, we would have led whoever planted it right back to the colony."

Baker paused, digesting this latest information. "It looks like someone got tipped off again—and now I'm sitting here wondering if maybe it could have happened on *my* end."

"Your end?" All this time, Dex had been concerned about a security leak in the squadron. Was it possible that the problem had been on Baker's side all along?

"Yeah, kid. I've been thinking that no matter how careful I've been, this operation has been just too dang big to insure one hundred percent security on both ends. I mean, I've only got a few select guys in the loop over here, and I trust each of them with my life." Baker paused for a moment. "But then, I'm sure you trust your folks, too. That's just my point. We don't know who or what keeps screwing up our plans, son, but until we find out, I can't keep putting you and your people at risk like that. We're going to have to cut off deliveries."

Dex had to agree. Losing Baker's semi-regular supply shipments would be a blow to the colony, but they would have to survive. Their own agri-plenishment efforts were progressing well, so food would not be the major issue, and Baker had previously delivered enough phirmium and other necessary materials to last for a while. It was, rather, the squadron that concerned Dex the most. They had spare fuel and parts, but without regular resupply, the Hornets and other vital equipment could soon fall into disrepair, leaving the colony defenseless.

"Aw, don't look so glum, kid." In spite of the seriousness of the situation, Dex was amused by Baker's comment. There was no way, through the encryption, that Baker could see whether Dex was glum or not. He smiled slightly as Baker continued. "We won't be cutting you folks off forever. We just need to figure out what's going on here. Then we can start fixing y'all up real nice again. I don't suppose you got any sensor feeds off that freighter before you used it for target practice?"

Dex winced. The freighter had already been compromised by the time the Angels had arrived. The hostile that Scot encountered had managed to get on board, and either he or someone else had planted the tracking device. It was possible that Baker could have used the internal sensor logs to determine exactly how and when that had occurred—even if the trail led back to his own organization.

"No. And we didn't leave very much of it intact for forensics, I'm afraid."

"Well, that part I appreciate, son."

Dex nodded. He and the Angels had needed to work fast, but their Slammers hadn't left any evidence of the freighter's contents to be traced back to their anonymous supplier.

"We may have another lead, however." Dex produced the side arm Scot had taken. "This is the reason I contacted you. It's a Hagg-Sauer BP-105. My insubordinate lieutenant picked it off a guy he tangled with during his EVA aboard the freighter. We don't have the ability to trace it here. I thought you might want to take a shot at it."

Baker thought a moment. "A user trace on a weapon taken from a covert aboard a vaporized freighter while on an illegal, nonexistent mission? Sounds like a long shot."

"Yeah, I know. But it's all we've got right now."

"You're right, you're right..." Baker didn't sound convinced. "Plug her in, and I'll get my guy to give it a look."

Dex turned the pistol over in his hand, exposing its underside. The identifying data module—strictly required on every weapon produced in the UC—had not been removed and did not appear to have been altered. He connected a fibroc cable to a micro-jack in the pistol's grip. The ID module's data was transmitted to Baker in less time than it took Dex to compose his next thought.

"Baker," Dex said, looking back up at the comm screen, "something just isn't adding up. If someone can hit us this easily, why haven't they finished the job yet? What are they waiting for?"

"I don't know, kid. Maybe they know where you're going to be, but they don't know where you're coming from." Dex could hear the determination in Baker's voice. "You folks keep that location of yours under wraps, you hear?"

"Count on it."

"And in the meantime, forget about that freighter and its sensors. You've got enough mission data from your own Hornets to go over."

Dex sighed. "I don't know. I've been over every byte of it myself, and I've got nothing so far."

"Just you? What about that lieutenant commander of yours—the clever one, *Ninja* I think you call him—and how about that big tough commander? Isn't mission analysis usually a team function?"

Whether it was mission fatigue or simple paranoia, Dex suddenly felt very isolated. He shook his head, trying to clear unprompted visions of Hagen or Onigen quietly transmitting intel to some sinister recipient.

This is stupid, he thought. Was he going to start doubting his most trusted officers now? Yet, he couldn't deny that this latest fiasco had shown just how vulnerable the squadron was. Dex didn't know if it was an agent in Baker's organization or his own, but someone was tipping off the enemy, and until the mole was uncovered, Dex could trust no one.

"No—this one I have to do alone."

Baker leaned in so close, it seemed as though he was going to come through the screen. "Belay that! You can't operate that way, hotshot. I know things look bad right now, but you're not a solo act, understand? You get your top team together and take another look at your data. And in the meantime, I'll get my people started on that pistol trace."

Dex nodded slowly. "Yeah, you're right, of course." It was his turn to sound unconvinced.

"Listen, kid, this isn't the time to forget who your friends are." Baker's tone lightened. "Where's that faith of yours?"

"I don't know, Baker. Sometimes it feels a bit elusive."

"Well, get it back, son. You and your people are going to need it." Baker moved to terminate the transmission. "And get some rest. You look like hell."

Chapter 18

A small speaker on Nikky's flat monitor chirped once.

"Now I've got you." Nikky whirled in his chair and began entering strokes on his keyboard. His efforts were instantly rewarded as a new stream of data cascaded down the screen. He smiled with satisfaction, leaning closer, warming even further to his task.

Ever since his expedition with Darik Mason into the restricted sub-levels of JenKore, Nikky had been more obsessed than usual. The difference was that now his obsession had been redirected. While the elusive echo and its bizarre, violent imagery still held a percentage of his interest, his main concern had shifted to a new endeavor.

It was that list—that series of bios that Nikky had seen during his misadventure with Mason. He couldn't get that list out of his head. Actually, it wasn't even the entire list. It really came down to just one name—a name Nikky had not encountered in a long time and had not expected to come across again, at least not in anything but a memory.

Back in the dim confines of that underground hallway, with Darik peering impatiently over his shoulder, Nikky had hurriedly scanned through the list of names and images, intending a simple once over and then a fast escape. He had quickly realized that it was a list of targeted individuals, but as interesting as that information was, it wasn't worth compromising Darik's and his escape. But then he had seen a bio that made him go back and scan the list again—a move that almost got both of them busted. The extra delay had been worth it, however. Nikky confirmed that his eyes hadn't been playing tricks on him. One image in the bio had borne a striking resemblance to that of a young man in a holopic hanging on the wall back in Nikky's own flat.

Scanning back, it had taken Nikky only an instant to memorize the data in the file. He hadn't shared the information with Darik—in fact he had brushed his employer off when he was asked about it—but Nikky was sure of what he had seen. It was the bio of Drager St. James, a flight sergeant who had served in the disgraced 714th Fighter Squadron. It was the bio of a man who, years earlier as a teen, had left Earth with his father, allegedly fleeing religious persecution. Nikky had been told by his own mother that his half brother, Drager St. James, was now dead. But, on that list, the image of Flight Sergeant St. James had not been bordered in red. If the information was credible, Nikky had been looking at evidence that— at least according to JenKore's database—Drager was still alive and was currently an outlaw with the "Angels."

Nikky needed to find out if that was true. And if Drager was alive, and was one of the targets on that list, Nikky was determined to find him and, if possible, find a way to help him.

His research so far had been exhausting. Running without sleep, and devoting little time and energy to his actual job responsibilities, Nikky had used his fabricated ACG codes to open a low-level comm port from JenKore's system to the UCN database. Utilizing JenKore's favored contractor status to his advantage, he managed to maneuver through enough back-door gateways to track down some interesting details surrounding the 714th Fighter Squadron's final hours on Earth. Information restricted at the highest levels had begun to loosen up under his relentless incursions. In the past two days, he had read, word for word, the classified orders that had decommissioned the squadron. Digging deeper, he had located correspondence showing orders behind the orders, revealing more of the motivation behind the unprecedented grounding of one of the UCN's most decorated squadrons. Nikky had groaned when he finally saw the reason. It was so like Drager to be caught up in a *religious* controversy. Some things never changed.

While the decommissioning of the Angels could have been the end of story, it wasn't. A subtle data trail had caught Nikky's attention and led him to uncover a small anomaly in the system—a barely detectable hack that had been so masterfully executed that if Nikky hadn't known better, he would have sworn he had done it himself.

The hack had been breathtakingly simple—just launch codes and a message. That and a group of coordinates that stubbornly resisted Nikky's every effort to decrypt. Frustrating as that final bit of missing information was, Nikky knew he was getting closer. Every hack had a signature—an unalterable nuance that could be detected by someone of Nikky's skill, no matter how hard the perpetrator tried to cover his tracks. Nikky had committed the signature to memory and set about trying to locate its presence elsewhere in the system.

Find the hacker, find the squadron, find my brother.

Now, in his office, eagerly watching the data flowing across his screen, Nikky knew he was close. The program he was running was designed to tell Nikky if there were any other traces of the Launch Code Hacker to be found. In a moment, he would have the results of his latest scan. If the hacker's signature was anywhere, Nikky could imagine tracking him down and following that trail to the Angels and to Drager.

Such fantasy was cut short when the scan abruptly ended. The results were not encouraging.

Nothing—not a trace of the hacker's signature anywhere in the system. At the bottom of the screen, a single cursor flashed insolently, mocking Nikky with its complete lack of information.

With a groan, Nikky slammed his head on his keyboard—hard. Normally immune to the effects of sleeplessness, he felt weariness now that bordered on despair. Maybe it really was a dead end. Perhaps he should shut down, go home, feed Louise, and sleep for about a year.

An insistent beep from the monitor suddenly clamored for his attention.

What now?

Nikky had not been expecting any kind of activity on his original data monitoring program, but he had kept it running simply out of habit. What he now saw stopped him short. Shaking away the fatigue, he refocused his concentration on this new development.

Someone was attempting an unauthorized query into the JenKore system right there, right in front of his eyes. For an infinitesimal moment, Nikky considered that it might even be Darik, but he just as quickly decided that Mason was neither that stupid, nor this skillful. Whoever the hacker was, he was extremely good. If not for Nikky's extra-curricular monitoring routines being up and running, the interloper might have been in and out without JenKore's sophisticated security protocols even detecting him.

Time to go to work.

Nikky's fingers flew on the keyboard. Satisfied that he had the proper lock-downs in place, he cracked his knuckles and typed a single phrase.

And just who might you be?

Reenergized, Nikky chuckled softly as his monitor revealed several quick attempts by the hacker to break off his connection. He leisurely typed another message.

Oops. Too late. You are locked and traced. Care to tell me what you are doing, or should I just retrieve that information as well?

He was rewarded by another flurry of activity on the monitor. Nikky waited patiently for the intruder to realize that he was locked down and triangulated, and that not even destroying his own workstation could prevent his discovery and exposure. If the hacker was as good as he seemed to be, Nikky anticipated that the realization would be coming right…about…now.

A response appeared on Nikky's screen.

Fine. Do your worst.

"Thought you'd never ask," Nikky murmured under his breath as he entered a new sequence. He smiled as he imagined the newcomer's workstation desperately trying to withhold the details of its user's intended infiltration but ultimately yielding to the persuasive power of Nikky's own program. His smile faded, however, when he saw the results on his screen.

Section Seven? What in the world is Section Seven?

With his right hand, Nikky activated another subroutine. Wanting to buy the program enough time, he used his left hand to hammer out a new message.

Okay, I can see you were performing a user trace on a weapon. Why risk that on the JenKore mainframe?

The response frame remained blank. The hacker, apparently, was done talking.

Oh, come on now. Don't be like that. I'll have your ID in a second or two. You might as well be sociable.

Nikky noticed one of the status indicators on his screen turn from red to green. The hacker was actually working his way out of the lockdown. From Nikky's perspective, that was impossible, but he would have to reason that out later. For now, he needed to accept the fact that his adversary was simply *that* good. Keying a new sequence, he watched with relief as the indicator returned to red status. He shook his head in admiration and sent another salvo.

Now, now, we'll have none of that. You're just making it harder on yourself—more evidence for the judge.

Nikky's subroutine continued to churn in the background, digging deeper into the hacker's own files. Meanwhile, Nikky's brain was engaged at even faster speeds. He thought he knew every system, every nuance of JenKore's expansive presence, but Section Seven was an enigma. He felt a familiar and not altogether unpleasant racing of his pulse as he realized that he was pursuing yet another mystery.

A flutter in the corner of the monitor caught his attention. A small cyan-bordered box revealed a series of intersecting polygons and platonic solids, shifting perspectives faster than most human eyes could detect. Nikky smiled again. The nuance was unmistakable, and he wasn't surprised. He had the hacker's signature.

I knew it was you! You're the Angel Launch Code Hacker! You're good. You're very good.

The text bar finally showed a response.

Great. You're a fan. I'm thrilled. So let's just say goodnight now and forget any of this happened.

Okay, now we're getting somewhere. Nikky kept his eye on the subroutine's progress as he entered his next transmission.

I don't think so. If you want to stay out of prison, I have some questions for you. Again, why are you risking a weapons trace on the JenKore mainframe?

The response was terse.

You're so smart—you tell me.

Nikky considered. Here he had a hacker breaking in to the JenKore system, ostensibly to track down a simple pistol ID, and according to Nikky's screen, the trace was leading to a Section Seven—a department about which Nikky knew absolutely nothing. He took a shot.

You followed the trail to "Section Seven"—what is that?

The response bar remained blank for several seconds. All the while, Nikky's subroutine continued its work. He tried again.

Do you really want to go to prison? Or worse? What is Section Seven, and why are you tracing a pistol back to it?

The text box still revealed no response from the hacker. Nikky was about ready to switch the entire affair over to his official workstation, have the intruder busted, and claim a nice little reward when the corner of his monitor fluttered again. As Nikky's program continued to burrow deep within the hacker's system, new tidbits of data scrolled across the screen— including a name Nikky did not recognize. He cocked his head and raised an eyebrow before typing his next question.

Baker? Who, or what, is Baker?

Though it was, of course, impossible to sense emotion through a screen, Nikky could almost feel his adversary's resignation as he came to grips with the fact that his most proprietary information was being sliced, dissected, and processed one byte at a time. Before long, Nikky would know everything anyway, and then what would be left to bargain with? The hacker's response appeared on the screen.

Baker…is my boss.

Nikky released a breath. *Finally, some honesty…and some progress.*

Then he's the one I want to talk to. Or would you rather we took this up with my bosses?

*   *   *

The meeting was scheduled for 7:00 a.m., Friday morning. Darik was certain that it would be his last day at JenKore. After another interminable wait at Clara's desk, the meeting itself would be brief. Jenkins would deliver a terse, condescending monologue that would begin with a list of Darik's recent failures and conclude with his immediate termination. While Darik wasn't exactly thrilled with the idea of having ten years of service to JenKore wiped away in an instant, he was partly relieved. His career, following a meteoric rise up the corporate ranks, had stalled the last two years, held back by his inability to halt an abrupt rise in M-2 "accidents." He now realized, of course, that he had been fed false information every step of the way. Ten years of long hours, little sleep, and even less of a social life, and how did JenKore repay him? By hand-picking him as some sort of sacrificial lamb. No—he would not grieve over leaving the company that had so callously betrayed him.

The pit currently residing in Darik's stomach, then, was not related to his impending meeting with Jenkins. Rather, he had spent every waking moment of the past week under constant worry that his and Nikky's corporate theft would be discovered. Since the break-in, he had passed his work days pretending to repair a perfectly healthy M-2 program while keeping an eye on the lift door across the office, waiting for armed personnel to storm through and nod in his direction. Or perhaps he would return to his apartment one night and find Graves once again waiting in the shadows. Or most likely, whatever it was, Darik wouldn't see it coming at all. Every minor detail of every day, however, had been disconcertingly normal, which only added to his paranoia. He couldn't afford to let his guard down even for a moment. Realistically, though, he knew that the situation was beyond his control. The cover-up and, consequently, his life were placed squarely in Nikky Weis's twitchy little hands—and that was the most frightening prospect of all.

To make matters worse, Darik couldn't help dwelling on the pointlessness of it all. A week's worth of anxious days and sleepless nights, and for what? What exactly had he discovered? Physical modification to the M-2 and a database that may or may not be a hit list—

223

information that was more or less worthless to him. The one piece of information that could have helped—the name of the person behind the M-2 redesign—was maddeningly absent from Nikky's hasty onsite download. Without that name, he had absolutely no leverage. Even if he could use the little evidence he had to prove that the M-2s were being modified and used in an illegal manner, what was he supposed to do, blackmail Jenkins?

Darik's stress level only increased as the week wore on. Sweating out day after day, hour after hour, alone in his office, he finally boiled over on Thursday morning, chewing out Liana over the improper formatting of a memo. He apologized soon after, but the incident made him realize that he desperately needed a change of scenery. He decided on an early lunch, hoping to clear his head—and take care of some unfinished business.

*   *   *

The Black Swan was unusually crowded for a Thursday, and Darik couldn't help scanning the busy dining area. He was under no illusion that he could actually detect some sort of plain-clothes agent, but looking kept him from feeling completely powerless. After a few passes, though, the faces of the middle-aged business types began blending together, and he gave up entirely. What was he expecting, anyway—a shady-looking man sitting alone in a corner? The anonymous crowd was making him feel more and more anxious, and Darik considered bailing on the lunch. He stayed only because leaving before his meal would have called even more attention to himself. And besides, he didn't want to further alarm Eliot, who had already taken notice of his nervous behavior.

"She's not working today."

Darik refocused on his friend across the table. "Huh?"

"Shari. That's who you're looking for, right? Well, don't bother—she doesn't work Thursdays."

"You've got her schedule memorized?" Darik asked incredulously. Eliot immediately turned defensive.

"Don't blame me for being observant. I just happen to take an interest in people. Shari doesn't work today or Sunday, and our lovely waitress today, Calli—short for Calliope—works Tuesdays, Thursdays, and every other Saturday. Calli's studying law, and she lives with her older sister, Lauralyn, in a little flat over in East Compton."

Darik arched an eyebrow. "That's actually rather impressive." He nodded at the waiter one table over. "And him, what's his story?"

Eliot frowned. "No idea."

Darik shook his head as they settled back into their chairs and opened their menus. Sitting in silence, Darik once again felt all the pent-up anxiety slowly rising in his chest. He hadn't even realized that his paranoia had momentarily disappeared, and neither could he now imagine it leaving again. Darik closed the menu, keeping his eyes lowered at the table.

"So…I might be in a little trouble."

"Yeah, I heard." Darik's heart jumped at Eliot's response. What exactly had he heard? His friend continued. "Word around the office is that you've got a meeting with Jenkins tomorrow. You think you're getting fired?"

"Yes." Darik's abruptness seemed to catch Eliot off guard. "But that's not what I'm talking about. I think I'm in *trouble*."

Eliot shifted in his chair, and Darik caught a glimmer of recognition in his eye. He leaned in.

"Eliot—look at me. Do you know something?"

Eliot's cheeks flushed red.

"Tell me."

His friend took a deep breath, held it, and then blurted out, "I should have told you as soon as it happened."

Darik didn't know whether he should be frightened or angry. "As soon as what happened?"

Eliot took a moment to collect his thoughts while Darik waited impatiently.

"Well, remember a few weeks ago when you decided to do a little field research on the M-2s?"

"Your idea, as I recall."

"Yeah. Well, right around that time, I was approached by a couple of guys."

"Who?"

"No clue. All I know is that they were dressed sharp and had valid JenKore IDs. They said they wanted me to keep an eye on you and report anything unusual."

Darik tilted his head slightly. "So, what, you were spying on me?"

Eliot nodded meekly. Darik's mind raced through the events of that week, and he recalled the unusual state of his office when he returned from Cacarus.

"You were in my office, weren't you."

Eliot's pitch raised as he began speaking more rapidly. "I didn't even know what I was supposed to be looking for. I just shuffled a few things around and left. Honest. I was the worst spy in history."

Darik rubbed his temple, attempting to reign in his anger. He was struggling to come up with a scenario in which he could give Eliot the benefit of the doubt.

"Why would you go through all that trouble? Did they threaten you?"

Eliot suddenly perked up and then slowly started nodding. "Yes...yes they did threaten me."

Darik's glare bore through Eliot's forehead. He stopped nodding.

"They paid me."

"Damn it, Eliot!"

"I felt guilty as soon as it happened. And I didn't even spend it on anything fun. A new espresso machine, I think. And it's defective—the drinks are too hot. I burn my tongue every time."

Darik felt a powerful urge to stand up and pummel his soon-to-be-former colleague, but he resisted, rationalizing that he needed to ascertain just how much Eliot knew. Both of their lives could depend on it.

"What did you tell them?" Darik asked through clenched teeth.

"Nothing—I swear to you," Eliot pleaded. "What could I say? I had absolutely no information. History's worst spy, remember?"

Darik studied Eliot, who, having completed his confession, had difficulty meeting his eyes. Watching his friend squirm, Darik felt his rage begin to subside. More than anything else, Eliot seemed pathetic—more worm than snake. Darik's gut told him that, despite the lies, Eliot had not placed him in any serious danger.

He let out a long sigh. "All right. I believe you."

Eliot looked up, his eyes widening. "Really?"

"Yeah, against my better judgment, but yeah."

Eliot exhaled loudly. "Thanks, buddy. You know, even if I had found something, there's no way I would've turned you in."

"Sure."

Their waitress, Calli, approached the table, but Darik shook his head and waved her away. Eliot watched her leave and then lowered his voice. "So, why all the trouble? What did you do?"

Darik stared in disbelief. "You've got to be kidding me."

"Oh, right. I suppose you wouldn't tell me."

They sat in an uncomfortable silence, Eliot idly fiddling with a salt shaker and Darik keeping his gaze fixed on his colleague. He originally had an ulterior motive for asking Eliot to lunch, but the confession seemed to have changed everything. How could he possibly trust him now? However, as Darik weighed his options, he realized that this new wrinkle in their relationship could work to his advantage. Eliot may not have been the ideal candidate, but with time quickly running out, Darik didn't have the luxury of being selective.

He cleared his throat.

"Listen to me. That was a rotten, selfish, cowardly thing you did. You jeopardized our friendship and my livelihood, and for what? A damn coffee maker."

"Espresso machine."

"Shut up. Now, here's how you're going to make it up to me." Darik pulled out a blue data chip. "See this? This is the cause of all the trouble. This is what those guys were hoping you'd find. And I'm going to give it to you."

Eliot appeared confused. Darik pressed on, purposefully denying him a chance to process the unexpected turn.

"Now, I know you're terribly curious, and the first thing you'll do after we leave is open it. Don't bother. It's locked." When Nikky had given the chip to Darik, he had assured him multiple times that the encryption was impenetrable. "If things take a bad turn, you're going to receive a password that unlocks it. And if that happens, I'm counting on you to release the information to the public."

Darik pushed the chip over to Eliot, who tentatively picked it up. He looked back up, his eyes moistening. His voice trembled as he spoke.

"I can't believe after everything I did that you'd trust me with this."

"I absolutely do not trust you." Eliot blinked away a tear while Darik continued. "But if something happens, I know you're the best hope for getting this information out. I'm counting on you."

Eliot recomposed himself. "I won't let you down," he said, sliding the chip into his pocket.

Darik had his doubts, but, again, his options were limited. Satisfied with Eliot's seemingly genuine response, he reached into his coat and tossed a credit chip on the table to cover the tip.

"Goodbye, Eliot."

A breath caught in Eliot's throat. It seemed to dawn on him that this was potentially the last time they would ever see each other.

"Hey, you can't leave yet."

Darik raised his brow as Eliot scrambled for a reason.

"You haven't eaten anything."

Darik kicked his chair back. "I'll grab a sandwich at the Tower."

"Wait—this is your last full day of work, right? That's cause for celebration."

Before Darik could respond, Eliot reached out and grabbed their passing waitress by the arm.

"Calli, my dear. Bring us your finest, most expensive bottle of Vorinian."

Calli stooped down and whispered something to Eliot, whose eyes suddenly widened. He turned away from the table and whispered, "Well, how much is your *second* finest bottle?"

Darik fought hard to suppress a grin as he settled back into his chair and reopened the menu.

*   *   *

"That's far enough. Have a seat."

Nikky held a hand in front of his eyes in a futile attempt to shield them from the blinding light. While he had anticipated this sort of treatment, experiencing the actual reality of it played havoc on his already overtaxed nervous system. Down each darkened corridor, through each strange doorway, his fight or flight instinct was screaming—mostly for flight. Still, he had to see the situation through to its conclusion. What he was beginning to suspect was too horrifying, and his mission—if he could call it that—was too important. And, after all, this meeting had been *his* idea.

Squinting between his fingers, Nikky could just make out the outline of a single chair, placed in the middle of the seemingly empty room. The three high-intensity beacons assaulting him from the far wall guaranteed that he would see little else.

Here we go again, he thought. *This guy must get his decorating advice from Mason.*

He made his way unsteadily to the chair and sat down as the voice continued.

"I'm sure you know what this is." A small black device about the size of a handpod slid across the floor, coming to a rest between his feet. "And I'm also sure you won't have a problem setting my mind at ease."

Setting his *mind at ease? What about* my *mind?*

Nikky bent over, picking up the device. As he suspected, it was a simple DNA scanner. Slipping it over a finger would allow a bloodless analysis, confirming his identity. He complied and slid the scanner back into the darkness beyond the lights.

"I...I don't suppose you'd be willing to return the favor?"

"We both know that isn't going to happen." A silence followed as Nikky imagined his host to be reading the scan results. Seemingly satisfied, the voice relaxed, and Nikky was able to detect a trace of southern drawl. "So, I know that you're Nikky Weis, and no, you're not going to find out who I am."

Two of the beacons winked out, considerably reducing the strain on Nikky's eyes. As his pupils adjusted, he could now detect a man's form, seated just behind the final light, in a chair that looked much more comfortable than Nikky's. A larger looking figure, he wore dark clothes and a wide-brimmed cowboy hat that worked with the intense beacon to shadow his face.

"But, for the purposes of this meeting, you can call me *Baker*."

Nikky nodded. The hacker he had blackmailed had apparently kept his word. Friend or foe, this *Baker* was the missing link in a chain that he hoped would lead him to his brother.

Baker went on. "I appreciate you not busting my man when you caught him in your system over there. I have to say, he's done a lot of work for me, and the young fellah's never run into a buzz saw like you. He was sure you were going to turn him over to the Sec-goons." Baker's voice dropped a couple of tones. "But then, that was never really your intention, was it."

There was no reason for Nikky to be coy. "No, it wasn't. I'm only interested in finding my brother."

"Your *step*brother, you mean, right, son?"

Baker had apparently done his homework. For a man who apparently employed people who could hack UCN launch codes, it must have been a relatively simple matter to cross-reference old census data, confirming who Nikky was and who he was looking for.

"Yes, my stepbrother," Nikky swallowed. Baker already knew everything, but saying the name still felt like a risk—a jump of faith into this transaction from which there was no turning back. He cleared his throat and continued mechanically. "Drager St. James, Flight Sergeant, formerly United Coalition Navy. Last known assignment: 501st Fighter Wing, 714th Fighter Squadron—a.k.a. the "Angels.""

Nikky watched the man bring his elbows to the arms of his chair, resting his chin on folded hands. He seemed to be regarding Nikky, sizing him up before deciding how to proceed. Nikky broke the silence.

"Do you know him?"

Baker took a deep breath. "No, son. I don't know him personally. But I know who he is. You might say that I'm a friend of his captain."

"Do you know if he's all right? Is he alive?"

"He's alive, at least for now. As far as being all right, I guess he's as fine as you could expect—for an interstellar fugitive."

Nikky felt a rush of emotion. For a decade, his stepbrother had been dead. His mother had believed it, and he had believed her. The news had devastated him, driving him further into his work, further into himself. Without realizing it, he had made a practical decision to never share meaningful interaction with other people again, if he could help it. And for the most part, he had succeeded. Nikky didn't need people. He would watch them, study them, eavesdrop on their business and social affairs, but he would never, *never*, care about them again.

All of this had changed when he saw Drager listed among the living on that JenKore list. But that "official" information was somehow not as convincing as hearing this man he didn't even know tell him that fact in person. The spark of hope flamed into reality, and with it, a renewed sense of urgency. With his recent research, Nikky had begun to put disparate pieces of information together, and he knew that a hit list, as bad as that was, was not even the most terrifying danger that Drager and his surviving squadron were facing. He leaned forward, his eyes watering from emotion as much as from the remaining spotlight.

"Do you know where he is?"

"I might."

"Will you tell me?"

"No."

Nikky couldn't believe it. Who *was* this guy? What kind of game was he playing?

"You don't understand," Nikky pleaded. "He's in danger. They're all in danger! More danger than even you could know. If I can find him—if I can get word to them…"

Baker's voice softened. "No, son, it's you who doesn't understand. You can't know his location. No one can. You wouldn't want to betray him. You would never intend to give out that information, but if you were compromised, well, there are *ways* to extract it."

The implication was clear, and Nikky had to reconsider his position. He put his head down, rubbing his eyes. With Baker's dark reference, the echo feed that had begun this entire mess for Nikky—a feed that he had finally managed to compile in its entirety—rushed unbidden into his mind. He had been able to solve the visual imagery from the start, and even though it only showed the violence from the perpetrator's point of view, it was enough to turn the stomach of anyone with a conscience. But it was the audio that had proven the most challenging—and the most terrifying. In order to decipher the sound file, Nikky had fought to extract one recognizable language track from literally thousands of layered, guttural utterances—each one eerily familiar but nightmarishly out of the reach of his understanding. When he finally isolated the standard language element and fed it through with the visual—when he finally knew what the murderer was *saying*—it all came together. The target list, the M-2 mods, the echo—it had all suddenly made sense. Nikky knew what these people—these forces—were capable of. And with that knowledge, he doubted that he would be able to withstand even the most casual of interrogations. No, Baker was right. Nikky couldn't know the location of Drager and his friends. He simply didn't trust himself. He didn't know who to trust.

Nikky lifted his head again. Through the blinding mix of light and shade, he tried to look Baker in the eyes.

"Please. There's got to be something we can do."

Baker moved for the first time, leaning forward, his features almost entering the light. "I want to help, son. I think I *can* help. But I have to know everything that you know."

Nikky reached into his pocket, pulling out a data chip—one of only two copies in existence, the other belonging to Mason. Up to this point, he hadn't been sure if he would use it or not. He had kept the chip hidden, actually cloaked from sec-scans, in a tiny diverter sleeve he had painstakingly sewn into his jacket lining. It was all there, the M-2 mods, the target list, and of course, the terrifying echo feed. The information was explosive—and dangerous—but Baker was right. To have any chance at helping, he had to know everything. Nikky bent down and slid the chip across the floor.

"Now, you do."

"Thanks, kid. I'll do what I can."

The room went completely dark.

*   *   *

"Captain, may I speak with you?"

Dex had been dreading this moment. In fact, since the Milk Run, he had done everything he could to steer clear of the main hanger in a vain attempt to avoid the very conversation he was about to have. Late for a meeting, he had tried to skirt unseen across the hanger floor, using Hagen's and Seltrice's Hornets as barriers. Almost in the clear, he had taken a furtive glance around the landing gear of Hagen's craft, ready to make a final push for the side door, when he heard the voice behind him. Exhaling, he turned to face Flight Sergeant Drager St. James.

"What can I do for you, Sergeant?" Dex fully expected—and deserved, to his thinking—a matronly scolding from the stocky mechanic. After all, this was the second straight mission from which Dex had returned with a badly shot up Hornet. Dex knew how hard Drager and his crew worked, with minimal manpower and supplies, to keep the entire squadron flight worthy. If the captain himself kept bringing back a damaged bird and adding to the sergeant's already impossible workload, Dex thought, then let the chastisement begin.

Usually, Drager would let him off with some tongue-clucking and a few comments about taking better care of his equipment. If the damage were bad enough—and it certainly was in this case—he would throw in a few unsolicited suggestions for remedial flight training and possibly a review of basic defensive maneuvers.

But not this time. Dex detected a guarded, almost haunted look in the little sergeant's eyes.

"Captain, after your return I began working on your Hornet. I had the shields and launchers back up and was going to start on the rear cannons."

Dex simply nodded, knowing from past experience that Drager would find his own way around to the point.

"I discovered that the cannons were still working—it was the targeting sequence that was malfunctioning. Naturally, the trace led back to the main sensor and comm bus. It was functional, but pretty much hanging by a thread, application-wise. You were fortunate to have lights at all after that drubbing."

Dex resisted an urge to check his chrono. He knew most of this information from reading the emergency systems display during the mission and didn't need to be reminded. He was already running late, but then, Drager wasn't the type to make idle conversation. He was heading somewhere with this.

Drager continued. "I didn't want to take any chances with it, so I decided the best approach would be to re-image the entire bus and then push the configuration files from a known working unit."

Dex saw Drager swallow and tilt his head in the direction of Adahn's Hornet. "The closest ship belonged to Officer Manasser."

"Okay, Sergeant, I'm following you so far," Dex said. "What's the problem?"

Drager responded by leading Dex over to Adahn's ship. "Here, have a look." He activated a diagnostic tool, its fibroc cables still snaking into the Hornet's cockpit. On the display, Dex watched a series of test patterns rapidly oscillating, concentric shapes turning with points intersecting at seemingly random intervals. At the bottom of the display, a line of numbers grew and shrank with the progress of the test.

"There!" Drager pointed at the display. "Did you see it?"

Dex hadn't. Flight Systems Topology and Diagnostics, while required, had not been his favorite class at the academy. He shrugged. "You're going to have to enlighten me, Drager."

The mechanic kept his eyes glued to the display. "We'll have to wait for it to come around again. Wait for it…" Drager's head swayed back and forth, in time to the display's oscillations, and a tuneless melody whistled between his teeth, providing a soundtrack to the silent data. "Very soon now…There!"

He punched a button on the tool, and the display froze. "Right there, Captain. Do you see what I mean?"

Dex could see it now. A delay, only micro-seconds long, but definitely out of normal specs, was affecting Adahn's sensor and communications module at regular intervals.

"That's odd. What's causing it?"

Drager looked down, his expression one of self-recrimination. "That's the problem. I don't know. It's like there's a virus—a subroutine or something—running inside the unit, but I can't find it. I've been through the entire system several times. It's like I can see the effect of it—you can see the delay right there, yourself—but I can't find the cause. Of course, I didn't send this on to your Hornet. I used Commander Lebrian's to configure yours—his checked out clean. In fact, they all checked out clean…except for this one."

Dex frowned. "What are you saying?"

Drager bought himself up to his full height. He was a full head shorter than Dex, but his squared shoulders and serious, remorseful expression added gravity to his words.

"Captain, I've never seen this anomaly before, but I've never actually *looked* for it before. I was thinking…if this delay was present in Officer Manasser's system during the Erebus mission, when Lieutenant Commanders Alderson and Simmons were lost, then…"

Dex remembered the Erebus encounter again. He wished he could forget. The high-risk, high-reward mission, with the Raven ferrying supplies back and forth while the rest of the squadron covered the supply dump, had knowingly left the Angels patrolling too long in one location, and the inevitable attack had come. Facing only a single flight of Marauders, the Angels should have handled them easily, but Scot and Adahn's Hornets had strayed inexplicably out of formation, leaving enough of a gap for the enemy fighters to exploit. Scot had been disabled by the initial barrage, and Adahn had seemingly been too far out of range to take action. The Marauders had knifed through the defenses, killing Fran and Kevan, destroying their Hornets before the remaining Angels could return fire.

Drager looked up at Dex, his eyes brimming with tears. "Captain, *this* Hornet was in the best position to respond. If there was even the tiniest delay—a glitch I should have prevented—then I must take full responsibility for the loss of our two pilots."

"Drager." Dex placed a hand on the little sergeant's shoulder. He smiled as reassuringly as he could, but inside his mind was reeling. "We ran the full debrief—many times. No one could have saved Smiley and Aces. You have no way of knowing if that delay was there already or not, but even with a fully functional fighter, Adahn couldn't have gotten to them in time."

"But, still—"

"Flight Sergeant St. James!" Drager snapped to attention as Dex adopted his most authoritative tone. "Hear me on this. It was *not* your fault. Are we clear?"

"Yes, sir."

"You will cease speculation on what you may or may not have done in the past and concentrate on the task at hand. Do you understand?"

"Yes, sir."

Dex nodded curtly. He had worked with Drager St. James for years. He knew the mechanic's extraordinary abilities and was certain that he had not been in any way negligent in his duties. He also knew that what Drager needed now was activity, to focus not on his own doubt and remorse, but on solving the mechanical or technical mystery that still remained. And Dex certainly needed an answer to that mystery.

"Drager, I need you to find that glitch. Find out what is causing it and how it got there. Contact Ronnie Wilco and get him down here. Go over Officer Manasser's Hornet from nose to tail—I want that bird fixed. Got it?"

"Yes, sir. Thank you, sir."

"And Sergeant," Dex said, "if you and Ronnie discover *anything* out of the ordinary on that Hornet—if this is more than a random glitch— report it to me immediately."

Drager saluted and went back to his work. Dex remained for a moment, staring at Adahn's Hornet and hating the direction his thoughts were taking. He placed a hand on the fuselage and closed his eyes, as if willing the craft to release its secrets. He thought of Fran and Kevan—the memory of their vaporized fighters once again rushing unbidden into his mind. His jaw set as he counted the number of times mission intel seemed to have leaked, with the enemy appearing out of nowhere.

He considered ordering the fighter and its pilot grounded immediately, then decided against it. He would wait to find out what Drager and Ronnie would discover, then deal with the problem decisively. If it was a simple glitch in the comm system, they would repair it. But if it ended up being anything else—.

Dex spun on his heel and abruptly left the hanger. If it was anything else, then God help the person behind it.

Chapter 19

Clara, who normally guarded her superior's door with the ferocity of a three-headed hound, had actually been *civil* to Darik. It was at that moment that he knew he was in real trouble. Expecting the worst from the caustic secretary, he had arrived at 6:50 a.m.—a full ten minutes early for what would likely be his termination meeting with Mr. Jenkins. But Clara, rather than giving him the Cerberus routine, had greeted him with sympathetic eyes, her normally razor-tinged voice almost tender as she informed him that Mr. Jenkins was ready. Then she had called him "Honey." Darik shuddered at the memory.

Jenkins waited behind his expansive desk. Every element of the office was just as Darik had last seen it weeks earlier. The plush white carpet, the dark Riksenian wood, the elaborate décor, the stifling heat, and the sculpture—*that* sculpture. Darik tore his gaze away from it and faced his employer.

"Sit down, Mr. Mason."

Darik could not recall—not once, not *ever*—being invited to sit during a meeting with Jenkins. Trying to stay calm, he dropped as casually as he could manage into a chair in front of the ivory-inlaid desk. The soft cushion, made from the tanned flesh of some exotic beast, gave way under his weight, effectively positioning him on a plane several inches below that of his superior. Darik had no doubt whatsoever that the effect was intentional. Folding his hands on his lap, he braced for impact.

Jenkins drummed his fingers on the desktop, his neatly trimmed nails clicking like horse hooves.

"The last time we spoke, Mr. Mason, I was under the impression that we had an understanding. Was I incorrect in that assumption?"

"Sir?"

"I do not like to repeat myself, Mr. Mason. Was I somehow mistaken about your commitment to our agreement—your dedication and loyalty to this organization?"

Darik involuntarily squeezed his interlaced fingers tighter. What did Jenkins know? There was no doubt in his mind that he was going to be fired, but if Jenkins knew about his and Nikky's recent espionage, unemployment was just the beginning of his peril.

"I…I don't think so, sir."

"Do you even recall our previous conversation?"

"Yes, sir. My assignment was to determine the cause of M-2 mining unit malfunctions and take whatever steps necessary to ensure their continued operation."

"And exactly *what* progress have you achieved toward that objective?"

Darik swallowed. What could he tell this man? That his side trip to Cacarus had shown that the very units he was accused of losing in the field had never actually arrived at their assigned destination? That he and Nikky had discovered, beyond any doubt, that the M-2s were being modified well beyond any intended design specs? That while he and Nikky were crawling around uncovering this information, they had also found a list that gave every impression that JenKore was somehow involved in the location and termination of Coalition citizens? Darik felt that anything he could offer at this point would only make his situation more precarious. Without knowing whether Jenkins had a clue as to his extra-curricular activities, he didn't know how to answer.

He didn't have to. Jenkins was on a roll.

"Nothing! Absolutely no progress! Those machines represent the single most substantial investment in the entire JenKore group, and you had but one responsibility—one!—discover the reason for their failures. I supply you unlimited resources to accomplish your task, and what do you do with that latitude? You disappear for days at a time with no discernible accountability, and you end up back here with absolutely no results— nothing to show in return for the trust I placed in you. Just what the hell have you been up to, Mason?"

A sense of rage began to build within Darik, gradually replacing the panic he had been feeling. Whether it was the oppressive heat, his internal turmoil, or a combination of both, Darik found his breath coming in shorter gasps.

"I asked you a question, Mr. Mason."

Darik's vision narrowed. He could feel his heart beating faster as the top of Jenkins's desk seemed to elongate and shorten before his eyes. In the back of his mind, Darik knew that the effect was only an illusion brought on by his heightened stress, but the weird image of Jenkins coming in and out of focus, first close, then far, brought on a sickening feeling of vertigo. Obviously, Jenkins did not seem affected by the phenomenon. His voice was as cold as the vacuum of space.

"I expect an answer."

"Fine!" The words exploded from Darik's mouth before he even realized they were forming. "You want an answer? Here's your answer! I've been *working*! Day and night, I've been working on this stupid problem. I haven't slept, I haven't rested—I've been killing myself for this job. You say you gave me latitude. Ha! You can't sit there and say you gave me latitude and then bust my ass for actually using it. And unlimited resources? Are you kidding? I was blocked at every point!"

Something wasn't right. Darik's instincts were screaming to him that Jenkins should be reacting differently to his outburst. The man simply did not tolerate dissension of any kind, least of all from sniveling junior executives. Jenkins should have been standing Darik down, berating him into cowed submission. Instead, the JenKore CEO just sat there, listening with a smug, almost pleased expression on his face. Inside, Darik's better judgment was pleading with him to just shut the hell up.

He ignored that judgment, too wound up to hold back the weeks of pent-up frustration that continued to pour out.

"You can't sit there and accuse me of not doing my job when the very structure of the assignment has insurmountable barriers at every step!" Darik actually pounded the arm rests of the ridiculous chair. "I needed information, it was my job to gather that information, and you know what I've realized—there *was* no information! I went through every official channel! All I found were dead ends—stone silence every time! I mean, I wouldn't know *anything* if Nikky and I hadn't…"

His voice trailed off like a tired siren. *Crap.*

"What was that, Mr. Mason?"

Darik drew a ragged breath. "Nothing. I'm sorry."

"Don't apologize." Jenkins actually smiled as he rose from his seat, coming around the desk to rest on the corner just to Darik's left, placing himself in even closer proximity, and increasing Darik's discomfort considerably. "You've been frustrated, haven't you."

No kidding.

"Yes," Darik responded honestly.

"And you hate me, don't you, Mr. Mason."

Darik side-stepped the comment. "I just want to know what's going on, that's all."

Jenkins leaned forward, an uncharacteristic bit of sweat beginning to glisten beneath his short-cropped silver hair. "All in good time, Darik, all in good time. When you first started here at JenKore, we knew you had potential. That's why we put you on the M-2 project in the first place."

What in the world was *this*? By all accounts, the meeting should have been over by this point, with Darik out on his rear. No job, no salary. His Perseus shuttle, repossessed. The mid-town apartment, history. Everything he had worked for, gone. That was the only future Darik had been able to envision walking into Jenkins's office. But why was Jenkins *complimenting* him? Was there any chance at all that he was going to be able to keep his job? More likely, Jenkins was simply treating him like the wounded mouse he was, playfully dragging out his demise as long as possible, or at least until it ceased being entertaining.

Darik couldn't look into those pale eyes. Turning his head to the right, his gaze came to rest on the sculpture occupying the space next to the desk. During their last meeting, Jenkins had referred to it as an idol of some sort—a "Travarian god," he recalled. At that time, its violent, incongruous angles and weirdly pulsating aura had dredged up within Darik a mix of feelings, ranging from sensual pleasure to abject horror. Now, compared to Jenkins's disconcerting countenance, it offered the only comfort he could find in the airless room. Darik continued to focus on the captivating piece as his employer continued.

"You're ambitious, Darik. You always have been. That's why these latest setbacks have been so difficult for you."

Darik had to admit to himself that at least that part of Jenkins's lecture was true. His memory drifted back, unbidden, to a conversation he'd had with Eliot a few years earlier. At the time, Darik had boasted that he would make vice president before he was thirty. He had told Eliot that the reason he would rise faster was because he, Darik, was willing to do anything— whatever it would take—to climb the ladder, while his good friend seemed perfectly content to coast along, enjoying the ride. Since then, Darik's career had floundered while everything Eliot had touched turned to gold. He suddenly realized how Eliot's success, in light of his own stagnation, had always secretly infuriated him.

"It's not too late, Darik. You can still resurrect your career. You can still demonstrate to me the brilliance I first saw in you."

The bluish-black tines on the idol pulsed as Darik considered Jenkins's words. The dread he had been experiencing leading up to this meeting began to dissipate, leaving room for a glimmer of hope—and something more.

"You can have everything you ever dreamed of, Darik. The success…the prestige…the power. Is that what you want?"

It is.

"But you are going to have to make some changes, Mr. Mason—some decisions. You might *believe* you have been committed to this cause, to this organization, but there is another level of performance, of dedication. A level you haven't yet reached. Look at me!"

At the command, more growled than spoken, Darik involuntarily turned his head. Looking into Jenkins's face, he couldn't determine if the flashing eyes before him had actually turned cobalt-blue or if they were merely reflecting the pulsating colors emanating from the idol.

"You were to report to me your *complete* findings on the M-2 project, Mr. Mason. I do not believe you have done so. So now I ask you, what *exactly* do you know?"

Darik hesitated, a nearly audible humming sound growing in the right side of his skull.

"Do you *want* to succeed, Darik? Do you want to rise to the top of this company?"

Yes.

The humming gradually coalesced into subtle voices—distant and unrecognizable.

Yes.

"Y…yes." Darik heard the weakness in his own voice.

"Answer my question. Do your job. What have you discovered regarding the M-2 units?"

Don't answer! Leave! Now!

Another voice? Darik closed his eyes, shaking his head violently. Opening them again, he stared once again into the face of his employer. Jenkins's mouth was moving, but his voice seemed to be coming from the

241

other side of the desk, mixing with the cacophony of utterances now flowing from the sculpture.

What do you want, Darik? What do you really want? You won't have this chance again. You have to decide—now!

Darik knew what he wanted. He knew what he had always wanted. And if it were possible, he would still have it. He bowed his head.

"We…uh, *I* found out the units are being modified—beyond anything in the official specs. For what purpose, I don't know."

"Is that all?"

"No…I found a list—a list of people."

"*People?*" Jenkins and the voices breathed.

Darik looked up again. "A list of targets, actually. Many of them had already been terminated."

The idol pulsed. Darik felt a palpable sensation of pleasure. He shivered.

"Do you know who those people are?"

At the moment, Darik found that he really didn't care.

"No, not really."

Jenkins leaned in even closer. A bead of sweat fell from his forehead into Darik's lap. "They are criminals…followers of *Christ*."

The idol screamed. Darik felt a quick twinge, a twisting in his stomach. A twenty-year-old memory, and an anger he thought he had left far behind, welled up inside him. Then, he felt nothing.

"So?" The indifference in his own voice surprised him.

"So they are enemies of the state. They are enemies of this organization. And if you accept this promotion, Mr. Mason, they are *your* enemies as well."

Something stirred again inside Darik, replacing the emptiness from a moment before.

"Wait…promotion?" Darik fought to regain control of his senses. As the idol continued to oscillate to his right and Jenkins closed in from the left, the bizarre sounds and voices seemed to be coming from every corner of the office at once. He couldn't be sure what he was hearing.

Promotion.

He struggled to separate one voice—Jenkins's voice, he thought—from the others.

Inner circle…total authority…M-2/A…assassins…

Darik's head swam. He didn't know if his eyes were open but found he couldn't see. He heard the voices mention an obscene salary and his heart raced.

Tour the Bellona installation...witness their capabilities firsthand...

He could no longer feel the chair. He wasn't sure he was even in the office anymore.

Enhance them...indestructible...carry out their directive...

He tried to speak but could not. His throat felt like it was in a vise.

Power...success...wealth beyond measure...

He wanted to scream his answer, but the sound would not come. He felt himself descending, deeper and deeper into a dark, terrifying, yet mesmerizing abyss.

Or death—the choice is yours.

He felt the word forming deep within his chest. His constricted windpipe loosened, and he prepared to answer with force and confidence. Instead, he barely managed a whisper.

"Yes."

Darik opened his eyes. What was he doing on the floor? He had no idea how long he had been there. Jenkins was still seated at the corner of the desk, making no effort to help him up. As Darik struggled to his feet, Jenkins rose as well, finally extending a hand for Darik to shake.

"Congratulations, Mr. Mason." Only his voice remained—the idol was motionless and silent. "You are our new vice president in charge of the entire M-2/A initiative. Do not let me down."

Darik took the offered hand. It felt metallic and cold.

"I won't," he said. "You can count on me." He turned and left Jenkins's office. He walked deliberately down the hall, striding past several checkpoints with a renewed authority and sense of purpose. In the lift, he found himself considering a move to a new flat he had his eye on— way too expensive at his old salary but quite befitting of his new status. In the lobby, Darik threw back his shoulders and left the Tower, eager to begin his trip to the Bellona station to inspect his M-2/As.

And it was night.

Chapter 20

Dex was startled from a restless sleep—a comm request was demanding his attention. Staggering to his desk, he activated the console, opening the waiting message. It was from Baker.

NEW INFORMATION. INITIATE CONTACT IMMEDIATELY.

Dex frowned. These two-way conversations were becoming a habit—a dangerous habit, considering the security concerns on both ends of the communication. Keying the proper sequence, he tried to imagine what would possibly cause Baker to solicit contact again so soon. Did he have information on the side arm trace already? Whatever it was, Dex decided, it had to be really important. Fighting a yawn, he glanced at his chrono—0400. Without knowing Baker's location on Earth, he couldn't figure out what time it was there, and he was far too exhausted to attempt the calculations, even if he did know.

The comm chirped and Baker's intentionally distorted image instantly appeared on the screen.

"Dex, I've got news, son."

No preliminaries, no security questions. This had to be urgent. Stealing a quick look at the voice print indicator, Dex verified Baker's identity as much as possible, drew a quick breath, and answered.

"All right. I'm secure on this end. What have you got?"

Baker didn't waste a moment. "I've got the answer to who's been chasing you all this time."

Dex was puzzled. "I didn't think that was a mystery. UCN policy is pretty clear regarding desertion and theft of government property."

"That's just it, kid. I don't think the UCN has been sending out all those Marauders. Now don't get me wrong, I'm sure the Navy brass still wants you folks in a bad way, but I don't think they're expending the resources we thought they were."

"I'm not sure that I'm following you."

"Think about it, Dex. In the two years you've been out there, you've had at least a half-dozen engagements with Marauders, right? How many of those encounters involved actual Navy pilots?"

Dex paused to consider. "Well, none so far. All of the ships have been unmanned."

"And have you noticed anything unusual about those unmanned ships?"

Dex remembered his and Jani's recent encounter with four Marauders in the Vorina system.

"Yeah, the same problem as always—we have yet to spot a control ship. We can't figure out how they've overcome the lag time between remote operator and fighter. They must've made some pretty significant upgrades that we don't know about."

"They have, but it's not remote control upgrades, my boy. The upgrades have been to the *pilots*."

"But we just said there weren't any pilots in the Marauders."

"There weren't any *human* pilots, Dex. Someone has been sticking M-2s in the cockpits of those buckets."

Dex digested this information. It *did* answer a lot of questions. "So the UCN has been modifying M-2s into combat pilots?"

"I don't think so, kid. All of my intel says that the military won't get anywhere near crossing a line like that…again."

Baker had a point. Sending machine pilots into combat against humans violated their programming at the most basic level. It was one thing to send a drone, with a human being somewhere making the actual decisions and sending instructions. It was entirely another matter to program a separate, artificial intelligence to seek out and to kill. That was far too much autonomy to grant to a soulless machine—history had proven the consequences for such recklessness. Dex found himself rethinking the situation, doubting that the UCN—at least the UCN *he* remembered— would take that chance no matter how much they wanted to find and capture the Angels.

"Okay, I see your point. Where are you going with this?"

Baker continued. "Here's what I've been able to find out. The UCN is *not* sending M-2 piloted Marauders after you people, but *somebody* is— somebody with enough access and ability to disable their fail-safes."

"And you know who that is?"

"Yeah, Dex, I do. It's JenKore."

"JenKore? The manufacturer? Why? What's their stake in this?"

"I'll give you my theory on that in a second, but right now you need to know that those clunky pilot mods are the *least* of your concerns."

Dex recalled the sneak attacks, the ships damaged, the pilots lost. Now, Baker was saying that modified M-2s had been at the controls. The M-2—a machine that never tired, never needed to sleep or eat, and if destroyed, could be replaced by a dozen more to continue pursuing the Angels indefinitely—what could be more menacing than that?

Baker leaned forward in the monitor. "JenKore's been reprogramming the pilots, working outside of the laws, making it possible for them to hunt you guys. I've got solid proof of that. But it gets worse, Dex, *much* worse."

"Okay, Baker, you've got my attention. What's going on?"

Baker drew a breath before continuing. "They didn't stop at reprogramming a few pilots. They've got another entire line out there—a whole new modification—and I've got to tell you, son, from what I've been able to gather, compared to these new units, those pilot mods you've been wasting out there are child's play. These new M-2s are killing machines, Dex. They're nearly indestructible, and they seem to have only one purpose."

Dex felt a sense of foreboding. "I think I can guess…"

Baker confirmed his suspicion. "They're programmed to hunt you down and kill you, son—and not just your squadron, and not just the colony. We found a list of every Christian out there—every soul that didn't return under Prop 413—and every one of them is targeted. It's your faith, Dex. JenKore is coming after you because of your faith."

Dex was beginning to feel light-headed. He tried to focus, tried to make sense of such madness. "I don't understand. Why JenKore? I can see the UCN wanting to track us down, to charge us with treason, but why would a contractor get involved in a *religious* conflict?"

"All I know, kid, is that *someone* pretty high up their corporate chain of command has it in for you folks—bad enough to violate every robotic law since the Asimov Accords. Understand, Dex, this doesn't seem to be a UCN black-ops deal. Trust me, I would know by now if it were. JenKore is in deep. They may have sympathizers in the military, but they are doing this on their own. From what I can gather, there's already an army of those monsters, and they're modifying more—which tells me that once they finish hunting down all the Christians out there, they could be gearing up to do the same job here on Earth. There's another war coming, Dex, and I don't think your old friends in the UCN even see it coming, or would be inclined to stop it if they did."

Dex considered all of this. Baker was usually reliable, but so much of this just didn't make sense. Why would a successful military and domestic supplier like JenKore risk so much just to hunt down people of faith? The situation on Earth had cooled considerably in the three years since Prop 413. Once the initial crisis had passed, the camps had been closed, and Terran Christians were even beginning to meet in churches again. The only ones still considered to be fugitives were those who had defied the order to return in the first place. There had even been talk in the Terran Council of a new amnesty program—excluding, of course, more notorious groups like the Angels.

"I don't know, Baker. It sounds like a lot of speculation to me. I'm going to need to see some proof."

Baker sighed. "Yeah, I was afraid you would." His hand moved to key a sequence on his desktop. "I'm sending you a data burst. It contains a holo I got my hands on. You can open and view it on your end, but I have to warn you, son. It's pretty graphic, even for a military man like yourself."

After a short pause, a file icon flashed over Dex's workspace. Touching the file, Dex opened its contents. The holo feed was grainy but clear enough to watch. It appeared to have been originally encrypted and then decoded by some means Dex couldn't hope to understand.

The holo moved forward from a single point of view. From the data running across the bottom—some familiar, some not—Dex reasoned that he was observing a recon stream, possibly from an M-2.

Baker's next comment confirmed his conclusion. "This was recorded by one of those new bastards. Brace yourself, kid."

The holo showed dimly illuminated hallways gliding by with a smoothness that was consistent with the signature motion of M-2 units. The machine did not appear to be hurrying, but something in the manner in which it turned each succeeding corner betrayed a certain sense of purpose. One part of the display at the bottom of the feed showed a measure of distance, decreasing steadily. The M-2 was in pursuit of a moving objective somewhere in front of it.

The holo turned a corner, and Dex could see a human figure staggering in the distance. As the M-2 drew closer, Dex could make out the image of a man, wounded in his side and frantically attempting to key a sequence into a closed door that barred his escape. The distance to the man closed as he turned to face his pursuer.

Dex caught his breath, his eyes widening in recognition. His stomach tightened—he *knew* this man. Despite the poor lighting and grainy holo, the face was clear as day. It was a face he had last seen on Earth, the night Prop 413 was ratified. It was the face of a man who had fled Earth, forsaking his life and career in order to keep his family safe from the coming persecution. It was the face of his best friend, Jonathan "Bulldog" Buhl.

In the holo, he saw Jon draw a weapon and fire. The bolt ricocheted away—the holo didn't so much as flicker.

Dex could see that Jon could barely lift his arm, but he fired once more. At this point, the holo rapidly closed the distance to his friend. Without warning, a thin pointed rod of shining metal extended with lightning speed from the left side of the holo, undoubtedly protruding from an appendage on the M-2. Dex cringed as the rod pierced Jon's shoulder beneath the collarbone. He watched in horror as his best friend—the only close friend he'd ever really had—was lifted, groaning in agony, from the ground.

For the first time in the holo, the M-2 spoke. While clearly mechanical, the voice was deeper, more multi-layered than any Dex had ever heard, like thousands of voices mixed as one.

You are a Christian, the monster intoned.

Jon struggled to reply. "Y…yes," he answered.

You cling to an imaginary god and a dead religion.

The holo showed the rod quivering, sending new spasms through its victim. Jon somehow gathered strength to respond.

"I…I believe in God the Father Almighty, maker of heaven and earth," he gasped. "I believe in Jesus Christ, His only begotten—"

Will you renounce your faith in exchange for your life?

Dex's fingernails dug into the soft flesh of his hands. Tears welled up in his eyes as he watched his friend's reply.

"No," Jon groaned. "Go to hell."

"Good for you, Bulldog!" The words were out of Dex's mouth before he realized it. In the side monitor, Baker suddenly sat up straighter.

What followed was the most horrifying imagery that Dex—a Navy captain, accustomed to seeing energy bolts ripping through fighter canopies and wreaking havoc on the flesh within—had ever seen. From the right side of the holo, he watched a pulsating blade appear and move toward Jonathan's neck. The blade, while longer, bore a striking resemblance to the knife now resting in the box on Dex's desk—the blue metal displaying the same eerie effects while its low-pitched hum assaulted his inner ear. With the audio playing, Dex couldn't tell if he was hearing only the sound of the recording or if the mysterious blade in his possession had begun vibrating in harmonic sympathy with the tones from the holo. He felt a strong impulse to open the box, to check on the knife, but he would not tear his eyes from the horror unfolding on the screen.

The image turned red as the blade made contact with skin, but not red enough to blot out the gruesome picture before him. Dex tried not to hear the sickening gurgling sound that followed as his martyred friend's head was slowly and methodically severed from his body.

The holo ended abruptly. Dex couldn't breathe. He grasped the side of his desk—his equilibrium gone. Trying to regain his balance, his hand brushed the box containing the ceremonial knife. Even this incidental contact sent waves of nausea coursing through his body—nausea accompanied by a slow-boiling rage. Dex wanted to smash something. He wanted to cry. He wanted to climb into his Hornet and kill anyone who had anything to do with what he had just witnessed.

Baker's soft voice interrupted his rage.

"Dex...did you *know* that young man?"

Dex's breath came in a ragged gasp. "He was a captain in the UCN...a pilot...like me. He was...my friend."

"Aw hell, son. I didn't know. There's no way I would've let you watch that if I—"

"No. I needed to see it." With difficulty, Dex began to compose himself. Staying consciously clear of the box to his left, he could feel the effects of the metal dissipating. But his anger and revulsion at the holo remained. "Where did that come from, Baker? When did it happen?"

"I don't have those answers, Dex, but I mean to find out. I have a contact here, and we've been working to blow this whole thing open. That

249

part's going to take time, and until we know who we can trust, we can't just go taking this thing to the military brass."

Dex shook his head, only half-hearing what Baker was saying, his mind still in that hallway with Bulldog.

"But we have a more pressing matter, Dex. I said that there's an army of these things out there, and they've got an unlimited supply of basic M-2 models to draw from—to modify into killers. From what I can gather, everything up to this point has been a kind of beta test, but now I figure they're getting ready to deploy. If you folks are going to survive this next onslaught, we've got to find a way to cut them off at the source."

That got Dex's full attention. "And that source would be?"

Baker regained some of his inherent exuberance. "Well, the base where they're doing the modifications, of course! My contact here has the location...and I have a plan."

Dex leaned in close to the screen, the image of Bulldog's execution replaying over and over in his mind's eye.

"I want in."

"Yeah, kid. I thought you might."

A half hour later, having discussed all the necessary mission details, Dex terminated the comm. Baker's plan, as usual, was as bold as it was intricate. It would require a considerable amount of personal risk to Dex himself, as well as to the remaining Angels, but based on what Dex had just seen, there were no alternatives. Rising from his desk, he let his eyes fall again on the seemingly innocuous black box. The mystery of the knife inside needled at him. Was there a connection between it and the blade he had seen in the holo, or was it merely his imagination? Either way, Dex could not allow himself to dwell on it. Time was short, and his only consideration had to be stopping the production of those monsters. That, Dex thought, and possibly getting a shot at the one person Baker had been able to identify as behind the whole mess.

Get me within range of him, Bulldog, and I'll make sure you have justice.

Dex paused. Looking once more at the black box, he carefully raised the lid. Steeling himself against the inevitable wave of revulsion and dread, he quickly picked up the pulsing blade, wrapped it in the strip of dark material lining the box, and stowed the knife in his shirt. Even through the wrapping, he could feel the cold metal against his skin—a sensation that strangely radiated warmth within his chest.

Yeah, we'll get him, Jon. You'll have your revenge.

Chapter 21

Louise had been unusually active all evening, burrowing in and out of the shallow mud of her aquarium. Nikky couldn't decide whether she'd been spooked by something or was on some sort of turtle mission. Most likely, it was just the extra food stick he'd given her for dinner. He normally didn't overfeed Louise, but he hadn't remembered the first feeding until she was halfway through her second stick. That hadn't been Nikky's only mental lapse of the day. On the way into his building, a man had asked him for the time, and Nikky had to stop and dig out his handpod before answering. Most people wouldn't have given this a second thought. But Nikky didn't measure himself against most people. He never bothered to wear a chrono because his internal clock was usually accurate within a minute. However, having been put on the spot, Nikky hadn't even been certain of the hour, which for him was somewhat troubling.

The reason for these uncharacteristic miscues was no mystery. He had been preoccupied as of late, driven by a single purpose—to find his brother, Drager. He had been working tirelessly to assist Baker in that effort, regarding anything else as a distraction. Watching Louise once again crawl up out of the pool of water and into the mud, Nikky wondered if she would recognize her old master.

A door chime broke his reverie. Nikky's first move was not toward the door but rather to his workstation to view the security feed. He remained confident that he'd covered up his and Darik's involvement in the R&D facility break-in, but it would be foolish to let his guard down. The feed revealed a courier M-2 waiting outside his door. In the first few days after the break-in, Nikky had found himself being startled by the sight of M-2s, associating them with the heavily-armed models depicted in the stolen schematics. But M-2s were so common, so thoroughly integrated into every aspect of daily life, that the shock value had soon worn off. The

M-2s he and Darik had uncovered were so fundamentally different—if not in appearance, then in programming—that they may as well have been an entirely different species of machine.

Studying the screen, Nikky quickly reasoned that though an evening delivery was a bit unusual, it was not unheard of, and certainly not cause for alarm. He deactivated his security system and answered the door.

Cradling a package in its mechanical arm, the courier spoke in its distinctive layered voice.

"Please state your name."

"Nikky Weis."

The courier's response was immediate. "Identity confirmed." It handed the package to Nikky. "Have a pleasant evening, Mr. Weis."

Nikky turned around and examined the package. The first thing he noticed was the lack of a shipping imprint. Had he been thinking clearly that evening, he would have known that he was not currently expecting any packages. He would have remembered that couriers were supposed to stop deliveries at 8:00 p.m., and it was now 9:15. He would have noticed the courier M-2 still standing in the doorway, blocking the sensor that permitted the door to slide shut.

But he hadn't been thinking clearly that evening, and he only came to these realizations a split-second before the package exploded in his hands.

*   *   *

Nikky opened his eyes to find himself completely surrounded by white light. He swiveled his head, searching the sea of white for a point of reference. There was nothing to his left or right, above or below. Looking down, or at least what felt like "down," he observed something even more disconcerting than the absence of his floor—not only was there nothing beneath his feet, but there were no feet. His body had disappeared. He had never given much thought to the concept of an afterlife, aside from reading a few quaint myths and legends in an elective literature course. But now, hovering over a white abyss as a disembodied consciousness, he was beginning to strongly consider the possibility of life after death. If he was experiencing some sort of afterlife, Nikky was anxious to learn whether he found himself in heaven or hell.

A dull ache in his neck made Nikky realize just how naïve this train of thought had been. Of course he wasn't dead. Just because he couldn't see his body didn't mean it wasn't there. Casting aside any irrational fears from a moment ago, he began focusing on actual concerns, such as whether he would ever again recover his sight or hear a sound other than the high-pitched whine that had begun resonating in his skull. His eyes and ears essentially useless, he sought input from his other senses. Blood and saliva sloshed around his mouth—a good sign, further confirming the existence of his physical body. An attempt at a deep breath triggered a coughing fit as his respiratory system rejected the acrid, smoky air.

Smoke. If there was a fire, it would be all but impossible for him to escape. He used his face to gauge the air temperature, feeling for excessive heat on his sensitive nose and cheeks, but he detected nothing aside from the usual warmth of his temperature-controlled flat. Carefully inhaling a second time, he determined that the smoke was not thick and black as the result of something burning, but wispy with a faint chemical trace, as if the odor had been manufactured.

Right—the courier. The explosion. Fearing the worst, he took inventory of the remainder of his body. He slowly shuffled his feet, tapping his toes on the floor. How he'd remained upright through the explosion was a curiosity, but he had more pressing concerns. Nikky next focused on his fingers—clenching them into fists and stretching them back out—and was immensely relieved to feel that both of his hands were intact. He rubbed his hands against his chest and abdomen, searching for wounds. Finding nothing, he pieced together the various bits of information and reasoned that he must have been the victim of an explosive stun device. This theory was soon confirmed as the effects of the device began to wear off. The whining in his ears began to subside, and the interior of his flat faded into view.

"I commend you, Mr. Weis. For the first time in my long career, a home security system proved impossible for me to crack. I generally prefer not to be quite this…loud."

Nikky nearly lost his balance as he turned to follow the voice. Though he was still finding it difficult to focus his vision, he was able to make out a large figure across the room, standing over his workstation.

"You have a rather unique setup. I must confess, I'd never before seen one of these in person." Nikky saw the man set down his keyboard before turning to face him. "You know why I'm here."

The man could be there for any number of reasons, but Nikky knew better than to incriminate himself. He kept silent.

"My apologies. You must still be a little groggy. Let me remind you."

Stepping closer, he suddenly came into focus. Nikky instantly recognized him as the man who asked him for the time earlier that evening. His attire had changed, and he appeared much larger now than he had hunched over the front steps, but it was the eyes that gave him away—those pale, ashen eyes.

"Two days ago you intercepted an intruder in the JenKore network. The incident went unreported."

Nikky relaxed slightly. Out of all the shady activity he'd been involved in lately, this was the least serious—and the easiest to explain. Still a little unsteady, he spoke up, stumbling over the first few words.

"That's not true. I logged an incident notice immediately afterward."

The man began deliberately pacing. "And the full report?"

"I'm finalizing the draft. It'll be ready by my next shift."

"You wouldn't happen to have a copy I could look at, would you?"

Despite feeling overwhelmingly intimidated, Nikky mustered some anger in his response. If the issue was truly an unfiled report, this was all ridiculously—and criminally—excessive.

"No, I don't have a copy. The only draft is on my office workstation—company policy."

"JenKore is fortunate to have an employee who is so mindful of the rules." The man stopped and hovered over Louise's aquarium. "I've read your report, Mr. Weis. It's rather bland. Not a single mention of your unauthorized messages with the intruder, nor a word about our mutual friend, Baker."

Nikky felt faint. What did he know about Baker? He raced to recall his messages with the hacker. Yes—Baker had been mentioned by name. Was the man bluffing? Perhaps he had merely come across the name *Baker* and was now attempting to use it to draw out more information.

The man continued. "I don't blame you, Nikky. A man will do anything to find his family."

Nikky couldn't believe what he was hearing. He'd been meticulous in covering his tracks, and yet here this man was, casually referencing all of his deepest secrets. These revelations at least made one thing clear—there was no longer any point in playing dumb.

"What do you want from me?"

The man attempted something resembling a smile. "It's simple—you give us Baker, and we'll help you find your brother."

"Who's *we*?"

"Your JenKore family, of course. We have unlimited resources. We have the power to reunite you with your brother. We just need your help."

Not a chance, Nikky thought. Yes, he was certain JenKore would love to find his brother. He had seen the list. He had seen what JenKore did to those it found. Nikky shook his head.

"You don't seem to understand. You have no choice."

The man held up a handpod and played an audio recording. Nikky immediately recognized the voice—Darik Mason.

I needed information, it was my job to gather that information, and you know what I've realized—there was no information! I went through every official channel! All I found were dead ends—stone silence every time! I mean, I wouldn't know anything if Nikky and I hadn't...

The man stopped the recording while Nikky's stomach churned. Every step of the way, Mason had stressed secrecy as their number one priority, and then he went and so carelessly gave them up. The slip-up had undoubtedly cost them both their jobs, and if the violent entrance of this large man was any indication, it had likely cost them their lives as well. For all he knew, Mason was already dead. If there was any minor consolation, it was that Mason's confession had sounded accidental. It wouldn't change their fates, but at least he hadn't been *intentionally* sold-out by his one-time partner.

The man tucked away the handpod. "Your friend has betrayed you. But I can help. I can make this all go away. Give us Baker. Is he more important to you than your brother?" He reached into the aquarium and picked up Louise. "Is he more important than she is?"

The man unsheathed a knife from his right hip and raised it to Louise's lightly-armored belly. At the sight of the dark blue blade, Nikky was not overcome by fear. Rather, he experienced an entirely new emotion—rage. He charged at the man, clenching his hands into fists. The man calmly dropped Louise, who landed on her back, her legs flailing, searching for a foothold. Nikky flailed his arms as well, but his fists likewise found nothing but air. Nikky's momentum carried him past the man, who easily sidestepped around the wild-eyed assailant. He wrapped his right bicep around Nikky's throat and jerked him upright, holding Nikky's upper-back firmly against his broad chest. As part of the same motion, he grasped Nikky's left hand and held it firmly out away from his body, his thumb digging into a pressure-point on his wrist. But that pain was nothing compared to the pressure on his windpipe. The man was flexing his right bicep, denying Nikky the ability to breathe. After several long seconds, the pressure eased ever so slightly, allowing Nikky to wheeze out a few short breaths. Out of the corner of his eye, he could see that the man still held the blade in his right hand, clutching it just inches from Nikky's face. Any lingering instinct to struggle melted away, and he gave in to his body's desire to go limp.

The man spoke again, his cold lips pressed against Nikky's ear. His sulfuric breath lingered in Nikky's nostrils—further taxing an already over-burdened respiratory system—and his voice resonated with a low and terrifying timber.

"You will give us Baker."

Nikky couldn't have spoken if he'd wanted to. He felt ill, as if he'd once again been stricken by the stun device. The room drained of color, and his throat burned. He just wanted to collapse, to pass out—whatever would put an end to this nightmare.

"This is not a dream, Nikky. This is not a vision."

The man yanked his left hand over toward his head, bending his arm at an awkward right angle. The bicep eased off of his throat as the man positioned the blade over Nikky's wrist.

"Let this be a reminder."

Nikky screamed in his head, but his lips produced no sound. All he could do was wince as the blade sliced cleanly into his flesh. The pain associated with the agonizingly slow cut was expected; what wasn't expected was the intense pulsation emanating from the blade. The vibrations coursed through his body from head to toe, producing a sensation unlike anything he'd felt before, as though some invisible hand were violently shaking every bone in his body. Nikky couldn't bear to watch the damage being inflicted upon him; it was only when the vibrations ceased that he knew the deed had been completed.

Gathering his last bit of courage, he turned his head and watched as his left hand was dropped into a bag and stuffed into the man's coat. The man then produced a thin package, tearing it open in one efficient motion. Nikky wondered what further horrors awaited him, but to his surprise, the man leaned over and cradled Nikky's left arm, sealing the bloody wrist with an air-tight medicated wrap. When the man released his arm, Nikky struggled to stay standing under his own power. He stumbled forward, and the man caught him.

"We're your family, Nikky. We'll take care of you." He lowered Nikky into a chair. "Do this one little thing for us, and we'll help you become whole again—as good as new."

As he turned to leave, he stooped over and picked up Louise, who was still struggling to flip over. He turned her around in his large hand, angling her against an overhead light. With his free hand, he reached over and lightly caressed her belly with his index finger before setting her down on her feet.

"I trust you'll make the right decision," the man said, disappearing through the door.

And then, finally, Nikky passed out.

Chapter 22

Scot Calgaro suddenly found himself on his back with Jani McLeod straddled across his chest. It was not, however, the pleasurable encounter that he had always envisioned. The sharp pain in his shoulder, where her elbow still immobilized him, chased away any possible enjoyment their close contact would otherwise bring.

The pressure released as McLeod got back to her feet, extending a hand to help him up.

"Another fall, Lieutenant?" She didn't even seem winded.

Scot wanted to rub the sore shoulder, and about a dozen other sensitive spots, but he resisted, choosing instead to crouch into a ready position, arms partially extended, warily eyeing his opponent.

"Whenever you're ready."

The two combatants circled one another slowly, the gym mat compressing beneath their feet, the exercise room revolving in their peripheral vision.

McLeod smiled. "I don't know why we haven't done this more often."

"Uh-huh." Scot wasn't amused. Seeing an opening, he moved in, grasping one of Jani's shoulders while hooking a leg behind her calf. She went down easily, attempting to exploit a momentary lack of balance to pull Scot down as well.

Maybe the first five times.

Scot was ready. He allowed himself to be pulled down but used their combined momentum to continue rolling. Never releasing his grip, he ended up on top of Jani, his forearm pressed across her neck. The wider look in her eyes told him he was exerting just a bit more pressure than was necessary. He didn't really care.

"You're going to have to do better than that, Rabbit."

Jani's eyes flashed. Pushing off the mat with her feet, she managed to buck just enough to momentarily take Scot's weight off of her. She rolled quickly to the left, scrambling back to her feet. Now it was her turn to sound a little winded.

"You *know* I don't like that call sign," she breathed. "Use it in the cockpit, fine—that's not going to change—but not here."

They circled again, both alert, both looking for another weakness to exploit. Scot regarded her with a placid expression.

"What *would* you like to be called then?"

Jani straightened from her stance and cocked her head, one auburn eyebrow arching slightly.

"How about *Lead*?"

That hurt. Scot couldn't stand the fact that Captain D'Felco had, in essence, demoted him following his unauthorized boarding of the freighter on their last mission. Sure, he was still a lieutenant, albeit a *grounded* one, but once he was back in the cockpit, he would no longer be flying lead. His former wingman, Adahn, was now paired up with Dex. The pilot who would be lead—*his lead*—was standing across the mat from him with an expression on her face that was far too smug for his liking. So far, his plan to take out his frustration with her on the exercise mat had not been going very well, but that was about to change.

"I don't think so." He moved in for the attack. This time, both adversaries remained on their feet. Scot managed to seize Jani's left wrist just as she moved to grip his right shoulder. Seeing her right side unguarded, he struck quickly with his left, this time connecting with his forearm to the side of her face—once again, too hard. Jani staggered back, her expression turning dark.

"What exactly is your *problem*, Calgaro?"

Scot dropped his hands for a moment. "Problem? I don't have a problem. What's the matter, *Lead*? Can't handle it?"

She pounced like a cat. Before Scot could react, she was somehow behind him, one hand painfully pulling backwards on his arm, her other arm wrapped around his neck. He could feel her breath on the back of his neck, then felt her lips move close to his right ear.

"No, I can handle it," she whispered fiercely. "The question is, why can't *you*?"

Gasping against her chokehold, Scot struggled to get another foothold behind Jani's leg.

"I can handle anything you throw at me, McLeod." He managed to get his free hand behind him, finding a grip somewhere on her exercise tunic. Finally getting the footing he was searching for, he spun, simultaneously twisting out of her grip on his left arm. While Jani held her position around his neck, he reached around her head as well, attempting to gain the same advantage she held. The effect brought their faces together, anger written on both. She looked at him with contempt.

"Anything? Anything except *command*, you mean."

The turn around had left their free hands each gripping the other's wrist. Both thumbs found pressure points at the same time.

"Command is wasted on some people." Scot gritted his teeth against the pain.

Jani's voice was strained, evidence that his thumb was delivering the same discomfort to her wrist that he was feeling. "I didn't make that call—the captain did—after *your* colossal screw-up. If you don't like the decision, I suggest you take a good look in a mirror. In the meantime, you got a problem with me as lead—let's hear it right now."

They continued to circle, feet shuffling, bodies pressed, both maneuvering for an opportunity, neither finding one. Scot twisted his wrist, hoping to lessen the sharp pain enough to speak without revealing his discomfort.

"My problem with you, *Lieutenant*," Scot began, knowing that their equal rank would not be lost on Jani. "My problem with you is that you've never shown even the slightest inspiration in your flying. You've spent your entire career as D'Felco's pet—and who knows what else? He covers for you—I think I can guess why—and you're so enamored with him that you think like a schoolgirl instead of a pilot. You're so afraid of making the *wrong* move in front of him that you don't do *anything*. You're too careful out there—and someday, that's going to get someone killed!"

"And *you* are an idiot!" Jani's thumb pressed harder, driving her point home. "Does it *ever* occur to you that Dex might actually know what he's doing?"

Scot's eyes bulged as Jani's arm suddenly constricted around his neck. His jab about the captain had struck a nerve.

"He wants you to learn something, Scot—something that might keep you alive longer than your God-given flying talent ever could. He wants you to learn discipline. And like it or not—whether *I* like it or not—you're going to learn that with me."

God-given talent? Was that a compliment?

Scot eased up on Jani's wrist. Her eyes still flashed anger, but he could have sworn he detected something else—an emotion he hadn't seen there before. He allowed his own voice to soften.

"With you, huh?"

The pain subsiding, Jani's expression relaxed. Maintaining her grip around his neck, she spoke—her lips within millimeters of his.

"Yeah...with me."

Scot considered this for a moment. He considered a *lot* of things. Her cheek was flushed where his forearm had struck earlier—probably the beginning of a bruise. He felt Jani release his wrist just as he let go of hers. His hand moved slowly toward her face.

Both of their handpods sounded an alert while the gym's comm system simultaneously sprang to life, the strong voice of Commander Lebrian demanding their attention.

"All pilots report to the ready room. All pilots report to the ready room—on the double."

Without a word, the two pilots grabbed their gear and headed for the door—their duty, for the moment, eclipsing all other thoughts.

*   *   *

Hagen Lebrian was standing with Ronnie at the front of the ready room, his back to the door, when Jani and Scot entered. Looking up from his handpod, he turned his head enough to acknowledge the two pilots. The commander met Scot's questioning glance with a nod.

"Yes, the term *all pilots* includes you, Lieutenant Calgaro. For this mission, you and Bennet may consider your grounding to be suspended, at least temporarily." Hagen turned back to the pod.

Scot took a seat without comment while Jani slid into a chair to his left. Most of the squadron had already assembled. Apparently, Hagen had distributed some new assignments, as Seltrice and Adahn were seated together near the front, with the Voor twins directly behind them. Lee Onigen sat a couple chairs away from Scot. He guessed that the Lieutenant Commander would be leading the second flight—Jani's and his flight—with Geff back in his customary spot as Onigen's wing. But where *was* Geff? And for that matter, where was Dex?

Scot's first question was answered as his friend somewhat sheepishly entered the room, sliding in to take the chair between Onigen and Scot. Geff leaned over, keeping his voice at a whisper.

"So what's going on, Flash? I got a second summons on my pod and figured I was actually supposed to be here."

Scot kept his voice equally low. "Apparently, they still have need of our skills. We've both been restored to flying status."

Geff grunted. "Must be pretty important to give us a reprieve this soon. Where's the captain?"

"Both of you gentlemen will find that out shortly." Onigen's tone was as sharp as his hearing. "In the meantime, I suggest you listen."

As if on cue, Commander Lebrian turned to face the squadron.

"Ten-*hut*!" Onigen called the pilots to their feet.

"At ease, everyone. You may be seated." Hagen got right down to business. "Captain D'Felco is not here. He departed, alone, in his Hornet sometime last night."

A few pilots shifted uneasily in their seats. Solo flights were dangerous and, by Dex's own orders, unauthorized—even for the captain. Hagen continued.

"I spoke with him, briefly, before he left, and he gave me the following orders." He cleared his throat and read from his handpod. "All pilots…" Hagen paused, glancing up from the pod long enough to shoot a withering look in Scot and Geff's direction, "*all* pilots are to report for launch at 1500 hours. Flight Sergeant St. James and Ops Tech Wilco have performed all necessary repairs following the Milk Run and have cleared each of your Hornets for flight. All ships have been rearmed with a full complement of Slammers, as well as one Heavy Ion Bomb per fighter."

Hagen held up a hand to quiet the murmuring throughout the room.

Adahn raised his hand. "That's a lot of firepower, sir. Can we ask what the target is?"

Hagen leveled his gaze at the flying officer. "You can ask, but you're not going to get an answer. All mission details are sealed. Upon launch, fighters will form up in their respective flights in orbit of this planet. At that point, the full mission briefing along with jump coordinates will be relayed to each Hornet. Until then, you have your orders."

Something about all this secrecy galled Scot. That many Slammers meant *action*. The HIBs meant *big* action. If they were heading into something hot, the pilots had a right to considerably more intel than this

263

before launch. Despite his tentative flight status, he was just about to stick his neck out, *again*, and say so when Seltrice beat him to the punch.

"Oh come on, Sarge. You've got to give us a *little* more than that!"

Hagen shook his head, a grim smile on his lips. "Not a chance, Viper. First of all, you know pretty much everything I know at this point. Secondly, even if I did know more, Captain D'Felco's orders stand." He nodded in Onigen's direction. "Lieutenant Commander."

Onigen stood to address the pilots. "Some of you have already received new flight assignments." For the second time, Scot and Geff endured a not-so-subtle jab, as several pilots smirked in their direction—this was getting old. "But with the captain's absence on this mission, we will have to adjust, so here is the updated squadron alignment. Flight one will consist of Commander Lebrian, with *both* Viper and Ghazi on his wing. Sunfire and Moonlight will make up the second element in Sarge's flight. I will command flight two. Prince will be on my wing." Geff grunted again, this time with satisfaction. Scot couldn't help being jealous of his friend—his status hadn't changed at all. Onigen continued. "And the second element will consist of Rabbit as lead with Flash on her wing."

The smirks from the other pilots turned to unabashed smiles in Jani's direction. Scot half-expected them all to jump up and start giving her high-fives at any second. Out of the corner of her eye, she shot him a self-satisfied look. Watching her smug expression, he wished he hadn't gone so easy on her in the gym.

"Enjoy it while you can, Rabbit," he hissed out of the side of his mouth, "and try not to get us both killed."

"Just do your job, Calgaro. I'm sure you'll do just fine—if you can manage to keep up with me."

Onigen regarded the two with undisguised annoyance. "Is there a problem here, Lieutenants?"

Scot looked straight ahead. "No, sir! Ready to serve with Excellence and Honor, sir!"

Jani nodded as well. "No problem, sir. No problem at all."

Hagen took control once again. "Further questions will be addressed during the orbital briefing. For now—"

Seltrice couldn't help interrupting. Her voice was respectful but insistent. "Sir, if I may ask, just where *is* Captain D'Felco?"

"You may *not* ask," Hagen snapped. "You have three hours to prepare yourselves, to pray, and..." he directed his attention to Scot and Jani, his tone leaving no room for misunderstanding, "to *resolve* any lingering issues. Countdown to launch commences now. You are dismissed."

Chapter 23

Darik stretched his legs out in the luxurious comfort of a lounge chair. Arching his back, he could feel the tension between his shoulders dissipating. The absolute void of etherspace played havoc on reality just outside the port window, but inside the well-appointed JenKore transport *Golden Crow*, everything in Darik's world was coming into focus.

It could have been the utter relief of knowing that his financial problems were finally behind him. Maybe it was the euphoria he felt after summarily firing his former boss, the exquisitely annoying Mr. Marcus Stirling, or perhaps it was simply the relaxing sensation that came with downing his third Vorinian—Darik couldn't decide. He only knew that he felt terrific.

"Can I get you another, Darik?"

Or maybe that was it, Darik mused as he regarded Liana. Still officially his secretary, she had readily accepted his invitation to accompany him on this fact-finding journey—no questions asked. The new salary, the cruiser—Darik could get used to these trappings of power. Eyeing the sharp brunette filling his glass for the fourth time, he wryly considered that she might also become one of his executive perks.

She finished pouring Darik's drink and proceeded to help herself as well. Settling into another chair near his, Liana toyed with the rim of her glass, her dark eyes coming to rest on her employer.

"So, did you enjoy it?"

Darik tilted his head slightly. "Did I enjoy what?"

"Firing Stirling. He's been on your case for quite a while."

Darik chuckled. "You should have seen the look on his face."

Liana leaned forward, eager to hear the details as Darik continued.

"I actually waited until he called me into *his* office. I knew he couldn't go an entire day without riding me for something. He obviously hadn't gotten the word yet, so he was just sitting there with that infernal, condescending face of his. I let him finish up with his latest list of my screw-ups and shortcomings, and then he started to tell me how I should do my job. At that point, I held up my hand and said, 'Uh, that's just not going to happen, Marcus.'"

"*Marcus*? You called him *Marcus*? What did he do?"

"At first, nothing. I don't think he knew *what* to do. He sat there for a moment with his jaw just about hitting the floor. Then he told me he wasn't sure that he liked my *attitude*."

"So what did you do?"

"I told him that I *was* sure that I didn't like *him*. I told him he had a choice to pack up and leave quietly, or I could have security show him the way out. Naturally, he still didn't believe me. He picked up his handpod, probably to give Jenkins himself a call, but of course I already had his account cancelled—dead air. That's when I had the sec-guys come on in. He was literally kicking and screaming on his way out."

"So, what did you do then?"

Darik took another sip from his glass. "I took over his office. I always liked that corner view."

Liana laughed, and Darik liked the sound. The lilt of her voice reminded him of a particular light melody that he had always enjoyed. The overall effect relaxed him even further as he warmed to his subject.

"You know what the worst part of working directly for Stirling was? The man was basically so incompetent, so single-minded, that he managed to force me in the wrong direction this entire time."

Liana raised a single thin eyebrow. "How so?"

"With Stirling, it was always *mining units, mining units, mining units*. He kept on hammering at me about missing mining units."

"Well, he *is*…or *was* the VP of Mining Operations."

The Vorinian had put Darik in a talkative mood. "But that shouldn't matter. My job—the assignment *Jenkins* originally gave me—was to track down a series of M-2 failures. Stirling just assumed they had to be mining unit failures."

"But wouldn't that make sense? Weren't the missing units supposed to be mining M-2s?"

"Yeah, they were *supposed* to be…but they weren't. Do you remember when I took a few days out of the office?"

Liana nodded. "As I recall, you were at home, working tirelessly on the project. That's what I told Stirling, anyway."

Darik looked around the lounge, experiencing a light sense of paranoia. He quickly dismissed the feeling, realizing that no one could possibly be listening in. It was standard procedure to sweep all JenKore ships for surveillance devices before launch. Through the open hatchway at the front of the lounge, he could see that the ship's cockpit was empty— as it should be. As a smaller, *Midas*-class luxury transport, the *Golden Crow* didn't require a pilot or crew. Though Darik looked forward to trying a few maneuvers himself on manual control, the *Crow* was fully automated and could take them directly to their destination and back without Darik even needing to sit in the pilot's chair. He and Liana were absolutely alone on the cruiser. Shaking away any lingering paranoid thoughts, he turned his attention back to his secretary.

"Liana, I wasn't at home. I lied to you."

Liana's laughter caught him off guard. "Well, of *course* you lied to me. The problem is you're lousy at it. I just assumed you were cutting out for a few days to unwind. That's why I covered for you. So what did you do, spend a few days in Amsterdam?"

"No...what? No! I took a side trip to Cacarus to find out what was *really* happening to the M-2s."

"Always the workaholic." Liana seemed disappointed. "I take it there was more to your trip than you were banking on?"

"Liana, the four base M-2 models I was investigating never arrived on Cacarus. They were never modified as mining units. At first, that's all I knew. Now, I've come to find out they ended up being modified as pilots—flying Marauders, I guess."

"I take it that's not exactly in their original design specs. No wonder there were failures."

"Oh, you don't know the half of it. Some of the M-2s out there are being..."

He stopped himself, staring at the nearly empty glass in his hand. He had said too much already.

Back to the original subject.

"Anyway, without actually telling Stirling that I had been to Cacarus, I still wanted to clue him that maybe we were chasing down the wrong type of failures—maybe even in the wrong division. I thought he'd be appreciative—that it would take him off the hook. Do you want to know what he said?"

Her eyes sparkled. "I can't wait."

"He said he didn't give a rat's ass about what I thought. He said that my job was to take care of *mining* units, and as long as I was in the mining division, that was my only concern. And if I wanted to play around with other theories, I could do it at home...permanently. The idiot wasted my time for weeks, handcuffing me without having a clue about what was really going on. I wanted to kill him, but in the end I had to settle for firing him and having him dragged out on his own ass."

Liana smiled. "So, yeah, you enjoyed it."

Darik stretched, feeling at ease once again. "You bet I did. I'm tempted to hire him back, just so I can fire him again. This time, I'd make sure that—"

The vibration of his handpod interrupted him.

"Damn it." Darik picked up the offending device, taking in the pod's information with a furrowed brow. "That's weird. It's an alert. Something triggered the tamper detection on my luggage."

"How is that possible?"

Darik considered a moment. "It probably just shifted in transport. Tell you what, I'm going to walk down there and take a look. I could stand to stretch my legs, anyway."

Liana gathered herself to rise. "I'll go with you."

"No." Darik poured the remaining contents of the bottle into her glass. "Stay here, relax. I won't be long."

Liana settled back, crossing her legs in a way that Darik found particularly pleasing. "I'll be waiting, boss."

Darik was counting on it.

*   *   *

The *Golden Crow*'s baggage compartment was located one level down, near the stern. Like most luxury transports, its opulent furnishings were reserved for the upper guest levels of the ship. In the lower utility levels, the walls were bare, the lighting scarce, and the climate settings much less comfortable. Darik tightened his collar in an effort to conserve body heat as he made his way along the dark corridor. He found himself regretting at least the third and fourth glasses of Vorinian as he unsteadily placed one foot in front of the other. The ship was fitted with the finest internal stabilization technology, but like everything else, this amenity was reserved for the upper decks. Already annoyed, he let out a curse as his head bumped against a low beam he had failed to notice. This was stupid, banging around down here, just to check out a false alarm. So what if his bag had shifted? No one was down here to mess with it. At worst, it would turn out to be a rat—a rare but not unheard of occurrence in luggage compartments. If that was the case, Darik really didn't care to deal with it. He just wanted to find the baggage area, check on his stuff, and get back to the comfort of the lounge—and Liana.

The hatch to the luggage compartment opened easily, revealing a well-organized room. Past several empty rows of stowage bins, he found his and Liana's bags. The M-2 handlers that loaded them had done a neat job of it, securing them properly for the trip.

Darik frowned. His luggage did not seem to have been disturbed, but *something* must have set off the tamper alarm. He was leaning in to check the electronic seal when a small movement to his left caught his attention. Startled, he turned in that direction, his eyes searching his surroundings for a blunt object. If there was actually a rat scurrying around down here, bumping his luggage and setting off alarms, the fleet steward back on Earth was going to be joining Stirling on the unemployment line.

The bin to his right had a couple unused stabilizing bars inside. Grabbing one, Darik felt the heft of it in his hands. It would do. He made his way cautiously forward, cradling the heavy bar, anticipating the sudden flurry of rodent feet and getting ready to bash the thing's head in.

Darik sensed movement between the next two bins. Raising the bar, he jumped into the space, involuntarily yelling as he sprang.

"Auuuuugh!" the rat yelled back. "What are you, crazy?"

Darik knew that voice. It *was* a rodent.

"Nikky." He slowly lowered the bar, his heart beating a hole in the side of his chest. "What the hell are you *doing* here?"

In the dim light between the bins, Darik could just make out the little tech struggling to get to his feet.

"I'm waiting for you." Nikky placed one hand on the side of a bin and continued to hoist himself up—somewhat clumsily, even for him, Darik thought. "I figured if I tinkered with your bag a bit, you'd come running, and here you are."

"But how did you get on board? How did you sneak past…" Darik stopped himself. "Okay, stupid question—here's a better one. *Why* are you here, Nikky?"

With a grunt, Nikky made it to his feet. He must have been sitting in that cramped space for a while. "I'm here because I need your help."

"My help? Help with what?"

Nikky stepped out from between the bins, coming fully into the light.

"With this." Nikky held up his left arm. Where his hand should have been, Darik saw only a bandaged stump, the dried blood soaking through the wrapping beneath a transparent airtight seal.

Darik caught his breath. He thought, for a moment, that he might be sick.

"Geez, Nikky. What happened to you?"

"I had a visitor. You might know him. Maybe he's even a friend of yours, I don't know. Tall guy…bald…*really* pale eyes."

Darik backed up against a bin. His heart was still pounding, but now it was for a different reason.

"Graves," he breathed.

"So you do know him."

Darik nodded. "Yeah, I know him. But he's no friend of mine. What happened, Nikky? What did he want?"

Darik wasn't sure he wanted to hear the answer. Even with his new position of authority, the thought of Graves still being out there, shadowing his moves, reporting everything directly to Jenkins, terrified him. Graves obviously wanted more information from Nikky, and he wanted it badly enough to torture him. What had Nikky said?

Nikky winced as he lowered his arm. "He was looking for information—information I had on…a source."

"A source?" Darik digested Nikky's words. "What source? Was he asking about me?"

Nikky's face soured. "Why does it always have to be about you? No. He was looking for someone else. Someone I came across during the work I was doing—work that I was doing for you, I might add."

Darik didn't care for the implication, nor did he appreciate the way Nikky was looking at him, but he still wanted more information.

"C'mon, Nikky. What did he want? How much did he know about *our* work?"

"I told you, already. He didn't ask about you at all. He was only interested in my other source."

Darik decided to believe him. He still didn't know how much Graves knew about his and Nikky's extracurricular espionage—and wasn't even sure why it would matter. After all, hadn't Darik already told Jenkins about everything he and Nikky had discovered? But the thought of Graves probing even deeper into his life had set him on edge. Now, hearing Nikky say that Graves had a different target for his scrutiny made him somehow feel more confident.

"Okay, so he was looking for someone else. Who?"

"Like I said, a *source*."

Darik let it go and tried a different route. "So, what did you tell him?"

"Nothing. I don't just blurt things out under stress, you know."

Again, with the look. What the hell is that all about?

"So you kept your mouth shut. Good for you. Then what happened?"

Nikky gave him an *are you kidding?* expression and held up his blood-soaked stump.

"Oh, yeah. Man, Nikky, I'm sorry about that."

Nikky winced again, unconsciously rubbing the end of the bandage with his remaining hand. "Yeah, well, you *should* be."

"And what, exactly, is that supposed to mean?"

Nikky cocked his head and stared directly into Darik's eyes. When he spoke, it surprised Darik to hear a reasonably good imitation of his own voice.

"I needed information," Nikky quoted. "It was my job to gather that information, and you know what I've realized—there was no information! I went through every official channel! All I found were dead ends—stone silence every time! I mean, I wouldn't know anything if Nikky and I hadn't…"

So that was it. Darik remembered the conversation in Jenkins's office. The CEO had obviously traced down Nikky and then dispatched Graves to interrogate him. And Graves had been sure to tell Nikky how they had gotten their information. Internally, Darik's own guilt about letting Nikky's name slip out battled with his irritation over the way the tech was now looking at him, as if daring him to deny it. The irritation won.

"Wake up, Nikky! You think, for a moment, that they didn't already know *exactly* who you were? They knew *everything*! Yeah, I said your name—I'm *sorry*, okay? But it doesn't change anything. They were on to me—they were on to both of us. Graves was coming for you, no matter what I said."

"Well, you didn't need to lay it out for them on a satin pillow, either."

Darik felt the need to sit down, but the luggage compartment didn't offer much for accommodations. Instead, he leaned farther back on the bin behind him. This new position gave him a better view of the aisle behind Nikky. He noticed a small transparent carrying case on the floor behind the tech's feet. In the dim light, he couldn't see what, exactly, was in the container, but it was definitely moving. Reminded again of the possibility of an actual rat's presence, he started, in spite of himself.

"What the hell is *that*, Nikky?" Darik held the bar in his hand at arm's length, pointing it at the case.

Nikky looked down. "Oh, that." He shrugged. "That's Louise, my broth…uh, *my* pet turtle."

"Your pet turtle."

Nikky nodded.

"And you brought it along."

Nikky shrugged again, and Darik rubbed a throbbing temple, concluding that it just wasn't worth it. He decided to continue, instead, with his original thought.

"None of this answers my first question, Nikky. Why are you *here*?"

Nikky swallowed hard. "He took my hand, Darik. He said I could get it back if I gave him my source."

"Then give him the source, Nikky! What's the difference?" He wanted Nikky to understand that, as long as Graves wasn't looking to dig up more dirt on him, nothing Nikky could tell the guy would matter. Darik was in charge now, and if Nikky had another source, that person was expendable. But the tech slowly shook his head.

"It's…it's not that simple. I have to protect my source." Nikky glanced at the floor for a split-second before looking Darik directly in the eyes. "It's…personal."

"So you have your integrity. Yeah, I get that. But is it worth your hand, Nikky?" For a brief moment, Darik had a visual picture in his mind of Nikky's fingers flying over that ancient keyboard of his—but with only one hand. Darik's nauseous dizziness welled up again, this time with force. Nikky didn't seem to notice.

"No! I can't reveal my source. There's too much else at stake. But that's why I'm here. There's another way. I can beat these guys! But I need your help."

Darik swallowed back the bile, his sympathy for Nikky disappearing along with it.

"*These* guys? Nikky, *I'm* these guys. I'm the vice president in charge of the entire division for crying out loud. I don't know what you're planning, but leave me out of it. I'm sorry about your hand, but if you hitched a ride to try to get me to turn against my own company, then you've wasted a very long trip."

Nikky stood to his full height—not all that impressive.

"You think I don't know that? I know all about your new position. I'm still capable of doing some digging. I'm not an idiot. You've got a job to do, and as usual, you're going to do it, no matter who gets hurt in the process."

"And I've already said that I'm sorry about your hand! But what exactly do you want me to do about it?"

Nikky's voice softened. "It's not just about me—or you. There are all those people on that list, too."

Serves them right, Darik thought. *Terrorists, every one of them—just like the ones who—*

He shook the thought from his head. There was no way he was going to be able to explain things to Nikky. Darik realized that, despite all the annoyances, he'd actually grown fond of the little tech, but he also knew that Nikky was hopelessly naïve. This was not the time or the place for a long debate or, worse yet, a soul-searching look into Darik's own family history. He tried a different approach.

"So okay, Nikky, if that's true—if I don't care about you or anyone else—why should I help you now?"

Darik could see fresh blotches of red under the seal at the end of Nikky's arm, evidence of an increased heartbeat.

"Because we can help each other. A big part of your new job is keeping those M-2 mods up and running at top efficiency, right?"

No point in denying the obvious.

"Yeah…so?"

"So, I took another look at that new program you guys are using on the M-2s. It's good, all right, but not quite as good as you would like."

"And what do you mean by that?"

Nikky raised an eyebrow. "I found a glitch—a potential hardware compatibility problem, actually. It's really not that surprising, considering the complexity of the modifications. I mean, someone with a little more skill could have probably—"

"*Potential* hardware compatibility?" Darik interrupted him. "What are you saying?" A thought nagged at the back of Darik's mind. All along, he had sensed that chasing down mining unit failures had been a waste of time. Even the lost pilot mods didn't seem to tell the entire story. Now, Nikky was indicating a problem with the M-2/As. "Nikky, are you telling me we're going to see failures with these new modified units?"

Nikky nodded. "They may have had some malfunctions already, for all we know. But it wouldn't be all of them, and not all of the time—just intermittent problems. That's probably why your buffoons haven't detected the glitch. Of course, I was able to nail it down with one hand tied behind my back, so to speak."

Darik wasn't amused. "So which pieces of hardware will fail?"

Nikky held up his remaining hand. "Uh-uh. This is where we help each other, remember?"

"Great. So what do you want, Nikky?"

Nikky opened his mouth and then closed it again. He looked at Darik for a long moment. Coming to a decision, he shook his head once more. "No, I'm not ready to tell you—*you're* not ready. Not just yet."

"Forget it." Darik pushed himself away from the bin. "I don't have time for this crap." Darik was cold, he was tired, and he had run out of patience. He was almost to the hatch when Nikky's voice stopped him.

"Focus on the laser cutter. It's not the only glitch, but it will point you in the right direction."

Darik turned and stared down at him. "Is that all?"

"That's all you're going to get, for now."

Darik took a couple of steps back into the compartment. He considered forcing more information out of him but quickly dismissed the idea. Beating up a one-handed runt was hardly becoming of a vice president, no matter how tempting the thought was. He was reconsidering his options when he heard another voice behind him.

"Darik, what's taking so long?"

Liana made her way gingerly through the baggage hatch. Halfway through, she stumbled slightly—her recovery complicated by the fact that she was holding two glasses and a fresh bottle of Vorinian.

"It sounded like you were talking to…oh."

Seeing Nikky, she stopped short. Nikky managed a half-hearted grin, started to hold up his left arm, reconsidered, and waved to her with his right hand instead.

"Uh…Liana," Darik said quietly, "this is Nikky. He's going to be…traveling with us."

Liana pointedly set the bottle and glasses down. One of the glasses rolled off the bin and shattered on the smooth metal floor. She didn't seem to notice, never taking her eyes off the wounded tech.

"Terrific," she said. "Welcome aboard."

Chapter 24

The Bellona sunrise bathed the antiquated high rises of Port Henri in a warm glow, momentarily gentrifying the dilapidated port city. Dex observed the effect through the forward viewport of the cargo freighter *Deliverance Nine* as it slowly descended toward its designated landing pad. The freighter—the ninth ship in Baker's not-so-subtly named *Deliverance* shipping fleet—was completely automated, just as the *Milk Wagon* had been before its regrettable demise. Nevertheless, Dex had spent the entire journey in the pilot's seat. Not only was he most comfortable there, but the lack of space elsewhere on the freighter all but forced him to the cockpit. As Dex was well-aware, Baker packed his ships to the brim.

The freighter touched down, completing the longest leg of Dex's journey. The last etherspace jump had begun in the uninhabited Purborus system, where Dex's Hornet was currently parked on a rogue asteroid. The *Deliverance Nine* had made a slight alteration in its route to pick him up, and the ensuing jump had given Dex some much needed time to clear his head and focus on the mission at hand.

He felt guilty about leaving the squadron behind, especially the manner in which he'd left—stealing away like a thief in the night. He was sure that more than a few of his pilots felt abandoned by their captain, and rightly so. His sudden disappearance, however, had been a necessary evil. The entire mission was made possible by a fortunate coincidence— Baker's shipping fleet made a monthly delivery to Bellona. At the time of Baker's last transmission, the *Deliverance Nine* was being loaded for departure, meaning that the mission either had to begin immediately or be postponed a full month. Delaying the freighter a few days was not an option. A late delivery would've called too much attention to the freighter, which would've defeated the entire purpose of infiltrating Bellona as discreetly as possible. Waiting a month held a certain advantage—it would have provided the squadron some much-needed time to meticulously plan the mission. However, given the squadron's recent issues with security leaks, that extra month may have been more of a hindrance than a benefit, presenting the traitor with ample opportunity to make off with a detailed mission plan.

And more importantly, Dex could not, in good conscience, wait an entire month to halt the production of those abominable machines. Every day that he delayed meant that more M-2s were being modified, which meant that more innocent people were being hunted down and murdered. Burdened with this knowledge, Dex had a responsibility to his brothers and sisters scattered across the stars to strike against such evil as swiftly as possible.

But the plan, so hastily crafted, was far from perfect. The entire mission hinged on the ability of an agent to infiltrate an on-planet facility and conduct sabotage—the type of guerrilla operation for which Dex was severely under-qualified. Hagen, with his infantry experience, would have been the natural choice, but there was no way Dex was going to send his second-in-command on what was essentially a suicide mission. At least, that was the rationale he eventually settled upon, however weak it might've been. After all, he couldn't count the number of times that he had ordered his pilots into similarly dangerous situations—what was the difference if they were in a Hornet or in the mud? The truth was that Dex had never considered anyone else for the mission.

He needed to destroy those machines, and he needed to bring to justice those responsible for their existence. Unfortunately, Baker's information was frustratingly lacking in that regard. Only two names were mentioned in the entire file. The first was Kirrone Jenkins, the CEO of JenKore, a household name famous as much for his philanthropy as his wealth, having funded schools, libraries, research facilities, and the like on nearly every planet in the Coalition. He wasn't sure of Jenkins's level of involvement with the secret M-2 project, though it would be naïve to think that he had no knowledge of it whatsoever. And yet, he found it hard to believe that a man as charitable and civically minded as Jenkins could be capable of such evil.

The other person, and the only one directly attached to the M-2 project, was someone by the name of Darik Mason. The accompanying holopic was surprising for just how unremarkable it was. It revealed a man close to his own age with sandy blond hair and a lean jaw that he tilted up ever so slightly with an air of self-confidence. He appeared to be nothing more than a run-of-the-mill corporate drone—far from the portrait of a mass murderer. But what had he been expecting—red eyes and horns? Dex burned the face into his memory, certain of what he would do if their paths ever crossed. He knew that such thoughts were taking him to a dark place, but he owed it to Bulldog.

However, before he could consider exacting any form of revenge, he first needed to pass through the backwater port without any trouble. Grabbing the handles of a long bulky case, Dex headed to the aft loading ramp, which had already been lowered by the freighter's automated systems. He paused at the top of the ramp, taking a moment to survey the landing pad. He was encouraged by what he saw—no customs officials, no sign of any security whatsoever, just a few mechanical Pack Mules hauling crates from one end of the pad to the other. Emboldened by the lack of personnel, he shuffled down the ramp, side-stepping a charging Mule on the way down. Dex had no doubt that the dull machine would've trampled him had he not moved. Watching the Mule amble into the cargo hold, he found it interesting that the port didn't employ M-2s. He figured that either the old port simply couldn't afford them or its M-2s, so conveniently close to the manufacturing station, had been recalled by JenKore for modification.

After a quick scan, he spotted an exit on the far side of the pad and moved as rapidly as he could while lugging around the bulky case. He made it only a few awkward paces before a voice echoed behind him.

"Hey! You with the case, stop!"

Dex reluctantly turned around and saw a man poking his head out from behind a stack of crates. He set down some unseen object and marched toward Dex. As he neared, Dex could see that he was wearing some sort of uniform, complete with a side arm strapped to his belt. He was pale with a wispy blond mustache and sunken eyes. An ID badge gave a single name—*Stubbs*.

"What, you thought you could just sneak on out of here?" Stubbs demanded.

"I'm sorry. I didn't see anyone."

Stubbs bristled, and for the first time, Dex noticed just how short he was.

"Check in," the man said, thrusting a data pad at Dex. "And let's see some ID."

Dex set the case down and handed over his ID tag. As Stubbs looked it over, Dex filled out the data pad. He wasn't overly concerned with the form, having committed every detail of his alias to memory. One question, though, caused him to hesitate.

Christian?

He'd been anticipating this. His cover required him to answer "no"—registering as a Christian would attract far too much attention to himself. Still, Dex was surprised at how easy it was to select the box—he had been expecting to feel much more guilty about it.

He handed the pad back to Stubbs.

"Davis Webb, huh? Well, Davis Webb, this landing pad is reserved for auto shipments. But I'm sure you just boarded the wrong ship by mistake, right? I understand—it's easy to get travel liners and cargo freighters confused. So, why don't you come with me, and we'll get this all straightened out."

Stubbs reached down to unlatch his holster.

"If you'd check the manifest, you'd see that I'm accounted for."

It was a shot in the dark, considering that Dex hadn't actually checked the manifest himself. He was hoping that Baker had planned for this possibility. If not, the mission was about to get a whole lot messier. Keeping one hand next to his holster, Stubbs used his free hand to flip through a few screens on the data pad. After a few tense moments, he frowned and set the pad aside.

"So tell me, why would an honest person make such a long trip stashed away on an automated cargo freighter?"

"The owner of this ship is transporting some delicate cargo. He wanted it handled *carefully*," Dex said, nodding in the direction of the cumbersome Mules.

Stubbs tapped the case with his foot. "Open it."

Dex knelt down and popped open the case, revealing dozens of sparkling crystals.

"Whoa," Stubbs murmured.

"They're Dionysian crystals. Very rare. Very fragile. So you can understand why my boss wanted these hand delivered."

Stubbs nodded. His face still registered surprise, but Dex could already see the wheels turning. *How could he profit from this? Could he shoot this lone traveler and make off with the case? Would he be able to erase the security feed?* Dex locked his eyes onto Stubbs, ready to spring at the slightest provocation.

Stubbs's first move, though, was not an act of aggression. Rather, he reached down and dug through the case, presumably searching for any hidden contraband. If he conducted a thorough search, he would find more than enough. But to Dex's relief, Stubbs didn't make it very far, pausing his search to pick up one of the crystals. He held it up by one of its thin spires, gasping first in admiration when the iridescent crystal shifted from clear to opaque and then in horror as it shattered in his hand. He stood in disbelief as thousands of dust particles sifted through his fingers and floated to the ground.

"Can I have your full name please?" Dex asked in an even tone.

It took Stubbs a moment to realize that Dex was speaking to him. "Huh? What's that?"

"*Stubbs*—is that your first or last name?"

"What do you need my name for?"

"For our records. My employer will want to know who to contact for payment. I hope for your sake you have a good insurance plan."

Stubbs nervously glanced up. Dex guessed that he was spying a security camera.

"I'll also need your print," Dex said, pulling out his handpod. "And it would be helpful if I could speak to your supervisor."

Stubbs backed up a few steps.

"Yeah, sure. I'll go get him right now. Just wait here."

Stubbs turned and half-jogged, half-ran across the pad.

"Can I get your print first?" Dex shouted after him as he escaped through the exit. Wasting no time, Dex snapped the case shut and once again began hauling it as quickly as he could. He knew he didn't have long. Stubbs was undoubtedly trying to cover his tracks by erasing the security feed. Dex wasn't sure if the little man would have the guts to come back and try to silence him permanently, and he didn't want to wait around to find out.

Shuffling through the exit, Dex was confronted by three similar-looking corridors. There were no signs or markings of any kind, which came as little surprise. He took his best guess. In a ring-style port, the left and right corridors usually led to other pads, while the center corridor funneled passengers to the main exit. But that was assuming that this port adhered to certain standards, and if his brief experience thus far was any indication, he wasn't overly confident. His hunch, however, paid off as the main entrance soon came into view.

He slowed his pace, looking for any sign of trouble—extra-long glances from officials, impromptu barricades, or perhaps even Stubbs himself would be waiting with backup. He was a touch insulted, then, when the only thing between him and the exit was a pudgy man behind a desk, reclining in a chair and engrossed in some viewing material on his handpod. Dex was about to set down his case to retrieve his ID tag when the man absently waved him through without a single glance up. Dex happily obliged, and just like that, he was free of the confines of the port authority building.

The doors opened up directly onto one of the main streets of Port Henri, a characteristic common to older port cities. Normally, the design was an annoyance, leading to excessive traffic and delays. But this time, Dex didn't mind the congestion, taking the opportunity to disappear into the bustle. He weaved his way through the foot-traffic for a few sub-districts before ducking into a side alley.

After confirming that the alley was clear, he opened the case and dumped out its contents, spilling the crystals without a second thought, several of them shattering before they even hit the ground. It was a clever trick devised by Baker—faux crystals that lost their integrity when removed from the temperature-controlled case. Dex, for his part, had made up the *Dionysian* label, figuring—correctly, as it turned out—that he wouldn't be dealing with an expert in rare gems.

From the bottom of the case, he removed a satchel that contained some credit chips, a couple of specialized devices, a disassembled battery rifle from the squadron's weapons locker, and the ornate knife that had mysteriously shown up in Baker's cargo crate. Looking over the contents, the knife now seemed like a silly addition—he couldn't even clearly remember his rationale for packing it—but, at the very least, one could always find use for a cutting instrument in the field. He secured it in his waistband.

The rest of the items had much more immediate and practical uses. The credits he would use to rent an airbike—it was five hundred kilometers from Port Henri to the small town of Little Thooft, and another two hundred kilometers from there to JenKore's planet-side facility. It was at the facility that he would make use of the devices and—if he was lucky—the rifle.

Chapter 25

"Tell me this won't take long."

Liana was reclining sideways in the copilot's seat, her legs draped over an armrest, as Darik guided the *Golden Crow* toward JenKore Manufacturing Station 33 in orbit over Bellona. As soon as the ship dropped from the ether, Darik had assumed manual control, eager to fly the sleek cruiser—if only for a moment.

"Why? You have somewhere more important to be?"

Liana lightly rubbed her foot along Darik's right calf. "Well, now that you mention it, I was thinking our own private island on Virgilia. Surely you could afford one, Mr. Vice President."

Liana's signals had become increasingly clear as the trip progressed. They had always enjoyed somewhat of a flirtatious relationship at the office, but it had never developed into anything more. Darik had held himself back, certain that she already had a boyfriend. How could she not—a woman of such poise, intelligence, and beauty? But the longer they were together on the cruiser, the more he found himself not caring whether or not there was someone else. She was here with him now, and that was all that mattered.

He smiled, though he kept his eyes fixed on the station, watching the distance tick down on the translucent display.

"That does sound tempting. We'd lie on the beach and watch the sunset. And Nikky could mix drinks and serenade us."

Liana wrinkled her nose. "Actually, I was picturing a Nikky-free island. We would have to drop him off along the way—Virgilia must have at least one habitable moon."

"Now that's just mean."

"Oh, it wouldn't be that bad. We could wave to him every night."

A couple of long tones interrupted the exchange, informing Darik that the autopilot had taken control of the ship for the final approach. As the station neared, Darik saw that the design of JMS-33 was far from elegant—nothing more than a narrow strip bracketed by two block-shaped docking bays. The autopilot steered the *Golden Crow* toward the smaller, entrance bay.

"So, you're sure I can't come with you?"

"I don't think that'd be a good idea. If you get bored, why don't you go see Nikky?"

If he ever comes out. Nikky hadn't left his cabin since their little confrontation earlier.

"Oh, what a wonderful idea!" Liana replied with a sudden burst of enthusiasm. "Yes, Nikky and I will have a grand old time. We'll share a bottle of Vorinian and have a lively conversation about current events, and then maybe we'll cap off the evening with some vigorous fingernail chewing."

The stars around them vanished as the ship glided into the docking bay. Darik rose from his seat. "Just…behave."

Liana swiveled around and blocked him in with her legs. "Are you sure that's what you want?"

For a moment, Darik considered postponing the tour, but soon thought better of it, deciding that, as a newly-promoted vice president, he should probably exhibit a measure of professionalism—at least this time.

He picked up Liana's left leg and gently set it down behind him.

"See you soon."

Exiting the cockpit, he glanced aft toward the cabins and saw that Nikky's door was still shut. Part of him wanted to stop over and say something, but he didn't particularly feel like talking to a door. And besides, he didn't even know what, exactly, he wanted to say. Instead, he turned to the exterior door, which, according to a green light on its control panel, had released its seal and was safe to open.

Darik pressed the panel and was taken aback by the darkness that awaited him. Docking bays, in his experience, were usually so brightly lit that they often gave him a headache. But here, it was quite the opposite. A thin row of burnt orange bordered the rectangular bay door, and a few other dim lights were scattered around, presumably to mark landing zones, but they did little to illuminate the gaping cavern.

Darik gingerly stepped down onto the metal floor. Upon his exit, the *Crow*'s exterior door wasted no time latching shut behind him, removing the strongest source of light from the bay. He stood still, reluctant to proceed until his eyes adjusted to the darkness. As he waited, the *Crow*'s engines powered down, the shrill whine fading away until there was only silence. He knew his ship was just a few meters behind him, that Liana and Nikky were just seconds away, and yet Darik had never felt more alone. He took a deep breath and slowly shuffled forward.

"Welcome, Darik."

The voice was impossibly close. Darik spun to his left and saw the outline of a man not more than an arm's length away.

"Follow me."

The man turned and walked off, disappearing after only a few brisk paces, leaving Darik very little time to process the startling encounter. His pride rejected the idea of blindly following some creep who didn't even have the decency to introduce himself, but that inclination was overpowered by his fear of being left alone in the docking bay. After a moment's hesitation, he scrambled after the man, struggling to keep him in sight.

They traveled in that manner for what felt like several minutes, the man always on the verge of evaporating into the shadows. They never entered a door or a corridor, nor did they ever seem to change direction on their way across what was increasingly becoming an improbably enormous docking bay. Darik had begun to suspect that he was being led around in circles when the man suddenly stopped, nearly causing a collision. A new source of light emerged as a pair of doors slid open in front of Darik. Wordlessly, the two of them entered a small lift.

A single overhead light illuminated his host for the first time. Darik instantly recognized him—Kristof Haman, the creator and architect of the M-2. It was a staggering discovery. Haman had always been something of a personal hero to Darik, who regarded the M-2 as a work of genius. He had long considered it an injustice that Haman never received the public recognition he deserved for his contribution to humanity. It was, then, exceedingly bizarre to suddenly find himself standing next to the man he so admired—especially since, only moments before, he had taken a severe disliking to his mysterious travel companion. As the lift continued upward, Darik couldn't help glancing over. It may have been the lighting, but Haman was much more odd-looking in person than his holopics had suggested. A scraggly layer of gray hair wrapped around the back of his pale bald head, and his thin lips were perpetually upturned as if he were always smirking at his own private joke. Seeing Haman face to face gave Darik the impression that his lack of public exposure may have been for the best.

The lift doors opened, revealing a long factory floor rumbling with the sounds of machines at work. To Darik's annoyance, the assembly area was nearly as dark as the docking bay. He figured that there was probably some strategic purpose to keeping the lights turned off, but it wouldn't have surprised him if it was just another way for JenKore to pinch some credits. Haman, for his part, was undeterred by the poor visibility, strolling confidently along the assembly line while Darik once again followed closely behind.

"As you can see, JMS-33 serves as a legitimate manufacturer of laser cutters." Haman had to all but shriek to be heard above the noise. "The entire operation is automated for obvious reasons. You should feel honored—you're one of only a handful of people who have ever stepped foot on this station."

Darik was about to express an insincere bit of gratitude when he became distracted by a pair of small white lights drifting through the air. As he stared, it quickly became clear that the lights were not floating freely but were attached to a hefty mechanical arm that was swinging directly toward his head. He instinctively covered up and ducked, narrowly avoiding what would have been certain decapitation. Remaining crouched, he craned his head around, looking for any other potential hazards.

Haman, oblivious to the near-fatal accident, continued on a leisurely gait up the line.

"You'll want to watch your step," he shouted without turning back. "The factory floor does not have the most human-friendly design."

Thanks for the warning.

Darik cautiously stood up, only to realize that he had once again lost sight of Haman. He had last seen him next to the main assembly belt, but now he was gone, as though he'd never been there, leaving Darik alone, surrounded by the ceaseless activity of the machinery.

Despite the potential distraction of Haman's disappearance, Darik had maintained his awareness of the equipment closest to him. Even as he scanned the dark recesses of the room, he sidestepped the bulky arm, which was swinging back to its starting position. As he moved, he caught a glimpse of Haman standing on the far side of a pair of enormous metal presses.

"Are you coming, Darik?" Haman's tone was a little too impatient for Darik's liking, considering that he had snuck away without a single word. He looked around for a passageway but couldn't find any route to Haman—at least, not any reasonable route. There was a narrow gap between the presses that was possibly wide enough to squeeze through, but he thought it highly unlikely that Haman had taken that path himself. A second search, though, revealed no visible alternatives. He could feel Haman's irritation mounting, but he was too proud to simply ask the way. Unwilling to wait any longer, Darik decided to take the only available option. He breathed in, turned sidewise, and slid in between the giant presses.

It was an even tighter fit than he'd thought, forcing him to tilt his head back, with his chin rubbing against one side and the back of his head against the other. As he inched along, the press behind him slammed down without warning. The impact was so loud and violent that Darik felt as though every bone in his body had shattered by mere proximity. He might have stood there in shock indefinitely had it not been for the very powerful urge to flee before the second press came thundering down. Doubling his pace, he scraped through the remainder of the crevice, ignoring the painful abrasions, until he emerged on the other side, disheveled and shaking.

As he took a moment to compose himself, he caught a glimmer of amusement in Haman's eyes. There was no doubt in his mind that Haman had purposefully withheld an easier path. Why Haman was bothering with all these little games was beyond him. There was no reason for him to feel threatened. Darik didn't want to wrestle away control of the M-2/As; he was only there to learn more about the machines. Perhaps he could find a way to communicate that to Haman. Or maybe Haman wasn't threatened in the least, and this was simply the way he treated all of his guests—in which case, Darik planned on avoiding any repeat visits.

For all his trouble, he had been led to a nondescript door marked *storage*—though he had a feeling that the label was misleading. Haman waved his handpod in front of a sensor, and the door slid aside, a bright light pouring out of the opening. Darik, whose eyes had only recently become acclimated to the darkness, recoiled from the sudden burst of light. Keeping his brow lowered, he opened his eyes with difficulty and saw that the light had now been partially blocked. The silhouette was within reach directly in front of him, and as he focused, he realized that he was staring into the black spherical eye of an M-2.

Neither Darik nor the machine moved. It was not a modified M-2/A but rather a stock M-2—a machine Darik had encountered on a daily basis for all of his adult life. Nevertheless, he was overcome by an irrational fear of the machine. It may have been the ambience of the station or the lingering effects of Haman's mind games, but Darik could not shake the sense that the M-2 meant him harm, as though he were some sort of intruder.

Haman strolled by, whispering something to the machine as he passed. At the command, the M-2 abruptly turned away, giving Darik his first clear view of the room. In contrast to the rest of the station, the walls were stark white and lit with the intensity of an operating room. The side walls were lined with rows of shelves that held a variety of parts and tools and weapons. The M-2 that Darik had met at the door positioned itself in front of a workstation while a second M-2 glided back and forth across the little room, collecting objects that Darik couldn't identify.

Standing like a statue in the center of the room was a nearly completed M-2/A. Several taut cords connected its frame to a couple of adjacent terminals, giving the impression that the machine had been tethered to the back wall. This was Darik's first glimpse of an M-2/A in person, and he saw that it resembled the stock M-2 in many respects. Its head consisted of the same bulbous omnisensor, enabling it to "see" in all directions at once in a wide range of spectra; its powerful frame was similarly sleek, though its torso had been widened to accommodate a small shield generator; and its feet likewise employed dozens of writhing "feelers" that reached out and absorbed impact, which made possible the distinctive elegance of an M-2 in motion.

The most obvious modifications, of course, involved its combat capabilities. Its left arm housed a multi-purpose firearm, which supported a variety of batteries and attachments, while its hands allowed it to operate any conventional weapon with maximum efficiency. Its most powerful weapon, however, was not a standard military weapon at all but rather one of the station's industrial-grade laser cutters, capable of penetrating the hardest materials known to man. The cutter made it virtually impossible for targets to barricade themselves from an M-2/A, which is why it was such a shame that the device was prone to malfunctioning, if Nikky was to be believed.

Despite its showy weaponry, Darik knew that the biggest changes were hidden away in the M-2/A's programming. Some changes were rather pedestrian, such as the command to record all raw data from its omnisensor for future analysis, while others were of the utmost consequence, none more so than its sophisticated—and highly illegal—combat-related subroutines.

Only when Haman spoke did Darik notice they were standing side-by-side.

"You can't hide from its sensors. Your weapons can't pierce its shield. It's armed like a tank yet runs with the speed and grace of a Hermesian gazelle. It will not grow tired, nor will it be hindered by fear or remorse. It is the most fearsome predator ever devised by God or man."

Darik was surprised to hear Haman refer to "God"—especially considering the intended prey for these predators—but it was hard to disagree with the assessment. He was glad the machines were on his side.

He cleared his throat and spoke to Haman for the first time.

"It's an impressive achievement—it seems as though the M-2 is finally being used to its full potential." Darik hadn't intended his comment as flattery—it had long been a strong belief of his that M-2s were under-utilized—but Haman certainly seemed pleased by his remarks. Darik realized that, if nothing else, the two of them could always find common ground in their shared appreciation of the M-2.

He continued. "How many M-2/As has JenKore produced?"

It was a plain question asked out of simple curiosity, which is why Darik was so baffled when Haman didn't supply a straight answer.

"I'm not at liberty to say."

The fact that Haman was withholding such a trivial piece of information made Darik all the more determined to discover the answer. He tried another approach. "Well, can you at least tell me how long we've been producing this model?"

From the limited files Darik had recently been given access to, he'd learned that the transition from M-2 to M-2/A was a long one—a process that included reprogramming, outfitting, and testing. His educated guess placed the turnover time at approximately one week per unit. If he could find out when JenKore began producing the M-2/A, he could make a rough estimate of the total number of units—provided that JMS-33 was the only station that oversaw the conversion, as he'd been led to believe.

Haman again stonewalled. "I'm afraid that's privileged information."

Darik wondered if Haman had always been speaking in such an irritating, nasally tone and if he had only now become aware of it. Whatever the case, he hated the voice, and he was beginning to hate the speaker. It was time to put an end to all of his ridiculous little games. He turned and faced Haman directly, accentuating every inch of his height advantage as he leaned in.

"Listen. Jenkins personally promoted me to vice president, which means I'm in charge of this entire operation. I say the word, and we shut the whole thing down. So, I'm going to need some straight answers, and I'm going to need them now."

Darik surprised himself with the intensity of his outburst. It did not, though, have the intended effect on Haman. Rather than submitting, he adopted a condescending, almost parental air in his response.

"I'm sorry, Darik, but Kirrone is very strict about this kind of need-to-know information. Now, if you want, I can put in a good word for you the next time I see him. Would you like me to do that?"

And there it was. After his promotion, Darik had foolishly assumed the veil would be lifted, that he would have access to the inner-workings of JenKore—or, at the very least, that he would be given the information necessary to perform his job. But now it had sunk in—he was going to be kept just as much in the dark as ever. Jenkins, Graves, Haman—they were all in a special little club, and no matter how many promotions he received, no matter how high he climbed up the corporate ladder, he would never be able to join.

He attempted to mask his devastation with a measure of civility.

"No, that won't be necessary. I trust Mr. Jenkins's judgment, of course."

Haman shuffled to Darik's side, placing a hand on his back.

"I know it's frustrating, but you must understand that secrecy is of the utmost importance. The government is not blind to our overall efforts, but if they were to learn that we were constructing an illegal army of machines, well, that would complicate matters."

"An army?" Darik allowed himself a slight smile. Even if Haman hadn't divulged a precise number, he took the revelation as a minor victory. The station apparently had been very busy over the past several years.

"Yes," Haman continued, unfazed by the slip-up, "an army unrivaled in the history of mankind—at least, it would be if we unleashed its potential."

There was an unmistakable trace of resentment in Haman's tone. *Trouble in paradise?* Darik pressed the issue. "How so?"

"In the field, my machines are used in a ridiculously inefficient manner. But Kirrone has his reasons, naturally. He is exceedingly particular about how he wants each...*encounter* conducted."

A long blade sprang out of the right forearm of the M-2/A, the tip stopping mere inches from Darik's abdomen. Until that moment, the machine had remained completely motionless, which made the sudden burst of movement all the more startling. The dark blade contained the same traces of blue as the idol in Jenkins's office. Darik guessed that the blade was of the same origin—he could, in fact, already feel the familiar effects of the peculiar metal on his body. His heart was pounding, and his vision began to blur.

When he regained focus, he was shocked to see that he was no longer in the same room, nor even, it seemed, on the station. The workstations, the walls, Haman—nearly everything was gone, replaced by unblemished white, as though he were travelling through the ether. The only thing that remained from the room was the M-2/A, which stood the same distance away. As Darik stared in wonder at the machine, the white around them dissipated like a lifting fog, revealing their surroundings. They were now in the middle of an abandoned city, enclosed on all sides by hollow, burned-out structures. Looking up, Darik saw the night sky and marveled at what had just happened. It was unlike anything he had experienced before—he certainly hadn't been transported in this manner during his previous encounters with the dark metal.

He tried to move but was overwhelmed by a sharp pain in his right shoulder. He looked down and saw that a metal rod was sticking straight through him. His gaze followed the rod out to its origin—the left arm of the M-2/A. The machine was using the rod to hold him in place.

Darik could hear the vibrations even before the blade flashed in front of his face. Only then did he fully understand the machine's intent. He was the victim. The prey. Darik tried to tell himself that this was only some sort of weird hallucination, but the searing pain in his shoulder felt all too real.

The machine slowly and deliberately raised its right arm, pressing the blade up against Darik's neck. He was utterly exhausted, and his entire body was trembling, but beneath those physical sensations, he was experiencing an altogether unexpected feeling—a deep and profound peace. As he struggled to make sense of this, he noticed a man in white standing behind the machine. There was a brilliant flash, and a bright shaft of light came bursting through the M-2's head. The machine melted away in front of him. Darik squinted, trying to catch a glimpse of the man who had rescued him, but all he could see was a blinding light. The harder he stared, the more it became clear that he was looking at an overhead light fixture.

The room had returned—the walls, and the rows of shelves, and the M-2/A, which remained motionless in the center, connected to the workstations. Darik felt a rush of embarrassment and was hoping that the little episode had been confined to his head, devoid of any accompanying physical actions. To his relief, he soon became aware that Haman was no longer in the room—though it was unclear if Darik's strange behavior had been the reason for his departure.

A quick look around revealed an open door along the right wall. He didn't have a full view of the side-room, but from his angle, he could see a handful of stock M-2s lined up against a wall. He guessed that they were in the process of being reprogrammed. After a moment or two, Haman emerged. If he had witnessed anything odd from Darik, he didn't let on.

"So, what would you like to know about my machines?"

Still feeling out of sorts, Darik meandered around the room, half-heartedly examining various pieces of equipment while he tried to regain his composure. As he wandered, he noticed a row of laser cutters on one of the shelves. The sight of the cutters helped clear his head. *Focus on the laser cutter*, Nikky had said back on the *Crow*, hinting at hardware concerns. Determined to refocus on the business at hand, Darik picked up one of the devices and turned to face Haman.

"Well, to begin, it's come to my attention that the M-2/A might be prone to certain failures."

Haman gave a thin smile. "I beg to differ. My machines have successfully completed every mission they've been assigned."

"That may be, but haven't there been performance issues with the laser cutter?" It was a shot in the dark. Nikky had said that the M-2/A program had the *potential* for compatibility errors, but it was possible that the glitches had yet to surface—if they even existed at all.

Haman sighed. "You're right, Darik. There have been a few isolated cases in which the cutter experienced an unexpected power drain. But all that did was give my machines the opportunity to be a little more...creative."

Darik pressed on, pleased that Nikky's information had paid off. "I don't doubt the ability of these machines to accomplish their objectives. But I think we can both agree that we want the M-2/As operating at their peak." Darik flipped the cutter over in his hand. It was lighter than he'd expected. "Would you mind if I ran some personal tests?"

"I can assure you that every conceivable diagnostic has already been conducted. I'll send you the data if you'd like."

Darik sucked in his cheeks. He'd spent the last two years relying almost exclusively on the information of others, and it had nearly cost him his career. That wasn't how he planned on operating this time around. He looked Haman directly in the eye.

"I'll be glad to look at your data, but I'm also going to need to examine one of these devices for myself. So, with your permission, I'll study this one, or I'll just pick one up on my way back to Compton. It doesn't matter to me."

There was a pause, and Darik could see that Haman was visibly annoyed. For a moment, he thought that Haman might order the M-2s to forcefully remove the laser cutter from his hands. But when Haman finally spoke, it was clear that the main source of his annoyance was not anger or distrust or even wounded pride, but rather sheer boredom.

"Then, yes, by all means, go ahead and play with your toy. We certainly don't have a shortage of cutters around here. But there is a better way to see what these weapons can do." He strode toward the room's exit. "Come, let us travel to the planet-side facility. I'm eager for you to see my machines in action."

Tucking the laser cutter in the crook of his arm, Darik followed Haman out of the room. Behind him, the M-2/A's blade slowly retracted back into its arm.

Chapter 26

The striking blue-green atmosphere of Pella stretched out below Scot, but the panoramic beauty of the world was lost on him. In the cockpit of his Hornet, he fidgeted, anxious to learn the details of the Angels' latest mission. He glanced to his left. Flying in tight formation, he could just make out Jani's grim, determined expression in the soft interior lighting of her own ship. He imagined that she was mulling over the same concerns that he was.

As always, taking all ten Hornets out left the colony totally vulnerable. However, with only one squadron, and that one already two fighters short, there simply weren't a lot of alternatives—particularly if the Angels had a "big" mission. And with full loads of Slammers, one HIB each, D'Felco already out there somewhere, and all the secrecy—this certainly qualified as "big."

Scot waited impatiently for the in-flight briefing to begin. He was already positioned astern of Ninja and Prince. He and Jani had followed the lieutenant commander and Geff into orbit, flying in formation the entire way. Ahead, Viper and Ghazi were joined together behind Sarge's fighter—Seltrice to the right, Adahn to the left. As much as it galled Scot to be flying Rabbit's wing, he had to admit that he was happy to be at least temporarily relieved of the burden of flying with Adahn. He noted with pointless satisfaction that his sensor screen showed his former partner to be just a fraction of a meter out of position.

Just behind them were Sunfire and Moonlight, completing flight one's star formation. There was no need to check their positions—whatever the Voor twins may have lacked in aggressiveness, they certainly made up for in precision.

Nine Hornets, Scot thought, correcting his earlier assessment. Depending on where Dex was—and what his intentions were—there was a very good chance that the remaining Angels were going into battle *three* fighters short. Just what did the captain have in mind when he took off, alone, in the dead of night, leaving the rest of the squadron even more short-handed than before?

With little fanfare, the mission data feed finally engaged—simultaneously, he surmised, with the ones on board the other eight Hornets. As flight coordinates and other data streamed across the screen, Captain D'Felco's recorded voice played in his earpiece.

"Angels, this is Deadeye. I apologize for this clandestine approach, but recent security breaches and the importance of this mission necessitated this unorthodox briefing."

Scot's screen flickered, and the flight data was replaced with an image of a standard JenKore M-2 service unit. Dex's briefing continued.

"You are all, of course, familiar with these units. Some of your families may have even owned one or two."

Scot smirked. *Not my family. We never had the scratch to afford one of those.* He did remember, however, a few of them hovering around the Bennet compound when he had accompanied Geff on leave to visit his parents. The M-2s had poured drinks, maintained the lawn, parked shuttles—no task was too trivial for the machines. Scot recalled being somewhat envious at the time, but he couldn't see what any of this had to do with their mission.

Dex went on. "What you have not known is that during our engagements with the Marauders, we have actually been flying against reprogrammed M-2s."

Scot heard several clicks in his headset, an indication that multiple pilots were attempting to chime in with comments, but a red indicator on his mic switch told him that Commander Lebrian apparently had everyone on listen-only mode for the moment.

The recording continued. "To answer the question that I'm sure many of you are asking, yes—that does violate every robotics law on the books today. However, our intel does not indicate that the Coalition government is behind this reprogramming, nor do we have any reason to believe that they are responsible for sending them out after us. Someone else has been dispatching these things. For the time being, their identity will remain classified, but make no mistake, the altered pilot M-2s intend harm on this squadron and this colony."

Scot had an instant recollection of Fran's and Kevan's Hornets evaporating before his very eyes. Flight recordings after that mission had shown zero evidence of a control ship within range. The Angels had always wondered how unmanned Marauders could possibly have gotten the jump on the squadron without another, manned ship in the sector, exercising close proximity control. Now they knew the answer. If this mission was intended to blow apart some Marauder-flying bolt buckets, then Scot was all in.

Dex had apparently anticipated his pilots' sentiments. "Now, I know most of us would like nothing better than to take a little revenge out on these things, especially for Smiley and Aces, and you very well may get that chance, but any Marauders you might encounter are not, repeat *not* your primary mission objective. Reprogramming of pilots is only the beginning of what we are up against." Scot heard Dex pause, as though the captain was gathering himself. "Base M-2s are also being physically modified—modified into efficient killing machines. These modified M-2s have one known objective at this time—the elimination of every Christian dispersed throughout the Coalition, including our own colony. I will spare each of you the details, but I have seen what these machines can do, and if their assembly is allowed to continue, they *will* accomplish that objective."

Scot whistled softly, the sound echoing inside his flight helmet. Pilot M-2s coming after the squadron—that was bad enough. But now, he couldn't help picturing a vast army of soulless automatons mowing through a defenseless colony. Shaking the image from his head, he concentrated on the mission screen as it changed once more, this time revealing a narrow nondescript station in orbit above a medium-sized, yellow-ochre planet.

"This is Bellona." Dex's voice continued. "The station you see is called JMS-33, and it is your mission objective. According to our intel, this station is the site where M-2s are being reprogrammed and modified. In short, we destroy this station and we stop, at least temporarily, the manufacture of these killing machines."

Scot grunted with satisfaction, stealing a glance at his ordnance display. The Heavy Ion Bomb, issued to each Hornet for this mission, was securely in place.

"The station may appear defenseless, but it is not. We can expect heavy resistance. In addition to externally mounted turrets, the station is armed with an array of two dozen missile launchers hidden within its structure. Mission analysis has concluded that nine Hornets would be completely outmatched by the amount of fire-power from those launchers. We've identified, however, a vulnerability in this defense. The organization behind these modifications values secrecy above all else. Because of this, Station 33 is normally unmanned—a fully automated operation. The missile launchers are controlled from a planet-side facility."

This made sense to Scot. The personnel on the planet probably had no idea what they were guarding up there. Through his headset, he heard a subtle change in Dex's voice.

"Now, Angels, we come to the reason for my sudden departure. I have obtained an access code into the planet-side defense system. Once inside, I should be able to deactivate the launchers, giving you a clear shot at the station. As you hear this, I am placing myself into position to hack into the system, but time is of the essence. The code is scheduled to change at midnight, Bellona time. If you accept this mission, you will follow jump coordinates straight to Bellona immediately following this briefing. This will place you at your target at 2300—enough time for me to input the code, deactivate the launchers, and let you light up the station."

Scot's heart was already beginning to race. Dex in the mud, the threat of a couple dozen missiles locking on at any time, the prospect of launching his first live HIB—it sounded like fun.

"By now, Sarge and Ninja have given you the new squadron alignment. This mission is voluntary. You may respond to Commander Lebrian whether you are in or not. He will relay the final total to me by a series of static bursts on a tight, closed bandwidth."

He paused, and now Scot was certain he could hear controlled emotion in the captain's voice. "Angels, we have a duty. We must protect our brothers and sisters who are unable to protect themselves. We owe it to them, and we owe it to our fallen comrades. The madness behind these machines must be confronted, and it must be confronted now. Much has been said about our being on the defensive. I have heard your concerns about never getting the chance to launch a preemptive strike—to decisively fight for our continued freedom, and our very existence. *This* is your chance, Angels. I await your response. Deadeye, out."

Scot's mic indicator toggled from red to green, and he beat the other pilots to the punch.

"Sarge, Flash. I only have one question. Why would Captain D'Felco put *himself* on the ground? I mean, with all respect, he's *not* the most qualified person on the team for that kind of grunt work—and Lord knows, we could use him out there in a Hornet."

Hagen's response was quick. "I'm sure that he has his reasons, Lieutenant—reasons we are not here to speculate about. Understand, pilots, that the planet-side component of this mission has extreme danger—danger that the captain has chosen to face alone. We, ourselves, must expect resistance from the station, and if the captain is unsuccessful, or even delayed in his ground mission, there is the very real possibility we will take heavy casualties. The captain has left the decision to proceed in each of your hands. One thing is certain—this mission will fail if that code changes before we arrive."

Scot heard Jani click in. "Not to mention we would be leaving Deadeye with no escape support."

It was Geff's turn. "That's another thing. In that briefing, I really didn't hear anything about an evac plan for the captain."

Hagen was back on the channel, his voice subdued. "No…you didn't." He paused while the implication sunk in. "The captain included more information on my mission feed. I doubt that it was intended for everyone, but under the circumstances, if you are going to accept this mission, I think you have a right to know the rest of the situation. We don't know how many of those monsters have already been built. For all we know, there may even be other manufacturing sites. Because of that, the captain's orders are as follows: We are to destroy the station, then jump out *immediately*. We are to return to the colony and begin preparation for the possibility of an all-out invasion. Under no circumstances, repeat, *no circumstances*, *Lieutenant Calgaro*, is there to be any attempt at an evac or rescue mission for the captain. This is in and out, real quick. He doesn't want to risk any delay that would leave the colony vulnerable or lead to us getting tracked back home."

"Sarge, Viper. So what, then? We just *leave* him?"

"Yes. That is *exactly* what we do. I can tell you that Dex is completely committed to this mission. For him, it's…" Hagen paused again. "It's…personal. I won't say any more, but understand this—he will not be leaving Bellona until that station is destroyed, and I believe the best way to give him a chance to get out of there alive is to do our jobs and blow it to pieces. So, what's it going to be, Angels? I'm going after that station. Are you in or out?"

Scot keyed his mic, prepared to say, *Are you kidding? Just try to go without me*, but his response was lost amid the chatter of the other seven pilots, each racing to be the first to say yes.

*   *   *

The message was brief. Sidnir had it solved before his terminal had even begun the decryption process. To anyone else, the transmission would appear as nonsense, a random burst of visual static. But Sidnir knew this agent's signature well enough to sift through the interference—where others would see only static, he pieced together a single seven-letter word. As Sidnir considered the implications of the message, the program caught up to him, displaying the word in plain characters.

BELLONA

He swiveled in his chair. Herk was still attempting to crack Weis's workstation—a challenging task that had been made all but impossible by the presence of Graves, who was silently hovering over his partner's shoulder.

"Sir, I just received a message from Blackfriar."

Graves immediately marched over—information from Blackfriar was almost always time-sensitive. As Graves arrived at his station, Sidnir stole a glance across the room at Herk, whose shoulders had already released some of their tension. Graves leaned down and studied the screen.

"That's it?"

"Yes, sir."

Graves remained silent. There were a number of concerns that merited discussion—the unusual brevity of the message, the lack of mission details, even the potential that Blackfriar had been compromised—but Sidnir knew better than to interrupt his boss's mediation. After a long moment, Graves turned and stared into the distance above Sidnir's head, his eyes not focusing on anything in particular.

"It seems as though they've finally taken some precautions. But it's of little consequence—this will suffice. Send word to Bellona. Tell them to expect the entire squadron."

300

He paused and caught Sidnir's eye. "And activate the Marauder squadrons in the Agrius system."

Sidnir nodded and tried, unsuccessfully, to suppress a smile. For two years, D'Felco and his squadron had remained maddeningly elusive. But suddenly here they were, willingly marching into the lion's den.

Graves paced toward the room's internal lift. "Send me continual updates."

"Sir?" Sidnir was surprised to see him leaving the nerve center at such a critical time.

Stepping into the lift, Graves pivoted back around and held the door open for an extra second. "I'm heading up. Mr. Jenkins will want to hear of this development in person."

*   *   *

Darik Mason watched Bellona's distant red sun creep behind a range of foothills, the fading light casting long shadows behind the scorched bunkers that surrounded the facility. The top level of the facility's control tower offered Darik a panoramic view of the entire compound, and the effect was unsettling. Up until now, the capabilities of the M-2/A had been a mere abstraction. But looking all around and seeing nothing but endless rows of burned-out, crumbling buildings caused Darik, for the first time, to fully consider the destructive power of these machines. The place was less a research facility than a warzone.

Perhaps his outlook would change once he could focus his attention on the intoxicating beauty of an M-2/A in action rather than the sobering aftermath.

If the test ever happened.

He had spent the last several hours wandering about the control room as Haman made preparations at a pace far too leisurely for his liking. At one point, Darik had lost his patience and demanded to know the reason for the hold-up. With an air of condescension, Haman had responded that the facility only conducted tests at night. Darik would have been more irritated at his complete disregard for common courtesy had he not come to expect that kind of nonsense from Haman. Despite his own frustrations, he felt worse for Liana and Nikky, who, lacking the necessary security clearances to visit the facility, were still cooped up in the *Golden Crow* on the orbital station.

"Kristof."

There were three techs in the control room, and all of them had been periodically calling out for their boss.

"Not now," Haman hissed from another station.

"Actually, you're going to want to see this." Darik detected an unusual urgency from the tech, an older man with a gray-stubble beard. Haman either didn't notice the alarm in the man's voice or didn't care. He entered another series of commands before finally shuffling over to the nervous tech.

"What?" he demanded.

The tech whispered something. Darik couldn't hear what was said, but he saw the annoyance dissipate from Haman's face—replaced by what emotion, he couldn't quite tell.

"What's going on?" Darik asked, knowing that Haman wouldn't freely volunteer any information.

For a moment, it seemed that Haman was going to ignore him, but after a brief hesitation, he abruptly turned to face Darik, the devious little grin returning to his lips.

"Well, Darik, it appears that we're going to be receiving a visit from a squadron of heavily armed fighters."

"D'Felco…" Darik muttered, recalling the name of the ex-Navy captain and one of JenKore's high-priority targets.

Haman smirked. "Very good. You must have been doing your homework."

Darik didn't care for Haman's casual attitude.

"Well, what's the procedure here? Do we evacuate?"

Haman exchanged an amused look with the youngest tech, a cocky looking kid with bleach-blond hair. "Oh, that's a little dramatic, don't you think?"

Darik took a mental inventory of the facility's defenses, or lack thereof. No walls. No turrets. Not even a perimeter fence. He understood the rationale—if the facility too closely resembled a military installation, it would attract the wrong sort of attention—but it left them absurdly vulnerable. As far as he knew, the only weapons in the entire compound were in the hands of a couple of guards patrolling the perimeter.

Darik shifted under the weight of his satchel's shoulder strap. Inside the satchel was one additional "weapon"—the laser cutter he had taken from the station—but they were all in serious trouble if it came down to that.

"No, I don't think it's dramatic. Correct me if I'm wrong, but this facility lacks even the most basic defenses."

"The orbital station, not this facility, will be their target. And let me assure you—its defenses are impenetrable."

Darik thought it incredibly reckless of Haman to be gambling their lives on such a guess.

"And what if you're wrong? What if they send ground forces?"

"I sincerely hope they do! A single one of my machines could lay waste to an entire Marine battalion. So I don't think a handful of pistol-packing flyboys will pose much of a threat."

Darik had not considered the M-2/A as a line of defense, and he had to admit that the thought of it stalking around the compound made him feel a little more secure. Even so, he wanted to point out the very real possibility that D'Felco and his squadron might attack the facility directly with their fighters. But Haman, apparently, considered the matter closed, turning his attention back to the blond tech.

"Cycle through all the codes and post a double watch on the outer buildings." Though Haman maintained his casual body language, he issued the command with an authoritative tone.

"Should I power up the station's launchers?" the tech asked.

"Not yet. Coordinate our defenses with Compton. I have a feeling they'll want to have a hand in this one."

As Haman and the techs continued to make preparations, Darik stole away to the far side of the control room and sent a comm request to Liana on his handpod. It took her a little longer than expected for her to accept the request and appear on screen.

"Done already?"

Darik couldn't fault her the icy tone. It had been over seven hours since he'd left her alone in the *Crow*'s cockpit.

"Liana, listen. There's going to be an attack."

"What? What do you mean *an attack*?"

"We just learned that a terrorist group is on its way to Bellona. They're flying stolen Navy fighters. And the station's their target."

Liana looked off screen, taking a moment to digest the information. When she finally spoke, Darik admired the strength in her voice. She was calmer than she had any right to be.

"Okay. All right. So, I'll meet up with you at the facility. I'll have the autopilot take us down right away."

That certainly seemed to be the best course of action. The *Crow*'s autopilot couldn't jump into the ether or deviate from its waypoints without Darik's key codes—which, unfortunately, were embedded in his handpod. And it didn't make sense for her to remain on the station—that is, if Haman was correct in assuming that the station was the only target. But something about Haman's reasoning didn't quite add up. If the terrorists attacked the orbital station, why wouldn't they attack the facility as well? After all, both were integral in the production of the M-2/As, and putting an end to that production was undoubtedly the reason for the attack. If the squadron did strike at both, he liked the station's odds a lot better.

"Honestly, I think you'll be safer up there. The station is well-defended. I'm not as confident about this facility—we're pretty vulnerable down here. And there's no saying they won't attack here as well."

It was clearly not the answer she'd been hoping for, but she gave a slight nod to show that she understood.

Darik continued. "Keep the ship's engines powered up and have Nikky monitor the sensors. If things start looking bad, don't hesitate—engage the autopilot and get out of there."

They locked eyes, and Darik momentarily forgot the great divide that separated them. He knew that he should say something more, something meaningful. Specifically, he felt a powerful urge to say he loved her. But he resisted—the word sounded ridiculous in his mind. Since leaving Earth, they had spent a grand total of a day alone in each other's company, so rather than providing comfort, such a loaded word would only complicate an already difficult situation. After a moment of consideration, he chose his words of reassurance.

"It'll be all right. I promise."

It had seemed like the right thing to say. He had even tried to deliver the line with an extra measure of confidence. But watching Liana's face, it was terribly obvious that his words were as hollow as they sounded.

Chapter 27

Dex lay prone in the deep shadows of the foothills, his body aching from being pressed against the same patch of earth for the past three hours. It was a particularly dark night. The moons of Bellona were too small to reflect much light, and the facility, hidden away in the countryside, was far removed from the hazy glow of distant cities. The near-absolute darkness reminded Dex of nighttime at the colony, where external lights were forbidden. He had spent many restless nights walking the colony's pitch black perimeter, lost in anxious thought.

He checked his chrono. A countdown indicated that the Angels would drop into system in less than ten minutes. It was almost time.

Half a klick away, the facility blended into the darkness, its control tower a silhouette against the night sky. JenKore's testing compound, like the colony, operated without external lighting—for similar reasons, Dex imagined. Only the top level of the control tower offered the faintest illumination—the characteristic dim orange glow of emergency lighting. The lack of lighting along with the general disrepair of most of the buildings gave the impression that the facility had been abandoned.

Dex, however, saw a different story through his rifle's holosight. While the facility wasn't exactly bustling with activity, it clearly maintained regular operations. Four guards patrolled the outer buildings, looking more alert than he would have preferred. They didn't have the appearance of men going through the motions of a long shift on yet another uneventful night. Rather, they were sharp, precise in their rotations, actively searching for threats.

Dex was reasonably sure that he hadn't done anything to alert the facility. He had been meticulous in approaching his current position. And the micropulse pad wrapped tightly around his upper chest should have masked him from any passive bioscans, causing him to blend in with the natural vibrations of the surrounding plant-life. He had never worn a pulse pad before, and at first, he found its gentle massage to be soothing. But now, after several hours of continuous use, his chest had gone numb, and he was finding it difficult to breathe. Despite his current discomfort, he was not about to remove the pad. It wasn't perfect—if the facility conducted a focused scan in his area, his heartbeat signature would be unmistakable—but it gave him the best chance at remaining undetected.

The micropulse pad, though, would be entirely useless if he were spotted by the guards. Watching a pair briefly exchange a few words as they passed each other, Dex hoped that they were simply more professional than expected. If, on the other hand, they were on high alert because they had received special information, the mission was in serious jeopardy.

At least there had been no sign of one of those modified M-2s. Dex, however, knew full well that just because he hadn't seen any, it didn't mean that one wasn't lurking somewhere. According to Baker's report, stealth was a specialty of those machines.

As the minutes dragged on, he tried to keep his full attention on the guards, looking for any indication that he had been detected, but he found his eyes often drifting up to the control tower. For much of the evening, a man had been pacing back and forth along the windows of the top level, sometimes looking over the facility grounds but mostly peering up at the stars. With his holosight at maximum magnification, Dex could make out just enough of his face to make a reasonable guess at his identity—Darik Mason, the man responsible for the killing machines.

At one point, he turned his head in Dex's direction and suddenly became very still. Dex studied his face carefully, and the longer he watched him, the more he couldn't shake the feeling that Mason was staring directly at him. Dex knew it was impossible for the man to see him from that distance without enhanced optics, and yet the moment sent his heart racing—which, in turn, caused the micropulse pad to contract, making it even more difficult to breathe.

That particular physical discomfort, though, was nothing compared to the intense burning he suddenly felt in his stomach. At first, Dex assumed it was just adrenaline, but he soon determined the true cause—the knife tucked into his waistband. The blade was physically radiating heat, feeling as though it were burning through his undershirt and setting his skin on fire. His natural response was to grab the knife and cast it away. But the

306

intensity of the heat soon subsided, the fire giving way to a more soothing warmth that permeated his body. He left the knife in his waistband, allowing it to warm him against the cool night air.

Moments later, he shook himself out of a daze. He had been drifting. For how long, he wasn't sure, but the intense disorientation he felt upon snapping out of it was instantly familiar—it was the second time in recent memory that he had awoken from a mental fog in the middle of a dangerous mission. He wasn't sure why this was happening to him, but he was reasonably certain of one thing—if he checked out a third time, he likely wouldn't wake up again.

Checking his chrono, Dex determined that he couldn't have been "out" for more than a couple of minutes—still plenty of time to complete his mission before the Angels arrived in system. The facility grounds appeared unchanged, and he couldn't help noticing that Mason was still standing by the same window.

The knife, which had cooled since he'd woken from his mental haze, again began burning against his stomach. The sensation focused him, sharpening his sense of purpose—clarifying the reason he'd come to Bellona in the first place. This was the opportunity for justice that he'd been craving, and Dex feared that if he didn't act now, he may not get another shot at Mason. He lined up the holosight's crosshairs on his head.

Dex took a deep breath, held it, and was preparing to pull when he noticed a subtle flicker out in front of Mason. The window was shielded, he realized, which meant that his bolt would be deflected away. Worse, Dex reasoned as he all but physically shook himself back to his senses, regardless whether or not the shot hit its mark, firing on the tower would prematurely alert the facility to an attack.

Dex sternly reminded himself that Mason was not the primary objective. He had become dangerously distracted, nearly throwing away the entire mission before it had even begun. The squadron was on its way—the *entire* squadron, according to the comm he'd received earlier that day. He wasn't surprised, but he did feel a sense of pride, knowing that each pilot had recognized the gravity of the situation and had volunteered for this mission, apparently without hesitation. Now it was Dex's responsibility to keep them as safe as possible by ensuring that their mission could proceed with minimal resistance from the station.

He had already been fortunate in one regard—even at half a klick out, his specialized device was in range of the facility's network. The Worm, as Baker had called it, was foreign to him. He recognized that it had the same basic graphical interface as a handpod, but the similarities ended there. While a handpod was designed to be multi-functional, the Worm was made for a single purpose—infiltrating secure networks. There was a time when Dex would have questioned how Baker had obtained such an expensive, illegal piece of equipment, but he had come to take for granted Baker's seemingly unlimited resources.

The Worm, programmed with a code Baker had managed to obtain from an unnamed source, would grant Dex access to the facility's system controls. From there, he would be able to deactivate the orbital station's missile launchers, presenting a near-defenseless target to the Angels.

Dex saw the color of the countdown display change from green to red. Time to begin. Keeping his right hand firmly on the pistol-grip of his rifle, Dex flipped open the Worm with his left hand, using his thumb to navigate through the screens. With the code already pre-entered, the Worm was supposedly foolproof. According to Baker's instructions, all Dex had to do was press *Execute*, and the Worm would automatically access the network and input the code. After that, it would be up to Dex to navigate the system as quickly as possible and find the controls for the launchers.

The Worm was ready. Dex closed his eyes, thought a quick prayer, and pressed *Execute*.

A message in red characters immediately popped up.

Invalid password. Access denied.

Dex froze, staring at the message in disbelief. If he didn't get those launchers deactivated immediately, the Angels—his friends—would be pummeled. But it was impossible for him to access the system without the correct code. He tried to remember if he had been given any alternative passwords. No—it had always been the single one. As he scrambled for options, it suddenly occurred to him that perhaps, prior to the mission, the code had been entered incorrectly into the Worm. Fortunately, during his mission prep, he'd had the good sense to commit the code to memory.

He tried again, this time manually entering the code one character at a time, carefully checking each stroke.

He again pressed *Execute*.

Invalid password. Access denied.

That was it—he was out of ideas. If the network followed standard protocol, he knew that one more failed attempt would lock him out and alert the on-duty techs of an attempted unauthorized entry. So, without another password to try, there was no point in making a third attempt.

He felt completely hollow inside. The micropulse wrap constricted, squeezing tighter and tighter around his chest. He scarcely noticed.

The digits on his chrono rolled to zero.

Chapter 28

In case he had forgotten, Scot was instantly reacquainted with his demotion the moment the Angels dropped from the ether. As the squadron's trailer, he was presented with a fantastic view of eight pairs of glowing purple tailpipes. Up ahead, Hagen led the way with Seltrice and Adahn on his wing, followed closely by the Voor twins. Onigen led flight two with his usual wingman, Geff, while Jani and Scot brought up the rear as the flight's second element.

Bellona lay directly ahead, still distant enough at the moment for Scot to take in the entire planet. From the squadron's angle of approach, the planet was only half-illuminated. Its right side—tilted up at a 30 degree angle from Scot's perspective—shimmered in the darkness, its ochre color shining like a faint star while its left side was completely black, as though God had erased half the planet with a single broad stroke.

Scot's sensors located the objective—the JenKore manufacturing station—and highlighted its position in his visor's HUD. Though the station was positioned over the dark side of Bellona, squarely in the planet's umbra, Scot was just able to make visual confirmation thanks to the light reflected by the nearest moon. The station looked incredibly fragile next to the planet—an ant in the shadow of an immense boulder that was delicately balanced on edge, its flattened bottom hovering menacingly over the tiny creature.

The Angels maintained comm silence as they approached the station. Their sensors told the pilots everything they needed to know, and Hagen was not the type to clutter up the comm channel stating the obvious. The station steadily grew in Scot's canopy, looking something like a blocky free weight—only if one side were twice as heavy as the other. So far, none of the Hornets had been actively targeted, a good indication that Dex had been successful. Scot performed a focused scan, searching for the concealed missile launchers. The scan came up empty. That should have been more good news, but something didn't sit quite right. In the recorded briefing, Dex had said that he would deactivate the station's launchers. He had said nothing, though, about powering them down completely. Perhaps that bit of information had been implied, but it wasn't Dex's style to be vague.

He was about to voice his concern over the comm when Hagen beat him to it.

"Abort. Abort. Pitchback to three-one-six."

No one questioned the order, and it was executed without hesitation. All nine Hornets rose as one, the pilots pulling back on their sticks until the station was directly aft. Mere seconds after Scot had begun his turn, a beeping tone blared in his cockpit, a warning that his Hornet was being targeted. The beeping morphed into a solid tone when the station had achieved a lock, and then changed again into a rhythmic buzz.

"Archer archer!" several pilots called out.

Out of the two dozen incoming missiles, Scot identified a couple that were tracking his Hornet. His HUD highlighted their positions, represented by two arrows pointing directly aft, accompanied by a pair of countdowns that gave the estimated times until impact.

Hagan's voice did not waver as he once again issued orders over the comm.

"Continue run. Trash the Slammers with your rear guns."

Scot's instincts urged him to do otherwise—to break and use counter-measures to evade the missiles—but he knew Hagen was right. They needed to get out of the station's missile range as quickly as possible. Defensive maneuvers might defeat the first batch of missiles, but as long as the Hornets remained in range, the station would keep pumping out Slammers—and the Angels couldn't avoid them all. No pilot, of course, wanted to see an incoming missile, but a lone Slammer or two launched at a distance from a single direction was not cause for panic, given the rear-firing capabilities of the Hornets. If the Angels maintained their cool, they would be able to pick off the missiles one by one.

Scot kept his Hornet as steady as possible. Using the rear cannons never felt completely natural, and he knew he wasn't alone. Most of the Angels only used pre-programmed firing solutions for their rear cannons, shooting them off blindly as a last resort to try to scare a bandit off their six. Dex was the only pilot Scot had ever known who could be engaged in combat maneuvers and still aim his rear cannons with some degree of accuracy.

The HUD indicated that the missiles were spaced about two seconds apart and closing fast—there wasn't going to be much room for error. The lead missile skirted into the end of his firing range. Using his rear display, Scot nudged the circle pipper over the Slammer and squeezed off a long burst from his cannons, counting *one-thousand-one* in his head before letting up on the trigger. He soon discovered that a shorter burst would have been just as effective. The first of the yellow bolts impacted the missile, causing it to detonate well behind Scot's Hornet. His moment of triumph was overshadowed, however, by a surge of panic when he lost track of the trailing missile. He frantically searched his HUD for the target, knowing that he had mere seconds before the missile would collide with his fighter.

A secondary explosion eased his fears. The trailing missile, he realized, had been detonated by the explosion from the first. Feeling relatively safe for the moment, Scot examined his battle map and saw red blips rapidly flickering out until not a single missile remained. The Angels had made it look easy, but Scot knew full well how close they had all come to complete catastrophe. If they had strayed just a little closer to the station, the amount of missiles from multiple directions would have been overwhelming. There was no doubt in his mind that the entire squadron would have been wiped out in a matter of seconds. He breathed a prayer of thanks for Hagen's quick thinking.

His battle map lit up with a fresh set of contacts. This time, however, the contacts were coming from the wrong direction. It was not a new batch of missiles but dozens of Marauders dropping from the ether directly in front of the Hornets. In the blink of an eye, the Angels found themselves in an impossible situation, bracketed in between the Marauders and the station. Scot counted four full squadrons—they were outnumbered more than five to one.

His cockpit again began blaring with warning tones. The Marauders were already on the edge of missile range. Even if the Angels had wanted to bugout, fleeing the system was no longer an option. With the Marauders already in missile range, the Hornets' autopilots would not be able to hold a true course long enough to jump into the ether.

Not that the Angels had any desire to run.

Ever since Scot had learned that the Marauders were piloted by M-2s—the same basic model of machine that had been brutally murdering countless innocent Christians—he had been itching for a fight with the Slugs. He was certain the other Angels felt the same way.

Hagen gave the order they were all craving to hear.

"Angels, you are cleared to engage the Slugs—guns only. Save the heavy stuff for the station."

A wave of chills swept through Scot's body. He was trembling—not out of fear but exhilaration. Here he was, given the rarest of opportunities, about to engage in the grandest dogfight in recent memory, the largest, no doubt, since the Frontier War. Why should he be afraid? He was flying the S/A-81 Hornet, the Coalition's most advanced fighter, and he was an Angel—a former officer in the 714th of the 501st, the Navy's most highly trained, most elite fighter squadron. He was born for this moment. There was no way, then, that he was going to be intimidated by a bunch of machine-driven Slugs.

He had no doubt that the M-2s were terrifying on the ground, but the Angels still owned the heavens.

A red cloud obscured the top half of his battle map. Scot zoomed in to see what must have been a hundred incoming missiles. The Angels did not scatter, nor did they turn and run, but they raced forward, charging into the teeth of the enemy.

*   *   *

The station was eerily quiet considering the battle that raged just beyond the confines of the hull. There were no sirens or flashing lights or announcements over the comm system. The cavernous docking bay was as dark as ever, and the assembly floor continued to churn out laser cutters without interruption. There had been only one slight deviation from the status quo—a series of shuddering noises from deep within the station's infrastructure. The groaning had lasted but a few seconds and had not returned.

Had it not been for the sensor screen in the *Golden Crow*'s cockpit, Nikky and Liana may not have been aware that the attack had even begun. Relying on nothing more than the silent movement of red and blue figures, they watched the battle unfold. Over fifty fighters and twice as many missiles streaked toward each from opposite ends of the screen, colliding at the center where they frantically circled like a swarm of insects. To some, the rising and dipping and crisscrossing may have held an odd sort of beauty, the multi-colored patterns looking like a choreographed dance of death.

Nikky, however, did not see a dance. He saw enough firepower represented on that screen to destroy the station a thousand times over.

He looked up at Liana, who was hovering next to him, studying the screen just as intently.

"I think it's time to leave."

She nodded. "Agreed."

There was only one other destination pre-programmed into the *Crow*'s navigation system—the planet-side facility's landing pad. Leaving the station would now be as simple as activating the autopilot and strapping in for the ride. Using his good hand, Nikky began punching in a series of commands.

"What are you doing?" Liana demanded.

Nikky was disappointed. In their brief time together, Liana hadn't seemed that dumb. Naïve? Perhaps. Mean? Definitely. But not dumb. "I'm turning on the autopilot," he explained, gesturing broadly to try to make his point as clear as possible.

"I can see that, you idiot. What are you trying to do, get us killed? We'll be sitting ducks out there."

"Yeah, but without the autopilot, how are we—"

Liana stood up, cutting him off. "Move."

Nikky found himself complying without fully realizing it. He rose, and Liana brushed past him, sliding into the pilot's seat while he took her old chair. She canceled the autopilot and positioned her hands over the flight controls. After a brief check of the relevant systems screens, she ignited the ventral thrusters. The ship gently rose and hovered over the docking bay floor. A slight smile played on her lips as she shifted her attention up to the cockpit's forward window.

"Here we go."

She turned the stubby control stick for the lateral thrusters, causing the ship to violently dip forward and spin around. The wild turn sent both Nikky and Liana hurtling, leaning almost horizontally in their seats, held in place only by their restraining belts. The ship settled into place, and they slowly sat back up.

"Sorry." Liana didn't look at Nikky and there wasn't even a hint of apology in her tone, but he saw that her cheeks had turned a light shade of red.

Somehow, the turn had managed to point them in the general direction of the bay door. A handful of stars were visible through the opening, but nothing more. To Nikky, it looked terribly empty and cold outside. He was beginning to have second thoughts about relinquishing the pilot's seat.

"You're licensed for this class of ship, right?"

Liana refused to meet his eyes.

"Right?"

She responded the second time by slamming the throttle forward, jerking Nikky into the back of his seat as the *Crow* blasted through the bay door.

*   *   *

So far so good.

Scot and the Angels had survived the initial wave of missiles thanks to a tactical error by the M-2 pilots. In launching their Slammers at the edge of missile range, the Marauders had succeeded in keeping the Angels from jumping into the ether, but it also had given them a few extra seconds to organize and prepare defensive action. Hagen had countered by ordering a Thach Weave, sending flights one and two crisscrossing in a continuous scissors maneuver. The weave placed each flight in an ideal firing position to pick off missiles trailing the other flight.

The Thach Weave was their best defense, but never—not even in the combat sims—had it been tested against such an overwhelming number of incoming missiles. For the Angels to survive, each pilot needed to be flawless, sustaining pinpoint accuracy for several minutes rather than seconds—an eternity in combat time. Miraculously, they had not yet allowed any of the Slammers to score a direct hit, but several had been shot down dangerously close to the Hornets, damaging shields and other critical systems. None of the Angels had come through unscathed, but flight one had taken a particularly severe beating, having attracted a disproportionate number of missiles. Still, defeating the opening barrage of Slammers without suffering any casualties was an enormous victory. They had absorbed the Marauders' best punch, and soon they would be in position to throw a few of their own.

315

The two forces merged, setting their sector of space ablaze with lightning flashes of gold and crimson. Scot had never seen so much cannon fire. He shot off several bursts, not aiming at any one target but hoping, rather, to scatter the wall of Marauders in front of him. The Slugs didn't so much as twitch while returning cannon fire of their own. Running through the intertwining patterns of red fire seemed impossible, like trying to dodge every drop of rain in a thunderstorm. And for Scot, it proved to be impossible as several bolts splashed across his forward shields, nearly draining their power completely.

He couldn't afford to take another series of hits like that. Fortunately, the Angels had a brief moment of reprieve, blowing through the last of the Marauder squadrons. Scot exhaled. Now, finally, the Angels could go on the offensive.

Flights one and two again turned into each other, but this time each flight completed a full cross turn, heading back at the Marauder squadrons. The Slugs were fearsome in a head-on engagement, but the more agile Hornets held a clear advantage in a furball. Completing the cross turn, they caught a flight of Slugs trying and failing to turn with the Hornets.

Hagen opened up with his forward cannons, peppering one Marauder's shields until they visibly collapsed. While he paused briefly to recharge his cannons, Adahn finished it off with a short burst of his own. *Figures Ghazi would steal the first kill*, Scot thought before realizing that now was not the time to be petty—there were plenty of Slugs to go around.

Seltrice splashed the Marauder's wingman while Onigen and Geff teamed up on another straggler.

Three down, only forty-five to go.

The remainder of the trailing Marauder squadron aborted their turn and began running, while ahead, Scot saw that the first two enemy squadrons were turning in opposite directions in a wide arc. Onigen, apparently, had spotted the maneuver as well, voicing his observation over the comm.

"Sarge, Ninja. Bandit squads one and two are floating for a possible bracket."

"Roger. I see it," Hagen replied. "Angels one and two hard left to one-eight-eight. Cut off squad one."

Scot realized that the M-2s had been using the trailing squadron as bait, letting the Angels pick them off one by one as they set up their trap—the soulless bastards. Rather than pursuing the stragglers and allowing the two leading Marauder squadrons to sandwich them in, Hagen led the Angels on a new intercept course.

The first Marauder squadron, determining that it no longer had enough time to complete its flanking maneuver, turned into the Hornets. The engagement was brief—the Hornets and Marauders racing past each other in a matter of seconds, exchanging mostly ineffective cannon fire—but it seemed to last much longer for Scot. One of the Slugs had turned directly into his flight path. After the beating his Hornet's shields had taken the last time, Scot was not confident he could survive another head-on engagement. He could break early, but that would give the Marauder the advantage and, worse, would separate him from the weave, leaving the other Angels exposed. No—he wouldn't break. This one he had to win.

His senses heightened as time seemed to slow. He had tunnel-vision, seeing nothing but the Marauder in front of him. The pipper left a ghost trail behind as it stretched across the HUD and settled over the enemy cockpit. He pressed the trigger. Normally, the operation of his Hornet's cannons sounded like a buzz saw, each bolt firing so rapidly that the noise blended together in a single whirring hum. But now he could hear the rhythmic pumping of each bolt. He watched the tracers cut a path through space, intersecting with the red bolts from the Marauder, which lanced toward him and flashed just over his head. The M-2 had aimed a touch high. It would not have the opportunity to correct its error.

His pair of yellow tracers drilled into the Marauder's shields, boring in deeper and deeper, until a single bolt burst through. Scot swore he saw it vaporize the head of the M-2 pilot. He kept the trigger depressed, splitting the Marauder in two. As he watched the Marauder burst apart at the seams, time resumed its normal speed, and Scot realized that he was on a collision course with the remains of the fighter. He rolled his Hornet, slicing between the two halves of the Marauder, which exploded into thousands of fiery pieces just behind him.

He was the last one through the small wave of Marauders, and the Hornets again executed a cross turn. This time, the Marauders didn't try to turn, but ran in an attempt to gain some distance and set up another head-on pass. With the Marauders yielding the advantage, it was tempting to give chase, but Scot resisted the urge. The two flights remained disciplined, continuing the weave in whatever direction Hagen called out. The pilots took their shots when the opportunity arose but never split off to pursue individual targets. The maneuver relied on all nine Angels

317

watching over each other. If even one pilot broke away, the weave would unravel, and each of the Angels would be swarmed by the enemy.

Scot stole a glance at his battle map. He counted seven confirmed kills. They were still heavily outnumbered, but each successful pass evened the odds just a bit more. As he studied the movement of the Marauder squadrons, looking for another possible trap, a new contact caught his eye. The blip was located at the back quarter of his map, away from the action. Zooming in, he saw that it was not a Marauder or a stray missile from the station, but a *Midas*-class transport. It was leaving the station in a hurry, making a frantic run for Bellona. He narrowed his sensors on the transport, performing a bioscan. There were two people on board.

He toggled to his Slammers and locked onto the transport, his index finger lightly caressing the trigger. Destroying the transport would be a gross violation of the squadron's rules of engagement, but Scot considered this to be special circumstances. The squadron's rules were designed to protect the innocent—civilians and police forces and military personnel who, by simply doing their jobs, had the misfortune of crossing paths with the Angels.

But this was different. There was nothing innocent about those people in the luxury transport. Their very presence on that station meant that they were actively contributing to the slaughter of hundreds, maybe thousands of innocent people. Christians. His brothers and sisters who had never wanted anything more than to live and worship in peace. Someone needed to defend those who couldn't defend themselves—and who better than the Angels?

A lone Slammer would go unnoticed in the chaos of the battle— particularly if it had not targeted any of the fighters. It would streak forward and punch straight into the heart of the lightly-shielded transport, bringing justice to the murderers harbored within.

Scot certainly had convinced himself that it was the right thing to do, but he knew that he could never get away with it. Even if no one else had noticed the transport, he would eventually be found out when the flight recordings were reviewed after the mission. And, having already been demoted for insubordination on the Milk Run, he would never so much as glimpse a Hornet again.

The transport was quickly escaping from missile range. If Scot was going to take it out, he only had one option.

"Sarge, Flash. I've got a bogey leaving the station. Permission to ID and engage."

Scot waited a few moments for Hagen to locate and scan the transport.

"Negative, Flash. My thumper reads warm."

The response was entirely expected, yet Scot still found himself burning with anger.

"With all due respect, sir, this isn't some police force defending their system. These people are murderers."

Seltrice and Adahn voiced their support for Scot. This was good, he thought. If he could get enough of the others behind him, perhaps they could sway the commander.

Geff entered the channel next, but it was not the affirmation Scot had been hoping for.

"Flash, we don't know who's on that transport. They may deserve to die, or they may not—but it's not for us to decide. Trust me—you don't want that kind of blood on your hands."

Scot didn't care for his friend's holier-than-thou tone, and he was about to let him know it when Hagen put an end to the discussion.

"No one is to fire on that transport. That's not my order—that's Deadeye's order."

No one dared utter another word. The reference to Dex had a sobering effect on the squadron. It was clear that his mission on Bellona had not gone according to plan. And if Dex had indeed sacrificed himself, the Angels were determined to give their captain a send-off worthy of remembrance. They refocused their full attention on the Marauders— giving extra-long bursts from their cannons as they blasted through another squadron—while on the fringes of the battle, the transport sailed away, fading into the dark underbelly of Bellona.

Chapter 29

A cool night breeze swept down from the hills, blowing through the tall prairie grass that blanketed the land west of the facility. Dex moved, using both the noise and the motion of the rustling grass to cover his approach through the field.

He had begun formulating a new plan the moment Baker's code had proven to be ineffective, determining that he needed to locate the facility's relay building—the communications link between the facility and the orbital station. If he couldn't access the system directly with the Worm, he could attempt to break the link by sabotaging the relay building itself. And without the control tower's human operators feeding commands to the station, the missile launchers would be rendered inactive—at least that was the theory. With nothing more than that rough objective in mind, he had packed up his gear and set off down the hillside, leaving the rented airbike, his only viable means of escape, far behind.

Dex stopped moments before the wind died, crouching an arm's length from the field's edge. Through the thin blades, he could see the outlines of the facility's perimeter buildings, the nearest only about fifty meters away. With his objective growing ever closer, he found himself becoming increasingly frustrated at his deliberate pace. Each passing second placed his pilots in greater danger, and it seemed incredibly selfish to remain so cautious. He was tempted to expedite the mission, to burst out of the field and sprint the short distance into the compound. But he remained still. There was nothing left but open ground between him and the facility, and charging blindly ahead was sure to get him spotted and captured—which would make him useless to the Angels.

Dex slowly raised his rifle, careful not to disturb the surrounding grass, and used the holosight to search the perimeter buildings. As he steadily swept back and forth, he hoped that this all wasn't necessary—

that his pilots, upon learning that the station's launchers were still active, had immediately turned around and jumped out. It was, after all, the only sensible thing to do—which is why he was certain they were still up there.

A building to the left caught his eye. It was small, no larger than a storage shed, and nondescript, save for one telling feature—an emitter on the rooftop pointed skyward. It hadn't been the emitter, though, that first caught his attention but rather a pair of guards—one a full head shorter than the other and both dressed in gray paramilitary uniforms—patrolling tightly around the building. He'd found his target.

Getting past the guards was not going to be easy. They maintained good spacing and kept constant visual contact with each other. The shorter of the two also regularly peered in his direction, guessing, correctly, that any ambush would likely come from the field. Dex waited impatiently for a moment of disconnect between the two guards, an opportunity to take out one and then the other before either realized what was happening.

The taller guard reached into his pocket and pulled out a handpod. It looked as though he was flipping through a few messages. It wasn't the perfect opportunity—Dex would've preferred for one of them to stray around the corner of the building—but he couldn't wait any longer. He lined up the crosshairs over the man's left temple and fired.

The blue energy bolt screamed from the field and slammed against the man's head. He lurched and crumpled to the dry ground. Dex's rifle was not silenced, and upon hearing the high-pitched blast, the shorter guard immediately dropped prone. His right hand pointed a carbine toward the field while his left hand rose to his ear, triggering a comm. A second stun bolt struck him between the eyes before he had a chance to speak.

Dex stood and sprinted toward the facility. Crossing the open ground, he could feel the eyes of the control tower upon him. After spending most of the day skulking in the shadows, it felt, in an odd way, freeing to suddenly be so exposed.

Here I am. Come and get me.

He closed the gap in seconds. Nearing the shorter guard, he slid to his knees and began digging through the man's back pockets, searching for his handpod. Finding nothing, Dex rolled him over. The man's right arm lay limp across his chest, and Dex roughly flung it aside. There was no danger of him waking any time soon. The effects of stun bolts varied depending on the victim's physical makeup and the location of impact. A shot to the head always rendered someone unconscious—the only variable in this case was for how long. Looking over the man, Dex figured that he would wake up in an hour or so with a nasty headache and a new tattoo on his forehead.

He found the guard's handpod in a chest pocket. Clutching the device, Dex circled the relay building, looking for an entrance. He discovered its only door on the east wall—the wall facing the interior of the facility. If Dex had felt watched before, the feeling only intensified as he slid the guard's handpod over the door's sensor. All his bravado from moments ago had vanished. He was no longer running toward danger but standing still, his back turned, waiting for some unseen threat to creep in and pounce.

The control tower hovered behind him. By now, its personnel had certainly learned of the commotion and were staring down at the intruder. Perhaps Mason himself was just now ordering his execution. At the feet of the control tower, rows of bunkers stretched out toward him, their scorched ruins likely concealing his executioners—the machines, standing motionless in the dark, silently watching, waiting.

The sensor flashed green, and the door slid open. Dex ejected the stun battery from his rifle, replaced it with a standard clip, and entered.

*　　*　　*

By Scot's informal tally, every pilot had splashed at least one Slug except for Jani, who was concentrating almost exclusively on gunning down incoming missiles—much to the gratitude of her squad mates. Despite the squadron's early success, Scot was nervous about the direction the battle had taken. It had been over a minute since the Angels had scored a kill—a bad sign considering the wealth of potential targets.

The reason for their recent struggles was obvious—the M-2 pilots had adapted. Rather than continuing to attempt to get position behind the Angels, which had left them open to crisscrossing cannon fire from the weaving flights, the Marauders had been making passes at their flanks. Recognizing the shift in tactics, Hagen had been ordering the squadron into an almost constant sequence of hard turns. For the most part, the wild maneuvers had been successful at keeping the Marauders off their flanks, but the evasive action didn't give the Angels any opportunities to engage the Slugs offensively.

To Scot, it was suicide to maintain defensive positions indefinitely. Most of the Hornets' shields were on the verge of collapse—each fighter a stray cannon burst or two from destruction. If they didn't start eliminating large batches of Marauders soon, the Angels, by sheer attrition, would be wiped out.

His HUD tracked flight one, the blue-highlighted Hornets arcing to his left. The two flights were on the outer edges of the weave—the point at which they were all the most vulnerable.

As if on cue, Geff's voice blared over the comm.

"Viper, archer archer—your nine, low!"

From the inner edge of flight two, Geff had a clear view of Seltrice's fighter across the gap. Scot quickly spotted the missiles and understood the special urgency in Geff's voice. The Slammers were headed for Seltrice's blindside—the midsection of her Hornet that wasn't covered by forward or rear cannons. She wouldn't be able to shoot the missiles down herself.

"No joy! No joy!" she shouted back, signaling that she couldn't get a visual on the missiles rising toward her. The comm didn't make sense to Scot. Her HUD should have automatically located and highlighted the incoming Slammers. If Seltrice couldn't see them, there was only one explanation—she was panicking.

Flight two, just now beginning to curve back in, was still too far away to cover her. And flight one's tight formation meant that the missiles were in their collective blindside. If Seltrice couldn't trash them herself, there would be no saving her.

A flash of motion caught Scot's attention. Just ahead, Geff's fighter rolled hard left, breaking from the weave and cutting a sharp intercept course for flight one. His twin tailpipes emitted almost pure white light as he engaged his afterburners. Even with the speed boost, Scot doubted that Geff would be able to intercept the missiles in time. Geff appeared to realize that as well, opening up with forward cannons well beyond maximum effective range, hoping for a lucky hit.

From Scot's angle, it looked as though Geff had fired directly at Seltrice's Hornet. The yellow bolts converged on Seltrice, all but scraping the belly of her fighter as they passed below. A micro-second later, they impacted the lead missile. The resulting pair of explosions, only meters away, rocked Seltrice's fighter, sending her hurtling into the center of flight one. Scot winced, watching in disbelief as Geff's heroics had

323

improbably led to total disaster—Seltrice careening toward a massive collision that looked as though it would envelop all of flight one.

Her Hornet awkwardly lurched back as Seltrice attempted to regain control, the starboard wing of her fighter swinging narrowly over Adahn's canopy. Behind them, the Voor twins eased up on the throttle, giving her plenty of space to maneuver. Following another slight overcorrection, she was able to guide her fighter back into formation. Seltrice was safe for the moment.

Geff, on the other hand, was caught in a kill zone, his Hornet all alone between the two flights. Scot knew that his friend was a dead man if he didn't receive cover immediately. Onigen anticipated Scot's next action.

"Angels two, hard left in place to oh-eight-one. Prince, right to one-six-six."

Onigen's order cut down the angle of the weave, turning flight two as hard in as possible to reform with Geff. Sarge ordered flight one to close the gap as well. The two flight leads would not permit the Angels to break the weave—not even to rescue Geff—but they were making every effort to bring the squadron to him as quickly as possible.

Geff turned hard right, closing the distance to flight two. The turn, however, brought him into the path of a trio of ballistic Slammers, unguided missiles that had lost their intended target. Scot saw them first, the three points of light stalling as they identified a new target and then diving sharply, like birds of prey swooping down from the sky. There was no time to warn his friend through the comm, no time to think—only to react. His thumb twitched, and he fired.

Scot had led the Slammers a little too much, but the angle was true, and he kept the trigger depressed, ignoring the draining bar. The missiles closed, reaching out to grasp their prey, before each evaporated in a flash of light—one, two, three—burning up in Scot's wall of fire, a shield over Geff's head.

Scot was not able to enjoy the moment. Even as the third missile detonated, he spotted   a pair of Slammers rising toward the belly of Geff's fighter. He lined up his pipper and fired again, only to hear a sickly groan from his forward cannons as they managed to squeeze out just a single bolt. Scot cursed his drained batteries and rerouted his Hornet's limited shield power to his cannons, hoping to speed up the recharge. In his peripheral vision, he saw Jani send a long burst in Geff's direction. The pair of missiles vanished from his HUD.

And still more missiles poured in. Geff, alone in the gap, had been singled out by the entire pack of circling Marauders. Scot watched helplessly as a Slammer from below sliced through the Angels' desperate cannon fire and tore off Geff's port wing, sending him spinning out of control. Two more missiles streaked in from opposite directions, meeting simultaneously over Geff's canopy. There was a blinding flash.

Scot's sensors showed that Geff's fighter was broken into a million tiny pieces flung in all directions, but when he looked up, he saw nothing, as though in that instant his friend had crossed into the ether.

*   *   *

The interior of the relay building was a mess. Dex had purposefully kept the lights off to avoid attracting any more attention, and he was now paying for that decision, bumping into loose stacks of crates and getting tangled in hanging bundles of cords. As he neared the back of the single room, a faint glow aided his progress. He soon found the source. Shimmering at eye-level over the back wall was a screen that provided real-time status updates for all of the key systems in the facility and orbital station. He searched for an interface terminal but found nothing, meaning he could monitor the systems from the screen but couldn't gain access.

Of course not—that would've been too easy.

He stole a glance behind him. No one was at the door—yet. Dex felt certain that his time was coming to an end—not the time needed to complete the mission, or the time until more guards arrived, but *his time.*

But it was pointless to dwell on that—it had never been his time anyway.

He switched his battery rifle from semi to fully automatic. Locating the largest power source in the room, he aimed and fired. The flurry of red bolts shrieked as they exited the barrel, pounding the equipment in a deafening staccato and setting off a shower of white sparks, each burning an evanescent trail through the air.

The screen remained lit, the white lines of text unchanged.

Dex had had enough of the constant setbacks. He fired again, this time indiscriminately, spraying bolts back and forth in a wide arc. His ears were ringing, and his face burned against the heat, and still he fired, shouting at the top of his lungs, hollering wordless noise, smoldering with anger against the relay building, the facility, the station, and beyond, against all the underlying evil and injustice—he emptied himself into the equipment.

He stopped. The fading sparks revealed smoke rising from the equipment. There was a sharp pop, and the screen flickered out.

That was it. He'd done everything he could for the Angels. Regardless of how the next few minutes played out, whether he would escape with his life or not, he could be at peace. Dex turned toward the door, but a faint click and hum caught his ear. He resisted looking at first, fearing what he would see. But he knew he couldn't leave unless he checked.

Turning back, he saw that the screen had lit up again. After cycling through a sequence of start-up displays, it projected the same information as before—all facility and station systems operating as normal.

Dex figured that there had to be a back-up power source somewhere beyond the relay building. Where it was located, he didn't have the faintest idea—nor did it really matter. Seconds from now, he would be captured. He would be captured, and he would die, knowing that he had completely failed his friends.

Dex closed his eyes, feeling entirely small. His whole being pleaded with God. He didn't pray for a miracle in the system, or safety for his pilots, or even his own deliverance—his thoughts were not coherent enough for him to ask for any one thing in particular. Rather, broken and overwhelmed, he offered up only a single word.

Help.

He opened his eyes. He didn't feel any different after the prayer. There had been no rushing wind, or blinding lights, or thundering reports. But he did notice one small change. On the right side of the screen, a third of the way down, one of the lines had changed color from white to red. It was the line representing the orbital station's missile launchers.

At the end of the line, a word flashed.

Inactive.

Dex knew he should run, that if he had any hope of surviving, he needed to leave the building immediately. But he stood in place, staring at the screen, his hands trembling as his mind tried to comprehend what had just happened.

*   *   *

Inside a small luxury transport nestled at the base of a rocky bluff on the surface of Bellona, a single hand pulled back from an ancient manual keyboard. The fingers twitched slightly before moving to the left to rub a damaged stump—a phantom pain where the other hand should have been.

Chapter 30

Over the past quarter hour, Darik had observed a steady shift in mood among the control room techs—from unabashed giddiness at the arrival of the Marauder squadrons to mild concern when the initial ambush resulted in zero enemy kills to outright nervousness as Marauder losses continued to mount. Even when the first enemy fighter had been destroyed, there had not been an outburst of celebration, as Darik might have expected, but rather an almost palpable sense of relief—they finally had proof that the Hornets were not invincible after all.

Darik had been carefully monitoring the screens as well, his attention divided between the clashing fighter squadrons and a lone contact that had been drifting toward Bellona's atmosphere. He wasn't sure what Liana and Nikky had been thinking—flying a defenseless transport through the middle of a raging battle—but he was relieved to see that they had made it through the fray unharmed, landing moments ago a few kilometers from the facility.

Haman, oddly enough, had not been actively watching the maps, adopting an air of indifference about the outcome of the battle. He had, instead, planted himself behind the young blond tech, preoccupying himself with the upcoming M-2/A test. Darik was more than a little confused by Haman's apparent obsession with seeing the test through. The orbital station was under assault—how could anything else be more deserving of his attention?

"We can certainly postpone the demonstration, given the circumstances," Darik offered.

Haman didn't bother to turn around. "No, no," he said, rechecking his chrono. "Testing must not be delayed."

The blond tech nodded to his boss. "It's ready."

Haman clasped his hands together as he turned toward Darik. He seemed genuinely excited.

"There will be three test subjects this evening," he announced. "My machine is prepped and ready, but it will only be activated on our command." He motioned Darik toward the terminal. "The honor is yours."

Darik felt a little unsure, but it seemed silly for him to refuse. Why else was he there if not to see the M-2/A perform? He was being paid an exorbitant salary to oversee thousands of operations exactly like this one. If he didn't have the stomach for it, he had better start thinking of a new career.

He triggered the command.

Haman's face gleamed darkly. "Watch the screen."

The blond tech orchestrated the viewing experience, selecting from a dozen live security feeds. The first angle to appear on the main screen was at eye-level, as though they were one of the guards patrolling the facility grounds. No mere man, however, could have moved with such fluidity. The image glided forward, never bumping or shaking as it traveled in and through and over the rows of bunkers. Darik realized he was watching a feed directly from the M-2's perspective. He was mesmerized by the image, feeling a sense of weightlessness as he floated with the machine through the facility.

The tech then switched to a wide view, showing a row of identical small buildings. Their purpose was soon revealed. Three doors simultaneously slid open, releasing three prisoners from their cells. Because of the distance, it was difficult for Darik to see any of the people clearly, though he could follow their general movements. Two of the people saw one another and embraced. The other had started running as soon as he'd stepped out.

"Have you ever seen a live sacrifice?"

Though his eyes remained on the screen, Darik knew that Haman's question had been directed at him. He shook his head. For the first time, it fully struck Darik that he had likely sentenced these people to death. Up until now, he had not given much thought to the machine's intent, assuming, if anything, that it was going to capture the subjects—the terrorists—for interrogation. Didn't that make more sense? Wasn't that more beneficial to the Coalition in the long run? But he had never completely fooled himself—deep down, he had known all along what was going to happen.

Haman continued. "There's nothing quite like it. As you watch, pay particular attention to the eyes. The panic, the pain, and finally the doubt—the moment the subject realizes that he will not be saved, that his life has been built on a lie, that he will die for nothing."

Darik tore his gaze from the screen. Haman was in a distant place, his eyes unfocused.

"This will be the first ritual for this particular machine. As the blade passes through, you'll be tempted to remain focused on the eyes—to watch the life drain away. But I encourage you instead to watch the blood pour down and temper the blade. Watch it boil and steam, purifying the surface. When you consider the work that is being accomplished—this, the final step toward universal peace—it's enough to bring a man to tears. Let me assure you—it's a transformative experience."

Haman met his eyes. Darik, unable to speak, managed only a slight nod.

The M-2 was closing in on the subject who had immediately taken off running. The blond tech zoomed in for a closer look at the target. He was an older man—tall and thin with short gray hair. And, disturbingly, he looked familiar.

"Yes, Darik, it's the mechanic you questioned in the mines of Cacarus. A terrorist as it turns out. We're in your debt. We never would have uncovered him without your help."

Darik was beginning to feel dizzy. He didn't feel at all prepared to watch an execution, and he certainly hadn't been expecting to see anyone he recognized. The man's name escaped him, but he could picture their meeting clearly. The mechanic had been a little odd, he remembered, but also friendly and helpful—the only person he'd met on Cacarus who hadn't made his skin crawl. Had the old man been hiding out in the mine because he'd committed past atrocities, or was his crime simply being a Christian?

The screen switched back to the M-2's perspective. The machine easily overtook the old man. Following a brief interrogation, he was executed.

Franklin, Darik remembered. *His name was Franklin.*

Next to him, Haman audibly exhaled. "Can you feel it, Darik? This is a great moment for the Coalition. A known terrorist has confessed, and justice has been done."

Wordlessly, Darik continued to stare at the screen. The machine had begun pursuing the other two subjects—a middle-aged couple fleeing together.

Across the room, the older tech with the stubble beard suddenly hollered out, visibly startling Darik. The relay building had lost power, he reported.

"A saboteur?" Haman questioned aloud—his voice revealing more anticipation than concern.

He ordered the blond tech to drop what he was doing and scan the relay building. When the scan came up empty, Darik feared for the young man, so murderous was the look in Haman's eyes.

"There," Haman hissed, jabbing his finger at the screen. The tech narrowed the scan where Haman had indicated and managed to pick up a flutter—the heartbeat was faint but distinctly human. A smile crept across Haman's face.

"Tag him," he ordered. Then, catching Darik's gaze, he added, "What a delight—an unexpected test subject!"

The older tech at the far terminal called out again. "I've lost the station's missile launchers."

"Then you'd better find them," Haman replied, his tone light and mocking.

Darik saw the older tech shake his head and mutter something under his breath. He suddenly felt an odd kinship with the man.

The young blond tech next to Haman switched to a security feed of the relay building. From a high angle, they watched the door slide open and a man emerge. The image was currently too wide to make out any defining characteristics, but Darik could see that the man was of average height, if not a touch shorter. His movements were precise and purposeful. Proceeding cautiously, he pressed his back against the east wall, holding a rifle at the ready as he peered around the corner.

As the tech zoomed in, Darik, for the second time that evening, felt a glimmer of recognition—and then the screen flickered out.

Haman spun around and glared at the older tech. "Fix it!"

Turning back to the blond tech, he spoke in a more measured tone. "Stay with the M-2 feed—default angle and spectrum."

The moment Haman finished speaking, the room went black as the emergency lights and terminal screens simultaneously switched off. The darkness lasted a few moments before the emergency lights slowly flickered back on. The screens, however, remained blank.

Haman gave an exasperated look to the older tech.

"I'm working on it," the tech growled.

"No matter," Haman said, peering through the window at the facility grounds. "The problem will be dealt with momentarily."

He scanned the room.

"Where's Mason?"

"I think he's in the lav," the older tech said. "He was looking a little pale."

Haman grinned to himself. "Yes, my machines will have that effect on people."

*　　*　　*

The weave had quickly unraveled following the loss of Geff. Already strained by the squadron's desperate rescue attempt, the weave's integrity dissolved completely once Scot took it upon himself to avenge his friend.

Scot was finding it difficult to breathe. He thought of Smiley and Aces. It wasn't that long ago that he had watched them die. He remembered how he'd felt—the sting and the emptiness. This was worse.

He traced the three offending missiles back to the original Marauders. Each of the three Slugs had formed up with a different squadron. Scot wasn't sure if that had been deliberate—a ploy by the M-2 pilots to entice the Hornets into separating. If so, it had worked. Even as Scot raced toward one of the Marauder squadrons, he saw Seltrice veer off toward another.

Hagen apparently saw the writing on the wall.

"Angels, abort the weave. Strip and engage at will. Ghazi, saddle with Ninja."

Scot knew that he was the one responsible for breaking up the weave, but he didn't feel guilty in the least. The weave had become useless offensively. And with Geff gone, it would have been much less effective as a defensive maneuver as well. It was asking too much for the three remaining Hornets in flight two to cover the five fighters in flight one— something would've slipped through the cracks. Hagen could have evened the numbers by sending over a member of his flight, but that would've meant ordering someone across the gap—and they had all just witnessed the consequences of that.

No—rather than sitting back and getting picked apart, it was time to go on the offensive. Considering the odds, the question in Scot's mind wasn't whether or not he'd survive, but how many Slugs he'd take down with him.

Jani had engaged her afterburners in an effort to catch up. He eased off on his throttle, letting her take her rightful place as lead. He knew that he was more qualified than Jani to fly lead, but now wasn't the time to try to prove that point. To have any chance against the Marauder squadron, they needed to work together seamlessly, which meant swallowing his pride for the moment.

Glancing at his map, he saw that Onigen and Adahn had managed to pair up and were engaging the second Marauder squadron along with Hagen and Seltrice. Farthest away from Scot were the Voor twins, racing alone toward the third and final remaining enemy squadron.

The all-too-familiar buzzing alarm sounded again in Scot's cockpit, indicating more incoming Slammers. This time, though, there would be no cover—no second flight to pick them off. He saw that a half dozen Slammers—a group of four and two trailers—had targeted his Hornet, in addition to another four headed for Jani. Watching the blue missiles streak in, Scot was seized with doubt. He had never stared down so many missiles—at least not without the protection of the weave. And with each missile coming in on a different trajectory, he knew that it was impossible to shoot them all down.

He was going to die. He was going to die without having fired a single shot in honor of Geff. And he was going to die knowing that his rash decision to break up the weave had condemned the other Angels to death as well.

He might have continued down that line of thought, passively allowing the missiles to strike him, had it not been for Jani's level-headed instructions.

"Flash, on my mark, break right and deploy bugs."

Scot regained his focus as the two Hornets and the missiles converged. "Break!"

He turned hard right with Jani and triggered his countermeasures, dumping dozens of micro-jammers in his wake. The tiny spheres acted similarly to a full-sized jammer pod, disabling sensors in a localized area. Activated upon release, they had an immediate effect on his Hornet, knocking out his battle map and sensor screens. Without the aid of his

HUD, Scot turned and checked his six. He saw the first four missiles pass through the cloud of jammers. Rather than turning with him, they continued forward, going ballistic as they lost contact with his fighter. The range of the micro-jammers was limited by design, and Scot soon regained his sensors. His HUD highlighted the remaining two missiles, which he shot down with ease. He saw that Jani had enjoyed similar success.

The Marauder squadron, meanwhile, had closed to cannon range. With his shields still drained, Scot knew that a head-on engagement was suicide, yet he dutifully remained on Jani's wing as they charged the Slugs. The two sides exchanged a hail of cannon fire before Jani, aware of Scot's predicament, broke off early—saving Scot but yielding the advantage to the Marauders.

Seizing the opportunity, one of the Slugs swooped in on his tail. By reflex, he snapped off a burst from his rear guns, managing through sheer luck to score a few glancing hits. He fired again, pumping more yellow bolts at the Marauder until it peeled off—directly into Jani's path.

"Splash one!" she called out seconds later.

Scot smiled at Jani's enthusiasm—it must have been a relief to finally get her first kill of the battle. Even so, that had been way too much work for one Marauder. And the only reason they'd managed even that kill was because he'd been uncharacteristically accurate with his rear cannons. The chances of that happening twice were slim.

His cockpit blared again, announcing another round of enemy missile locks.

"Flash, what state bugs?" Jani asked, wondering how many micro-jammers he had left. Scot didn't have to look. Not wanting to take any chances with the last batch of missiles, he'd emptied his entire load.

"I'm winchester."

"Yeah, me too."

There was a hint of resignation in her tone—the only time Scot had ever heard defeat in Jani's voice. It broke him. He wasn't going to let her go down like that.

"C'mon," he said. "Let's light 'em up."

He opened up with his rear cannons, spraying wildly at the trailing enemy squadron. Jani joined in—the two of them determining that if their time had come, they weren't going to get caught with their cannons fully charged.

Their indiscriminate fire was largely ineffective. A stray bolt occasionally splashed across a Marauder's shields, but it was nothing that should've deterred the enemy—which is why it was so puzzling when the warning alarms in Scot's cockpit ceased.

His HUD showed the Marauder squadron disengaging, hooking back on a new heading. He would've liked to have thought that they'd been intimidated by the frenzy of fire from the Hornets, but he knew that couldn't be the case.

As he and Jani turned to pursue the squadron, Scot checked his battle map, following their heading to see what had attracted their attention. The only thing he saw in that direction was the Voor twins.

He blinked and double-checked the map—the *only* thing in that direction was the Voor twins.

An entire Marauder squadron was gone.

Scot couldn't figure out what had happened. Had the squadron inexplicably jumped into the ether? He focused his sensors, which detected Marauder fragments scattered throughout the area. No, they hadn't jumped—they'd been destroyed. In roughly the same time it had taken Jani and him to barely scratch out one kill, the Voors had somehow managed to wipe out an entire squadron.

Every one of the twenty-five remaining Marauders was descending on the Voors, and now Scot understood why—Ravi and Purnima had become by far their biggest threat. The other Angels, Jani and himself included, raced to assist the twins, but Scot found it difficult to resist simply being a spectator.

The Voors were magnificent. They weren't joined at the wing, as Scot had come to expect from them, but they flew separately, wildly, seemingly out of control. From within the furball, it must have looked like utter chaos—how could they keep their own bearings straight, much less keep track of their wingman? And yet, from afar, Scot saw a certain elegance to what they were doing, an order to their crazy maneuvers. The movements of their fighters often mirrored each other, even when they were at their most distant, and they had an uncanny ability to sense when their partner was in danger and sweep in from nowhere to pick off the threat.

At one point, Scot gasped aloud in admiration as he watched Purnima purposely allow a missile to trail her, just so she could drag it into one of Ravi's pursuers. The Voors fought with creativity and precision and even,

Scot determined, a certain ferociousness. They were absolutely tearing up the Marauders.

When he and Jani arrived, Scot was unsure whether he should try to help the Voors or just stay out of their way. Watching the Voors eliminate the target he'd just selected for himself, he couldn't help wondering where this had come from. Sure, since joining the Angels, the twins had developed into capable pilots, but never had they shown the capacity for anything like *this*. Then again, Scot reasoned, they had never been given the opportunity—always placed in a supporting role, always shackled to the back of one flight or another. And now that Scot thought about it, there had been flashes of brilliance—the two of them saving Jani from her tailspin over Olympic Park, Purnima on the Milk Run evading missile after missile without the aid of sensors. Perhaps all the Voors had ever needed was a little freedom.

The comm had been dead silent for over a minute, which only added to the surreal quality of the moment. He was impressed that the Voors could execute their sophisticated maneuvers without speaking to each other, but their lack of comm chatter wasn't exactly out of the ordinary— they typically went about their business in silence. Scot might have expected, though, the other Angels to be cheering on the Voors—he certainly felt like doing so. But no one had uttered a word about what was happening, as if acknowledging it out loud would force them to come to terms with the unreality of it all, causing them to all awaken from their shared dream.

Scot, having grown accustomed to the silence, was startled when Onigen's voice broke through the comm.

"Sarge, Ninja. The station's launchers appear to be deactivated."

Scot scanned the station himself to confirm. Onigen seemed to be right—leave it to him to be the only one with the presence of mind to monitor the station during the Voors' spectacle.

"Roger, Ninja," Hagen replied. "But it could be another trap. Any volunteers to test the water?"

"We'll go," Purnima said.

"Negative, Moonlight. You and Sunfire continue pressing those Slugs."

Hagen was right. No one, at this point, doubted the Voors' ability to get the job done—rather, they were simply too valuable against the Marauders. The enemy, thanks mostly to the Voors, had been pared down

336

to about a squad and a half—a sizeable drop from their initial four squadrons—but they still outnumbered the Angels two to one.

"We're on it," Jani said.

Scot grinned. He'd wanted to make the run, but it would've been bad form, as the wingman, for him to volunteer his element. He followed Jani's wide turn, which pointed them, once again, in the direction of the station. He kept a close eye on his sensor screen, looking for any sign that the launchers might reactivate. His battle map showed that their path to the station was clear. To their rear, however, he saw that a pair of Marauders had disengaged from the furball and were closing in on their tails, eating through their afterburner reserves in an effort to catch them. Despite the threat they posed, Scot interpreted that as a good sign—why would the Slugs bother to chase them if the station could defend itself?

He called out the threat in case Jani hadn't seen them.

"Rabbit, two bandits closing on our six. Please advise."

There was a brief pause as Jani considered the situation.

"Continue run."

Scot was a bit confused by Jani's lack of urgency until he rechecked his map and saw a pair of Hornets—Onigen and Adahn—intercepting the outlying Marauders. The Slugs proved to be even more desperate to catch them than Scot had guessed, refusing to break even as Onigen and Adahn closed from above. From his ideal firing position, Adahn tore through the lead Marauder with a burst from his forward cannons.

"Splash one Slug!" he hollered.

Scot shook his head—the kill had been way too easy for Adahn to be getting that excited. Even while saving his life, his former wingman found ways to annoy him. Still, he was grateful for the cover. Onigen took out the other Slug without comment, clearing them once again for their run on the station.

At some point during the brief action, they had crossed into the station's missile range. There still had been no activity from the launchers, but that didn't prove anything to Scot. For all he knew, it was another trap—the station's operators luring them in for a closer shot. The good news was that missile range worked both ways. He and Jani prepared their attack.

"Sarge, Rabbit. I've swept the target," Jani reported. "The station's cool."

That came as no surprise. From the beginning, they'd anticipated that the automated station would be empty. The transport evacuating earlier had been unexpected, but Jani's scan had just confirmed that the two people on that ship had been the last ones on board.

"Affirmative, Rabbit. You're cleared hogs."

"Roger. Flash, arm your hog and paint the target."

Toggling his sensor screen to weapons mode, Scot zoomed in on the station and marked his target. Etiquette dictated that he should have waited for Jani to fire first, but wanting for himself the thrill of striking the first blow against the station, he released his fighter's Heavy Ion Bomb the instant he achieved a lock. Watching the HIB shoot forward, propelled by four small crimson rockets, he saw, to his mild disappointment, that Jani had already released hers as well.

"Hogs away," Jani informed the squadron. Then, quieter, she added, "Nice try, Flash."

This was Scot's first experience with live HIBs, and he studied their progress carefully. The hogs were large by necessity, housing a shield generator in addition to their rockets and sizeable explosive package. And though the bombs traveled at twice the speed of the Hornets, they seemed cumbersome to Scot, plodding along at a snail's pace compared to the darting Slammers and lightning-fast cannon bolts. Scot could only hope that when the HIBs finally reached their target that it would be worth the wait.

The bombs continued to travel unimpeded toward the station. Scot was now confident that the station's missile launchers were disabled, reasoning that if the launchers were still active, they would have shot down the HIBs long ago. As the bombs neared their target, the station automatically began pumping out a loose screen of cannon fire, but at this point it was a mere formality. The red bolts were harmlessly absorbed by the strongly shielded HIBs, and even if the bombs were somehow detonated prematurely, the explosion at that range would still cause critical damage to the station.

The flight paths of the two bombs had not diverged the entire way. Scot realized that he and Jani must have marked the same location. Wanting to make the most of their one shot, they had both targeted the weakest point on the station—the center of the long, narrow midsection between the two docking bays.

Barreling through the last bursts of cannon fire, Jani's HIB struck the station first, followed a split-second later by Scot's. The bombs did not detonate on impact but instead had been programmed to explode on a slight delay in order to maximize damage.

Scot held his breath as the bombs burrowed into the station. It was immediately clear when the bombs went off, though visually, it was not quite what Scot had expected. He didn't see a blinding flash or an enormous fireball but rather witnessed a simple instantaneous change in the fundamental nature of the station. In the moment before the bombs detonated, the station was a single continuous object. Then, in the next moment, the station was two roughly equally-sized objects—the large docking bay spinning out into space, while the smaller bay hurtled in the opposite direction toward Bellona.

The sudden and violent aftermath elicited a few appreciative gasps and whistles from the other Angels.

"Stay focused!" Hagen barked. "Don't let the Slugs catch you gawking." It was the commander's job, of course, to be concerned for the safety of the squadron, but it was rather clear by this point that the Marauders were no longer much of a threat. With less than one full squadron remaining, they were engaged strictly in defensive maneuvers, doing everything they could to try to hold off the Voors.

Hagen continued. "All ordnance is cleared. Let's sweep up the scraps."

Though the station was damaged beyond repair, the Angels didn't want to leave any usable sections for the enemy to salvage. Scot selected four points along the station's larger docking bay and fired a barrage of Slammers. His missiles were soon joined by dozens more, the blue points of light splitting off into two groups and ripping into the docking bays. The damage caused by the Slammers was substantial, but Scot, nevertheless, felt a touch disappointed by the ordinary series of explosions—he'd been spoiled by the raw power of the HIBs.

Onigen reported that he and Adahn had launched their HIBs, and Scot watched with interest, curious what the next pair of hogs would do to the docking bays. Shortly after the HIBs were released, however, a flight of four Marauders swooped in to intercept the bombs. Onigen ordered Adahn to pitch back, and the two of them turned hard away. Scot soon understood why Onigen had yielded to the Marauders. The flight was not interested in engaging the Hornets—they were attempting to knock out the HIBs. With sustained cannon fire, the Marauders managed to penetrate the shields of the trailing bomb and detonate it, which immediately set off the other.

The explosion was enormous, engulfing the entire flight of Marauders and setting off collision alarms in Scot's cockpit. While switching off the alarms, he located Onigen and Adahn on his battle map and checked their status. They'd been rocked pretty hard—both fighters were without shields and had sustained moderate hull damage—but they'd be all right provided that they could stay clear of any cannon fire. He checked their area, looking for any more stray Marauders. Finding nothing, he zoomed out, surveying the entire sector. Aside from the two halves of the station, there were no more red contacts. Scot felt a cool chill shoot up the back of his neck. The suicidal flight of Marauders had been the last of the enemy fighters.

Able to give the station their undivided attention, the Angels dealt thoroughly with the remaining sections. As Slammers continued to pound away at the larger docking bay, another pair of HIBs punched through and exploded in its center, converting the structure into millions of tiny fragments flung out into space in a spherical pattern. Soon after, the squadron's final two HIBs, launched by the Voors, struck the smaller docking bay, the last significant section of the station. The explosion sent burning chunks of metal hurtling into Bellona's atmosphere, the fiery pieces showering the dark side of the planet.

The meteor trails had not yet faded away when Hagen gave the order.

"Angels, reverse heading, find the groove, and jump on my mark."

There were no acknowledgements from the squadron. After a brief moment of silence, Jani spoke for them all.

"We're not seriously going to leave him, are we?"

They had known all along that Dex's orders were to leave him behind. But now that the time had come, it just didn't seem right.

"His orders were clear," Hagen replied. "Jump out immediately after the mission is complete."

Scot couldn't tell if the annoyance in Hagen's voice was because he was having to explain himself or because of the orders themselves. He did notice, however, that Hagen was still maintaining his original heading—traveling toward Bellona, not away—as were the rest of the Angels.

Dex's orders made complete sense. Nobody else in the squadron knew the location of the planet-side facility, and even if they found it, blasting down there would only expose Dex's position. And yet, not a single Angel could find the strength to turn away.

Scot stared intently at the dark half of Bellona.

Where are you, Dex?

The planet suddenly disappeared behind a wall of gray. Scot instantly recognized the enormous obstruction. A carrier—the UCS *Ganymede*, his sensors informed him—had dropped out of the ether directly between the Angels and Bellona. Scot's battle map lit up with new contacts—the carrier had launched three full Hornet squadrons just seconds after its arrival. Scot couldn't help noticing the Angels' old rivals, the Knighthawks, among them.

The *Ganymede*'s skipper clearly wasn't messing around. There were no warning comms, which was message enough. The Angels were flying stolen Navy property. There would be no terms—and no mercy.

"That's it," Hagen said.

No one argued. This was a fight they couldn't win. The Angels were not permitted to fire on manned ships, and this was one time Scot agreed wholeheartedly with the squadron's rules of engagement. There wasn't a single Angel who would feel right about gunning down Navy pilots. And, even if the Angels could miraculously find some way to slip past the advancing squadrons, they couldn't exactly conduct a search and rescue operation with a hostile carrier keeping watch over the planet.

And so the Angels, though victorious in their mission, began their journey home with heavy hearts, each pilot uttering a prayer for the safety of their captain, believing for the best but fearing the worst.

Chapter 31

Dex had entered the facility a dead man. If he had believed otherwise, he would have lacked the nerve to see the mission through—to expose his position in taking out the perimeter guards or to march through the relay building's only entrance, knowing that all eyes, human and mechanical, were upon him. But now, for the first time since he'd descended from the hills, Dex allowed himself to hope. Exiting the relay building, he still had encountered no resistance—no armed guards waiting outside the door, no M-2s emerging from the shadows. Sliding along the relay building's south wall, he entertained the possibility, as unlikely as it seemed, that his presence in the facility had gone unnoticed. If so, it wouldn't have been the first miracle to have occurred that night.

Looking ahead, he couldn't distinguish much of anything amid the varying shades of black, the fields and hills blending seamlessly into the night sky. He raised his rifle, holding it left-handed to minimize his profile, and peered through the holosight, its night vision capability enabling him to scan the open ground between him and the field. The only guards he spotted were the two men he had taken out earlier, still lying unconscious on the ground. It was difficult to suppress his anticipation—if he could make it back to the tall grass, he would by no means be free from danger, but he would like his chances a lot more. With the micropulse pad and holosight at his disposal, he felt he could stay one step ahead of the enemy once he reached the thick cover of the field.

When a second sweep of the area turned up nothing, he didn't waste time with a third. He lowered his rifle and prepared to sprint.

That's when he heard the scream.

Dex turned toward the sound, rifle shouldered once again. It was a woman's voice, originating behind him, deeper within the facility.

Adjusting the holosight, he looked through the row of buildings before him, searching for signs of trouble.

He soon found what he was looking for. The image was blurry—a result of the holosight having to project through multiple layers of obstructions—but Dex was able to make out just enough to assess the situation. Two figures stood cornered, one physically shielding the other. Advancing on them was the unmistakable shape of an M-2.

According to his range finder, they were nearly eighty meters away. It occurred to Dex that this was unquestionably his best opportunity to escape. With the machine preoccupied, he could turn back around and make a dash for the relative safety of the hills beyond the facility grounds.

There was no decision to be made. Without so much as stealing another glance behind him, he sprinted toward the couple in danger.

As he ran, Dex continued checking the holosight to track the M-2's progress. The machine slowed as it neared its targets, closing in at a deliberate pace far below its peak speed. Still, Dex was beginning to doubt that he could intercept the M-2 in time. The holosight made his objective appear deceptively close, but the buildings in his way had forced him into taking an indirect route. As he sprinted to the corner of the final building, Dex, through the holosight, saw the M-2 pierce the shoulder of its nearest victim, a middle-aged man standing in front of a woman of roughly the same age—his wife, Dex assumed. Dex could hear their plaintive cries— the man begging her to flee, the woman refusing to leave.

Dex didn't hesitate to act, rounding the corner with his rifle raised, ready to engage the target. But his way was suddenly blocked. A piercing, unnatural scream accompanied the appearance of a bright red beam, materializing directly in front of him at waist level. He came to an abrupt stop, sucking his stomach back as his momentum carried him ever closer to the searing-hot, razor-thin line.

Balancing precariously on the balls of his feet, Dex was able to shift his weight back and stumble away from the beam, back to the cover of the building. The beam continued to follow him, cutting through the corner of the building, forcing Dex to retreat even further. Seconds later, it disappeared.

Using the holosight, Dex watched the M-2 move its right arm back toward the middle-aged man. A laser cutter—undoubtedly the source of the beam—was mounted below the appendage, and from atop the same arm, a new weapon emerged. At the appearance of the long straight-edged blade, Dex began to feel heat on his stomach, but he forced it out of his mind. At the moment, he needed to fully concentrate on doing whatever he could to stop the imminent executions.

The problem was how. Dex knew he couldn't advance on the machine if it continued to block him in with the beam. But the arm that held the laser cutter had also produced the blade. Maybe, Dex thought, if the M-2's right arm was wielding the blade, it wouldn't be able to aim the laser cutter—at least not immediately. It was a gamble, but the alternative—to stand by and do nothing—was unthinkable.

Dex again rounded the corner, noting that the M-2 did not move its right arm toward him but rather kept the blade extended toward the man's neck. Dex quickly lined up the shot, but before he could squeeze the trigger, another part of the machine moved. A compartment on its left arm opened, releasing a small object into the air. Hovering for only a split-second, the object shot straight toward Dex, impacting the ground directly in front of him. A blinding light and deafening explosion left Dex lying on the ground, disoriented and unable to move.

His vision slowly began to clear, but his muscles refused to respond. Dex could only watch as the machine went about its evil work. As the blade inched closer to the man's neck, his wife launched herself at M-2, grabbing its right arm and pulling at it with all her strength.

In response, the machine released its rod from the man's shoulder, freeing him momentarily. With its left arm now disengaged, the M-2 batted the woman away, sending her slamming into a wall. Then, using the same arm, the machine pumped two stun bolts into her legs before whipping around and shooting its rod back into the man's shoulder, straight through the original wound. The rod had been retracted and reinserted in less than a second.

The interrogation began—the same questions, Dex realized, that Bulldog had been asked. Straining, groaning, but still unable to move, Dex watched the scene unfold with horrified, unblinking eyes. He heard the man confess to being a Christian and watched, silently screaming, as the machine removed his head. It then turned toward the woman slumped against the wall. With no fanfare or warning, it shot the rod into her shoulder and lifted her from the ground. Her cry of agony echoed through the grounds.

Dex felt a fraction of movement returning to his arms and legs. Ignoring the pain, he willed himself to roll over onto his elbows. He raised the rifle—an agonizing process that left him unable to hold it steady. His limbs were shaking uncontrollably, causing the crosshair to waver uncertainly back and forth across the target. He heard the machine begin its interrogation, which meant there was precious little time—he couldn't afford to wait any longer for his body to cooperate. And so when, for the briefest moment, the crosshair lingered over the M-2's center mass, Dex fired.

His aim was true, and the red bolt struck the machine square in its torso. An outer shield, however, deflected the bolt, sending it glancing off harmlessly into the sky. The machine continued its interrogation without missing a beat. The woman either refused to respond or was physically unable to find her voice. Regardless, her silence made no difference. Moments later, her body lay next to her husband's.

The machine retracted the blade and turned slowly toward Dex. Lying on the ground, he felt a rush of heat course through him from his chest through his legs, and Dex found the strength to move—rising, limping, running. He could feel the M-2 behind him. How close, he wasn't certain, and he didn't dare turn to look. It didn't matter—he ran as if the soulless beast were breathing down his neck.

Turning this way and that through the maze of shredded bunkers, Dex began to lose his bearings. He could scarcely think beyond a single primal imperative—*run*. It was unclear, though, if he was making any progress toward the edge of the facility. The bunkers before him were numerous and densely packed—the paths between them narrow and strewn with piles of rubble. More than once he stumbled over loose rocks, but he would not let himself fall—to fall was to die.

Knowing that he couldn't outrun the M-2 forever—he was surprised, in fact, that the machine hadn't caught him already—Dex looked for a place of refuge. His endurance fading, he needed somewhere to pause to catch his breath and his wits. Among the demolished bunkers, he saw a potential shelter blocking the end of the row—promising only because it was the first bunker he'd seen with its door still intact. Pushing through the pain—his lungs burning, his side cramping—Dex made a final hard push for the bunker. He didn't slow much as he reached the door, slamming his hand onto the side panel. The reinforced door slid open, and Dex jumped inside. He immediately turned to his left and pressed the inner panel.

As the door closed, he caught a glimpse of his pursuer. It wasn't making a mad dash toward him, as Dex had imagined, but was gliding effortlessly forward, the impact of each stride cushioned by the dozens of worm-like feelers on the bottoms of its feet. It drifted forward like a spirit—as an immortal, it had no need to hurry.

The door slammed down, and Dex double-checked to make sure it was locked. Looking over the bunker, he found only one more entrance on the east wall. It was a double-wide, heavily armored door, likely intended to be the main entrance for an entire complex of inter-connected bunkers had the facility been a traditional military installation. The door's side panel indicated that it too was locked. Even with the illumination provided by the panels, it was too dark for Dex to see if there were any cracks or holes along the far walls of the bunker. Using the holosight, he scanned the entire bunker, concluding that it was completely intact. It was the only pristine bunker Dex had seen in the facility, and he couldn't shake the foreboding thought that it had been constructed specifically for the purpose of testing the very machine that was now stalking him.

Nevertheless, he was safe for the moment. He had seen ample evidence of what the machine could do to a bunker, but he doubted that even it could cause such devastation in mere seconds. He paced in a tight circle, catching his breath as he considered his options. He couldn't outrun the M-2—despite its casual pace so far, he knew that the machine was capable of much greater speeds. And he couldn't outgun it—the machine wielded a potent arsenal and that was before factoring in its personal shield. No—if he was to have any chance at all, he would need to outthink, outmaneuver it.

Dex called to mind everything he knew about the machine. Whatever its advantages, the M-2 seemed bound by certain rules. Dex had now seen an M-2 murder three people, including Bulldog, and in each case, the machine had interrogated its victims before executing them with a blade. It was a rather inefficient method, considering the machine's array of weaponry. Dex thought back to his own engagement with the machine moments ago. The M-2 had corralled him with a laser cutter and temporarily incapacitated him with a stun grenade. It would have been easier for the machine to simply kill him if that had been its sole intent. All it would've taken was a flick of its wrist and the beam would've cut him in two, or he could have been hit with a standard, lethal grenade instead.

Perhaps, Dex determined, the machine was programmed to only perform a very specific type of execution. If so, it might be a weakness he could use to his advantage. If the machine could only engage in close-quarters executions, he would stand a chance if he could manage to keep some distance between them.

Emboldened by the thought, Dex began searching for possible escape routes, using his holosight to peer through the walls of the bunker. He saw that the east door opened up to another path, bordered on both sides by rows of bunkers. Beyond the last pair of bunkers was open ground—overgrown, brushy terrain that sloped down to a narrow river. His range finder indicated that it was only about seventy meters to the end of the row—he was closer to the eastern perimeter than he'd thought.

He swung the rifle back around to the west door, curious to see if the M-2 had made any progress in penetrating the bunker. The machine, however, was gone. He swept his rifle around in a complete circle, looking through all four walls of the bunker. And still there was not a trace of the M-2. Dex frowned—he was partly annoyed with himself for letting the machine out of his sight, but he also saw this as an opportunity. Regardless of where the machine had disappeared to, he had a clear path to freedom. He could either sit around and wait for the M-2 to return or he could make his move.

Creeping up to the east door, he paused and took a couple of deep breaths, preparing himself mentally for the final dash. When he felt ready, he reached for the panel, but as he approached the door, his stomach again started burning—the knife in his waistband once again emitting heat. He placed his hand over his stomach and felt the blade through his shirt. The knife was hot to the touch and was vibrating rapidly, almost humming. On a hunch, Dex pulled away from the panel. Leaning back, he pointed his rifle straight up, peering through the ceiling. There the machine was, crouching over the ledge of the roof, as still as a statue, waiting patiently for Dex to emerge.

The two of them stared at each other through the reinforced ceiling—Dex with his holosight, the machine with its omnisensor. After a couple of seconds, the M-2 abruptly stood erect and ran across the roof, leaping back down to the lightly armored west door. Dex tracked the machine with the holosight until a bright flash forced him to look away. For the second time that night, he heard the scream of the machine's laser cutter at work. He didn't need the holosight to see the results as a pinpoint of light began melting a perfectly straight trail down the door.

Faced with the impending breach, Dex wasn't sure what to do. He could make a run for it out the east door, but he had just witnessed the ease with which the machine scaled buildings. If he attempted to escape the bunker, the machine would see him, leap onto the roof, and track him down from behind in a matter of seconds. On the other hand, he couldn't simply remain still, waiting for the machine to break in. As he scrambled for options, he became distracted by odd behavior from the laser cutter. The once steady point of light began to flicker, and beyond the door, the screaming noise broke into an irregular staccato. After a few seconds, the cutter ceased operating altogether, having made only a single long cut down the door.

Able to use his holosight without being blinded by the beam, Dex raised the rifle and saw the machine running down the path, away from the bunker. He wasn't sure where it was going—possibly to recharge or replace its cutter—but whatever the case, he knew he wouldn't get a better opportunity than this. He rushed over to the east door and activated the side panel. The double-wide door groaned as it disengaged its locking mechanisms, taking much longer to open than Dex had anticipated. After several long seconds, the double doors began to slowly separate. In that same moment, Dex heard an ear-splitting crash behind him.

Whirling around, he saw that the machine had slammed into the west door, bursting halfway through before getting caught in the narrow seam. The interior of the bunker shrieked with the sound of metal grinding on metal as the machine jerked and writhed, frantically trying to free itself from the tangled mess. With the M-2 momentarily immobilized, Dex saw his chance. He slid through the narrow gap in the slowly opening east door, but not before the machine, with impossible quickness and accuracy, twisted and snapped off a shot from its wrist, the blue stun bolt striking Dex in his right side just below the ribcage.

He lurched through the doorway under severe pain. While the stun grenade from earlier had affected his entire body, leaving him still dizzy and sluggish, the effects of the stun bolt were localized and intense. His abdominal muscles were contracting, pulling his head down toward his midsection. His body urged him to collapse, to curl up on the ground and ride out the pain. But Dex would not relent. Staggering forward, he fixed his eyes on the open ground ahead.

An elongated scraping noise brought an end to the sounds of struggle from within the bunker. Nearing the last pair of structures, he limped ahead faster, even approximating a sort of jog as a surge of adrenaline masked the pain.

And then his right leg gave out. Struck by another stun bolt, the leg seized up, causing Dex to hitch and tumble face first into the dry rocky ground. He tried to will himself forward, to crawl, to drag his legs—to do anything—but his body refused to listen.

He raised his head, looking past the settling dust into the fields beyond. He'd been close—so close—falling about ten meters from the edge of the facility. Even now, he could hear the gentle flow of the river.

With agonizing effort, he rolled over to face the approaching machine—if he was going to die, it wasn't going to be with his back turned. As he shifted position, Dex realized that, through the fall, he had managed to maintain hold of his rifle. He knew from experience that the machine was shielded, that the rifle's high-powered bolts would be deflected away. And yet, he thought, if he could hit a weak point, say, a well-placed shot to the head, maybe that would be just enough.

He twitched, and the rifle exploded in his hands, destroyed by a single red bolt from the M-2. Dex cried out, partly in shock from the blast and partly in pain as the palms of his hand burned against the smoldering metal. He dropped the charred remains of the rifle to the ground.

The machine was moving even more slowly than before, almost as if it were taunting him. It was then that Dex remembered he had one other weapon left—the knife. He pulled it from his waistband, holding it delicately in his wounded hand. It was again warm to the touch and seemed to be throbbing in rhythm with his own frantically beating heart. Dex knew, of course, that the knife would be useless against the M-2—but, he suddenly realized, he could, at the very least, deny the machine and its makers the satisfaction of executing him.

He could go out on his own terms, not the enemy's. Wasn't there honor in that? He rotated his wrist, turning the blade inward toward himself. The M-2 made no effort to disarm him, and indeed, had stopped moving altogether.

Dex closed his eyes and took a few quick breaths, steeling himself. One decisive thrust and it would be over. Gripping the knife tightly now with both hands, he took a final deep breath and looked skyward. And it was there in the night sky that a glint of movement caught his attention.

Stars were raining down from the heavens—a meteor shower unlike any Dex had ever seen before, each trail of light originating from a single patch of space. He could think of only one explanation. The Angels had done it—the station was destroyed. Forgetting all other concerns for the moment, he paused to savor the breathtaking show. The display was brilliant yet fleeting, the entire shower, from beginning to end, lasting only a few precious heartbeats.

As the fireworks faded, and darkness once again replaced the light show above him, Dex became aware that the tip of the knife was pressing against his chest, just millimeters from his heart. The knife throbbed again, as if willing him to complete the job. Shaking off the dread feeling, Dex pulled the knife away. What had he been thinking? The station was gone—his friends had put their lives on the line to save countless others. How close had he just come to taking his own?

The knife, Dex realized. He hadn't been right since the cursed thing had first been shackled to his Hornet on the Vorina run. With a mixed cry of rage and anguish, he raised the knife and threw it at the M-2. The machine absently batted it aside.

Dex felt a vaguely familiar, but almost forgotten presence stirring in his soul. He struggled to push himself to a fully seated position, praying for the strength to face his own death with the same courage that Bulldog had shown.

As if also sensing that its hunt had reached a conclusion, the M-2 accelerated, closing the remaining distance between them with alarming speed. As it towered over him, Dex continued to struggle—urging, begging his paralyzed muscles to respond. Fighting the pain, he managed to pull his left leg underneath himself, pushing hard to rise up on one knee. Dex was determined to die on his feet like a soldier—like a man.

The machine did not allow him to get any further. Without warning, the shining metal rod shot out of the M-2's left appendage. Dex involuntarily cried out as the sharpened point pierced clean through his right shoulder—the downward angle causing it to punch out of his back just below the shoulder blade. Gasping for breath that wouldn't come, Dex felt several sharp points of pain as the rod deployed grappling hooks into his back around the exit wound, effectively securing him in place.

Groaning, he felt the thing lifting him up slowly—first to his knees, then to his feet, and further, until his unresponsive legs dangled inches above the ground.

The pain was unbearable. Dex fought to keep from blacking out. His eyesight was coming in and out of focus with every ragged breath. He tried to look directly into the single dark eye of his tormentor. The hellish thing had no features—no emotion, no remorse, no soul.

It spoke.

You are a Christian.

Dex wanted to answer but found that the words would not come. As he opened his mouth, the pressure and unnatural angle of his shoulder prevented him from drawing enough air to utter a response.

The M-2 apparently took his silence as an affirmative.

You cling to an imaginary god and a dead religion.

In his fading peripheral vision, Dex saw the M-2 raise its right arm. He heard the blade, felt its eerie vibrations before it even emerged from the thing's appendage.

As the bluish blade drew close to his neck, the pulsating effect began to radiate throughout his body, every nerve set on edge, sensitized to the moment when the blade would come into contact with soft yielding flesh.

It stopped, pressed up against his neck. He felt palpable waves of pain and shock whiplash to his extremities—his stunned muscles twitching violently under this new assault. The impaling rod retracted a few centimeters, pulling Dex even closer.

Will you renounce your faith in exchange for your life?

Through the pain, fear, and disorientation, a thought occurred to Dex. What if he did just that? He hadn't actually *admitted* to being a Christian. He hadn't said anything. What if he simply denied it? Maybe if Bulldog had been willing to say that, no, he wasn't a Christian, he would still be alive today. Was that all that the thing wanted? Maybe the damned machine would let him go. The pain would end, and the monster would back off, leaving Dex to recover from his wounds and crawl back to his freedom.

The rod shook and the blade pressed harder, cutting into his flesh and prodding him for an answer. A fresh wave poured through Dex, but this time it wasn't pain.

Crawl back to my "freedom." Yeah. That was exactly what the beast wanted. It had asked him if he would renounce his faith. Dex stared into the soulless eye, defying the machine, defying its creators, defying anyone watching on the other end. He gritted his teeth, forced in a final breath, and gave an answer—an answer that would honor Bulldog, his fellow pilots, and most of all, his Savior.

"No," he said, "I *am* a Christian. And you can go to—"

A piercing unnatural scream filled Dex's ears. At the same time, an intense flash exploded in his field of vision, blinding him completely. He sensed himself falling, unable to brace himself, certain that his head had just been separated from his body.

But no. He was on the ground. He was even breathing again. He could feel his arms and legs. Blinking rapidly, trying to clear white haze from his vision, Dex felt around desperately, trying to get his bearings.

His left hand came in contact with a smooth conical shape. Running his fingers along its surface, he felt a slight protrusion, an orb that could only be the M-2's eye. A moment later, his vision cleared enough for his eyes to confirm what his hands had felt. There, on the ground next to him, was the severed head of the M-2.

Dex looked up. The body of the M-2 was still standing, but completely motionless. The rod and grappling hooks that had impaled him had retracted, dropping him to the ground. The awful blade was still in place, but its vibrations had ceased. The bluish tint had faded—it rested, silent and cold.

How...?

Dex shook his head and blinked again—hard. In the dim light beyond the M-2, he could make out another form—a human form. Squinting, he recognized the figure.

Darik Mason.

The JenKore exec, the man Dex knew to be responsible for these atrocities, was standing a few meters beyond one of his own decapitated machines. He was holding an industrial-grade laser cutter—its emitter still glowing from its discharge.

Dex tried to sort out what had just happened. Without a doubt, Mason had saved his life, and Dex wanted to ask him why. He wanted to ask a thousand questions. But mostly, he just wanted to get back on his feet. With his right arm still hanging uselessly, Dex extended his left hand toward Mason, expecting his rescuer to help him up.

Mason didn't move. Dex let his hand drop, suddenly aware that Mason had not yet lowered the laser cutter. Staring at the glowing emitter now pointed directly at his heart, Dex realized that he may have simply exchanged one executioner for another. His legs still far too weak to allow any kind of escape, Dex searched again for options. With his eyesight clearing, he tried to read Mason's expression, looking for a tell, any clue that would tip his intent, his next action.

In Mason's eyes, he read only anger. Whether that anger was directed at him, Christians everywhere, or the universe in general, Dex had no way of knowing. He only knew that if Mason's thumb even twitched on the cutter's activator, it was over. Several seconds passed into eternity, each man staring down the other, Dex bracing for the kill shot, Mason apparently deciding when to take it.

Finally, Mason lowered the weapon. But even as the cutter hung limply in his hand, the expression of anger remained. Dex could see that Mason was considering saying something, his lower jaw working beneath tight lips and a twitching cheek.

Instead, Mason shook his head, turned, and walked silently away, pausing only to pick up the knife Dex had thrown before disappearing into the darkness.

Dex considered calling out after him, then decided against it—his craving for answers tempered by the thought that Mason could always change his mind. He drew in a ragged, painful breath—the impaling rod having likely punctured his right lung—and resumed the struggle to get to his feet. Finally rising up on trembling legs, he staggered to the edge of the clearing. His strength fading with each step, he stumbled at the top of the bank, falling down the brushy slope and crashing to a stop just short of the river's edge.

The river appeared to be deep, and despite its gentle flow, Dex knew that in his current condition, getting across would be difficult, if not impossible. But it was only a matter of time before armed guards or even another M-2 would be dispatched to finish the job Mason had postponed. The opposite bank was tantalizingly close—the tall grass beyond, beckoning.

Dex pushed himself once more to his feet, but in doing so, he felt the full extent of his injuries take their toll. A coughing spasm shook his body, his vision blurred, and his strength failed. Unable to stand, he tumbled headfirst into the cold water.

Beneath the water's surface, it was dark, serene. Dex remained still, the cold water washing over him. His body went numb, and the pain from his wounds subsided. He couldn't move—he couldn't even think. His body sank slowly to the bottom, his soul rising toward the stars. Above, the ripples on the surface expanded into ever-widening circles before fading completely away. The river resumed its normal flow.

A half-minute later, there was another disturbance on the surface of the water. Dex emerged on the far side of the river, crawling slowly up the bank, one handhold at a time. Still gasping for breath, he turned, looking back across the river. The silent M-2 still stood there, a narrow wisp of smoke rising where its head had been. Dex thought about Mason, alone somewhere in the darkness, probably already regretting the decision to spare his life. He looked toward the stars and felt again the satisfaction of knowing that his pilots had succeeded in their mission. The production of the horrible machines would cease, at least for now. The Angels had purchased time—for the colony and for Christians everywhere.

What price the Angels had paid for that victory, Dex had no way to tell. Was Jani alive? What about Hagen? And Scot? In the midst of his physical pain, a new awareness gently cascaded through Dex. His spirit had never felt so full. The nausea, the anger, the darkness that had accompanied that damnable knife were gone. In their place, Dex felt hope—hope and longing. He wanted nothing more than to be reunited with the squadron, to see his friends again. As another coughing spasm racked his torso, Dex could taste the metallic tang of blood rising in his mouth. With the extent of his injuries, he wasn't sure he would survive to see that reunion, but he knew he had to try. With a final prayer for the Angels, he slipped into the tall grass, one step closer to freedom.

Epilogue

Kirrone Jenkins sat alone in his darkly paneled office, relishing the feed from Bellona. He had silenced all other data and comm sources immediately after receiving word of the destruction of the manufacturing station in order to devote his full attention to this single exhilarating stream.

The real-time resolution was excellent. His pulse quickened as the hunt drew to a close. Watching from the M-2's perspective, he felt the bloodlust of a predator descending on its prey.

He leaned forward as the interrogation commenced, his pale eyes intent on the scene before him. He could clearly see the fear in the victim's eyes. Fear, despair, pain...and something else.

He cursed. It was almost always there, at the end, in the victim's eyes—that foolish, futile, elusive hint of resolve. He hated it.

But no matter. It would be over in a moment. His eyes widened as he watched the Travarian blade press against the man's neck, enjoying the thrill of seeing his body twitch from the contact.

The victim was clearly struggling to speak. What he was saying wasn't relevant. The audio would follow later and, of course, nothing the man could say would change the outcome—it never did. A single bead of sweat fell from his forehead and splashed on the ivory desktop as he savored the imminent and satisfying conclusion.

A sudden burst of static partially obscured the image. He experienced a brief sense of vertigo as the visual before him skewed to the right, appearing to tip slightly before falling quickly to the ground.

The image, barely discernible through the interference, slowly rolled and came to a stop. Through the static, he thought he could make out the hazy form of another man standing a few meters behind the M-2. At that moment, the display went dark—its corrupted feed replaced by two lines of text.

CRITICAL MALFUNCTION
M-2/A UNIT #2301 OPERATION TERMINATED AT SOURCE

He cursed again, more vehemently. His fists clenched in anger—meticulously manicured fingernails drawing blood from his palms.

In response, a voice spoke from within the empty office—a voice with which Jenkins was familiar. It breathed a single word.

Failure.

Jenkins shrugged, his nonchalance belying his apprehension. "It is only a minor setback, a short but unavoidable delay in the execution of our plans."

There will be no further delays. Your source is in position. We will add the fate of this infestation of Zealots and their misguided guardians to that of all of the others.

Jenkins nodded, eager to find agreement, eager to please. "Yes, Blackfriar has served his purpose to date. All that remains for him is to reveal their location." The single bead of perspiration now mingled with a pool of sweat accumulating on the desktop. "You must understand. We have the location of every other colony. And we will renew our production of the M-2s. It will just take time. In the meantime, we have thousands—*tens* of thousands—already completed."

Then unleash them. Do not prevent them any longer from carrying out their divine purpose. Unleash them all.

The room grew quiet, and Jenkins sensed once more that he was alone.

He considered what he had heard.

All of them.

Yes, he will activate them all. Colony by colony, the Zealots will be found. They will beg for mercy, they will deny their misguided faith, and they will blaspheme their false god. And colony by colony, thousands by thousands, right up to the depraved souls who had dared to defy him on Bellona, every one of them will die.

He growled, the words coming in an ancient language long forgotten on Earth.

Beside him, the idol burned.

Acknowledgments

Well over a decade ago, many of the characters in this novel, their circumstances, and the universe in which they live were simply rough ideas in the imagination of a young Christian sci-fi fan and his equally enthusiastic son. Without the timely encouragement, advice, and skillful contributions of so many friends and family, those rough ideas would have remained as just that, characters of unrealized potential who never found their way to the printed—or electronic—page. We want to express our gratitude to so many people who played a role in bringing this project to realization.

To Larry and Jenny Clair, and Drew and Mary Graham, thank you for your "beta testing" of our early manuscript. Your encouragement, but also your detailed and often humorous feedback helped more than we can say.

To Phil and Michelle Thooft, your constant encouragement and advice took this entire project to a higher level. A special thanks to you, Michelle, for your evaluation of our characters. Honesty isn't always easy, but the "Angels" grew because of you, and so did we.

To Joe and Carol Campbell, every week we would spend at Campbell's Lodge, the story would take a giant leap forward. Thank you for providing a place of rest, relaxation, fishing, and faith.

To Aaron and Jessica Broberg, for your friendship and for Aaron's phenomenally mad web skilllz. A shout-out to your first-class work at AandBe Studios for bringing the web side of this venture to life.

To Patty Miller and Dan Bergan or, as Allan and Aaron knew them in high school, *Mrs.* Miller and *Mr.* Bergan. Your encouragement and commitment to excellence engendered in us a love for the written word and a desire to wield it with respect. English teachers do make an impact!

Words cannot fully express our appreciation to our families. Mike, your cover art captured our imagination for this novel as if you had climbed inside our heads, grabbed the idea, and then improved it one hundredfold. Andrew, Jenni, Mark, Emma, Aidan, Bella, and Julia, your laughter and joy have kept us going throughout this process. Thank you for your love and support in the mad rush leading up to this publication.

And finally, to our partners in faith, in life, and in love, Becky and Jill. Your unabashed enthusiasm is the real reason we pressed on and completed this work, which we humbly and gratefully dedicate to you.

About the Authors

Allan Reini is an enthusiastic sci-fi fan with over thirty years of business and leadership experience. Allan lives in Hibbing, Minnesota, where he and his wife, Becky, are thankful to have three of their adult children and their six grandchildren in close proximity (with missionary son, Michael, available via Skype). He has admittedly raised a family of self-professed nerds, including his eldest son and co-author, Aaron.

Aaron Reini, his wife, Jill, and their four children also live in Hibbing, Minnesota. Aaron taught English for eight years at Hibbing Community College prior to moving into administration (though he still finds any excuse he can to get into the classroom). He has been writing collaboratively with his father since 2008. *Flight of the Angels* is their first novel.

Also from Allan and Aaron Reini

Hornet's Nest
Book Two of *Flight of the Angels*
Available in paperback and Kindle at Amazon.com
Audiobook available soon at Audible.com

"Blood Ace"
A *Flight of the Angels* short story
Available in The Crossover Alliance Anthology Vol. 1
and on Kindle at Amazon.com
Audio dramatization available at Untoldpodcast.com

Questions for Allan or Aaron?
Email us at mail@flightoftheangels.com

For more information including a glossary of terms, pilot brevity codes, and the history of the S/A-81 Hornet, visit us at www.flightoftheangels.com

Join the Angels: Like us on Facebook
http://www.facebook.com/FlightOfTheAngels

Follow Flight of the Angels on Twitter @PellaColony

One Last Note from the Authors: If you enjoy the *Flight of the Angels* series and believe it is worth sharing, would you take a few moments to tell your friends about it? We would also be very grateful if you could rate this book and leave a review on Amazon.com. Your words of support will help us get the next book in the series, *Phantoms of the Void*, out as quickly as possible. Thank you!

Allan & Aaron

.

www.ingramcontent.com/pod-product-compliance
Lightning Source LLC
Chambersburg PA
CBHW020324180626
46812CB00001B/44